BLOOD
OF MY
BLOOD

SONIA BLADE

Book Cover by Neptune Designs

ISBN 979-8-9987838-1-4

To my family and friends...with all my love, thank you for all you've done for me.

For Josh, my husband, who allows me to cultivate my creativity and paint the world crimson with my stories. Thank you for your support and your heart. I cherish both.

For Lina, my best friend. Without you, Blood Of My Blood would still be a messy first draft. You helped me realize that becoming an author doesn't have to be solitary...that there is community in creativity. I'm honored and grateful to be your friend and can't wait for us to write our vampire books together until we get old.

This book is for the survivors out there. No matter your battle. Never forget how strong you are.

CHAPTER ONE

I STUDIED THE PAINTING in front of me, just five feet away. In it, a ballerina, arms stretched above her head and legs posed carefully with one foot on its toes, gazed to my right. Her white floral dress, adorned with splashes of bright colors, complemented her pale skin and the hair pulled away from her face. In stark contrast to her delicate hues, streaks of blues and greens suggested she was in a forest clearing. Or at least, that's how those careful lines and strokes appeared to me. But then again, what the hell did I know about Edgar Degas?

Not much.

Just enough to pass art history before I dropped out of art school.

"*Danseuse Aux Bras Levés,*" I read aloud, squinting to read the small print of the placard beneath the piece. *Edgar Degas, 1834-1917. 1891. Pastel and charcoal on panel.*

I blinked and refocused on the blue of the landscape and how it had added depth to the leaves and trees behind the dancer. My eyes instinctively returned to her, drifting back to the almost serene expression on her face, as if performing ballet had been second nature in the middle of the woods.

"Miss, the exhibit is closing for the night."

The stranger's words had made my shoulders rise three inches and caught my breath in my lungs. Shit. How long had I been standing there?

"I'm so sorry," I replied, glancing at the other two Degas works before turning completely around toward the exit. "I just wanted to get one last look at them."

The silk of my evening dress slid against my skin as I left the Art of the Avery Foundation exhibit on The Avery Hotel's first floor. Every major city in America had an Avery, including Dallas, Texas. Stained wood, gold, and plush red velvet encompassed every inch of the Art Deco inspired decor around me. The interior presented a classic picture of timeless elegance—old money wrapped in a mixture of European pomp and Americana.

"You've got this. You're fine." I whispered the words to myself as I made my way back to the main lobby. Thoughts filled my mind as I pushed my feet forward. Was my lipstick too flashy? The blush on my cheeks felt boldly out of character. "You are that bitch," I encouraged. "You look amazing."

As soon as I said it, my stiletto heel wobbled. The rhythm of my walk faltered, losing its cadence. When a passing stranger glanced my way, I smiled and continued toward the other side of the building, as if I hadn't just almost fallen not twenty feet from them.

"You are that bitch about to break her ankle. Stop shaking." The pep talk deteriorated as my calf muscle tensed.

I crossed the dark wood parquet floors, wondering what had possessed me to stay there in the first place. *Oh, right.* It had been one of downtown Dallas's fanciest hotels, and I needed to feel like a million bucks. At four hundred dollars a night, it certainly made me feel like I had that kind of money in my bank account.

A long stretch of frosted windows sat above dark wood paneling not far from me, warm yellow light barely making its way through the glass. Antiquated lettering read Amaranthine Wine Bar and Eatery over the two large glass doors where I was headed. The vision of it, along with just about everything else in the place, reeked of a century past. Maybe longer.

I stopped short of the entrance to Amaranthine and took a deep breath, smoothed the fabric of my dress, and rolled my shoulders back. Tonight would be the night to start the rest of my life, ex-fiancé be damned. I looked beautiful and I felt great. Well...I should have felt alright. My anxiety simmered as I fought the tail end of a hangover. Two bottles of cheap white wine had done a number on me from the night before. But that hadn't stopped me. Not when so many other things had already tried. I ran my tongue over my teeth, shook my head to settle my curls, and put on a flirty smile.

Here we go.

I pushed open the swinging doors, took two steps inside—and that was it.

When I did, everything stopped. Wealthy, callous men all turned and looked at me with crooked smiles on their thin lips. I found myself not knowing what to do. My common sense screamed at me to put one foot in front of the other and move to the bar top not fifteen feet away.

It was a simple sequence of movements, but at that moment it was impossible.

I didn't belong here.

They all knew it.

I knew it. I wasn't fooling anyone with my expensive clothes and jewelry. I stood paralyzed. In that moment, I was the ballerina in her floral dress frozen mid-pose, ready to begin her ballet in the forest clearing.

As heat flared in my cheeks and my thighs threatened to shake, I managed to find my senses enough to make it to the countertop. As I did, I scanned the room. Twenty men occupied the place with two or three women littered into the mix. All of them were appropriate, blending in perfectly with the aesthetic as if they were made to frequent these kinds of places. In turn, they all watched me with varying degrees of perversion coming off of them, consuming me from coiled curl to manicured toe with just their eyes.

I cleared my throat.

All I had to do was avoid looking at any of them too long. But I couldn't stop myself from lingering on someone sitting toward the back of the bar top. His dark eyes found me, fixed themselves on me, but didn't violate me. Not like the others. The corner of my lip twitched, wanting to loosen my smile. I wouldn't mind sitting with him for the evening. He was a little pale and more timeless in his good looks than the hotel we stood in. A face not meant for cell phones and social media, but for drawing rooms and portrait paintings. I probably needed to stop staring at him.

I diverted my gaze to someone else—anyone else—as I neared the counter. There, I caught sight of another man. He was quite the opposite of the first one I'd noticed, but he still had his gaze trained on me. His sharp eyes were crystal blue, almost too bright to see a color from my distance. He radiated something different. Something mysterious and powerful. I looked away to the space in front of me, butterflies fluttering and flipping as they bounced against my stomach walls.

"Good evening, miss."

Unable to shake the feeling of being dripping meat dangling over circling sharks, I welcomed the distraction of the bartender's voice, allowing it to jolt me from my haze. The ambient noise of the luxury hotel bar faded back into reality, releasing me. I breathed easier.

"Hi."

My fingers shimmied down the fabric of my dress again before stretching and flexing. The other hand gripped tighter to my clutch purse. *Did I normally fidget this much?*

The young man smiled at me as I sat down on the closest barstool, the high slit of my dress teasing up almost too much. So much for letting Marley, my sixteen-year-old sister, help me pick the thing out. *Why did I take fashion advice from a teenager?* The girl was habitually in daisy dukes and crop tops on any day over sixty-five degrees, which was most of the year in Dallas, except maybe two months. Maybe.

The tight, revealing nature of the whole outfit flirted over the line of my comfort zone. I'd never been one to show so much skin, but was that because of personal preference or because I'd previously been in a relationship and didn't want to attract attention. I wanted the attention now.

"Can I get you something to drink?" the bartender asked.

I concentrated on his hands as they casually dried a highball glass with a white bar towel. Not even the cleaning tools were dirty in a place like this. The whole vision of him was a cinematic cliché; he even wore a black vest and slacks with a pristine white button-up.

"A mil—" I stopped myself.

Beautiful women in hundred-dollar dresses and three-inch heels didn't order lite beers. They ordered overpriced, complicated mixed drinks. Ones that came with a fruit or vegetable garnish and an air of superiority. And a dainty glass. Definitely one of those.

"Martini, please." Was the first thing that popped into my mind.

"Of course," he replied but lingered before moving to make the drink, waiting for me to give him further particulars. I grimaced, but only on the inside, as I grasped at nothing. *What the hell were the preferences on martinis?* The only things that came to mind were the overused preferences of a certain international man of mystery. But I couldn't bring myself to use the order. I'd look like an idiot.

"Vodka martini." The words came from some random place in my mind. "Dirty, please, but only a little."

Yes, that sounded right. My ex-fiancé, Matt, had ordered one of those for me years ago when he insisted I try something other than red wine or lite beer.

"Of course, Miss."

He turned and walked away, leaving me staring at the space he left, my eyes drying from lack of blinking. I sat, stuck in the weird place where I couldn't will myself to actually think of anything. As if I'd gone into standby.

Through the blur of unfocused vision, the shape of him returned, and I blinked. The black and white mass sharpened until it returned to normal. When he placed the delicate drink down on the white marble counter, I unzipped my clutch but froze because of the change in his expression.

"How much is it?"

"You won't have to pay for drinks here dressed like that." His tone was friendly, despite the words sounding as if they were disrespectful.

"I'm sorry?"

"Beautiful women in beautiful dresses who make the whole bar freeze when they come in don't really pay for drinks here. And I mean that in the nicest way possible."

My mouth opened to fire off a snarky reply before I stopped myself. "You think so?"

The version of me that would have been offended by that was the one that was engaged to be married. That version of me sat in booths not bar tops and she definitely didn't come to bars dressed to the nines, hoping to catch a man's attention to boost her confidence. But, I was a new version of Joceline. A version that wanted exactly that to happen.

"Absolutely, Miss," he smiled. "I'll leave your tab open."

Then he winked before walking away. It was a nice touch, I admit. It had me feeling more comfortable than I'd been when I entered, and I relaxed enough to notice my jaw had been clenched the entire time. I corrected myself, looked down and grinned as the confidence I sought after started to come to me. My cousin Trina would be happy to hear that her plan was working. She insisted that I'd find a sugar daddy at the illustrious Avery Hotel, like a friend of hers had, but I told her I didn't need all that. I just needed a rebound. A really good night to kick off my own journey to get my groove back.

I traced the veins of the marble as I rubbed my thumb against the base of my ring finger, fighting off thoughts of less pleasant things—the things I came to the hotel to forget. I must have taken a sip or two of the martini, fighting off the desire to pull out my cell phone and scroll, when someone approached behind me. Butterflies danced again as a shadow enveloped me. Their very presence in my vicinity weighed heavy. My eyes made quick work of scanning the room, trying to figure out who was missing from the faces I'd seen earlier, but I couldn't remember them all. With fluttering eyelids, I grabbed my drink and took another sip, trying to look casual.

"I'd love to take this seat, if you'd have me."

Have him? Me?

When I turned to face him, sharp crystalline eyes looked down at me. His thin, pink lips smirked with a quiet mischief. His choice of words made my brow furrow, but the foreign accent it was spoken in had me fighting off a goofy grin. Despite being obviously British, it wasn't English. I struggled to place it.

"Excuse me?" I fumbled with my words.

He lifted a brow at my stutter, the smirk spreading wider. He was sharply dressed, much like most of the men in the bar with us, but the cut of his suit fit it to his frame perfectly so that it didn't hug his body nor did it hang off him. I zeroed in on his face and the sharp angles that sculpted his pale skin. Paler even than the first man I noticed when I walked in, but it fit him well. His fierce features and high cheekbones pulled together his whole look, slight wrinkles on his face giving me an estimate of around mid-thirties, definitely nothing close to forty as far as age.

"May I?"

Long, slender fingers motioned to the empty bar seat next to me, and I followed them until they landed on the black leather of the backing. "Sure. I mean, yes. Please do."

His responding smile disarmed me and when he moved to sit, the motion wafted his scent my way. I wasn't sure if it was cologne, because I'd been used to the overpowering stuff most men wore, but his was more like a natural musk. Whatever it was, I drew in a breath to get more.

"Sir?" The bartender's voice sounded miles away, despite the fact that he had returned and stood not three feet from us.

"Scotch, on the rocks."

"Same as before?"

"Yes," the blue-eyed stranger insisted, then turned to face me when he added, "And call me Dom."

Before I registered his name, I rolled my bottom lip between my teeth. "Scotch. Is that where you're from, Dom? Scotland?" I asked, adjusting so I faced him. He leaned in, as if to tell me a secret.

"I consider myself Pictish, but you can call me Scottish, yes."

Of course, the accent was Scottish. It made perfect sense after he said it, but the other word, not so much. I hated to appear uneducated, so I gave a huff of a laugh but found myself admitting my ignorance anyway.

"Pictish?" *So much for the charade.*

"Yes, but I'm much more of a traveler."

I nodded. "I've never left Texas."

The admission weaseled its way out, and I cringed inwardly at how simple it made me look. Plus, I'd been to the casino in Oklahoma. Once.

"Would you like me to show you what I've seen?"

My hips shifted and my gaze fell to the ground, desperate to process how the question sent me spiraling. *Had they turned up the heat?* I'd only been in the bar for less than ten minutes. There was no way it'd gotten several degrees hotter.

I laughed again before bringing my gaze back up to him. "Maybe."

The bartender returned with a highball glass filled with amber liquor and a perfectly squared, oversized ice cube. "And when I share my experiences, what should I call you, lass?"

7

"Joceline." My name came out a little too fast for my liking and a surname followed. Luckily, I had enough wits about me not to use a real one. "DeLon."

"Joceline DeLon." He repeated my name back to me, and I caught skepticism about the last name.

He didn't believe me, but we both knew he didn't have to. It belonged to a friend of mine from high school. I hadn't spoken to them since graduation. It also, apparently, belonged to a woman who drank martinis. Maybe she had a job downtown or was visiting for work from out of state. My imagination whirred to life like a computer, coming up with micro-biographies for versions of myself I could play. "I won't be interrupting any plans by stealing your attention, will I?"

I remembered the martini in my hand and took a drink. *Would I appear desperate if I told the truth? Should I put on a completely fake personality and backstory to match my outfit?* "I'm unaccompanied." The truth somehow won.

"Not anymore." Honeyed confidence dripped from his words.

My head shook in agreement. He could accompany me anywhere he liked. The plains of the Serengeti, the bottom of the Pacific Ocean, or my momma's house. I didn't give a shit. All that mattered was being close enough to hold his gaze and breathe in his musk, to be within reach so he'd touch me.

"Cheers."

I lifted my glass to his when he offered the casual toast, the clink of our drinks muffled by his ability to steal my focus. Even my desire to glance away from him and try to play coy dulled because it meant looking elsewhere. Alabaster and crystal. He was miles from my normal type or my wildest fantasy, but goddamn it, I couldn't care less. My ex's face blurred in my memory, as if his betrayal had been years before, but only if I kept my eyes on Dom.

"Despite my gratitude for the opportunity, I must know what brought ye' to Amaranthine."

"People don't go to bars for regular ole' drinking anymore?"

"Not this bar."

I took the rest of my drink down in one gulp and placed it on the counter before responding. I didn't have enough wealth to be in this five-star hotel or its bar, but I'd never admit that to him or anyone else. It was already bad enough that I was the only Black person there.

"Should I go?" I flirted back with a teasing smirk. We both knew I wouldn't be going anywhere.

"Oh, I wouldn't do that." He lifted the highball glass to his lips but didn't appear to take a drink. I tried my hardest not to stare. "But everyone comes to places like this for a reason."

"What brings you here then, Dom?" I asked.

"Dinner," he answered. I smiled at the joke.

"Liquid diet?"

"It keeps me young."

The remark won a laugh from me. I finally pulled my eyes away to scan the room behind him toward the length of the upscale bar. All of its polished gold and marble greeted me, its wood shelves home to alcohol from brands I'd never seen except some of the bottles on the bottom shelf. The lighting was just enough to illuminate everyone, but not much beyond that and the overall aesthetic matched the art deco of the hotel's interior. The scene transported me into movies I'd seen and imaginary scenes I conjured when I wondered what exactly rich people got up to. Was there a secret room somewhere nearby filled with bottles of wine and liquor that matched the value of my car? Probably.

A wave of warmth ran through me from head to hips, eyelids fluttering at the sensation. I may have finished my first martini a little too quickly. "Well, I came here to drink." As much as I wanted to stay guarded, his inviting aura coaxed me to continue. "Drinks are good for more than liquid diets."

When the bartender turned my way, I discreetly lifted a finger to hail him. He nodded in acknowledgment and started in my direction.

"Drinking is good for many things. To feel, to not feel. Both...simultaneously," Dom explained.

There were plenty of feelings I craved.

Confidence.

Sexual gratification.

A man's genuine interest...to name a few.

Then there were the feelings I begged to be released from.

Abandonment

Rejection.

Inadequacy.

Just thinking about them sent dread into the bottom of my gut.

"Is that where you come in?" I raised an eyebrow.

"I can."

I gave him a side glance at the reply, noting his nonchalant confidence. That unspoken energy made my knees weak. He didn't need to be what I considered conventionally attractive because he'd change my life in one night. Nor did he need to convince me of anything. He wasn't begging to be a stud because he owned the entire stable. All that mattered was whether I cared to visit it. Possibilities raced through my mind until the bartender reached me, throwing a bar towel over his shoulder in his immaculate performance.

"Miss?"

His voice made me jump, as I had zoned out, considering just what Dom could do behind closed doors. I blinked a handful of times. The world returned and, embarrassed, I averted my gaze for a moment, landing on the dark-eyed man from earlier. Coincidentally, he looked my way and smiled.

Oh wow, what a smile. He had a face I could look at for hours. I had to slow down. All the desired attention might have actually been more than I could handle. I wasn't used to having someone eye me while another was talking to me. My body's core temperature wouldn't stop rising. I gave the bartender back my attention.

"Yeah, can I get another one?"

"Please, put her drinks on me," Dom offered.

"Th–thanks."

"It's the least I can do, seeing as you're accompanying me for dinner," Dom said.

"Still, thank you. You don't have to."

"There are plenty of things I do, not because I have to, but for the fun of it. Tell me, Fuil, is this what you do for fun?"

"Do what?" The unfamiliar Gaelic word threw me off. I couldn't even begin to assume what it meant in context. It sounded like nothing I recognized.

"Show up all alone to lavish hotel bars looking more stunning than the authentic Monet hanging in the lobby," he elaborated.

My cheeks tingled at the compliment and my subconscious begged me to be honest—although my gut signaled weariness. Why should I confide in a stranger who, deep down, didn't care at all about me? On the other hand, what did it matter if I shrugged some emotional weight off if he was inconsequential? Dom was a distraction and a means to an end, in the nicest way possible. I didn't want to marry him, and I'm sure he felt the same. We were two strangers in the night. Two adults who understood what happened when you met another good-looking stranger in a bar.

"No, it's not. But I'm not really the person I used to be anymore," I admitted, my thumb finding my left ring finger again. His eyes shot down when he caught the movement but returned.

"The mistakes of our youth. I can promise 'ye, you'll think much less of them tomorrow."

"I'll take forgetting them just for a night."

He offered me a slack-jawed grin, where I caught him running the tip of his tongue against the bottom of his teeth.

My confidence heightened the longer I looked at Dom and remained the center of his attention. His eyes took me in and didn't dare to look anywhere else. I hadn't seen that in so long. It'd been years since I'd been chased. My ex-fiancé hadn't put effort into keeping a spark alive after I said yes. Not even close to the effort he'd put into the private messages of other women after he deemed me damaged goods.

Fuck him.

My eyebrow twitched.

No, that sack of shit wouldn't ruin my night.

Forget about him.

Yes, I'd forget him for one night. If only it could be forever.

Don't think about that asshole when Dom's right here in front of you.

The train of thought initially came in Dom's voice but shifted into my own. The difference struck me. Had he said something out loud at the same time? My head shook to clear the brain fog. My earlier hangover must have had some lingering effects.

I turned in time to catch the delivery of my new drink, which I swapped as soon as it was set down. "I'm sorry. Did you say something?"

His head shook, furthering my confusion, but I pushed it down. It didn't matter whose voice said it in my head; the words were true enough, and my second martini would help me to not think of what's-his-face, anyway.

"Tell me about how beautiful Scotland is."

Ten minutes passed, then thirty, an hour, and then another. Time disappeared around us as my inhibitions fell to the wind, much like my sobriety. Dom charmed me with stories of the small village he grew up in, a town so scenic and simple it must've been stuck in time, far from city lights. He spoke of the most interesting parties and characters. I grew hypnotized by the words and the cadence of his accent. Everything faded away until I swore the only ones in the room were us—unless the bartender appeared to refresh my drink.

I had received my fourth, and what I had insisted was my last, martini and let my fingertips trace the stem. As I did, he described ruins of ancient Roman architecture, strewn with golden fabric and set with the finest furniture and china, elaborate decorations complementing the thousand-year-old structures. All for an exclusive soirée of Italian socialites. His vivid descriptions formed the visuals perfectly in my imagination. It was as if he plucked the memories from his head and placed them in mine. Lost in them, I swayed so hard on my barstool I had to catch myself. Usually, three drinks didn't have me slipping, no matter what their contents were, but I felt these.

"Politicians, celebrities, royalty. Dom, I'm speechless." I laughed. "I could listen to you talk all night."

He smiled, taking such a small sip from his glass I didn't even notice the drink go down. *Wasn't it still his first drink?* I had to let him take a break from talking long enough to enjoy his Scotch, but it seemed he enjoyed telling the stories as much as I enjoyed hearing them.

"I'm so jealous. You've lived such a full life and you're young."

"Not as young as I look, but you're as young as you feel."

I chuckled and said, "Then I must be old, because I'm not feeling the same."

"And how could someone brimming with such beauty and youth feel any less?"

The question forced a frown to my lips. For a moment, memories flashed like a highlight reel of my recent misfortunes. From two miscarriages and the emotionally and physically painful doctor's appointments that accompanied them, all the way to the shock of coming home one day after a work trip to find the apartment half empty. They all struck like lightning in a storm before fading back into my mind.

"Many reasons," I whispered. "Not that I need to bore you with any of them." I finished, my voice heightening. I took a drink, then placed the glass down.

"I have dined in every continent and seen things you'd only imagine in your dreams, but the time I spend with you is not a bore. The things I'll do with you will be nothing close to dull, I promise you that."

My breath sped up after his words, my head swimming. *Did he really mean that, or was it a performance?* At that moment, I didn't care either way. I swayed in my seat and smiled at him.

"I used to be engaged." I lifted my naked left hand into view, then shyly lowered it. "Used to." I chuckled and took a drink. "I guess the not-being-able-to-have-kids part nullified the agreement." The word vomit started, much to my horror, but his eyes stayed on me. I was surprised that the word "kids" didn't have him turning away.

"My late wife had the same affliction."

"Oh my God, I'm so sorry."

"Please, don't worry. That was so very long ago."

"Well," I started. "It seems we've both experienced heartbreak. I'm still sorry you've gone through that. Losing a partner must be awful." I took a generous sip of my martini and nearly spilled it sitting it back down.

"Oh shoot." God, I was feeling that vodka. I hiccuped, and a hand flew to my mouth. "I'm so sorry." I apologized before it happened again. "I should..." My voice trailed, losing mental clarity quickly. "I need to go..." I slapped my free hand on the countertop, then grabbed it to steady myself. "To the baths...bathroom."

Yes, the one with water and...toilets and mirrors, lots of mirrors. I gave my head a shake, but it didn't help.

I gazed up at him as I slid off my chair, feeling like a liquid. Those clear eyes took me in, unbothered, as if my inebriation had gone unnoticed. That or he didn't care. No, he wasn't an asshole; he'd been nothing but nice to me.

Take him back to your room.

The thought hit me in both of our voices as I walked to the rear hallway on wobbling legs. I tried my hardest not to look drunk, but there was no way that I didn't look off. *Why was no one doing anything? Could no one tell how fucked up I was?* Maybe it had been too long since I last stood up.

The further I made it, the harder it was to walk upright. My body wanted to slouch and fall over, as unconsciousness became more appealing with each step. By the time I reached the back, where I assumed the bathroom was, the world spun so fast I grabbed the wall to keep myself from falling.

When someone approached behind me, I hardly registered them until I heard my name muttered, but not by Dom.

"Joceline."

I tried to turn around to see who had called, but all my bearings fell away before I folded to the ground.

Barely able to manage it, I opened my eyes to see that both of my hands were braced on the arms of the dark-eyed stranger from the other side of the bar. My mouth opened to speak, but nothing came out.

I would have panicked if I was capable of it but I didn't have the focus. Again, I heard his voice through my brain fog so clearly, I thought it spoke directly into my mind.

"Do you want to live?"

His harsh tone gave the question a terrifying gravity beyond the words themselves. Was I in danger? His British accent was closer to

English, unlike Dom's, and oddly familiar, despite never having spoken to him before. Not that I remembered.

"Yeah," I slurred the word out.

No matter the reason for the question, my survival instincts were strong enough to have willed the answer out of me. He gripped my arms and used his hold to lift me to my feet and keep me steady.

"Then run, Joceline."

Something about him, the depth of his eyes or the earnestness of his voice cutting through the surrounding silence, made the warning carry immense weight.

"Run."

.

.

.

Run?

I...had to get away...

...from someone?

What was I...who was I running from?

I couldn't...I tried to remember...but it escaped me...

If only...I could think straight...

.

.

.

Without warning, I was no longer in the back hallway by the restrooms.

"You are quite beautiful, 'ye ken." Dom's voice hit me at the same time as my change in location. "You walked in, a desperate mess, and I knew I had to have you. I can almost taste your melancholy now; it'll pair nicely with your pain."

My vision blurred as he spoke, my thoughts losing coherence. There was movement happening around me, but I didn't feel like I was the one doing it. He held me up, like a limp teddy bear. My feet shuffled beneath me, body autonomy slipping away.

"What did you do?" I pleaded.

I wanted to panic, to reach out to anyone who could hear, but I couldn't scream. With each step we took to what I assumed was the elevator bay, lucidity drifted further away. Dom supported my dead weight like a cloud. In front of a mirage of gold, the lines of the doors wavered when they needed to be still. Keeping my eyes open and my head from rolling took all the energy I had.

"Only a little Rohypnol."

The indifference in his answer terrified me. On his face, he smiled. Not a wide smile, but a small one. One that didn't match what he just admitted to doing. In that nonchalance, a new side to him surfaced. Beneath the skin lay a manic satisfaction that could've made the ocean withdraw its waves against him. Warm tears fell down my cheeks, but I hardly registered them.

Why didn't I run away? That man in that hallway tried to warn me. I should've run. Did I try to? I couldn't remember. Not what happened in the hallway, not the last hour—nothing. It was all gone.

"Please," I begged, resisting when he yanked me into the first empty elevator car to arrive, although it didn't do much.

His movements were so strong and sudden, I swung into the cab as a dance partner would. Dom caught me in the same fashion. As we ascended floors, he held me up in his arms and led me in a silent waltz. We twirled and twirled, making me sick to my stomach. "Thank you, Fuil, for being so perfect. The perfect meal. Your anguish, your fear, your grief—it wets my waiting mouth," Dom continued but none of it made any sense. "It takes a refined palette to truly enjoy despair."

"No no no..." I repeated the words under my breath as we traveled higher. Unearthly strength allowed him to turn and spin me like a limp doll, uninterrupted by a single soul who may have helped me. *Please, could someone just hail an elevator? Please.*

"Room 1719, yes?" He spun me into the railing on the wall, and I let out a sluggish protest at the assumed pain, but everything my body tried to signal to me had dulled. Too quick to track, he snatched my clutch and grabbed my room key. The heaving of my chest became heavier while my breath spaced out. I didn't know if I'd be able to keep myself standing much longer, even with the bar as a support.

The elevator dinged and the doors slid open. He grabbed me by the waist, whipped me out of the car and caught me—all before I took

16

another breath. The little contents of my lungs rushed out as a gasp when my chest made contact with his.

"Forgive me, Fuil, I prefer not to sup where I lie."

Fuil?

What was that word?

Was he mocking me, speaking to me in foreign words as he described my murder?

Was he calm because he'd done this all before?

Mere feet from my hotel room door, we passed someone in the hallway, but I couldn't make out a single thing about them through the blur. My head barely turned as I tried to follow them, hoping, wishing, and praying they could make out the wordless plea for help in my tearful eyes. But nothing happened. They didn't help me.

I was going to *die*.

Before my world went deaf, mute, and dark, Doin spoke one last time with a smile.

"Come now, beautiful, it's suppertime."

CHAPTER TWO

A DEEP GASP BROKE through the silence, the breath painful in my lungs as if I hadn't done it in hours. On top of that, my skin burned like fire. Oh my god, there was so much pain. At that moment, every part of my body hurt—inside and out.

The hectic cadence of my heart matched my panic, the organ pounding against the walls of my ribcage. I knew it wasn't anything new for it to beat. But I'd never been able to feel it like that before. The discomfort forced me to groan. As the noise escaped, my vocal cords vibrated, and I cut it short.

Wait.

I was alive.

I was alive?

How was that possible? How had I survived that psychopath, especially in the condition I'd been in? I needed to get up and see where I was.

I regretted opening my eyes the instant I did it. Everything was so clear and bright around me; the air even seemed to shimmer with silver light. The only thing I could do was to force them back shut, if only for a moment of relief.

When I worked up the courage to open them again, I took in the space around me as best I could—but the sun set the room ablaze, and the air still shimmered with light. At least I could see I was still in my hotel room. The guide channel on the television glared at me in a million different colors and pixels; my peripheral vision blurred, but not as much as it should have been. I barely managed to focus on a single thing.

I kept my eyes open longer, struggling to concentrate with each blink. The longer I did it, the easier it became. I closed my eyes for five seconds, then opened them and as I refocused. I leaned into it, centering on a new point. To my right, every word of the emergency plan glued to the back of the hotel door was legible. My vision snapped to the front, then back to the sign. Against the plastic of it, I made out actual fingerprint smudges.

How the fuck were those visible from the bed?

Bed?

My eyes darted down but shot back up. I didn't know if I saw dark red or brown, wine or blood, but there was enough of it that the sight made my jaw tingle. And my dress I'd worn the night before was in pieces. My dark tan skin was exposed through rips made with such violence they looked like an animal had attacked me.

My gut jerked. I needed to get up and into the bathroom, quick. I knew the sensation from its appearance at nearly every one of my hangovers since I'd been on the losing side of my late twenties. Before anything came up, I leaped up and ran to the bathroom.

The next hour of my life turned into a disgusting hellscape of bodily fluids. Never had a hangover been so intense in my life. My body rid itself of all the waste it could find. Worse than the stomach bug of 2014, I expunged anything and everything, violently. I dripped thick, rancid sweat from every inch of my skin as I clutched porcelain. The sweat smelled strangely like iron when I'd never had that happen before. I'd take weird sweat and throw-up over being an obituary, but still it wasn't pleasant.

I crawled into the shower with no more liquid left in me, needing to get clean. Once I turned the water on, I finally looked down at myself for the first time since waking up, starting at my outstretched hand. The tawny skin remained undisturbed after dried blood brightened and then washed down the drain. I searched the rest of what was exposed through the rips. Everywhere my eyes roamed was free of injury. I wet my hair, braced to find an injury to my head, but nothing burned or ached on my scalp.

Panic set in again. I rolled what remained of the cream satin material off my body. I had to find something, anything, to explain what was on the bed. If it was blood, the blood had to be my own. There was no way it didn't belong to me. He said he was going to hurt me.

Pupils darting, I couldn't tell my tears from the shower water trailing my face. Not only could I not find any proof of injury, assault, nothing...I couldn't remember a thing. It all faded to black as soon as I made it to the door with that monster.

My hand reached up to the temperature control lever, and I turned it further right, the water taking no time to heat. I turned it again, then further, stopping only when I didn't think I could bear any higher. I wanted to...tried to turn it up more.

Teeth bared, I ignored the pain on my sensitive skin after a minute and turned the mechanism until it stopped. Around me thickened with steam through the shimmering air, and I released my emotions within that haze. Each sob I gave forth was heavy in my lungs. When I attempted to slow my breathing, the air skittered as it traveled through my mouth, giving an audible warning that the emotional distress took precedence over my physical turmoil.

Had he done something to me that left no marks? How? There was no way that was possible with the horror show on the bed. That deep red color covered everything, including me. I was covered in dried blood. *How were there no marks?*

Between sobs and dry heaves that rocked my torso, I tried to remember. I just needed one detail, something cohesive, but all that stopped at my room door. Everything else was gone. There were no answers to all the questions.

But I knew that I was lucky to be alive.

How I'd escaped it, who knew, but I had. All his charm and allure that oozed out of him was honey on a trap. I fell for it so easily, as if I wanted him to take me and end my series of misfortunes. I served myself up on a silver platter as the perfect victim.

No. I took all of my drinks directly from the bartender. I didn't leave my seat, not until I was already drugged. He admitted to doing it. Roofies, he said.

While my eyelids stayed open, my actual focus faded, and I pushed myself to concentrate on small details. He never drank anything out of his Scotch, did he? He pretended to, but after hours the glass was never empty. And his voice in my head, was that some kind of manipulation tactic? Was he saying things that I thought I was hearing in my thoughts?

I scoured the memories. Minutes came and went as I lay under that molten waterfall and eventually the heat didn't register anymore.

There wasn't any soreness or pain that signified a sexual assault. Yes, my chest and head ached, and oddly enough my gums, but that was it. No bruises. My thighs were untouched by purple and red. Not that the absence of those meant it didn't happen.

Where did the blood come from?

Deep down I knew at least some of it came from me, although I couldn't find the wound. If not to hurt me, why would he drug me? He had to have done something. The way he talked, he made it seem like he wanted to eat me. Maybe he had a cannibal fetish of some kind and chickened out?

Over half an hour passed before I pulled myself out of my thoughts. I'd softly traced every piece of me I could reach and found not a scratch, bump, or bruise. Not a thing. Only more questions.

Was some of the blood Dom's?

Did I put up a fight? Could I have even tried to?

Was the strange vision change and my discomfort in my own skin a side effect of the drug?

The glittery, wavy air around me definitely had to be. And why were my senses turned up? I could follow each individual water droplet and still see the tile behind it. That wasn't normal.

Why, why, why?

Nothing made a lick of sense, which caused my anxiety to snowball until I nearly beat at the shower walls with my fists. Defeated, I reached up and used the control lever to help pull myself to my feet, the remnants of my dress below. For a moment, I simply stood there. My stomach retched after a while, but as much as I wanted to vomit, I had nothing left in me. Not a drop.

I walked out of the bathroom and my eyes went straight to the bed and the blood soaking into it. I wished it had been wine, but I knew it wasn't. On the bedside dresser, the almost full bottle of merlot I'd brought with me was opened, but corked, and definitely not empty. I'd had two bottles the night before, but those were white wines. It didn't smell like wine, either. It smelled like blood. Blood and something else, something I couldn't place.

I took a deep breath to fill my lungs with air and resolve. I needed to get my shit together. The blood didn't come from a laceration on my skin. The jury was out on internal bleeding. Although, if I lost that much blood from internal injuries, I should've seen it in my vomit. I caught minimal red, not enough to cause alarm. Plus, I'd be suffering hypovolemic shock if it was all mine. There had to have been pints of the stuff all over the place.

Maybe it was internal, but not enough to be life-threatening? I had no idea if that was plausible, but it was the only thing that made sense.

Rage filled me.

There wasn't proof he "attacked" me that the naked eye could see, but there may have been some that I attacked him. A charming, successful man like that, I'd be vilified. They'd spin it to say I'd taken the drugs voluntarily and became violent. It'd be turned on me, an uninfluential woman of color, faster than I could find any concrete evidence. If I could find any. I didn't even know his real or full name. "Dom" wasn't either; I knew that much. Plus, my rape kit would be added to a never-ending catalog of other unsolved cases collecting dust at the hospital. Because what would they do with my partial information and accounts but put it on the back burner?

The world stopped and two possibilities appeared in front of me. Whichever I decided, there would be no turning back. I had to see it all the way through. My mind flooded with all my recent bad luck, the losses I took because of the naivety I held that others had integrity or deserved my trust. The last six months had shown me I'd only ever had two trustworthy men in my life, and only one was left.

My father had been buried for years.

With a racing heartbeat in my ears and fire in my soul, I acted. I threw off my towel and dressed in my last clean set of clothes. The first thing I needed to do was figure out the bloody bed. The comforter had been thrown aside, leaving only the sheets for the bloodshed. I raced into the bathroom and shoveled my things into my bag, then turned the shower back on. Makeup and hair products were tossed into my suitcase, clothes and shoes piled in on top, and chargers stuffed into it once it was mostly zipped up.

A quick search on my phone, which I was grateful remained in my clutch purse, gave me tips for the fabric. And, maybe put me on a watch list. Cold water and soap. Alright then. Getting the material spotless would be impossible, but that wasn't necessary. I only needed to make sure nothing was viable. I couldn't let them find anything from him on it.

Twenty minutes later, I had soaked and scrubbed the regular and fitted sheets, collected and bagged anything disposable and wiped down all surfaces. Damp sheets placed back in place, I grabbed the merlot bottle, uncorked it, and poured it all over the bed like an arsonist with gasoline. Then I tossed the spent bottle on the floor.

It'd work.

It had to work.

From where I stood, I didn't think it looked like a murder scene. I'd pay hundreds for the sheets and maybe a new mattress cover, but I'm sure the hotel had seen far worse than wine stains.

Yes, this would work.

I turned, grabbed my things, donned my oversized sunglasses, and walked out of the hotel room, hoping never to return.

CHAPTER THREE

THE DIM LIGHTS OF the hotel hallway buzzed and glared behind the heavy tint of my glasses. To distract myself, I ground my teeth against each other and walked. In doing so, I brought back the pain in my upper gums, so I went back to focusing on walking. Left then right. One foot in front of the other.

It was so hot. It may have been January, but we were still in Dallas. They didn't have to make the heater put in overtime like that. If I hadn't lost all the moisture in me, I'd sweat the rest of it out. I blew out my cheeks, then released the breath as I reached the elevator landing. Just a little longer, only another five minutes or so and this nightmare was in the rearview. My throat squeezed when I pressed the button to hail an elevator car.

I doubted Dom would be in there, but still my eyes closed when the ding indicated its arrival. One eye opened to no one in the car, but I didn't enter. Couldn't enter.

"Come on, JoJo." I said out loud to myself, using my familial nickname. The words did little to encourage me. I pressed the button again a minute after the car left. My stomach flipped at the thought of getting inside the thing when it arrived. The bright sheen of all that gold and the way it looked as Dom forced me to dance with him was all I could think about. I would take the stairs instead.

I found the nearest stairwell and made my way down, relieved not to trigger any more memories from the night before, but not pleased that I'd have to go down sixteen floors. I thought by halfway down I'd have a side splint or shaky legs, but I had neither. Trailing behind me, my rolling suitcase was light as air. If only it had been so easy to handle when I'd brought it up there Thursday, when I checked in.

Stepping out of the stairwell, my eyes drifted over to the traveling art exhibit. A part of me wanted to see it one more time, but there was no way that I could in my state. Lord knew if I'd ever be able to step foot in an Avery Hotel again. If I wanted to feel fancy, I'd stick to the Gaylord in Grapevine or maybe the Omni.

I bee-lined to the front desk, avoiding what I thought were the stares of strangers, but that may have just been my anxiety playing tricks on me. Inside, the late morning sun blinded me as it beamed into the lobby so I put my sunglasses back on. Around me, the voices and echoes of the high-ceilinged area bombarded my eardrums, sending my shoulders up. I couldn't get the fuck out of there fast enough. My first attempt at happiness after my breakup would be marked as a complete and utter failure.

Heaven help me.

Once I reached the dark wood counter at the checkout, I placed my key card envelope down and slid it toward the desk clerk. Despite the dimmed lighting and absence of natural light where we were, my eyes struggled when focusing. The air around the clerk distorted like it did around me, glittering with a strange silver whiteness. My fingers came up to rub my eyes beneath my sunglasses, but it didn't help.

The clerk scanned the cards, then looked up at me wearing his best customer-service smile.

"Good morning, Miss Fuentes. You're up early. Checking out?" The comment gave me pause, and I wrinkled my brow. Considering the foot traffic around me, checking out at ten in the morning hardly constituted early.

"Yeah, and I had a little bit of an accident with some wine last night. Got it all over the bed. You can charge me for the sheets if you need to. I completely understand." *Yes, perfect. Mention it casually so they can assume what it is right off the bat.*

"Don't worry; Lord's got it under control," he answered. "You're good to go."

The sudden reference to the Christian God caught me off guard enough that I couldn't stop myself from making a face at him. Nothing made sense here. Was the Avery a portal into some weird Twilight Zone? They should put that kind of shit on the website. I had to get the hell out of there.

I turned my body toward the garage entrance, not looking forward to the drive home. Before walking away, I turned my head back to the clerk, lowered my glasses with one hand, then made the sign of the cross toward him, and said, "peace be with you." Flecks of bright white glitter floated around him still when I did, prompting me to blink about a dozen times. I pushed the glasses back up, turned my head, and walked away without another word.

Were hallucinations a side effect of roofies? I didn't have time to stand and stare while I thought about it. I wouldn't bother looking in the direction of Amaranthine, either. I wasn't about to relive that fresh hell on my way out.

Rolling bag trailing behind, it took no time at all to reach my car. I threw my stuff in the back seat of my decade-old white sedan while battling sensory overload from every direction. I had to get home. Walking outside drained all the little energy I had. My arms started burning the longer I was outside, even though I only needed to put my luggage in the trunk. I should have worn long sleeves. It only burned where the sun filtered in through the openings in the concrete. It may have been a mild January day, but the sun's rays covered everything. It was something I should have welcomed, something I usually enjoyed in the mornings, but I didn't. Not even a little.

"Shit," I yelled as soon as I sat down and turned the engine and stereo on.

The volume of it was a personal attack. When I turned it down, the fact it had been hardly a quarter of the way up made me antsy. The Rohypnol didn't want to let go, and my body couldn't stop fighting it. That was the only logical explanation. That or an allergy, maybe an adverse reaction. I'd figure it out later; I needed to focus on getting home in one piece.

When I pulled out of the parking garage and started navigating the confusing downtown streets, I ignored the growing heat that stung my exposed arms. All of the world around me moved in so many different directions. The traffic lights on the road glared, despite the daylight. My eyes burned, even from behind my glasses. Oddly enough, the street signs were easier to read than normal. Even though I could read them clearly enough, it didn't make navigating out of downtown any easier.

I hardly ever ventured this deep into Dallas. My family was from the mid-cities, like so many people who had to say they lived in Dallas just so that people knew the general area they were talking about. But things were so different in Irving, where I grew up, or even in Addison where I lived. This far into my twenties meant I only came here when it was absolutely necessary. And the fact that I drove instead of ride-sharing or taking the Dart made me feel so brave.

Thirty-five minutes passed before I pulled into my apartment complex. Having parked a handful of spaces from my building, relief washed over me like a waterfall. I grabbed my purse and had the house key already isolated on my key ring. Any exposed skin on my body itched worse than ant bites after the drive, but my left side itched especially bad as it was the side my window was on.

My eyes centered on the front door, at the left corner of the building. There was no reason why, but I knew when I got inside, I'd feel better. Fuck my suitcase; I'd get it later. I needed inside, fast.

I took off.

Fingers shaking, my house key scratched at the front door lock while I opened it.

Once inside, I slammed the door and surveyed my skin. The redness of a sunburn faded before my eyes until my bronze skin was left smooth. Almost too smooth. I took a deep breath. The action was meant to center me, but I only grew more discombobulated.

Around me everything looked the same.

All the lights were off, which was just as I had left them. The living room to my left remained in its depressingly bare state. All I had was the cheap couch Matt left and the twenty-dollar coffee table I grabbed from the store. I'd never been one for decorating. Just a few pictures on the wall to remind me of vacations I'd taken with an asshole who didn't have the courage to stick with me through the hard parts. I wish he'd have taken those down when he left. I hadn't bothered to either, to be fair. I needed to do something about sprucing the apartment up so it looked more lived in instead of a future exhibit for what hopeless millennials lived like.

I sniffled, fighting the tickle in my nose of a smell that shouldn't have been there. My face scrunched up. *What the hell was that? Something smelled awful. Was that rotten food?*

Maybe the fridge had gone out while I was gone. I let my nose lead me to the source of the smell, which was a box of macaroni and cheese in my small pantry closet. I grabbed it up, convinced something perishable had been forgotten or spilled beneath it. As the box lifted, I spotted the moisture stain of what I assumed was a busted cheese bag. The gag that left me came out comically loud. After throwing it out, my attention spread from the cupboard to the fridge six feet away to my left.

The cheese sauce smelled bad, but what permeated from that thing took the prize. Anticipating a dead fridge, I pulled a trash bag out from beneath the sink and loosened the opening. With my fingers on the fridge handle, the gentle pulse of electricity radiated from the appliance into me. It hadn't broken down. Dead or not, a putrid stench burned my nostrils and it came from the fridge. I whipped open the door and the whole thing rocked in place.

The inside looked normal, apart from some forgotten produce, but there was no way everything wasn't spoiled. The smell made my stomach spasm. I grabbed everything and tossed it into the open bag. It didn't matter how fresh it looked or what the expiration date was; I shoveled all the contents in. Each bottle I swept into the plastic abyss provided the smallest iota of cathartic cleansing. I'd emptied the entire thing by the time I could pull myself back to reality. I tied the overfilled sack up and threw it outside from behind my door. I didn't want to test the photosensitivity. Not after what it did to my arms in the car.

The apartment still stunk when I turned back around to look at it from the door. Every breath I took revealed something else gross. *How did I live like that? Why was I only noticing it now?*

There was dried sweat on jackets and dirt on the bottom of my shoes by the foyer. Somehow, I could smell God-knew-what from the couch. In my peripheral vision, I caught the rising speed of my chest heaving. A million things, everywhere, from all directions. Everything smelled too much. A stupid thing to think, I knew, but it was true.

29

It wasn't only the scents driving me crazy. My eyes were still playing tricks on me. The colors of my belongings were not quite the same, almost more vibrant. Not to mention the wavy, shimmery bullshit happening in the air around me. And...the electronics hummed? I could hear it but also feel it. The pulse of electricity almost moved through the air and into me, but only with the large electronics. Anything plugged in emitted a humming pulse that reached me even if it was idling. Because I'd turned everything off before I left, I only noticed it from the fridge, my laptop upstairs, and the air conditioner. I located each of them based off of the strange electric hum. And it wasn't right. None of the extra sensory stuff should have been happening. Something was wrong.

I squeezed my eyes shut and let out a yelp. At my sides, my hands shook, but more than that, my entire being vibrated with emotions. Rage, frustration, confusion. Each one flowing into the next like capillaries of river rapids. My mind kept going back to earlier in the morning, when I'd purged my fucking guts out. I needed to do that to the apartment. All I was, all I had, everything needed to be cleaned.

I started in my small kitchen using the same harsh cleaning products I had used countless times. This time though, the fumes left me gagging within the first five minutes. The hang-up did little to stop me, as I switched to boiling water and soap. It may not fully disinfect, but I managed the fragrance well enough.

It didn't take long until I fell into a groove and a few hours passed, allowing me to disconnect further from reality. Any time a memory from the Avery Hotel or my recent breakup reared its head, I scrubbed and wiped with more vigor to will it away. Idle hands led to a wandering mind, and I refused to allow it. Plus, the work took away the sickness.

As I finished handwashing my upstairs bathroom floor, my back arched up when a spasm ricocheted from my gut up my chest until it rattled my head. I threw the washcloth into the pot of soapy water next to me. It no longer had steam rising from the top, which meant it was losing temperature.

As soon as the lightning strike of pain settled, I resigned myself to dumping the pot and starting another. I needed to wipe the walls and baseboards of the second-floor bedroom and stairs before I could conclude my manic cleaning episode, and I still wanted more dopamine.

Right as I placed the fresh fill of water on the stove, my eyes moved to the front door thanks to my intuition. Someone was outside. There was no way I could hear someone approaching from the kitchen on the back wall, but every instinct inside me told me there was someone there.

I made for the door and as I closed in on it, a sudden burst of knocks came. I jumped, hand placed over my heart. *Did someone say they were coming over today?* I hadn't bothered to check my phone, but it had to have been well into the afternoon by that point. I knew I didn't invite anyone over the whole weekend, seeing as I planned my long weekend staycation. I didn't even have to return to work until Tuesday, so I had an extra day to recover. No matter who it was, I didn't want anyone over while I fought a trauma-fueled mental breakdown. I stood behind the door, but the knocking continued.

I rolled my eyes and sighed. If either of my teenage siblings were on the other side of the door, I wasn't driving them back home. Who had the audacity to show up unannounced, anyway? My gut told me it wasn't Marley or Byron.

My skin bristled, charged by an unseen heat that warmed the air between me and the person on the other side of an inch and a half of wood. For a minute I stood there, trying to see if my arms were having another allergic reaction because of the returning warmth. But it wasn't allergies. The warmth didn't come from something on the surface. It overwhelmed me in a metaphysical way. As it heightened, I swayed, somewhat dizzy, before shaking my head to clear the feeling. All the while, someone continued knocking in short bursts.

Not ready to face anyone but able to tell they weren't going anywhere, I whipped the door open with the fervor of an actress on a Telenovela. I expected to see my ex-fiancé or one of my siblings, but it was an oddly familiar stranger waiting for me.

CHAPTER FOUR

"YOU..." THE WORD DRIPPED off my lips as I stood dumbfounded in my tiny foyer, staring into endlessly dark eyes. "You're..." I reached for words, questions, and statements, but they all fell short. Disbelief, and the way red and blue smoke swirled around him like his own personal clouds, paralyzed me into a bumbling idiot. "You're the —" I tried to get the accusation or realization out, but my heartbeat doubled, making me lightheaded. Smoke and clouds, those dark eyes, the sun, the man...

I barely caught myself from collapsing, but not before he rushed forward to catch me if I didn't. The action mirrored his behavior the night before in the back hallway of Amaranthine.

"Who are—"

I backed up to get some distance between me and the man from the night before, the one I noticed before Dom, who had warned me to run.

"Do you need to take a seat?"

His face, paired with his accent, resonated with me in a subconscious place I couldn't pinpoint. A word came to mind, faint but recognizable. *Dove.* I kept it in despite how much the word wanted to come out. Against the harsh sunlight, I blinked and stared as the wisps of red and blue smoke played in the air around him.

I was losing it.

"Why?" I asked, forcing myself to bend my knees so they wouldn't lock in place and send me to the ground.

"You nearly fell out a moment ago, and the things I have to tell you may make you lightheaded again. At least we can get out of the doorway. I know the sun is burning your eyes and my skin." My head tilted, but I didn't speak.

"Sun allergy, yes?" he continued, "Sudden onset solar urticaria starting this morning?" As he spoke, I became uncomfortably aware of the sting of the afternoon light, but from where I stood, it didn't directly hit me. Still, it did make my eyes ache.

As I stood there, wondering how big of a red flag I had to ignore to let him in, he rolled up the sleeve of his button-up shirt and placed the exposed skin into direct sunlight. It reddened and bumped. I sucked in a long breath and held it in. The same thing happened when I pulled out of the parking garage hours earlier. My darker complexion hid how red it should have gotten, but his fairer skin showed it clearly. Just the sight of it made me grimace.

"I'm not going to hurt you; just watch." He put his hands up for a second, then placed the exposed skin further into the doorway, out of the direct sunlight. When he did, the hives receded and his skin calmed until the redness was gone. My eyes widened. I'd seen it on my own skin but seeing it on someone else and how quickly it happened just extended the Twilight Zone from the hotel to my apartment.

The display, coupled with a strange pull in my gut, made it impossible to turn him away and told me to let him in. Only long enough to explain himself, then I'd kick him back out. As crazy as the last twenty-four hours had been, I abided by my intuition. "Hold on."

I shut the door in his face as he started to say something. The sound of it slamming sent my shoulders up but I needed to protect myself somehow. In less than a minute, I had a chef's knife from the block in my kitchen. When I ran back over and reopened the door, the man took note of the new addition and placed his hands up.

"Come in." I pivoted to the side and gestured with the knife for him to enter toward the living room to my right, not the stairs to my left. As soon as he cleared the foyer, I reached forward and closed the door, feeling the sun's intensity as I did, and grimacing at its punishment. Even with a second of exposure, it forced heat into my skin. When I turned inside, everything appeared darker than it should have for a few seconds before adjusting, my slight nearsightedness returning until the sun's effect on my eyes passed.

"Who are—"

"Where do you—"

We both started at the same time.

"Who—"

"Where—"

I sighed when we did it again, then gestured again with the knife at him to go first.

"Where should I start?" he asked.

I kept my position by the door despite the earlier advice to sit. "Your name, for one."

"Not what I thought, but—"

"Then who the fuck you think you are...showing up at my house?"

His expression changed with my last answer. Peony-tinted lips smirked at me and my attitude and I studied him a moment. All the energy in my body tugged toward him, and despite the sensation being entirely new, I recognized it as a yearning of some kind. *Visceral yearning?*

My cheeks warmed the longer I lingered on his face and the tugging continued. He was more handsome up close than he'd been the night before, in a timeless sort of way. Or maybe it wasn't timeless, but out of ours. His dark eyes were downturned and hooded and the irises large, but not enough to make him look alien. Part of me considered that they only gave the impression of being so large because of their darkness. I was plenty used to seeing dark eyes. My deep chocolate eyes greeted me in every mirror and most of my family shared the same trait, except Marley, whose eyes were a few shades lighter. But his weren't brown. They gave off black.

In our mutual moment of silence, we both studied each other's faces. I wanted to know why my brain was reaching to recognize him. I had no idea why he looked at me in the same silence, with the same level of concentration, but it was definitely there.

The rest of his features were perfectly fitting to his face shape, none appearing too big or small. Despite being thinner, his lips were exactly as big as they needed to be. All complemented with scruff that kept him from looking too young. The scruff may have been the one thing modernizing his look, giving him the perfect blend of ruggedness and beauty.

No, I had to focus.

"My name's Rhys Llewelyn," he started. I shifted my weight to one side as the knife relaxed so it wasn't chest level but a little closer to the kidneys. I leaned a little too far to one side and corrected, lifting the knife back up and shaking my head to clear the sudden fatigue. "And I'm your Lord." My jaw loosened and I stopped with it held open, flabbergasted at the sheer audacity of his statement.

"I don't know if it's a guy thing, a white thing, or a British thing, but you can't come in here like a savior, after the fact, when you didn't save shit."

"No, it's a title."

"So, it's a British thing."

"No, it's not that. Please, have a seat. You're swaying." He pointed at the couch, reiterating his earlier request. I sighed but obliged. My body really wanted to rest after I spent hours cleaning. Plus, I'd do almost anything to start getting some straight answers.

As I moved past him, the urge to reach and touch him made me question everything. I didn't act on it, but it was so visceral I felt it in my veins, a magnetism that spoke to my body without words, telling me to just touch him. Pushing the foreign sensation away, I took a seat on the furthest part of the couch. He followed suit but gave me distance on the opposite side by the door. My knife, now resting on my thigh, pointed in his direction and my hand gripped it ready to plunge it into him at a moment's notice. Last night was never going to happen again.

"Explain."

"Lord is a title for what I am because of what I did." The cryptic answer twisted a knot in my stomach. *What did he do? Had I invited in the accomplice to my attempted assault? Did he come to me feeling guilty for what he and Dom did, seeking repentance?* I gripped the knife tighter.

"What did you..." I trailed when nausea rose in my gut from the idea of Dom surfacing. "Were you working with him?" I whispered the question, wondering where in the house my phone was for when I had to call 911 to come get this man after I stabbed him.

"God no." He answered, disgusted. "Dove, I would never."

That word, dove. Why did my mind flag it as familiar when I hardly used it? He used it like a pet name. His repulsed reaction to being grouped with what Dom did reassured my intuitive pull that he wasn't an enemy, but there were still many things left that he could be if he wasn't an enemy. I signaled with the knife for him to continue.

"What I did technically saved you." He hesitated, struggling to find words, his eyes moving as if they could visually find what he wanted or needed to say. Maybe he was as nervous as I was. "I apologize for fumbling. You see, you're my first Protégé. To be honest, I'm surprised but thrilled you're not a Creeper. I thought I got there too late."

My mind dissected what he said to find context and my head tilted more and more to the side. "Me...not a Creeper? Well, yeah. You're the one who showed up at my apartment unannounced. How do you even know my name and address? You better start making sense, or I'm going to use this thing."

"I'm sorry. Please, let me rewind. Perhaps I can shed some more light. Do you remember who I am at all?"

"Remember who you are? The fuckin' dude from the back of Amaranthine? You caught me from falling and told me to run. What else is there to remember? Do I look like I remember?" My eyes widened and I inclined my head. After a few seconds, I exaggerated the facetious expression by quickly blinking at him. His lips tugged with the information as he formulated his response based on it. The idea of there being more than what I could recall twisted knots in my gut. Did I even want to remember what happened in that hotel room? The blood and the remnants of my dress pointed to a level of violence I may not have been able to handle. My fingers trembled around the knife and I grabbed them with my right hand to hide the nervous tick. His downward glance as I did showed it'd been noticed.

"I'm the man from the hallway of Amaranthine, yes. I tried not to interfere; I did. I convinced myself it wasn't my place. But when you stood up and nearly fell, I couldn't take it. I knew he wouldn't let me walk you out of there, but maybe if you left on your own accord...it wouldn't be that I stole you from him. It wouldn't be an insult. It'd be your choice. He could find someone else. But no. He grabbed you as you headed for the door. I was going to intercept you before you got into your room, but it wasn't the same room."

I frowned, remembering the fact that I had to change rooms that morning due to the heater in my room not working properly. *How did he know that?* "I couldn't stop him earlier because I had to find your new room. By the time I found you, it was too late, but I had to make a last attempt..." He took another pause to plan his next words, and despite the continued growth of questions I had, I remained silent. "I—I couldn't stop what he did to you in a more direct way. You must understand, he'd have killed us both in the blink of an eye if I tried."

I sucked my bottom lip in and ran my tongue along it, trying to conjure the memories based on what he divulged. "What did you do?" The question fell from my lips as a delicate breath, so soft my lips hardly moved. Embarrassed, my eyes strayed downward.

"I interrupted it...him...before you—"

"Interrupted what?" My previous volume had been meager, but a sudden burst of agitation ripped through me at his vagueness. I stood, towering over him, huffing my breath, knife only inches from his cheek. "I don't know..." I stopped when my voice cracked. "I don't know where the blood came from, but I know he hurt me. I know he did, even though I can't find where it came from."

"You, Joceline. It's yours."

My jaw quivered. It couldn't have been all mine. There was too much. I'd have gone into shock. "No." Any normal person would have called 911 if they saw someone bleeding out. "No, it can't because—"

"Joceline, you're shaking," he pointed out, his face soft in a show of pity or sympathy. I didn't like either. I shivered and shook out my free hand. The tip of the knife trembled in the air by his skin, moving a little closer.

"No." I backed off, scared of how close I was to stabbing him because of my unsteady hands. I needed space and air. My heart hammered in my chest and my head throbbed.

"I'd be dead, okay? If that blood was mine, I'd...I'd die of blood loss." I stuttered, the throbbing becoming a pain.

There was too much blood on the bed. I'd been functioning on panic and adrenaline earlier when I was in front of it all, but each time the scene flashed behind my eyes left me flabbergasted. So much red.

I grimaced at the pain running from my head to my gums.

"You did," He spoke the words, and everything stopped. I dropped the knife. "But not for long.

I died?

The blood drained from my head and rushed down into my stomach. My body agreed with him, but not my mind. What I woke from didn't feel like a regular sleep. I didn't wake up; I restarted. Waking up was only painful when it was from death. Late-night doom-scrolling had exposed me to articles and blog posts about near-death experiences before. One recurring theme I remembered reading was the agonizing return to life.

My jaw tingled and my chin jutted out and then back in. To combat it, I pressed a hand to my mouth and swallowed. In front of me, Rhys started to reach out but withdrew. The strange shades of red and blue danced around him more erratically.

Had I died in that hotel room?

No. I would need medical intervention to be resuscitated. That's how it worked. My ears rang, then the breath I took was too heavy on my lungs. Through a mental fog, I heard a voice, not Rhys's or my own, but Dom's...

You should be thanking me. I am a mercy.

My eyes welled with water, but all I saw was red. The little memories I did have from the night before were dripping in it. Trails and splotches of crimson painted my world in that room. Everything else was lost. But if I pulled and pried, did I want to find more? Did I not make my choice not to try and see those memories that morning when I washed those sheets? But Rhys said he found me and helped me. How?

"What did you do?"

"When I got inside the room, there wasn't enough time to get you to the hospital, but there was a way that I could—" he said but stopped short as he struggled again with his words. Something begged to come forward in my mind but remained obscured behind a wall. "I turned you."

"Turned?"

"You had lost a lot of blood, but there was still enough there for the mutation to work."

"Mut—mutation?" The phantom sensation of blood loss emerged, a gentle floating into a dark, cold emptiness. An emptiness that spread both forever and into nothing. Into a place with no time nor space.

"I took what remained of your blood and gave you mine."

39

Was he insinuating that he gave me a blood transfusion in the hotel room? What kind of unhinged shit was that? My head craned back. A transfusion from a donor with a different blood type was fatal. It was pure recklessness to even attempt it.

"With the exchange, my blood would kill you. But it wouldn't be forever. You'd come back."

"What the fuck are you talking about?" I screamed, confusion shifting into anger. "You're not human anymore, because I'm not human either," he said. My head inclined slightly, frustration growing. *This delusional idiot supposedly saved me?*

"Oh yeah. So, what are we then?" I asked.

"Vampires."

"Vampires?" I repeated, dumbfounded. A bout of laughter begged to come out, but I pushed it down. I was too angry to laugh but sarcasm managed to still escape. "The monsters aren't the heroes, Rhys. Didn't you know?" I faltered when his expression remained unchanged by my reaction. "Do you seriously believe in vampires?"

"I don't *believe* anything; I know they exist. Using the word believe implies faith in something I can't see. I know they exist because I became one and then I made you into one, too. Now, you're the blood of my blood. You're a vampire." He became more direct with his words, as if getting to vampire was the hardest part and he could talk freely now.

The chuckle finally escaped me. *What a basket case.* My shaky hands came up and gestured towards him.

"You're a vampire." I exaggerated the last word. "And now I'm a vampire." I put my fingers to my chest. "You saw a woman bleeding out and thought, this is my chance. Let me give her a back-alley blood transfusion and try and convince her she's a creature of the night. That's what you're selling. That's the big rescue."

"You can't remember anything, and vampirism is far-fetched. I understand. But are your logical conclusions any better?"

"There's no bite." I snapped, as if I'd found the chink in his story's armor. "I'd have a goddamn bite." When I said it, flashes of pain shot through me, mostly in my mouth and temples, then traveling to my lower torso.

"You did. You had several, but they healed. The only scars you have or will ever have are the ones that fully healed before your mutation."

"No, no... I can't, this is..." I trailed.

Vampires weren't mutants; no story I'd ever read called the transformation a mutation. He was full of shit.

"You knew I was at the door before I knocked, didn't you? Your skin's allergic to direct sunlight. The aura you see around me, it's red and blue. It's not a hallucination, Joceline. Just like the aura you see around you."

He stood and instinctively, I backed up toward the fireplace, hands raised in preemptive defense. "I'm not going to hurt you. I'll never hurt you." He lifted his hands, open palm to me, mimicking the way he'd show an animal he wasn't a threat. Despite how odd everything was, the yearning compelled me to reach out and join my hands with his, and I hated it. "Do you feel that?"

I did, but I'd never admit it. "Feel what?" I zoned in on his palm and imagined the warmth of our fingers connecting, entwined. "I don't feel anything."

Why the fuck did I want to touch him? In spite of the attempted lie, my hand rose of its own volition, connecting with his skin before I had the chance to pull it back. As soon as we made physical contact, I gasped. It wasn't painful, but it was fire. My blood buzzed beneath the surface, as if it called to him and his to me. Shocked, I pulled away with my eyes stuck where my hand once was.

"No?" His own sarcasm surfaced. I didn't see it, but I could hear the smile on his lips. "You don't have bites because we heal. You healed. The sun makes you burn but it won't make you burst into flames. We're weakened by it...allergic to it. In direct sunlight we're almost human again. You feel me because I took everything you had left and gave you everything I had to give to save you."

"Why?"

The air grew heavy.

"I wouldn't imagine doing anything less."

My eyes flashed up to him. "Why?"

"I asked you if you wanted to live and you did. You are so strong. I let you down by allowing him to walk up to you, but I wouldn't let you die."

His face in the hallway appeared in my head, then faded into the face in

41

front of me. "My blood is a part of you now and yours is mine. We're connected and always will be." Despite the absurdity, I slipped into a passive acceptance in hopes it would help it make sense, until he spoke again. "Dom is a vampire, too."

I sucked in a breath as if I'd been underwater, common sense returning.

"What?"

"He's one of us."

"No." I shook my head. "No." It continued. "How dare you?" I moved toward him on the offensive.

"I'm sorry," he said.

"No. No, you don't get to come into my house and spew your crazy shit. I was—" I stopped, my head pounding again. "You don't come here and try and tell me he's some make-believe monster." I seethed.

"Please, Joceline."

"No. Stop it." I threw my hands up. My blood pressure must have doubled because my head swelled with tension. "Stop using my name like that, I didn't give you my name."

I hated that he acted like he knew me when I'd barely laid eyes on him before. I hated everything he said. I hated that even for a moment I thought about believing it.

"You did; you can't remember." He looked hurt, but I didn't care. He was taking advantage of my trauma to make me believe in fairy tales.

"Get out."

"You must understand what you are now. I can't leave you without explaining. I would have been there when you woke, but I needed to drink to restore my strength, or you would have found me unconscious. I hadn't expected you to wake so soon. Please understand."

"What I am *now*?" I spat the words at him, zeroing in on that part. "That piece of shit drugs me and does God knows what in that room and you didn't have the balls to stop it from happening, but that's dismissible, huh? You knew what he was going to do, didn't you?"

"It's not like that—"

"Did you?" I screamed, assaulting my own eardrums.

His eyes averted down before returning to me. "Not exactly." I sneered at him. "But, to an extent, yes," he admitted. A bomb went off in my whole being.

"Why?"

"Why what?"

"Why didn't you stop him?"

He sighed, his posture showing obvious defeat. I wanted him to drown in the shame that radiated off him. It was so palpable I didn't only see it, but my body recognized it as if it was a scent in the air. No matter what my intuition said about him or who he was in the grand scheme of what occurred, he needed to admit to what he allowed to happen and how he minimized it.

"Cowardice, I suppose," he answered. His brow quivered as his eyes scanned side to side for more of an answer. "Fear." He glanced down. "Most of us in that bar knew what would inevitably happen. Amaranthine is a hunting ground for the privileged of our kin." Heat spread in my cheeks as I listened to him, disgust brewing. "The majority of them would've done the same, but he's older, stronger, and far more powerful. No one dared to challenge him, including me."

My eyelids fluttered to ward off an onslaught of tears.

When I walked into that place, an alarm should have sounded, because I'd been released into a slaughterhouse. I was never supposed to walk out of that hotel.

"Y'know what...he was a vampire," I said, walking forward. I didn't know if he couldn't predict my actions or if he did and allowed them, but he didn't react. As I closed the distance between us to get right up in his chest and poke at it. "He was, you are. All of you are because you let him kill me. You all sucked that innocence right out of me. You all stole it away like a vampire in the night!"

"Please, you m—" he started.

"I don't have to do shit. Y'all didn't." His hand moved as if to extend out to me, and I looked down at it and scoffed. The edge of my lip tugged up.

"I deserve your rage," he said. "But the consequences of last night will resonate for the rest of our lives."

Our lives.

As if we were truly connected. No, he only played the savior. He only, allegedly, saved what was left, the edges of the puzzle. He didn't save *me*.

"Get out." The sensation of something moving down my cheeks was present but the wetness of my tears had been lost through the heat.

"You must listen..."

I put my hand, palm down, against his sternum and pushed. Luckily, the warm magnetism didn't seem to work on his clothed skin.

"If you really did anything helpful," I said and sighed with a shake of my head, "then thanks. But that's the last shred of human decency you get outta me, which you don't even deserve. If you want to hear it so you'll get the fuck out of my house...then thank you." I put venom in the words. "Thank you for supposedly stopping something you never should've let happen in the first place. *Supposedly.*" My brows shot up at the end to express my disdain. He grounded himself and his chest gave resistance to my hand. My eyes thinned, and I tried harder to move him. He didn't budge.

"Again, I accept your anger. And I'll let you get it all out and answer your questions, but first you must accept what you are," he said. My lips twitched as I fought a snarl, giving more and more effort into my push. He didn't have to put visible effort into being still. "Despite your new strength, you won't move me." Desperate, I put both my hands on him and groaned as I exerted all my strength. My eyes squeezed shut, and I turned my head so I could use it for more leverage.

Nothing.

"Joceline." His voice went firm. "You can see the aura. You see it on me and you see it on yourself."

"It's...a...hallucination," I ground out through my teeth. His hands came up and seized me by the shoulders, pulling me off him as easily as removing a blanket. With all the effort, the edges of my vision darkened, but I fought against it.

"No, it's not." He gripped my shoulders tighter, but not enough to hurt me. It only heightened my temper, which made me lightheaded. "Look at me." My eyes were on him, but it was all out of focus.

"Look at me," he repeated. I blinked. "Look at my teeth," he instructed.

The canines differed from what they'd been only moments before. My headed turned but stayed studying the sharpened teeth. Despite the confusion, the anger remained. The drugs were playing tricks on me again; that was all. He told me there was something different about his teeth, and my mind was filling in the blanks.

My head grew heavy like bricks were being dropped into it, each one conjuring an even denser fog.

"Hallucinations," I whispered. "Adverse reaction or something." As I spoke, the world went fuzzy. "I'm not a...not a monster." I wouldn't be able to fight the dizziness much longer. "Not a monster. He's a monster." Everything started to gray. "A real monster, not a fake monster."

I'd faint at any moment, but I refused to concede to such ridiculous excuses. I fought the darkness as much as I could, but I was losing the battle.

"You're fading; you need to drink."

"Get out...now!" I yelled, using all I had left in me to lean down and grab the knife off the floor, the tip pressed to his gut.

"I'll give you some time to process this and rest, but I'll be back. I promise. I'll come back for you tomorrow. Just rest." I heard his words but wasn't listening to a single one of them. "Eating and drinking regular food will make you sick. Stay here and I'll come back." He continued as I backed him up toward the front door. Before he reached the door, he pulled his wallet from his back pocket, grabbing a card from it and trying to hand it to me. I pressed the knife harder against him, and he dropped the card to the floor. "That's my number."

I blinked a few times to sharpen my vision, but by the time he opened the door and left, everything had gone gray and fuzzy to the point all I could see were vague shapes. Before I could make it back to the couch to sit down, everything faded out and I dropped to the floor.

CHAPTER FIVE

THE DARKNESS BEHIND MY eyes stayed vacant only a short while before I had the strength to open them. When I did, I found myself in the familiar foyer entrance of the family home I grew up in. From my place on the floor, the ceiling greeted me first, the speckled popcorn texture of the paint accurately dating the house to its late seventies construction. A glance back toward the front door revealed the long-standing cobwebs the kiddos always forgot to sweep, but my mother never chided them for.

Moments earlier I'd been in my apartment; I know I was. The wannabe vampire Rhys had been there trying to convince me monsters were real. But it all got fuzzy around the edges. I must have fainted but that didn't explain my relocation. My stomach turned, permeating unease through my whole body. Something was off. I shouldn't have been there. Mom, Byron, and Marley all still lived at the house in Irving, but my apartment was in Addison. That was a thirty-minute drive away.

I opened my mouth to tell them that I was there, but nothing came out. Not even the sound of my expelled breath. I pulled myself up and looked from side to side. Everything remained intact around me as it should be. The formal dining room was to my left and the corridor to the bulk of the house was up ahead. Not much light filtered in through the windows even with the curtains opened, due to the large trees in the neighborhood. Just as it always was and would be until eventually they grew too much and had to be cut down or relocated.

I tried harder to force out a loud "mama," but again nothing came out. My mouth closed. The entire house was completely silent. Not quiet. Silent. Even ambient noise seemed absent. The television in the

47

living room should have been on, loud enough to provide a blanket of background noise but not enough to disturb anyone. I walked into the house almost every weekend to hear and see the same things. Why was this time any different?

My heart quickened. I should have felt it in my ears and temple with how fast it beat, but I didn't. I sat, horrified, unable to speak or hear a single thing. I stood up and ventured further, hoping things would change if I moved deeper inside the house.

My younger sister, Marley, always played popular songs in her room with the door closed, but the songs echoed down the hallways still. My mama, Annie, hated it but allowed it. Anything the baby of the family wanted, she got. No sounds carried over to me, though. The rise and fall of my chest grew faster. I should've heard so many things in the quietness.

Maybe I had died in that hotel room, and this was just another level of hell. Not that I had believed in heaven or hell before. Had that been the reason I'd been sent here? I drove home from the hotel and everything. I cleaned the blood from my attack off the bedsheets. It was real. I just needed to figure out how I got to my mom's house.

Nearing the opening to the side corridor toward the kids' rooms, my breath stopped, and I jumped at the sound of a fist hitting hard against the front door behind me. Every hair on my arms stood at attention. The volume of it bounced off the walls and reverberated around me. It was deafening until it stopped. I contemplated moving again in the returned silence, but the anticipation of hearing the pounding again kept me glued to the spot.

One second, silence. Two, silence. Three—

The knocking came, nearly sending me up into the air. I knew it'd come, so why did it scare me so much? My body twisted toward the door. Apprehension and dread coiled my insides as I zeroed in on the painted wood.

Who was there?

I wanted to backtrack and check it out, but my body didn't respond. The drive to move further into the house overpowered any desire to see what was outside. One foot in front of the other, I continued at an unnaturally slow pace. My body was heavy; the effort it took to walk doubled, if not tripled.

At my back, the knocking continued. Louder, harder, and quicker. It escalated to pounding, the rhythm hectic. It made my breathing react to the point I nearly panted. I checked the door, the wood bouncing on each impact. The visual made the noise louder.

"Joceline!"

As soon as I heard my name yelled from outside, everything froze. The voice struck immediate fear and dread in me. Whoever was on the other side couldn't get in. My family, they couldn't...I'd never expose them to the monster trying to get in.

Never.

Panic set in. Heat rose from my chest to my ears and face. What would it do to my siblings? Marley and Byron didn't deserve its rage. Neither did my mother.

Down the corridor the quiet hint of a different voice came to me, so low I hardly caught it.

"JoJo."

With the banging, part of me wondered if I truly heard it at all. The monster screamed my name again, causing my jaw to tense. The whisper belonged to my father. The father who last whispered his goodbyes years ago. No matter how delicate, the lost voice stole my attention.

I opened and closed my mouth, over and over, trying to call to my dad. I desperately wanted to hear my familial nickname said by him again. When I tried to lift my foot to make for the corridor, my leg refused to budge an inch. The yelling, the pounding, all of it fell silent at the drop of a dime. It wasn't until everything stopped that I noticed my hands shaking, and I pressed them to my sides to get it to stop, but it didn't work.

After a moment, the phantom's assault on my ears and the door began again, becoming more violent with each barrage until the wood had no choice but to give up. The sound of it splitting forced me to turn and when I did, I caught an arm as it reached through the opening to grab me.

It didn't matter the distance between it and me, or the fact that he physically couldn't reach me; terror overwhelmed every sense of my body. I reacted as if he were seconds away from grabbing me. My head started to shake, side to side.

"Let me show 'ye the things I've seen, Joceline."

It was Dom.

Oh my god, it was Dom.

His face appeared momentarily after he snatched his arm back, looking in through the hole in the door, looking for me. *How did he even know where I lived?* My registered address was for my apartment, not my childhood home. That wasn't right. Those words struck me in a way that I couldn't express. They were what he'd said to me at the bar. Fuck. The fear, disgust, and hatred all bubbled up in me until it erupted.

I grew lighter, able to move freely. From there, I ran to the first door in the side hallway, Byron's room. I tried to scream for him, but my voice hadn't returned. The door slammed silently into the wall beside it and I looked in on an empty room. The teenage wasteland of a seventeen-year-old occupant remained, but he was nowhere to be seen. The walls of his room were littered with posters of beautiful women rappers that he followed, and a few pairs of Jordans had been kicked around the room. But he wasn't there. Clothes piled up in the corner, discarded and dirty...but no Byron. Even his game console was next to his TV, which showed his favorite battle royale-style video game on the home screen. Still, no younger brother. *Shit!*

I turned and ran to the third door, Marley's room, to find the same thing. Lived in, but empty. I walked in and searched for any evidence she had been there recently but came up with nothing. No phone, bookbag, nothing. Her room was hardly cleaner than Byron's. Half her clothes were off the hangers in the closet, strewn over the ground to the point I hardly found a piece of carpet uncovered. Her TV showed her music streaming app, which said her favorite song was playing. No sound came from the speakers. Frustrated, I tried to scream their names with every ounce of strength I could muster, but it was in vain.

The living room? Maybe they were hiding in there?

I went back up the corridor to the opening, then left. As I entered the room, I saw no one. The next silent scream was for my mother, before I turned on my heels and headed to the kitchen and attached formal dining room. Near the front door, which I had passed to get to the kitchen, Dom's clawing at the broken opening took my attention and my stomach sank. He'd get through any second, and if he did...god no. He had come to finish the job and take those I loved with me in death. My survival of the assault was such an affront to him, he refused to accept it. I couldn't let him inside. They were hiding; that was enough. I needed to keep him from getting inside.

Running to the hole, I flexed my hands so my fingers became claws and scratched at his skin anytime it reached in. Each time I came down on his arm, he snatched it away with unnatural speed, but I kept going. More and more I fought, growing tired. Far too tired.

It didn't take long until I barely had the strength to keep my arms up and attack, but even with the exhaustion, inside I raged. He could do what he wanted to me, but I would do anything to keep him from my family. I couldn't let him do those things to my family. Soundlessly, I repeated the word no as he tried to force himself in. He pulled pieces of the door off in chunks until I saw most of his upper body, dressed as he was at Amaranthine in business casual clothes.

"Joceline," he roared.

I flung my arms at him in a continued futile attempt. I couldn't even scratch him. There wasn't a break in his clothes or skin. Nothing I did hindered him from getting through. Tears streamed down my cheeks. My arms wouldn't lift anymore; I used up too much of myself. It was gone. In defeat, Dom laughed and reached his hand to grab me by the shirt. His nails bit through the cotton fabric all the way through to graze my skin. Like a scared animal, I tried to pull myself away from him, cowering away.

"Joceline!"

Someone else's voice thundered behind me and warmth spread through me. As the heat reached deeper into me, the world filled with noise. In the same instant, all my strength returned. I gasped at the change, then lifted my arms to begin my assault on Dom. A moment later, someone was at my back, their proximity making me stronger.

I gritted my teeth and released a guttural scream, then dug my nails into his flesh as deep as I could. I wanted to tear every piece from his bones, to rip him to shreds. I had to destroy him to keep him on the other side of that door.

51

"Joceline," Dom roared again. His face appeared, fangs drawn as he screamed my name.

"You're a vampire," the person behind me said, and in those words I placed them. Rhys. "Dom is a vampire, too." Before I could truly react or turn to look at him, he pulled me backward in a single swift motion, and the world went completely black around me.

CHAPTER SIX

"RHYS, DON'T!"

I cried out and my eyes popped open. Against my cheek the laminate hardwood was cool, but every other part of me was warm. Much too warm. I unfurled from the fetal position, sweat on every inch of me. I took a moment to move through the mental haze and the longer I did, the more I pulled myself out of it. It was a dream. A nightmare. Clarity spreading, the first things that came to me were Marley and Byron, coupled with panic.

I smelled blood.

Where it came from, internal or external, I didn't know but I caught it. I may not have been a doctor, but internal bleeding didn't work like that, right? It didn't resurface after hours, did it?

My hands flew up to my mouth, searching for moisture, wiping at my face and pulling away to investigate. I moved my head from side to side to check my exposed arms. The longer I searched, the faster my breathing became. The inhales were deep, but the oxygen intake did little to nothing to help my spike in anxiety. The sweat wasn't normal. It was pink.

I collected a sheen from my face, then lifted my hands to my nose and inhaled. Blood. Not overwhelmingly so, but it was there. My nose wrinkled. Drug interactions be damned, I never heard of sweating blood. That couldn't be right.

Either way, I had to check on my siblings. Yes, I'd had a nightmare, but Rhys found my apartment. If he could, Dom could. And Dom was capable of far worse than Rhys.

Frantic, I pulled up to look for my phone. It stuck out, half-lodged under a rug. I snatched it. Activated by the movement, the screen illuminated to show a long list of unanswered notifications and the sight of them all overwhelmed me. It was six forty-five in the evening, which was well into nighttime by Texas standards for the time of year. That meant the weird photosensitivity would be gone. No matter the reason, it was there, and I didn't want to deal with it.

Able to focus a little clearer, I scrolled down the list and stopped when my group chat with my brother and sister showed up. Seeing the chat's nickname of "tHe LOVE boooooaaattt" made my heart skip a beat, and my breathing stalled.

Deep down I knew they were alright because I had only had a bad dream, but the world wasn't the same as when I last checked in with them. Not that the spooky monster and shit Rhys said were real, but it still changed forever. I pulled my finger over the bubble for the chat to open it.

> Byron: U home yet? Text us when ur home, mom's worried

> Marley: Find any sugar daddies with sum hot kids? I wanna go shopping

> Byron: Fuckin cringe

> Marley: Kiss my ass

> Byron: Yikes. JoJo, will u text us back so I don't have to read this shit

My eyes focused on the winking tongue out emoji Marley replied with as the last message. I sighed. No matter what I thought or dreamed, according to this conversation, they were okay. They were all safe. My fingers danced across the bottom of the screen and I sent off a vague reply.

BLOOD OF MY BLOOD

> I'm alive, y'all. Damn. Calm down.

I considered my answer for a second. I was alive, but that was as vague as vague could be. Beyond that, I was very much not okay. Divulging more meant I had to tell them what happened to me. I refused to do that; I couldn't subject them to knowing I had faced something like that without recollection. They'd send me to the hospital to get tested, then I'd be forced to report it to the police. My lips trembled at the thought. I couldn't do either of those things anymore. I made my decision before I checked out. The evidence was gone. I hadn't gotten any calls from an unmarked number that weren't marked as spam. The hotel hadn't called. They cleaned the room, no questions asked. I had no practical memories of the assault. I couldn't tell them anything without concrete evidence. I had truly locked the door on what happened. He was probably rich, successful, influential...all the things I wasn't. The police would mention that I had trashed the only viable evidence around and played it off when I checked out.

No, I wouldn't tell them.

They were still kids, not even eighteen years old. I couldn't do that to them.

My phone buzzed in my hands and I refocused my sight to read that the two of them didn't like my answers and the details it omitted. Too bad. They were not just teenagers, they were my siblings. Even if the night had been successful by any stretch of the imagination, I sure as shit wasn't going to disclose any of those details either. Not by a long shot.

Goddamn it, I needed to think.

An invisible pressure heightened on my temples, as if something wanted to pop my head open like a geyser. Despite the liberal size of my two-story apartment, I didn't think I could be there another ten minutes. It had always felt like home before, but now it didn't. It was worse than when Matt had emptied the place when he left. It was all...off.

Everything and nothing made sense.

But where did I go? If I wasn't going to tell my family about what happened, I wouldn't visit them. Too many questions and not enough answers I'd give. Not yet. I didn't have any super close friends that I felt comfortable going to, and my cousin Trina was at a work conference in Maryland for the week.

Lenny's Spot?

The place was a cheap, family-owned sports bar down the road. I'd been a million times. It was familiar but not as much as it had been before the breakup. My stomach ached but when I expected a growl of hunger to come, nothing sounded. I did, however, catch myself slipping into a volatile irritability.

"Screw it."

The last time I'd eaten had been the day before, roughly a full twenty-four hours ago. Drugged, hungover, hangry, whatever it was, I'd benefit from something in my stomach. Especially after how much I threw up. There was nothing of sustenance left inside me.

Lenny's Spot it was.

I threw out all my food anyway. What else was I going to do? Food couriers charged out the ass in fees with a tip on top; it was double the price of going somewhere in person. Plus, my job didn't pay enough that staying at The Avery didn't make my bank account cry a little inside.

Without another word, I grabbed my phone and purse and then headed outside. My mind raced with the nightmare, my attacker, and what Rhys said. Around me, the insects were deafening. Usually in winter, the nighttime offered some relief, but they screamed into the night air.

Face in a grimace, jaw clenched, I locked my door. A neighbor and his wife argued somewhere behind me, and I caught every word of their yelling match. How I could hear it from behind their closed walls blew my mind. Had the world been mute my whole life and my trauma had awakened me? Or was it the opposite and everything was fine and I couldn't process it?

Neither option sat right with me.

The cars lined up against each other were my next point of focus. Each one had their own paint jobs, all of them reflecting iridescent colors at me even in the absence of sunlight.

The single guy I'd been casually eyeing all week drove a sporty little number, a car I pegged as sleek black, but it wasn't. It was midnight blue.

There were flecks of green and royal blue glitter in the paint job, too. My cheeks grew hot when I noticed.

No.

The car was black. It had always been black and it would remain black.

I blinked a few times and refocused on the car, which glared back at me with its midnight blue color.

"Fuck, fuck, fuck." I repeated the expletive. I refused to give the thing another glance and walked to my car, eyes on concrete. What surprises did aged pavement have for me? A multitude of colors and textures, apparently.

I slammed the door of my sedan when I entered and my shoulders drew up. Once the engine was on, I remained on edge. The motor running was a mixture of a single thunderous rolling that didn't stop and a chaotic symphony of a million moving parts that made individual noises. I let out a guttural cry before throwing it in reverse.

After the resiliency I'd shown in the last year alone, I rejected the possibility of losing it. I drew in a stuttered inhale through my mouth and let it rest before releasing it from my nose. All that mattered was getting to Lenny's Spot. Everything else was background noise. Over time, the sound of the vehicle dulled, and I sighed. Driving was second nature enough that it calmed down my overstimulation.

If only my thoughts had taken the same cue.

"Vampires, really?" I randomly blurted out, then shook my head.

How could a grown man think something so stupid? It was comical to the point of being a prank. If it wasn't for being roofied and assaulted, I'd have thought it was one.

Maybe Dom and Rhys worked together in some weird trafficking scheme? I didn't know. Not that it mattered. I wasn't going to call him, I wasn't going to let him back into my apartment and I wasn't going to see him again. I'd never be so easily tricked by good-looking men, not after Matt and Dom. Rhys wasn't getting the chance to get one by me, either. They could all kiss my ass.

CHAPTER SEVEN

FLUORESCENT LIGHT BEAMED INTO my windshield, forcing me to squint as I pulled into a spot right outside the door of Lenny's Spot. Despite how convenient it was, it put me right in front of all the lights of the exterior, which all glowed with unnecessary intensity. Even with the air conditioning turned off, the grill smoke came through the vents as I eyed the brick facade.

The stand-alone building was nestled into the outer edge of a run-down shopping center, one of the countless army of half-occupied, hardly maintained ones across the metroplex. The dark brick might have been red at some point, but now the muddy brown color looked almost black in the nighttime. The painted blue of the stucco surfaces that housed signage was also on its way to brown. No matter where you happened to open one, they were the portrait of the area, the mark of the starving suburban middle class of North Texas. The fact that Lenny's remained, in light of small shops coming and going in the center, gave me a sense of reassuring consistency. After waking up that morning, though, it might as well have been the front of a Las Vegas casino.

My stomach muscles contracted, sending me back into place enough to get out of the car. Maybe the food carrier was a safer bet? Was I ready to be out and about again? I pushed the doubt away. The world didn't stop because I had a bad night. A terrible night. A fucking awful night. It kept turning, I kept moving, and I had no choice but to fall back into the motions of a normal life. They weren't vampires and neither was I. Plus, I couldn't afford to order in after my fateful stay at the Avery Hotel, not with student debt loans to pay off my failed college experience.

Once inside, the buzz of the TVs wasted no time in rattling my brain. I seated myself at a small high-top table in the corner furthest from the other patrons at the bar and about a dozen TV sets. It wouldn't get any quieter in a place like that unless I ate in the bathroom. I considered it for two seconds. The smell of harsh chemical cleaners lingered over the more enticing aroma of grilled food, but even that bordered on too powerful for my sensitive senses.

Barely a minute later, a bubbly server came up to my table, almost skipping. While I commended her for the cheerful front from a customer service standpoint, I needed it not directed at me in my current condition. When I focused on her face, I recognized her as the one who had served my fiancé and I a few times before the breakup. Matt always smiled so wide when she came up to the table or appeared in front of us at the bar top. I'm sure the fact that he followed her on social media had nothing to do with his enthusiasm. Not that it was her fault, but it still made a sour taste roll down my tongue.

"Hello, Joceline."

The shrill volume of her voice made my eye twitch. I opened my mouth to rattle off my usual order, and in doing so, I realized how dry it was. I swallowed and tried again, my tongue dancing in my mouth in search of moisture. "Can I get water and a cheeseburger? No fixings," I ordered. As she turned to retreat and put the order in, my arm shot out and snatched hers to keep her from leaving. I stunned myself with the quick action; I barely caught the movement with my own eyes. "Rare, please."

"R—right." Her eyes panned down to look at my hand as it held firmly to her.

I released, afraid I gripped her too hard. Had I hurt her? No, I wasn't strong enough to bruise someone that easily. That Rhys guy was full of shit. The server's youthful features scrunched up and I grimaced and put my hands into my lap, offering back an awkward smile that showed all my teeth.

"What in the actual fuck was that?" I hissed the words at myself after she walked away. A groan followed close behind. All around me, a multitude of sounds demanded my attention, but all I had the fortitude to do was lay my head down on the laminate wood of the high-top table. Again, I swallowed to combat my dry mouth. No relief came.

As I rested, the vision of the soon-to-be-devoured burger returned. Its warm, glistening juices seeped out of the patty as I cut it in half, returning moisture to my tongue. A coppery tinge spoiled the saliva, but it was better than how parched it'd been. The rare meat was new, though. Never in my life had I eaten a rare hamburger. My steaks were always cooked medium, as I didn't trust the meat anywhere enough to go any redder than that, but not hamburgers. My mind wandered to Rhys and the earlier nightmare, considering the possible correlation. Mentally, my eyes rolled. I wasn't nearly naïve enough to believe I'd been turned into some crazy creature of the night that fed on the blood of humans. That was crazy talk.

"Here you go."

My head shot up as the bartender approached the table, holding a sweating glass of water in one hand and a red, plastic basket with my burger and fries in the other. "Thanks, Brandie." I pulled the name from my memory without trying and as it left my lips, my brow furrowed. Brandie did the same as she placed the items down. I'd never used her name before, I didn't even remember knowing it.

"Uh, do you need—"

"No, thanks," I cut her off, wanting her to be as far away from me as possible.

"Okay, enjoy."

I cradled my face in my hands to chase away the embarrassment of the interaction when she left back to the bar area. "Fuckin' Christ."

I didn't need to linger on it; there were bigger fish to fry and things to eat. I refused to process anything else until I alleviated my more pressing bodily ailments. My eyes fell on the basket and its contents, and I stared unmoving for a long while. Nothing about it seemed off, but I simultaneously wanted to devour it and throw it away in equal measure.

"It's fine," I said under my breath.

Picking up a knife, I grabbed the burger and began sawing into it with the ceremony of a caveman. The fragrance of it grew stronger as I did. I paused.

61

Rhys's warning made me doubt whether or not to bite. Frozen there, my fingers dripped with juices, the patty a deep pink still steaming with heat. The scent of cooked meat was but didn't excite me. I repeated the thought, "it's fine," in my head. I almost turned to look when the entrance chimed but stopped myself. This was more important than the barfly who came in.

Chewing the piece down, relief seemed to come creeping in even if my taste buds didn't approve of the comfort food as much as my mind did. A small nod began, and I grinned as I chewed another bite and swallowed. Rhys was full of shit. None of that hocus pocus was real.

I took a large drink of my water to wash down the food like a competitive eater. With it all traveling down to my gut, my first victory of the day warmed me from the inside out. I'd be alright. Bringing the burger forward, I opened my mouth and took another bite.

My stomach bubbled.

I went rigid mid-chew. Inside me, a violent reaction brewed. My jaw tingled and my mouth watered as if to help lubricate the impending vomit. The food dropped from my stilled hands and I made for the restrooms, hand clamped to my face. The contents of my stomach made their way up my chest to my esophagus.

Bar patrons stared at me as I ran, but I didn't care. All that mattered was getting there before I erupted on a scale that would make Mount Vesuvius quake. One arm came down to force open the swinging door of the stall. I didn't bother checking if it was occupied nor did I lock it behind me. I hoped I ran into the right restroom, but time wasn't on my side. I needed a toilet.

I threw myself down onto the stained white tile of the bathroom floor with enough force my knees made a sickening sound on impact. Lurching out the small amount of food and water I'd had, and what remained of my stomach acid, I begged any and all cosmic beings to make it stop. Never in my life had I been so hungover or messed up that I threw up twice in a single day. I also had never been drugged either, so my opinion was skewed.

My insides clenched and my stomach contracted as it tried to void contents it no longer had, and for minutes I dry-heaved with tears in my eyes. When it finally stopped, I collapsed onto the floor, my arms splayed out, chest bouncing up and down as I panted.

I needed to get the hell out of that bathroom, and I needed to do it quickly. I should have never come there in the first place. The only thing I should've done was get into bed and hide after I left that godforsaken hotel.

Rolling, I tried to muster the strength to get up. My cheek pressed against the disgusting floor much longer than I'd like as I gathered energy. The smell of every chemical or bodily fluid in the room suffocated me like poison gas.

I rolled enough to be able to put my hands against the floor and push myself up and then used the momentum to get up to my feet. My legs and arms wobbled as I did. Wiping the back of my hand across my mouth, I moved to the sink and rinsed my mouth and face, studying my reflection as I did.

Why did I look rested?

My eyes were clear, not sullied by swollen veins or dark circles and my skin glowed clear and dewy. My appearance showed none of my pain and discomfort. My teeth and gums ached, head pounded, and the entire world screamed at me without saying a thing, all while a stranger looked back at me from the mirror.

I dropped my chin to my chest, took a deep breath, then lifted it back up. Refocused on the mirror, I tried to regain composure but for a moment the phantom image of Dom stood behind me, smelling my hair. I swirled around only to be greeted by empty air. My chest bounced up and down, pupils darting around the small bathroom as if he had hidden somewhere.

Before another minute passed, I was out the door, smoothing my t-shirt. When I got to the front a couple of patrons watched me return to my seat, but their gazes were fleeting. I wasn't the first suspected drunk to wander into Lenny's to try and eat, then end up getting sick. Only the disruptive ones held the attention of the regulars for long, everyone else was riff-raff.

I pulled a twenty out from my wallet and placed it on the table before grabbing my stuff and leaving. My stomach gurgled and bubbled as if it wanted fulfillment. I tried to eat; I tried to drink, and it rejected it. How could it still growl at me?

Once outside, I gasped when I brought in a large inhale, aware of how stifled I'd been inside. The bar had too many contradicting scents for me to breath normal.

The night sky was a deep hue of purple and blue above me. I used to love looking at it, but it startled me as I dissected shades of the two colors I'd never seen before. I pulled my car keys out of my pocket with shaking hands, but as I lifted them out a pain shot from the top of my mouth down to my feet. It damn near knocked me over when it did. The surprise disoriented me to the point I stumbled along the wall to the side of the building.

Part of me wanted to run to the car, but if another bout of vomiting started, I refused to do it in there. My heartbeat sped up again until it bounced against my temples and forced my eyes shut. After using my hands to guide me, I braced myself with my back against the brick.

The pounding grew louder and harder until I had tears in my eyes. I slid to the ground and smacked my hand against it. I needed the shock of the impact against the concrete to distract me, especially as my gums seared with pain. I kept smacking the ground with one hand and the other came up to rub my gums.

There was something very wrong. I wasn't sure if my teeth had cracked or moved, but it was something I'd never experienced before. I bit my bottom lip to keep in the screams and when I did, the skin broke and I whimpered.

"Miss, are you okay?"

I ignored the words at first, but footsteps still approached. In the air, cigarette smoke brought back my earlier nausea, and I lurched forward. Doubled over, his steps grew quicker until he was beside me with a hand placed on my back on the assumption that I was drunker than he was.

"Oh shit. How much have you had to drink?"

Blood dripped from my lips from the accidental bite and I cried out when a second wave of pain came. I couldn't figure it out, but my canines ached so much I couldn't control myself. I screamed.

"Miss?" he asked again.

I forced myself to my feet with the man's help. I focused on him and sucked in quick breaths through my clenched jaw. My mind continued to cloud; the fog so thick I couldn't form coherent thoughts.

I reached out to him and circled my arms around the back of his neck as if I needed to support my weight. It wasn't that I thought I would fall...not really. But the warmth of him, his smell, it made me so hungry it hurt.

"It hurts," I whined, voice low, jaw tight.

"What hurts?"

"Everything."

I heard his heartbeat and breath quicken. The pain, the pulses, the whole world screamed at me and I needed it all to stop! All the fucking sounds and sensations, all of it was too much.

"Blood of my blood."

"You're not human anymore..."

"Vampire."

My jaw slackened and I pressed my tongue forward until it met resistance against my two canines, but they didn't feel like mine. They were long and sleek. They were far too sharp to be mine. Mine weren't like these. I didn't recognize them as I rolled my tongue over them.

"I'm—" I started to say, eyes moving side to side as I tried to process my thoughts. "I'm so sorry."

The words left my lips as I struggled with what they meant. Nothing made sense, especially the lie that I was some Hollywood Halloween creature. My heart still beat in my chest; I wasn't dead.

How could I be a vampire?

Was I a vampire?

Peace came to me as I entertained the thought. The way my vision had sharpened would make sense. The fact that the food made me sick made sense too, if I was. It may have made sense.

"I'm so sorry." I whimpered after the apology.

"What for—"

Before the man finished his question, I let go of restraint and let my body go into autopilot. Exhaustion stopped me from fighting it any longer. I didn't have it in me to resist. Whether I fell to the ground, fainted, I didn't care. Instead, my hand came up and clamped his mouth shut to keep him from screaming as I slammed him up against the brick wall of the building. The actions came to me like a natural reflex...like an animal about to devour its prey. Visions flashed through my mind of all the pop culture versions of those creatures making a meal of their victims while everything happened around me. I watched it all happen like memories that had already taken place.

Vampire.

I imagined how they silenced, restrained and consumed humans.

Bloodsucker.

I saw the deep red trails that flowed down the skin of beautiful maidens hypnotized in their bed chambers. Then I moved closer to him, mouth ajar. The blood in my veins willed it all out of me.

Undead.

Unable to bear the sight of what I was about to do but unable to stop myself, I squeezed my eyes shut and bit into the side of his neck.

Monster.

I wasn't sure what I expected, but it didn't happen.

Instead, the man struggled against me as I held him in place. Restraining him as quickly as I did was a miraculous feat, considering the guy looked like he had twenty pounds of muscle on his arms alone. No matter how he tried, I didn't move an inch. My ex pushed me over with ease when we were roughhousing and playing, but a man bigger than him failed to drive me back.

Screams muffled against my hand, but it didn't phase me. I pressed my hand harder against him. I even bit down harder, wondering when something would come out. Wasn't that how it was done in all the movies and shows? A bite? Or was it not working because my dumbass wasn't a vampire? How could I let myself believe such a stupid lie to the point I assaulted a stranger?

When he tried to scream again, I pulled myself away to shush him. In doing so, blood spurted from the wound onto my face and shirt. My hand flew to clamp itself onto the bite, containing as much of the mess as possible. Bright red overtook my vision.

In the mayhem of the moment, his blood hit my tongue, and when it did, every muscle in my body relaxed. Despite only a little bit of it getting into my mouth, it warmed me, and I swallowed it. The satisfaction sent shivers from my head to my toes. It tasted like blood, yes, but not just blood. There was a clear undertone there of something different. So different. Not only did it taste like copper, but it reminded me of other things.

I put my mouth back onto the wound and began to suck at it. With each gulp I took, a memory came. One, the first bite of my mother's sweet potato pie at Thanksgiving. The next one gave me the same satisfaction as a morning kiss from my ex when we were together. So many things from something that should have only tasted like one thing.

I fell into a state of pure euphoria. There was an edge to it, like a fruity cocktail drink. It held a magic there that tingled on my tongue. I moaned. Loud and inappropriate, the sound came as natural as an animal's growl.

I took a draw at the open wound again and again, trying to get more to come out. When it worked, it drove me further into a frantic bloodlust. All I could think about was how amazing it tasted and how much it satisfied me. Each drink gave me more strength and a great sense of clarity.

I needed more.

Nothing else mattered, only more blood.

CHAPTER EIGHT

SECONDS FELT LIKE HOURS with my lips pressed against a weakening pulse. I fell into it in waves. Each heart beat a wave. Each swallow a wave. Nothing else mattered then and nothing else would ever matter again. All of my worries and confusion faded into a red sea as it flowed down my throat and into my being, making me whole again for the first time in too long.

I floated...lost in that red sea.

So much so that I heard, but didn't register, the sound of boots as they came running up behind me. Only when a voice came thundering into my ears and I was snatched off the man did I comprehend what I had done.

"Fuck, please not have taken too much." A Boston accent boomed from a stranger. Everything happened so fast, I struggled to understand any of it. Not the fact that he had me in a bear hug, his strong arms encircling me from behind, or that he was keeping my fighting body off the man I had attacked...the man that was unconscious on the ground.

Flustered, face covered in blood, I stopped kicking long enough for him to put me down and when he did, he moved around me so that he could kneel over the crumpled figure, one hand clamped over the man's wound while bringing the other to his lips. I stood, mouth open to say something but stayed silent as he bit into his palm.

No matter how much I tried, my mind worked like a rusted machine unable to turn over. I kept trying anything to process what had happened and what I'd done. All the while the newcomer took the wound he'd given himself and switched hands so that his blood commingled with the wounded man's.

Was he dying? I didn't know. I had no idea how much blood I'd taken from him or how much was fatal. It all happened so fast. I needed everything to slow down so I could think. Still in shock, my hand came up to cover my gaping mouth, and as it did even more red came into my vision.

Disgust should have overtaken me. I should have panicked like I had in the hotel room, but a calm high pushed away the dismay. I ran my tongue over my lips to get more before everything flooded back in.

"I—"

"Yeah, yeah." The newcomer interjected. "You didn't know."

My mind grasped at my other senses, not just taste. The air around him wasn't right. Much like Rhys, the desk clerk, and I had those clouds, he did too. But, his was different from ours. The...*oh what had Rhys called them*...the auras? The stranger's aura looked like someone with green powder had run up and clapped, releasing it all into the air. The color was obvious, though not as intense as the red and blue I'd seen. Was he not a vampire?

Vampire.

What I was. What Rhys and the clerk were. What Dom was, too.

I watched as the stranger withdrew his hand from the wound then licked it clean. My body wanted me to say something, but the words hit a wall in the silence. The hand that he licked didn't have a wound anymore. My eyes darted to the unconscious man, and I squinted. The bite marks I'd given him had scarred over. I blinked and tried to stare harder, as if it'd make a difference. No fresh bite marks appeared.

"No harm, no foul," the newcomer said.

The hand over my mouth lowered slowly to my side as I short-circuited. He was human; he had no aura. How did it heal so quickly? The stranger's blood? What little he put on it must have had some kind of healing effect but how?

"What the..." I stammered. "Who the..."

Things had to start making sense. Facing away from me as he was, I never got to see who had run up on me to interrupt, save the day, or whatever the hell was going on. Satisfied with his work on the wound, he stood and pivoted so I could get a good look at him.

"Listen here baby Prole, pipe down on the attitude for a second while I clean up the mess." I craned my neck back and scoffed.

Who the hell—

His face came into full view and the insult I started to hurl his way vanished. All I could do was make myself blink a few times, as if my eyes were sending inaccurate signals to my brain. What stood in front of me had me at a loss.

From the shoulders down, he mirrored a member of a British punk band from the early eighties. Pants half red plaid, half black, depending on the leg, were littered with patches and holes at the thighs. But his face... he was so conventionally attractive, which I never cared about before. On the fashion choices alone, of a heavily ornamented leather jacket and combat boots, I expected to see a head full of liberty spikes or a mohawk, but no. His modest chestnut hair screamed, "I pay taxes and hold yearly neighborhood barbecues for the Fourth of July."

The entire vision of him was an enigma.

He was the hottest punk I'd ever seen. A gorgeous, All-American looking anti-capitalist wearing jeans tighter than my own, who looked like he may or may not have called everyone bro until graduating college. A college that his family was a legacy at.

"What?"

I shook my head about a dozen times for good measure.

"Joceline, right?" He asked and my brows furrowed. "Look, Joceline, I'm here to make sure you don't kill anyone or yourself, alright. I'm sorry for calling you a baby."

"You know my name?"

"Y...yeah. I—"

"Where'd you learn my name?"

"Okay. Let's reign this in for a second. I'm not your Lord—"

"Lord?"

"For fuck's sake."

That title, Lord. Rhys had used it before to reference him and his new supposed relationship to me. It sounded so ridiculous, but if the new guy used it maybe it wasn't a joke. The unconscious man groaned from his place on the ground and both of our heads snapped to him. There was breathing and a heartbeat, which meant he was alive. Judging by the

71

steady rhythm, he'd remain that way long enough for me to get a few answers.

"My Lord..." I trailed, my brain reeling and pulling me in different directions. "Rhys?"

"Your—" He emphasized the word. "Lord is Rhys Llewelyn, yes. I'm here right now because he called me in to make sure you're okay while he's away."

My Lord. I didn't like it, but I may not have had a choice but to get used to it. I pulled back on my aggression, the fog and adrenaline settling in my bones, causing me to shiver and shift my weight. In my mouth, the weight of my canines was heavy and foreign. I reached up and touched them, my shoulders jumping when I realized they felt like real fangs would.

I tried to focus on the stranger who gave me the vibes of someone watching a feral stray dog to judge its temperament.

"I'm sorry." I started the apology, but I wasn't sure why. Against my wet skin, the January chill cooled spilled blood and the sensation only made my edge grow sharper. My nostrils flared over and over, getting faster the longer I refused to move.

Emotions crashed around me.

Reality cracked and split, then smashed like the mirror it had been, showing what lay behind the world I'd been taught. The world I knew, the city, the life—it was a lie.

Everything I knew had been a lie.

What Rhys had tried to convince me of was true.

He had an aura; Rhys had one. I had one, too. I had fangs and used them to drink that man's blood. Not only did I drink it, I enjoyed every drop of it.

My eyelids twitched in small movements, wanting to see the whole scene in front of me but somehow my subconscious refused the epiphany. My tongue moved restlessly in my mouth, as if the movements made it harder to taste the blood on it. I tasted it. It tasted beautiful.

I hoped the concrete would open and swallow me whole, releasing me from the nightmare, but it never did.

My eyes moved to the form on the ground, his breathing too audible for its distance. "Is he?"

"Yeah, he'll survive." The stranger answered before I had the chance to elaborate on the question.

"Did I just—"

"Bite that guy, yeah. Yeah, you did." The accent gave his words more sharpness than I cared for but my gut knew he meant no harm.

I tore my gaze away from the man and back up to the punk. The air that released from my lungs as I deeply sighed pushed the scent of blood off my tongue and into my nose.

It should have smelled gross, but it didn't. I should have been sick to my stomach, sick like I'd been inside the restaurant, but there I was, hungrier than I'd been waiting for grace to be over at Thanksgiving dinner. Starved. My throat begged to be coated in more of that crimson, to be drowning in it.

My fingers were covered in it. Dripping with it. I could just—

"Am I..." I trailed the question out as I tried to pull myself out of the sway of blood. "As bad as him?"

I looked at the stranger, hoping, praying he would say no. I needed him to say I wasn't as bad as Dom.

"Him?"

I shook my head. He didn't know. He couldn't reassure me.

"I don't know..." As I spoke, the gravity of my new reality continued to hit from all sides.

The paranormal existed. All my life and well before that it had always been there. All the scary things that went bump in the night were out there. Because of that, I'd been made to do something horrible. There were bloodthirsty creatures out there and I was one. Dom was one too. There were more things to fear in the world. I looked for only a fraction of the dangers. Monsters existed, lurking in the shadows of everyday life, blending in with society, picking people off like they were nothing. The Dallas I knew and loved was teeming with monsters.

My stomach turned.

I was one of those monsters.

"Joceline? Can I call you Jo?" he asked.

My head shook instantly. "Joce like Joss."

"Okay look, Joce. You need to go to Rhys. He's your Lord, he'll walk you through all this. He should have already walked you through it, to be honest. For what it's worth, I'm here to help; I'm Slevin Sweeney." I started to nod, eyes blinking, and as I did, I became aware of my tears. "C'mon. I'll drive you home."

I shook my head at him, and he raised a brow at me. I lifted my bloodied hand and pointed to my car. He sighed and a smile softened his expression. I sniffled. "You don't need to drive while you're in shock. You can get it tomorrow." I shook my head again. "I'm not going to let you drive like this."

Like this. Did he mean the absolute horror show that I looked like, or how I tittered on the precipice of a complete mental breakdown. My lips trembled as I swayed over the cliff of my impending downfall, an inch from losing my shit.

After a quiet pause, he extended his hand for me to take it, and I accepted it with a meek smile. I had no reason to, but I wanted to. So, I did. His hand was warm, a welcome contrast to how cold mine had gotten. He clamped his fingers around mine and gave them a squeeze before giving me a smile that made me return it back at him. "You'll be alright. I've got you."

"What about him? Is he going to be okay? I think we should take him to the hospital."

"Hold on a minute." He said, releasing my hand.

It took all of a minute, as I stood dumbfounded and watched as he arranged the guy in a way that made him look like he was sitting sleeping against the side of the building. All the while, the man groaned and gave the smallest of protests, obviously confused.

"It's fine, see. No need for another documented case of spontaneous blood loss."

"Am I going to get arrested?"

"I'll come back and wash off the blood. Let me just get you home first."

"Why are you..." I started to ask but remembered the answer. "Are you sure he'll be alright?"

"I've done this before. You can tell after a while," Slevin said, the other man groaning a little as he fixed their slumping to look natural. "Cross ma' heart. And he's wicked drunk. I'm sure you could taste it in him. I can smell it. He won't remember a thing."

"Oh, okay."

A bit barbaric, but I supposed I was thankful. I looked at the man as Slevin put the finishing touches on his staging, guilt washing over me. I could've killed him. I would've killed him if Slevin hadn't been there to stop me, wouldn't I?

I *was* a monster.

"Joce?" he said and I looked up at him with glassy eyes. "He'll be okay." He moved himself so that he obscured my vision, his hands coming up to squeeze my shoulders. When he did, I closed my eyes to try to center myself. "He'll wake up groggy with a blank spot in his memory and live to drink another day."

When he took his hands off me, my eyes opened and I gave the man a final look before turning away when Slevin started to walk. He insisted it would be alright, so I had no choice but to believe him, right? What did I know? I had no idea what a Prole was, but I did recognize that I was, in fact, a baby. The alternative was turning myself in before the man even woke up and admitting to doing it because I was Dracula's illegitimate cousin.

"Okay," I responded.

"C'mon baby vamp." He winked at me. "Let's get you outta public, you've got...red all over you," he joked.

As we walked to the far end of the parking lot, closest to the street, I put my focus onto what I saw to divert attention away from my emotions. Parked by itself, I couldn't mistake which car was his as the details of it became obvious.

A restoration in progress, the muscle car was a mess of mismatched parts. A red door panel here, a yellow hood panel there, and spots sanded down to the dull metal beneath. It mirrored its owner. The parallels brought a smile to my face, the positive expression at war with my already present emotions.

As we closed the distance, he moved in front of me to unlock and open the car door. I found the courtesy endearing. Which probably was because he was good looking, because I knew the old thing didn't have automatic locks.

When we were both seated, he turned the engine over. The sound, although loud, didn't startle me as I had expected it would. I released the tension in between my shoulders, which had been there for I don't even know how long, and my whole body relaxed as I did. I welcomed the full body catharsis. I wanted to sigh or moan but refrained. Instead, I listened to the music that had started to play from the ancient cassette player.

At nearly thirty, I shied away from pretending to be young anymore, but a cassette player with no accompanying CD player in a car gave me flashbacks. Like actual flashbacks to the old beat-up SUV my parents drove in the mid-90s.

The memory came out of nowhere.

I must have been three or four years old, tops. Yet, it played through my mind as if it happened a week before. I recalled every detail when our family, only three of us at the time, drove from Dallas to Detroit. We were visiting my dad's side of the family, they were an aunt and uncle, we only drove up to see once. But I recognized the song in the present because it'd been playing at the precise moment.

I hadn't considered how odd it was that I was hearing a funk song from the late seventies playing in a car that was opened by someone who looked like his name should have been Hunter, Chad, or maybe even Josh. The band was Earth, Wind, and Fire if I remember correctly.

Was that...the time he was from?

I pulled myself out of my memory to consider the possibility. Slevin never told me which supernatural being he was, but he had that green aura around him. Almost everyone in the bar didn't have it. Neither did pretty much everyone at the hotel when I checked out.

Humans.

What I no longer was.

The vision of Dom, with red splashed on his face, hit me. The contrast of the terrible memory forced me to suck in my breath with a hiss.

"Your heart rate's up. You alright?"

Slevin's question made me snap my head to the side. I returned to the present, away from my family and from Dom, only thankful to get away from one of them.

"It's a, uh, I just...the song." I sputtered out. He smiled, the gesture as relaxed as the way he drove with two fingers controlling the steering wheel and his hand barely on the gear shift. "Brought me back to a memory I didn't know I remembered."

"That happens a lot at first." He said with his eyes fixed forward. From my place beside him, I could tell there was something there, even if I only saw so much of his face. Maybe he was remembering what it was like when he first became one of us?

"Because I'm a baby vampire?"

The baby title hit me hard in a not so positive light. Did it mean I became some irrational, infantile thing that had no control over her body or mind? I had already shown how little I could regulate my new impulses. That might have been the perfect way to describe me.

"Yeah. We remember things we forgot. We access parts of ourselves that we never thought we could." He started to explain, and I nodded, despite the fact he couldn't see it. "We're different now."

We.

He was a vampire too, in some capacity. It put me at ease by a slim margin, but that little bit helped.

"Different, but not better?"

"Depends on who you ask." He answered. An honest answer, sure, but it could be used a million ways. I huffed at how vague it was.

"I'm asking you."

"Well, in that case, my case, better."

"Oh."

", I'm not better just because I'm a vampire. I'm better because of the things in my life that changed when I became one."

I narrowed my eyes at the also vague answer. It said a lot and nothing at all. All of these vampires were cryptic. Would I have to learn how to do that too? Say a lot and nothing. Were there classes?

Looking forward, it took half a second to spot that the apartments were half a mile away. I sucked on the inside of my cheek and stewed. On the radio, another song started by the same band and without turning I watched him nod his head in rhythm.

Vampires.

Dom. Rhys. Slevin. *Me.*

There were more out there, for sure. There were also the ones that made those I knew of. How many had I passed on the streets or talked to at work? The sun allergy was annoying, but it wouldn't kill us. I had driven home earlier and survived despite a gnarly but temporary sunburn. Decades of inconsistent tales and rules in cinema and folk-lore flooded my mind, ones that likely held as many lies as they did truths. I grew more overwhelmed the more I considered the scope of it all.

As we pulled into the complex, I sat up straighter, ready to go home and try to forget everything that had happened in the last twenty-four hours.

"Am I a monster?" I asked as we navigated the parking lot.

"You? Nah. Do you think you are?"

"Yeah." How quickly I said it without hesitation startled me.

"I think you're Joceline Fuentes. And if you ever think you're not, my number's 682-555-9453. If you ever need to talk to someone whose been there before."

I wrinkled my forehead, unable to share his confidence in me. It was such a strange thing for him to even have in the first place, considering he got introduced to me by pulling me off a man's body that I could have easily killed.

"Thanks, I guess," I said, then my head turned to the side when I realized he knew my full name. "So, you know my name *and* you know where I live." He pulled into the spot just outside my building where my car had been parked.

"I'm supposed to be looking after you. Your name and address are the bare minimum of information I'd need to have to do that."

As true as it rang, it still unsettled me.

"Well, thanks again for saving that guy. I don't think I'd live with myself if I killed him." Just saying it made me queasy. I unbuckled my seatbelt, realizing as I did, that I'd likely survive most car accidents, no matter if I wore it or not. Weird. I pulled my keys from my bag, then exited the car. Before I closed the door behind me, I leaned down into it. "Are you gonna take me to my car tomorrow?"

"Ha!" He exclaimed, jokingly. "Rhys's gotta come back by then to do that."

"Right. I should probably not go out again, for sure. Don't want to, like, attack anyone else." I stumbled with what I wanted to say. "Thanks, though. You can go. I'll be good, promise. No jumping guys outside bars," I added the last part to break the awkwardness. He laughed, and

I had to admit, it was infectious. I did the same as I closed the door and walked inside to my eerily uncomfortable apartment.

CHAPTER NINE

I'D BEEN DROPPED OFF at my apartment at roughly nine-thirty that night. By midnight, I had casually browsed a myriad of online forums, educational websites from the mid-two thousands, and about a million social media posts about my new species.

Species.

Race? Did that sound better rolling off the tongue? Not really; it actually sounded worse. My race remained the same, and my name, too. My features hadn't warped in my transformation, or mutation, or whatever goddamn word was the proper vernacular for being made into a vampire.

Vampire.

I hated that word more.

Every time I said or thought it, Dom's face taunted me. Sometimes smiling and flirtatious, other times manic and bloodied, but always there to remind me of what a monster was and how I'd been forced to become one.

Half an hour before midnight, I had barely stopped myself from throwing my laptop from the second floor, the half wall perfect as a punishing drop point for the computer.

The research proved to only further confuse my new identity. Who was I? A victim? A monster? A survivor?

Had I really survived my attack? Could I call myself a survivor when I came out the other side of that trauma and couldn't even call myself human?

Not long after I came home, I'd spent hours staring at myself in the mirror. At twenty-nine years old, I knew every inch of my skin that my eyes could roam without contorting into positions. The scars, the blemishes, all in an unspoken inventory of the trials and tribulations of my body and soul...of my life in visual form. It was my living experience written on my skin. Now, it stopped short because none of the things Dom did to me were there.

I woke up in a hotel room unable to return to who I'd been because of what he did. But, unlike the fact that I fell on a scooter nine years ago and skinned from my lower shin to my knee, that motherfucker killed me and I couldn't find a single scar to prove it.

I knew some of me didn't want to face those new chapters in my book. What would I have done if I'd seen the evidence of the way his fingernails cut open the softness of my stomach like a feasting animal and licked the gore it caused?

I'd forgotten it entirely, but the word vampire gave me visual slices. I remembered the strained look down when I could only move my head. Now I saw the carnage.

Who needed to revisit more of that?

Next door to me, on the other side of what I assumed were walls unburdened with insulation, my neighbors argued. As a background noise, I didn't track their words; I only recognized the tones of their voices and the way they shouted at each other in quick bursts of passion.

I turned on my heels and started another tiny lap on the carpet but looked at the bed. Could I find sleep? If I did, would Dom continue to haunt me? The terror from earlier may have been a precursor to what I'd see if I closed my eyes long enough to become a blank canvas for his obscenities.

Parts of me were tired, others bristling; I was in discord with myself and the world. "Fuck!" It wasn't a yell, but to me it screeched out.

I had no idea what to do next. I didn't want to be here. I, also, didn't have the fortitude to face demons. But, maybe, I had the strength to remember something I loved. *Damn it.* My car was at the restaurant.

Emotions surging, I didn't realize I had punched the wall next to me until I stared at the fist embedded in it. My exhale flitted out of me and I pulled my arm back, hand shaking as I did.

I saw the slightest hints of red across my knuckles. The scent of the blood was metallic and sweet, but also sharp. Did its supernatural contents seep into its smell?

My fingers rubbed around the scratches, desperate to see new wounds or a new scar, but the scrapes blinked out of existence. Only a drop of blood remained to indicate an injury ever happened. Blood could be washed away, gone in a second like all the proof left that morning had been. My nose tingled.

I needed it to be there. I needed it to remain as a testament to the volatile, violent, monstrous thing I became.

I fell to my knees, my fingers scratching at my exposed thighs, cutting through skin with no resistance. The superficial cuts healed so quickly they didn't even bleed, leaving no evidence behind. I sucked in my bottom lip and fought the self-pity for as long as I could muster, but there was no hope of achieving that when I was like this.

I hated what I became.

I started down at my unscathed legs, fingers braced into claws. As my hands relaxed, I breathed out. Expelling air from my body no longer felt natural. Did my body still convert the oxygen I breathed into carbon monoxide? Or was I breathing in and holding it in only to exhale it unchanged, much like how I'd remain?

I pulled myself to my feet and stood there, considering options.

I hated the thought of sleeping in my bed. Despite several washes since my breakup, the thing smelled like Matt. The detail had evaded me before but with my improved abilities, it hounded me. It snuck under my nose and attempted to pull me into a mindset I said bye to months before. Remaining in that apartment already had its challenges when it came to our separation without adding heightened senses on top of it.

My jaw loosened to allow my canines to shift and my fangs to lower. It didn't hurt like the first time I did it. A shiver ran down me, then back up until I shook it out of my shoulders. I'd have to get that under control if I planned to go in public again. If I ever wanted to. My leg twitched as it anticipated standing, but I stopped.

I didn't want to be in public.

Would I have to shield myself in the shadows like some bogeyman? No, I refused to. I wanted to be with my family, though. Of course, going to them was out of the question. If I couldn't control myself with strangers, what did I expect to happen if I dropped fang in front of my siblings or worse, my mother. They'd think I was possessed by a ghost or worse, a demon. There were a million things they'd come up with. I bet they'd never guess it right.

No. As much as I wanted to, I couldn't run into their arms, not without putting them in danger. What if Dom found them, like I had seen in my nightmare?

"Jo Jo." My father's voice sounded in my head as if he stood next to me, "Baby girl, what are you doing?"

I closed my eyes and allowed myself the leniency of doubt.

I knew my father wasn't there, as he had died years before. But my body conjured him forward as a sign that maybe I needed to turn to those that weren't tangible.

I patted my bed frantically to look for my phone. It was there somewhere, in the fluff and distracting comfort of cloth and down. My fingers grazed the corner of the hard metal, with its material coolness. I pushed hard down on the mattress, the resulting bounce made the phone achieve airtime before I snatched it mid-air and pulled it into myself, the screen illuminating.

Hours earlier, Slevin said his phone number. I recalled it without hesitation, despite how casually he'd told it to me. The recollection of the ten digits was as natural as breathing, even if I didn't consciously commit it to memory as I typed it in. I liked that I could remember it with such ease, but it still weirded me out that I didn't fully understand how that worked yet.

"I need you to come back." The words came out as soon as I heard the click alert me that he had answered the call. I hoped my tone wasn't especially desperate, but who cared? If I could just explain what I needed—

"I'm outside."

Chapter Ten

"Joce." Slevin greeted me with a smile as soon as the door opened. My head craned back when the door revealed him, surprised by his natural enthusiasm.

"Slevin."

After the emotional turmoil I had soldiered through, I didn't have the strength to pretend to be welcoming. I didn't want to invite him inside or explain what I needed from him in detail. All I had in me was the strength to get where I needed to go. Everything else would remain in suspension until after that.

"Can you take me to my car?"

"Where do you need to go?"

"It's not impor—"

"I'll have to follow you there to keep an eye on you. Your sedan isn't going to outrun me, either," he said.

I closed my eyes and sighed.

It made sense. In my sensitive and volatile state, I shouldn't have operated a motor vehicle anyway. Did road rage hit differently for a freshly changed vampire? As a Texan, I could do without more of an inclination for aggressive, offensive driving. I already screamed threats at everyone who lacked common sense, especially if I drove on I-35.

When I opened my eyes, I kept my gaze averted downward. "I need to go to the cemetery to talk to my dad."

A moment passed where I didn't breathe, didn't move, but I also didn't hear him do those things either. I tried not to read into it, but I wondered if it coaxed pity out of him. However, given the fact that he was a vampire, he likely buried far more family members than my single one.

"C'mon."

The softness of his voice forced my eyes up, and I conceded to him. Him and that damn face with that damn Boston accent that should've been obnoxious and over the top with all that clothing but somehow made him feel more real.

Damn it.

"Okay."

As we drove, I didn't have the heart to converse aside from the directions that I gave him. What did I have to talk to him about? The mountain of questions I had about what we were seemed too much to ask of a stranger who'd been tasked with helping me. He'd already said that Rhys was the one to talk to about it all. Perhaps those questions had intimate answers or required a bond to explain. I had a whole new culture to learn. There were rules and customs, and a list of things to properly navigate the new underworld. If underworld was the right word. With what little knowledge I had, it seemed as accurate as it came, despite it making all those involved sound criminal and seedy. Myself included.

We weren't all monsters.

Slevin had said so. I didn't know much about him, yes, but when he said it my gut believed him. Rhys, I believed him now, too. But what did I think of him? He seemed genuine but also, my body viscerally reacted to him, so that could've been some chemical response. What part of it was real?

"Left here." I said, hardly looking up in time to read the street sign down the road from both the cemetery and my childhood home.

If I had driven, I would've kept going straight. Straight and then a right at Elm St, followed by a left half a mile down. I'd go right up to the curb of my mom's house and who knew what that could've brought about.

No, dad was the only one to tell.

"You can park here." I instructed as we rolled up to a modest chain-link fence bordering the small cemetery nestled into a forgettable neighborhood in suburban North Texas. Nothing fancy. Quiet enough for rest and quaint enough to be affordable. What more did the dead need? What else would they want? Despite his failing health, we never got him to talk too much about these kinds of things. Things like where to be buried and what to put on the tombstone. He faced what he could of his mortality, but that was too much.

Mortality.

What I didn't really have anymore, I guessed.

"I'll be here. But, if it gets too close to daylight, I'll come get you."

"Fair enough. I'll take my phone and try to keep an eye on the time."

"No rush. You're my only plans tonight." He said and I gave him a closed-mouth smile teeming with awkwardness, then got out.

As I approached the fence, I stuffed my phone into my pocket and braced to jump. With my new strength and abilities, I didn't know how to gauge the effort I needed to put into it. Despite trying to be humble, I overshot by three feet and then tumbled down, barely avoiding a headstone.

Crumpled on the ground, with my face heated in embarrassment, I got to my feet and used everything in me to not look back at the car. Did Slevin see my botch that jump? I really needed him to have not seen that.

I navigated the rows and sections of the cemetery in darkness as if I worked there and made the conscious effort to not read any markers. It should have been easy, but my eyesight made it impossible to ignore all the names and dates. Usually, I went off the shapes and colors, but I got disoriented by all of my father's neighbors. "Fuck." I backtracked a couple of rows to right myself. As I got close, my heart and stomach sank for the first time in years at seeing his plot. I wasn't sure when the last visit was where my approach carried such an ominous tone.

I stood and stared at his headstone for a long while. Then, I returned to myself and fell to my knees. The cold of the grass seeped through my jeans, but I wanted to feel it. It connected me to my father. "Hey, Pops." I sniffled through my greeting, the night wind tickling my nose. "It's me, JoJo." If he was in front of me, I'm sure he'd still recognize me, right? Was I still his baby girl?

"I can't tell Mama or the kiddos, but I can tell you…" I started, tears welling. "I went to The Avery this weekend. That fancy-ass place in Downtown, y'know. The one with the famous paintings in it. I stayed there because of my breakup with Matt. I wanted to forget about him and what he did." I continued and adjusted my position so I sat on my bottom, facing him, eyes focused on the attached portrait of my father in his late forties, full of life.

"It was fun for the first couple of days. I treated myself to all this stuff. I even got wasted on wine in my room one night." I laughed at myself a little but stopped when I realized what part would come next. "But I was drugged and I..." my voice trailed, becoming nearly inaudible. "I was attacked." My volume rose back up. Saying what had been done to me filled me with anger. "Assaulted, and, well, he tried to kill me." I buried my face in my hands and rubbed them up and down; the moisture of my tears smeared cold against my cheeks as another wind blew past. "Would've killed me." I amended. " But someone saved me. His name is Rhys." As I kept going, it was like a floodgate opened. "He's a vampire and to save me, he made me one, too. Like... I'm a whole-ass vampire now. I don't even really know what that means yet."

I recalled what happened to me since I woke up that day. The more I said, the more comfortable I became in the moment. The catharsis of being able to say it out loud, as if talking to someone I knew, filled me with enough warmth to combat the winter chill. I turned and leaned my back against the headstone.

"I don't know what I'm supposed to do, pops," I whined, lifting my back off the stone only to drop it back onto it, like a toddler throwing a fit behind a closed bedroom door. The polished granite resistance was so lovely against my back that I did it a second time.

"What do I do? As much as I knew that my father's voice wouldn't come to guide me in my next actions, I wanted something else to manifest an answer for me. But, if there were vampires and other supernatural things, what did that mean for my father's spirit?

My hands rested, palms down, on the ground above him. I held my breath and pressed my palms harder against the earth, willing a feeling to come that refused to answer my call. If the supernatural, and whatever else, existed now, then it did when he died. He was well and truly gone. I had no visitations and saw no apparitions. I was a member of that other world, and at his grave I felt no presence.

"What fucking good is being a vampire, now, anyways?" I grumbled, picking my hands up.

I wiped them against each other to clean the dirt off and lifted myself off the ground. As I got to my feet, I pulled my phone out to check the time, when it automatically illuminated. After my eyes adjusted, I read the time and sighed. Four-thirty in the morning already, where had the time gone?

I pocketed the thing and walked back to the car, clearing the fence more precisely the second time. I wasn't sure what exactly changed on the second attempt, except maybe I thought more about getting to the other side of the fence versus how high to jump, but it worked. Had I failed again in front of the running car, I would have asked him to leave me out past sunrise.

"Umph." The noise came out involuntarily as I misjudged how low the passenger seat was, collapsing onto aged leather. "How do you drive over speed bumps with this thing?"

"Carefully."

As soon as I closed the door, he sped off into the night, surprising me with his ability to recall the directions and apply them in reverse. I watched the yellowed streetlights as we went from highway to highway. There was a lack of highways in the Dallas-Fort Worth area, in our less than an hour drive, we switched highways three times. They all complicated and eased the traffic of the metroplex at the same time. As my first day, or night rather, as a vampire drew to its end, I found the emptiness of them all so early in the morning to be calming. I interrupted the silent drive only to ask if he'd let me roll down the window. He allowed it.

I wished the drive was prettier, but even with my drastically improved vision, I struggled to appreciate beauty in what I laid eyes on. Above me, however, was a canvas of darkness to get lost in. At nearly five in the morning, we had a couple of hours before the sun would be up. Every once in a while a flight would take off from DFW Airport, and I picked the planes out of the blackness and considered where they were going and who was on it. Maybe a vampire or two was flying out, a young one like me just trying to figure out the rest of their existence.

"Look at you, you remembered all that after I told you once. Is that—" I said as we entered my apartment ten minutes later.

"Normal? Yeah, but if you don't drink, you start to lose it."

"I'm guessing Rhys will explain all this to me later."

"I don't know why he didn't explain this already, but yeah."

"I didn't let him," I admitted as Slevin pulled into a parking spot not nearly as close to my building. Everyone was home sleeping on their beds, which meant their cars had already taken all the good spots. "I didn't believe him about the whole vampire thing and got pissed at him for even suggesting it. Then I kicked him out and fainted." I frowned and shrugged my shoulders, a silent "oops".

"Nice," he responded. "That makes a lot of sense in the context of your actions," he added.

I blew my cheeks out, then released it in a sigh. "Yeah... not the best move. I see that now."

He shrugged this time. "I tried to attack my Lady because I thought she was a demon that manifested while I was high. She turned out to be the opposite."

"Is Rhys a good guy?"

The question popped out of me faster than I had the time to reconsider it, but I wanted to know the answer and Slevin was the only one who could give it to me. Slevin gave me a wide smile and his arm came so that he rubbed the back of his neck before he spoke.

"Rhys isn't a bad guy." He clarified. "Indifferent, which is frustrating, but apparently, he's not indifferent to everyone who needs help."

"How do you know I needed help?"

"Because you're not happy to still be here. You're carrying a weight. If you wanted this, you wouldn't have it."

I started to smart mouth him back about how I was happy to still be alive, but I didn't know if I'd be lying. I bit the inside of my lip then got my keys out and unlocked my front door.

"Whatever." I dismissed, bested. "You want to just play guard duty inside? You can't see my door from your car and it'd be hella creepy for me and the neighbors if you just sat outside like a gargoyle."

He laughed but turned on his heels to walk away. "Nice offer, Joce, but I've got better eyesight than you think. Goodnight."

"Goodnight... old punk dude."

He threw up devil horns with his fingers and walked into the parking lot, leaving me standing at my open door. I didn't bother locking it as I entered and walked upstairs. Before letting emotional exhaustion carry me away to unconsciousness, I covered the windows upstairs with my extra blankets before falling face first into bed.

CHAPTER ELEVEN

I GROANED AND ROLLED over, using my arm to shield me from the sun's rays that heated my eyelids. The morning light was much brighter than I had expected after covering the windows with blankets, and what was that smell?

I took a deep breath and smelled something burning, which kind of made sense. Something hurt me that felt an awful lot like fire.

But where?

My skin?

I whipped my head from side to side to find where the sun had infiltrated my poor attempt to block it out, screaming as I did. A ray of light sliced through the air and landed right where my arm and face had been. The particles in the air were visible in a picturesque way, one that I would've appreciated if they didn't hurt me.

"Fuck." I whispered, looking down at my arm to assess the damage.

The burns had receded into my skin, but as I let my free hand touch the area, it remained hot.

"Damn it." I dragged out the two words with a misery in the exaggeration.

Beneath my covers, my phone vibrated and I snatched it up to reveal a slew of notifications and the current time: barely past one in the afternoon. Okay, not morning light. It may have been winter, but I still had hours before sundown. Did I not stay dead until the moon came up? I didn't think I considered myself dead, even as a vampire. I also didn't think I believed much of the pop culture shit that had been shoveled my way all my life.

My hand slid down the surface of my face, expecting the smooth glide of unblemished skin, but instead the pads of my fingers pulled something flaky and wet and sticky. "What the..."

I sprang up from the bed and ran to the mirror vanity built into the wall beside my bathroom, ten feet from the end of my footboard. Hands braced on faux granite counters, I leaned in and studied the reflection. While there were no open burns or sores, I recognized the dried scabs and blood. I grimaced.

Gross.

Using the hand towel on the ring next to my head, I softly rubbed it all off, dampening the fabric halfway through. Every time the scabs made a crunching noise, I fought off nausea. Fuck waiting for Rhys, I should've asked Slevin to text me a manual while he played private security in the car.

Running the water cold, I splashed it on my face a few times and gave it a few circular rubs to clean the canvas. Surprisingly refreshed by the cleanse, I lifted my head and as I refocused on my cleared skin, I stared in awe. I had sunburns on my arms and face less than five minutes before, but they were all completely healed. My bronze skin was enviable, and my chronic dark circles had disappeared.

"Old scars...no new scars."

I studied my hair next, natural curls and coils of it framing my head with tons of volume that I didn't usually have straight out of bed. Did I have split ends, frizz, dryness? My hand slapped the light switch by my side and bathed the curls in many colors. There were highlights I never noticed them before. I shook my head, and the curls bounced in perfect health. The sight made me smile.

Yesterday I died. *Dead*. Not for long, but I did to become a vampire. The day after I had beautiful hair, glowing skin and sharpened senses of everything.

The smile faded.

I trudged back to the bed to find my phone as the melancholy returned. I may have looked like a million bucks, but an innocent stranger paid that price for me the night before. Who knew the effect my attack would have on him? As I sat on the down comforter, cross-legged and shoulders slumped, I pulled the screen up to read my notifications. None of the people who wanted to reach me would be so lucky, not before I had a grasp on my new existence.

I fell back onto the bed with the phone above me, a huff of air leaving my lungs as I did. Bright screen only eight inches from my face, I pulled up my text messages.

> Why did Rhys ask you to watch me?

He was called on by someone he couldn't say no to.

> Called on? Like vampire jury duty? Is that a thing?

Vampires don't got that kinda government. But it was a summons. I don't know all the details, just that he had to go. Why? You regret meeting me?

I blushed and shied my eyes away before typing.

> That's not what I meant. I wasn't trying to say that. I just thought it was weird.

It happens. I'm glad it did.

> Why?

Because you're not so bad.

I scrunched my eyes closed then opened one to see if he elaborated, but he didn't.

You can't say that when your intro to me was pulling me off a dude

No ones perfect. =P

You looked like you could use a friend.

I smiled at the text. A *friend*. He wasn't lying about that.

Youre right tho. I didn't ask to be this.

most of us don't.

Did u?

As soon as I sent it, I wanted to resend the question. I had no right to ask him such a personal question.

That's none of my business. don't answer that

I overdosed on heroin. I don't think i could've given consent even if I wanted to. Not that I would have said no. Who says no to not dying lol

Oh shit I'm sorry. I shouldn't have brought it up

Don't be. That overdose saved my life. =) worst mutation ever tho. Purging drugs had me smelling like shit for days

> Congrats on the OD then

> Thanks XD

I facepalmed at the emoji but was grateful my joke didn't offend him. I could almost imagine the smile he probably had when he texted it.

> I'll stop bothering you. Didn't mean to wake you up or anything, I know you were just helping Rhys watching me.

> Bother away, no harm here. If I were busy I wouldn't text you back.

He was right about that. I still felt like I was bothering him. I also felt like I wanted a friend. Not a supposed Lord or Sire or whatever. Someone who knew what I was going through and didn't force it on me. Not that I blamed Rhys too much. Well, I did. But he also saved me after he fucked up so he earned a few points back by not letting me buy the farm.

> So, who is Slevin Sweeney?

Slevin texted me for hours about his life in Boston, when he'd been human. I enjoyed learning about him on a conversational level, like we hadn't met each other in the worst way possible. Like we both didn't have to drink human blood to survive. At the end of the day, he was just an old punk who got a second chance. He wasn't a serial killer or villain, not a billionaire or some suave playboy like I'd probably watched in a movie of a vampire. He was just a guy who got an extended ride to life.

> Ma died after I mutated, but I got to go to her funeral. I still keep up with a few friends up there. The punk scene isn't the same up there anymore, but I still know some of em. They keep me up to date on the remaining family there. Not that there's much of them now that Ma's gone. Just Daphne. But I can't see her.

Daphne?

> My daughter. Lost custody of her around the time I mutated. As you can imagine, addicts don't make court dates. Good thing too. What would I have done with a human kid as a baby vamp? XD She's good tho. Good kid. Got a family all her own now.

You don't see her?

> Daphne? No. Can't do that to her. Confuse her like that. What would I say? Hey, I'm your father but I look like we're the same age? Ha!

His text brought me around to my own human family. What the hell was I going to do about them? I missed them so much. I missed Marley's stupid little dances that she learned from the girls at her school and how she'd break into them during lulls in conversation when we hung out like they were her idle animation. I missed sending her ugly selfies to embarrass her, hoping she opened them around people. Or the game we made up when she was little and still played at the house on holidays. It took us hours to make the game board and cards. I'd never let anyone throw it away.

I miss Byron's obnoxious yelling at the television when he lost matches on his video game. Even when I was at the house, all he wanted to do was retreat to his room and play it, but I still heard him. I missed how he would always try and ask my opinion on outfits. Sometimes he'd come out to the living room showcasing them one by one before a date. The shoes always brought the outfit together, he said.

And mama. We shared stories about pops and laughed until our stomachs hurt and we could barely breath. We would try out new recipes I'd find online for family dinner, listening to the funk music she and my dad loved so much when they were younger. She even broke out into dance a few times, which is definitely where Marley got it from. Even with her age, she moved to the music, which was like she was still a teenager. I tried to keep up with her but dancing was never my strong suit. *Just like you father*, she'd say. *You dance just like Richie. Which means you can't!*

> I gotta go. Talk to you later.

> Thanks for keeping me company

> Anytime.

I groaned and rolled over until I was off the bed and standing. My entire being hummed with frustration and apprehension and I needed to get out of the apartment, even with the sun out. My job had me traveling all over Texas and southern Oklahoma, so I was losing my mind while I was on so-called vacation. If I were quick, I could get my car home. I had to cover myself in three layers of clothes and get a rideshare. If I left it too long, I risked getting towed. I doubted there was a supernatural clause in the towing contract for the strip mall. The restaurant was five minutes away, and clothes shielded me enough to not actually burn.

I'd be fine.

Twenty minutes later, I left my apartment as someone named Jarad pulled up. I didn't bother with checking the license plate to make sure that it matched what had been given. If the driver attempted to harm me, I'd be liable to tear their head off before a finger landed on me.

I pulled the hood of my sweatshirt down further as I entered the car and cleared my throat. Despite being aware of how suspicious I looked covering every inch of skin I had, I stayed vigilant. The clothes helped with the burn, but I felt the strength leave my body, even with window tint.

"Sorry, I have a sun allergy."

I hoped the excuse was adequate.

"I had a friend with that." Jarad said, the nodding of his head visible as I looked at him in his rearview mirror. I nodded in unison, mirroring the action to make him comfortable and he accepted it by putting the car in drive and sending us on our way. We ended the conversation there.

As we pulled into the large shopping mall parking lot, I broke the silence when I breathlessly exclaimed, "Oh, thank god, it's there," when I saw my car.

"Too much to drink last night?"

"Something like that," I grumbled back. He didn't know how wrong and right he was at the same time. "Five stars, thanks," I added, seemingly sarcastic though I'd be giving him the perfect rating.

"Take it easy."

I accidentally slammed the door behind me with my new strength, fingers clutching the car keys in my pocket like they were the only lifeline I had. The only exposed skin was my nose and lips and both were covered in a thick layer of two-year-old sunscreen I'd found under my bathroom sink. Even my hands, still hidden in my pockets, were covered with the only pair of gloves I owned.

They were cotton things I'd bought for a dollar at the supermarket when it was winter five years back. They weren't amazing, but good enough for Matt and I to act like kids and play in the snow when we were dating. Wearing them brought back unpleasant memories. No, the memories were nice, but that feeling they provoked had soured. Everything about that relationship had soured.

In a sudden act of defiance, I stood and turned my face up to the sun. I stared, unblinking, at it for what felt like minutes, testing how long I could last with dark but cheap glasses. It was the failing of the sunscreen on the bridge of my nose that caused me to look down eventually. It wasn't forever, but it was longer than I expected. I'd take the victory.

I spied a little piece of paper on my windshield and snatched it off. In messy print, I read, "Please don't tow. Friend is sick. will pick up tmrw." I huffed a laugh out of my nose. I didn't know for sure it was him, but I'd text Slevin my thanks later. He was my first vampire friend, whether Rhys sent him or not.

Unlocking and entering the car, I paused a moment before putting the keys in the ignition. In front of me, the facade of the bar and grill loomed but afforded no shadows. My eyes trailed from the large sign on top down to the door, then to the side of the building. Not a full day before, I attacked someone there. I could've killed them around that brick corner.

Do you think you can still see his blood on the pavement?

The words roared in my head, but they weren't in my own voice. They weren't me speaking. They were spoken to me in an accent I'd only heard one night and would never forget again.

Dom.

But how? He couldn't be there, because he would have no way of knowing I'd be there. Still, that didn't matter. The simple idea of him being here made me uneasy. Even the fact that we were both the same creature didn't strike the fear down. I didn't know what he was capable of, but I knew he was much more powerful than I was as a newly mutated vampire.

I spoke specifically in my mind as if my consciousness was a place for conversation. No one else was in the car with me.

I didn't kill him. I wasn't trying to kill him.

I turned and looked into the back seat of the car to find it was, in fact, empty, as I knew it would be. Of course, he wasn't there. How'd he know I was alive in the first place? He left me for dead in the hotel room. The exact memory, the words said, I couldn't recall them, but I knew he said something before he left me to die. Something said with absolute certainty that the coroner would be pulling me out in a body bag.

The first few kills are always by accident, y'know.

My fist came down hard on the dashboard, the material crushing slightly. "No."

Careful, little one. Don't want these nasty humans to see how dangerous you really are.

"No." I repeated louder. "You're not here. You can't—you're not here." I started the mantra and squeezed my eyelids shut so hard colors appeared in the darkness. "You're not here!" Something told me the words I repeated were wrong. The coolness of smoke rolled over my skin, although it was covered in cloth. My eyelids twitched, begging to open, but I refused. What if I was wrong? What if I opened them and he stood there?

Absolutely not.

He had no idea where I lived or the places that I frequented. There was no way for him to know that without asking me or someone who knew me. He couldn't be there.

Open 'yer eyes, Joceline.

"No."

Open 'yer eyes.

"No."

Open yer eyes!

His voice boomed in my head so loud and shocking, I couldn't help but to do as he commanded, hoping to release his terrible voice from my head. In front of me, standing tall with skin reddened by the sun, he stood. Different colors danced around him, but behind my sunglasses it was hard to register which ones they were. Still, his vampiric aura loomed like an ominous cloud around his tall frame.

Our gaze caught together and I froze. In my chest, my heart seized in a terror I didn't think I'd ever experienced before. His lips curled into a vicious smile, teeth white and shining, canines elongated. I tried to move, tried to breathe, to scream, but I only shook.

"Fuil."

"No, no, no..." I found my voice again, though it remained a whisper.

Then my eyes began to blink rapidly as if to clear the scene in front of me and allow something else to appear. By the time it stopped, he vanished, the change so sudden I tried to convince myself I'd been deceived the entire time. But I knew what I saw. I saw him there. Just there, in front of the car. My eyes watered, my face warmed, and a knot formed in my throat.

Human or vampire, that motherfucker remained.

I'd never be free of him.

Finally alone, my body temperature rose until I swore steam rolled off me. The metal sides of the car's frame closed in on me as I grappled with believing contradictory ideas. Every inch of my body knew he'd been there, while my mind refused. There was no way he knew enough about me to have been there. It wasn't possible. At war with myself, I failed to keep the tears at bay, and they streamed down my face.

Rhys may have saved my life, but at what cost?

My grasp on reality slipped, and the one who aimed to take my life in the first place now haunted me. This wasn't worth saving.

My chest heaved up and down as I cried, borderline sobbing. The longer I went, the more I gasped for air, but every breath fell short. My canines shifted, and my fangs lowered, causing a dull ache to accompany my mental turmoil; their appearance made me feel more shitty, but my emotions willed them out.

I didn't want the fucking fangs. I didn't want to be a vampire at all. How could I be okay with sharing anything with that monster... that beast... that demon from Hell?

If Hell was even a thing to me.

I didn't know anymore. I didn't know anything. I attacked that man unprovoked, all because I was a vampire. I could've killed him, and very well could have if Slevin hadn't shown up like a damn guardian angel.

When the blood flowed past my lips, over my tongue, and down my throat, I wasn't Joceline. Not the Joceline my parents raised. Not the one my siblings loved. I was someone else. I enjoyed that blood. The memory of taking it flooded my senses and my mouth watered. Even my saliva tasted like blood, too.

I balled my hands into fists, my jaw wired shut as I pulled myself out of the feeling. The lust for blood came raw and strong at only the recollection of my first time feeding. A part of me wanted to dive into the euphoria of it to escape my grief. Realizing that, the tears returned tenfold. Dom's voice in my head was right. I would've killed him, and it would've happened so fast. I didn't know where the point of no return was; I wasn't paying attention to my victim.

Victim.

A strong but accurate description for the human. My eyes flashed up to the side of the building, where I'd almost claimed a life. Was it only a matter of time before I had my mouth to the throat of someone else, but I didn't have someone to stop me?

I didn't want to kill. I didn't even want to land someone in the hospital.

Human.

Vampire.

I had transitioned from one to the other and didn't remember it. I let my hand find the keys, still dangling in the off position of the ignition. The sound of them rattling in place sent me into overstimulation, proving how unstable I was.

I had to get the fuck out of there.

Barely hanging on, I started the car on and sped off. A few minutes later, as I pushed ten over the speed limit, my fangs began to recede, though I still felt the weight of them. My body hummed with heat even with the air conditioning at full blast.

I wanted a million different things. All completely separate, but all with the same amount of desire. My hunger, my thirst, it bubbled under the surface. I hated that I identified it on instinct. It tugged at my brain instead of my stomach and tried to weasel its way into my thoughts every chance it got. But I also wanted to run home. My family sat central in my heart, and if I could, I'd drive past my complex onto the highway and keep going until I found myself in their arms. But I'm so hungry now. Would I attack them?

My mind flashed to Rhys and how much I needed to talk to him. It was dumb to rebuke him like I did, but anyone would have done the same in my position. If I accepted his words, no questions asked, that'd make me crazy. That whole situation was fucked. Plus, there was the strange way I felt near him, like being around my loved ones after a long time away, only there was no reason for it. Then, of course, there was Slevin. The random dude who appeared with confidence in me also made absolutely no sense. He had to literally pull me off a guy when he first met me. Yet, somehow, he had faith that I was the Joceline he didn't get a chance to meet.

The Shady Vineyard sign glared at me when I pulled into the apartment complex. The tears had dried and my mind was made. Parking in my usual spot, I cut the engine and pulled my phone out of my pocket. My fingers slid and unlocked the phone, then I opened the contact list and clicked on one of the new entries, the phone immediately starting to trill.

"Dove?"

CHAPTER TWELVE

I STARED DOWN AT the phone as Rhys repeated his pet name to dead air.

"Sorry, butt dial."

I yelled the lie into the phone and ended the call. The confidence I possessed only seconds before in seeking Rhys's company vanished, the polarizing of the emotions jarring.

"Shit." I whispered as I tried to step back and look broadly at my predicament. That and I didn't want to walk back inside in the glaring sun yet.

"Come on." The self-encouragement was weak, as I pulled my hoodie strings tight until the fabric blocked my vision.

I looked at the front door and whined. The run to get inside wasn't the only thing that troubled me. In my lap, the phone started to vibrate with text messages, likely from Rhys, questioning my call.

Maybe I'd woken him up. I figured vampires were supposed to sleep during the day, far from the damage of the sun, unlike my dumbass, who sat in her car with six layers of cotton on. My pits had to be sweating blood. It wasn't enough to bother Slevin; I had to wake up Rhys, too.

As I bounced my knees, I made sure that my house key was ready so I couldn't waste any time. I as inside so fast, it was a blur. The laminate of the door cooled my back through the sweatpants when I slid my body down the wood of the door. Gloved fingers loosened the hood until my hair sprang out and my claustrophobia waned. I sighed.

I needed to call him back.

Absolute trust in him wasn't on the menu, but neither was a complete shutout. He knew much more than I did about the whole vampire world and lifestyle, and he saved my life.

Still on the floor, I pulled my phone out. There was a groan, then I started the call back. It rang only twice before he answered. "Joceline?"

No pet name the second time. "It wasn't a butt dial."

"I know that."

I brought the phone up to my head and rested the cool surface against my cheeks, wishing I had the ability to telepathically express myself to him. I was unsuccessful at it. My stomach suddenly tugged before I responded. "I just ate yesterday, but I'm hungry. And I'm seeing Dom, well, hallucinating Dom," I amended quickly. "I'm spiraling."

I moved the phone away from my cheek so I could tap it against my forehead, brows knitting together. I hated admitting I had visions of Dom out loud to another person.

"Did something happen?"

"Happen, huh? No. I just went to get my car."

"Get your car?"

"Yeah, Slevin made me leave it at the bar."

"You went out in the middle of the day to get a car you don't a reason to use until nightfall?"

I sucked my bottom lip in and bit it, then pulled the phone away from my head to look at it. "More or less, yeah."

Rhys took his turn to sigh. "You're hungry because you're expelling your power."

"Pow—"

I could almost hear the frustration in his voice as he cut me off. "You need more blood."

"No, nope, no." I began, lip popping out. "I just fuckin' ate...drank. Fed off—" I groaned at the thought. "I just ingested blood. I don't want to do that again. I could have killed that guy."

"But you didn't," he reassured. "You didn't when most do."

"Yeah, but I could have," I repeated. "And probably would have if Slevin didn't stop me."

"I heard. But, you didn't," he repeated, exaggerating the words as if that would make me believe them easier. "That's what matters."

"Did you?"

"That's not—"

"Rhys, did you?"

Silence filled my ear as I waited for his response. He wasn't about to get away with not answering the question.

"Yes, I did." He exhaled. "Which is why I'm all the more thankful that you didn't, but if you're expelling power aimlessly like this, you'll have to feed more often. You fed then wasted it. It's basically snacking."

"Snacking?" My face scrunched up at him flippantly giving what I did a name like that. "Ugh."

"It'll be alright, dove."

"Dove?" I finally brought myself to ask about the nickname. "What is that?"

"Why call you dove?" He repeated the pet name and my head snapped to the side, an echo of the word hitting my head like a memory. I blinked a few times as the suspected reminiscence faded before I saw anything in my head except hotel lights. "I don't know, it just fits."

That wasn't it, but I had bigger fish to fry than his nicknames. "Am I going to have to kill? Do you need to kill?"

"No, I don't kill," he answered. "You snacked. I satiate. I don't kill anymore." A tiny pause, but still present. "And I'll teach you not to kill as well. I can teach you to have restraint."

Restraint.

I looked up, and my vision faded out as the memory of Dom forcing me down the hotel corridor took hold. How could vampires show restraint when they feasted on people?

"I promise," he added.

My vision sharped as the memory faded. Why hadn't Rhys bought me a drink at Amaranthine? Would he have had this supposed restraint that would've saved my life and allowed me to check out of the hotel the next day still human?

"I don't know. Maybe I wasn't supposed to be a vampire."

The v-word was heavy in my mouth and saying it brought the taste of that man's blood to my tongue from the night before. I hated saying it, I hated tasting that warm iron, but still, at the thought, my fangs slid out. Not far, but enough that my mouth felt foreign again.

"As if the other option was acceptable, yes?" I flared my nostrils at his attitude. "You're having a rough go of it. It's alright. We both know you didn't go to Amaranthine to die."

I sucked my teeth and rolled my eyes, though he couldn't see it. "What makes you think you know anything about me? You don't know me at all."

Rhys chuckled. "You'll see."

"The fuck does that mean?" I asked.

The line went quiet again and I thought about hanging up, but before I could, he spoke again.

"What are you wearing right now?"

"What?" I scoffed.

"What are you wearing right now?" He asked again, without a single sign of flirtation in his voice.

"Two pairs of socks, boots, thick sweatpants, leggings, long sleeves, gloves, and a hoodie."

"No glasses?"

I blinked in confusion. "I took them off before I got out of the car."

"All of that to go out into the sun because you aren't ready to give up and die."

He was right, but I wasn't about to tell him that. "I don't like the way it itches but burns at the same time. They feel different but the same and it sucks."

"Right." The word dripped with skepticism. "Technicalities aside, you've not taken your new life." I rolled my eyes at the truth of it. "I can teach you to be humane. What happened to you isn't the bare minimum of how we treat humans. Dom isn't all of us."

"Us," I said with hesitation. I didn't want to be in that "us."

"Listen, I'll pick you up at eight tonight. I have a lot to teach you. Wear black; we're going to The Pulpit. I've got to go."

"It's daytime; what could you possibly have to go do? Go back to sleep?"

"I have to return to work."

"Work?" I raised an eyebrow.

"Gainful employment, yes."

"You're a vampire."

Rhys huffed loudly as if I had offended him, "Very much so. Coincidentally, the two aren't mutually exclusive. Generational wealth only works if it continues to build. I have an exhaustive lifespan and a new protégé to support."

"You're going to support me?" I pointed at myself as if he could see.

"Did you think I'd save you from death and then abandon you?"

I shifted on the ground to sit cross-legged, one hand coming up and playing absently with my hair. "I have no clue. I don't know why you saved me in the first place."

He let out a single laugh. "It was a brash decision on my part, I will admit. Even so, no one deserves that sort of end. I'll see you at eight. Stay inside, please."

I made a face at the authority in his tone. "Yeah, yeah."

I pulled the phone down in time to catch the screen activate when the call ended. Some answers, more questions. I took a deep breath and then stood with more grace than I'd had in years. Not even my knees cracked. "Gotta get used to that," I muttered.

Shaking my shoulders out to release tension, I considered the conversation. "The Pulpit, huh?"

I threw myself on the bed when I got upstairs and partially undressed from the protective layers. I needed to see where he planned on taking me. The Pulpit had been labeled the first explicitly goth nightclub in the Dallas-Fort Worth metroplex, and every inch of it appeared to be the vampire hangout I expected. The pictures shown reminded me of an early 2000s vampire movie set. I remembered co-workers mentioning the club in passing years before. It wasn't my usual cup of tea, but I supposed tea wasn't going to be in my cup any longer, anyway. Who didn't like some darkwave now and then anyway?

Having explored everything about the nightclub I could find, my eyes ventured upward toward the closet. I knew that black girls were in the alternative scene, but they still tended to stick out enough. I needed to keep that down to a minimum.

I had a few items in the closet that would do just the trick.

By seven forty-five, I was pacing the living room with my hands crossed over my chest. I had scrutinized my outfit and makeup for nearly two hours. Pacing was the only other thing I could force myself to do. I couldn't stand to look at myself in the mirror anymore. The person staring back looked too close to me without being me. My skin didn't glow like that, and my eyes weren't that bright. My hair wasn't shiny and vibrant like that. I was on both sides of the uncanny valley.

Seconds before it turned seven fifty-five, a knock came to the door as my skin bristled with Rhys's proximity. I let my hand rest on the handle a moment while giving a controlled breath out, then opened the door. When he came into view, a handful of thoughts hit me. The one that took precedence was how disproportionately overdressed I was compared to him. I sucked my bottom lip in and gave it a soft bite.

"Joceline," he greeted, eyeing me.

In a mocking fashion, I curtsied, unsure of what else to do. I felt like an idiot. He opened his mouth to speak, but I held a finger up to stop him. I didn't need a smart-ass remark. If there was another outfit I could've worn in my apartment; I hadn't found it.

For comedic effect, I did a full spin to show off the baggy black cargo pants, combat boots, fishnet sleeves, and lacy camisole outfit. He held back a smile. When I finished, I straightened up and lifted a brow at him. He wore black slacks, black dress shoes, and a dark gray t-shirt beneath a black blazer. It was very much within the color he requested. I pursed my lips and averted my eyes elsewhere.

"All black attire." He grinned at me. *Fuckin' vampires.* "Shall we?" he asked as I caught a soft expression on his face.

Was I really about to get into a car with him and go to some random club? Why would he hurt me after saving my life?

If he had actually been the one to save me.

No, my body recognized him, it reacted to him. It didn't react to Slevin or anyone else. There was something there. I only wish I remembered what happened. Looking at him with gentle amusement, I found that I wanted to remember him saving me more than I wanted to remember why he had to.

"Sure," I answered, aware I also didn't have much of a choice. I wouldn't allow myself to attack another person from hunger. Never again.

The thought of supplies came to mind as I locked my front door behind me. What else did I need to go out and drink blood? Some wet wipes maybe, a towel, a change of clothes? Ridiculous as the ideas were, I seriously considered the wipes. Yesterday's experience proved insightful on how messy I could be.

"Should I grab some wipes?"

The question came out too fast. The look of confusion that swept his features made me pause as we walked to a dark SUV. "Wipes?"

I let out groan that vibrated in my throat as I looked at his frustrating but handsome English face.

"For, like, the blood." I squeaked out, my mouth wanting to rescind deep into my own face so it didn't say anything stupid enough again to warrant his expression. "No, don't," I fumbled. "I know drinking blood is messy, okay. Don't look at me like I'm asking stupid fuckin' questions."

He laughed as he started walking again toward the car unlocking it as we approached. "No wipes. No need."

I rolled my eyes at him and climbed in, unable to change the unamused look on my face. "Did you—"

"Make a huge mess? I feel like you know that answer so you don't even really need to be asking me that."

He laughed again. "Alright, James Bond. Are you going to explain all this shit now?"

"Bond, really?"

"Whatever, Alfred. Better? Let's go, I need details."

"Firstly, outdated...all of your references. That's coming from someone over two hundred and fifty years old. Secondly, I can talk at you for hours about what we are. History, culture, customs, politics. Most of it's not going to resonate with you until you see it for yourself. I'll tell you what I can on the way over, but a lot of it is going to have to wait," I blew raspberries as he continued talking. Then I raised my eyebrow, realizing what he'd said.

Over 250 years?

As in one century, plus another one, half of another one, and some more on top of that?

He was *older* than the American Civil War?

"Wait. I can't," I leaned forward. "Did you just glaze over the fact that you're 250 years old?"

"I am not 250 years old. I am two 263 years old, though I am only 238 years mutated."

"Mutated. You keep saying that word; mutated. No one really calls it that, do they? That sounds...clinical."

"Yes and yes," He nodded. "However, it's significantly better being mutated than damned, I can tell you that," he answered.

"We're not damned?"

He turned away from the road to offer me a smile. "No, we're not damned, demons, or evil. Not that I can tell, anyway."

I breathed out after hearing the words. I had never been religious. I knew it was a strange thing not to be growing up in a place like Texas, but my family and I kept to ourselves. Most of the family said they had their own personal relationship with God. I, on the other hand, never found a connection with anything personally, so didn't think there was anything out there. Either way, stories called vampires damned.

Turning into one would be a terrible way to find religion.

"I didn't think so," I answered, reassuring myself.

Rhys put his eyes back on the road, but they found me again. The picturesque skyline of downtown got closer and closer, tiny twinkling lights doting the shapes of the skyscrapers. The green lines of the Bank of America building stole my attention first, but quickly, I searched out the glove of the Reunion Tower. Able to see details much clearer than before, I noted the shapes of the buildings, some tall, some short, some thin, and some wide, but they all melted together to create a great skyline.

"You're not evil, and you're not like Dom."

I turned and looked out of the window. "Yeah, I know."

"Give it time, you'll become comfortable."

Time. Something I had too much of. Barring the end of the world, I had an endless supply of it. I chewed the inside of my cheek at the prospect of a physical eternity as it rolled around in my head. I'd already buried my father, and I knew eventually I'd bury my mother too, but not the kiddos. I didn't think I could bury them.

I released my inner cheek, and my face scrunched up at the nose. My younger siblings wouldn't look like my siblings for long. My knees started to bounce in my seat. Marley and Byron, the apples of my eye, the pains in my ass, the biggest pieces of my heart, they'd whither away and I'd still look like I did in that moment. How could I make sure they were okay if I couldn't show my face to them? How did Slevin manage to do it with his daughter?

"You had a million things to say," Rhys broke through my thoughts. "Now, you're silent"

"Just thinking about my family."

"Of course, I'd imagine you'll think of them often in the first decade or so."

"Decade or so?"

"I suppose it could be longer," I watched as streetlamps illuminated his face. "Maybe shorter. We're all different."

"You only thought of your family for ten years?" Rhys's expression didn't necessarily shift but I felt the change. It was shame. Shame and a little guilt. Waves of it swayed in my stomach until it made me not nauseous but uncomfortable. My eyebrows shot up when it dawned on me. The emotion didn't belong to me. It was his.

"I'm...I'm so sorry." I fumbled the apology. Oh, I didn't like these feelings at all. My mouth opened and closed a few times, stumbling to find the right thing to say. "I—"

"An empathetic connection is formed between a coupling."

"Coupling?"

"Yes. The connection shared between Protégés and their Lords or Ladies," he explained as we switched lanes.

"I'm not a fan of that word for it," I admitted.

"Coupling is perfectly suited for the term."

"It sounds like the name of some weird religious mating ritual," I mumbled.

Rhys's eyes found me before saying, "You know, you're quite right about that."

I nodded.

"I thought of them less than ten years ago," he added.

"You don't have to— it's none of my business," I interrupted, fidgeting with my hands. "No, it's all right," he reassured me with a small chuckle. "If there's anyone I can be honest with, it's you. I can't hide myself from you, as you experienced."

"I didn't want to," I sighed. "It just happened. Did I do something?"

"No, not at all. Our bond opens a channel of emotion between us. The stronger ones can reach the other side."

I mouthed the word "oh," and then embarrassment struck me. I'd been on an emotional roller coaster since my mutation. I frowned as I connected the dots of what he was saying. "Please tell me you haven't felt everything I've been going through this whole time."

"Like that embarrassment?" he joked, but I didn't laugh. "No. We have to be in each other's presence. You can also ignore it to a point, so as not to get overwhelmed."

I exhaled, thankful. "Thank God."

He smiled at me and tried not to pay it any mind by directing my attention to the approaching structures of downtown Dallas. I may not have visited many places in my life, but I enjoyed my city and the buildings that populated it. Even the ones that litter the outside of downtown, like the crystal palace, with its shining windows covering every surface they could manage to stick them on and the intricate white iron framework.

"What else can you tell me about us? Are we cursed or something?"

"Not at all. From what I understand, we were closer to blessed."

"Blessed? What do you mean?"

The Harry Hines exit approached, meaning we were entering downtown proper. "Blessed, yes. I don't know exactly what by, though. The records we have are old, but they were written accounts. Over time, stories warp. Some called them Gods; some called them other things. All we know is that they made themselves look like us to give us their blood.

They gave it to six people, and those were the first of their classes. We used to call them races, but we call them classes now." He explained. "Then they left. No explanation, no rules. They left the first of us to figure it out on their own and make their own assumptions. All of the old accounts can be taken with a grain of salt, of course. Just because the writing is old, doesn't mean it's true."

"You're telling me Gods came to Earth and gave us their blood to make the first vampires. Are we like blood angels?"

"What? No." He waved his hand in the air to dismiss the idea. "This is not Christianity. This is before all that."

"Before Christianity?"

"Yes. Quite a bit older. The records we have would put it over a thousand years before it. I wish I could tell you more, but I didn't dive far into the archives when I was at the Sovereignty."

"What's that?"

"The Sovereignty's a lot of things for us. They're a wealth of resources. They're protectors. Soldiers. Rulers. They keep everything tidy for vampires so that we don't lose ourselves. Of course, no system is perfect, but they do a good enough job of maintaining the sanctity of the species. Without it, humans would destroy us."

My brow wrinkled at his last statement. "I would think it'd be the other way around."

"A lot would, but humans greatly outnumber us. We are reduced to their strength in the sun. They could eradicate us if we show ourselves."

He said they greatly outnumbered us. How many of the seven or so billion people on the planet were human? "Are there hundreds of us?"

He laughed, then answered, "Hundreds, quite."

"Thousands?"

"Thousands." He repeated with confidence.

My brows shot up, and I blinked. There were thousands of vampires out there and the general population didn't know. My tongue pressed against the skin behind my bottom lip and moved from side to side as I considered the possibilities.

"Millions?"

As I asked, the single word stretched out, my breath stopping in suspense.

"Maybe. Even when I was an emissary, I didn't have access to exact numbers. Not that I tried to find them." He replied. "I doubt there are millions upon millions. Perhaps *one* million, but more than that seems unlikely."

"Huh," I huffed, matter-of-fact. "Okay."

The drive continued in an uncomfortable silence that even our weird ass connection couldn't quell. I'd catch him turn to look at him, but I couldn't quite make out the expression on his face. It played somewhere on the line of curiosity and maybe being sly, but each time I turned to answer his gaze, he would fix his eyes back on the road. Whatever it was, it wasn't strong enough to reach me. By the time we were headed down Commerce Street, I couldn't stand it anymore. Not only had I played telephone tag with Rhys on sight alone, but I'd also examined every millimeter of cuticle skin on my nails. My eyes refused to stay on a single point for more than thirty seconds at a time, and I had no control over it.

"I apologize for the awkwardness. I've never created a coupling myself before." My attention ricocheted off the dashboard onto him when he broke the silence.

"You've never made a vampire before?"

He shook his head. "No. I've been present during a mutation, but only to witness," he clarified.

"Why now?"

"I wish I could say that I had some strong calling to create a coupling, but it was so quick. It was the only way I knew to save you. It was an act of desperation but I don't regret it, dove."

The car slowed to a stop at the underpass as the urban landscape changed from bright lights and high rises to the gentrified facades of Deep Ellum, the club-going side of town overrun with bars, music venues, and buildings a lot shorter than the bulk of the inner city. I'd spent a few nights in Deep Ellum in my mid-twenties for sure. Not anymore, though. Every other weekend it was something crazy going on there.

Before I knew it, I no longer recognized where we were.

"You thought I called you a dove when we first met," Rhys spoke again, filling the silence.

I pulled my eyes away from the neon lights. "At Amaranthine? By the bathroom?"

"No, the night before that. I don't think you remember that night."

No shit. In my mind, the first time I had met him was in the bar.

"But, you will with time. You were pissed, though."

I perked up, confused. *Had he done something to make me mad?* "Pissed?"

"Drunk."

"Drunk?"

My hands came up to hold my forehead as my eyes closed and my head lowered. Was that what happened that night I had gotten wine drunk in my room and blacked out? Had I run into him in the hallway? What kind of interaction did we have? A hand lowered to pinch the bridge of my nose.

"If it's any consolation, it wasn't bad. I enjoyed it."

"What is that even supposed to mean?" I straightened my back. "You met me blackout drunk, and I thought you called me a pigeon. Based on that interaction, you decided I was worth turning into a vampire."

"In as many words..." The turn signal that Rhys triggered gave a laughable soundtrack to his rebuttal.

"That *sounds* bad," I said.

We turned into a half-empty parking lot between two buildings, directed by the exaggerated signals of the lot attendant. I took a long breath.

Blacked out, drugged, attacked, then sired.

What a weekend. And somehow, Rhys was there for all of it.

"You were fine." I caught him looking down and smiling before the expression disappeared.

I wanted him to keep going, to give me further clues about the gaps in my mind, but as we parked the car and exited, he offered nothing.

"Ready?"

Chapter Thirteen

I PUT MY FOCUS into releasing built-up anxiety as I walked up to the entrance of The Pulpit. The nondescript building had fake church elements fixed to its brick façade. It looked like a cathedral and a warehouse had merged together to become one. I admired the aesthetic. It intrigued me that even if I hadn't been there for The Pulpit in the first place, I'd be tempted to enter and see what kind of fun I could find inside.

The people who walked in the same direction as us and congregated close by the oversized metal doors, all dressed in different styles, though most were alternative by nature. My shoulders relaxed. I was neither over nor under-dressed. The sample size wasn't large, but I'd be just fine. Cyber goths were present, along with traditional goths, and I even saw some scene kids, which was wild because I thought they didn't exist anymore. It was a true amalgamation of different dark looks. Rhys still seemed relatively tame, though. Corporate? Too business casual, less darkwave?

As we approached the large doors, green wisps of smoke drifted lazily through the air around the bouncer, whose dark eyes fixed on us as soon as we entered his line of sight and never wavered. I recognized the color; it was the same as Slevin's. The bouncer stood over six feet tall, probably close to six and a half. His short buzz cut, chiseled jawline, light skin, and broad shoulders clearly indicated his Slavic background.

"Emissary Llewelyn, good evening." He greeted me, his fangs barely visible, yet I still caught a glimpse of them as he spoke.

I craned my head back at the title, not expecting him to be addressed so formally. Rhys had mentioned being an emissary on the way over, but there was no telling what that meant. All I could assume was that it was related to the Sovereignty thing he started explaining on the way over.

"Jordan," Rhys replied as we closed the remaining distance to the bouncer. He placed his hand over his heart in a theatrical show of what appeared to be friendship or some kind of affection.

"Please," He gestured to me. "I'd like to introduce Joceline. My Protégé."

"Congratulations are in order, then!"

"Hardly," Rhys joked dismissively.

My eyes moved between them as they conversed. I barely forced an awkward smile before Jordan's eyes bounced off me and back to Rhys. I plastered a facetious grin on my face and raised a finger to divert Jordan's attention back to me. "Uh, yeah. I almost died. I'd very much like a congratulations."

Jordan's smile grew until it beamed at me as brightly as the sun. "Fuckin' A," he boomed. "That's right. Congratulations, little bat. Welcome to the Thunderdome! Bleeders on me tonight."

Bleeders?

"Thank you, Jordan." Rhys dismissed, refusing to match Jordan's energy.

"Anything for Sovereign blood. Enjoy your night."

I raised an eyebrow, but Rhys was doing everything in his power to pretend like he didn't feel the curiosity radiating off of me.

Jordan gestured to the open doorway and gave the metal counter a couple of clicks.

Rhys's hand rested at the small of my back, guiding me forward, as he whispered in my ear, "It's going to be loud, yes. We'll head straight upstairs to help you acclimate. That should make it easier. Just try not to concentrate on it."

As he began speaking, we entered the club, and the overwhelming noise hit me hard; the bass reverberated through my body. My jaw tightened, and my shoulders instinctively lifted. Aware of my discomfort, Rhys's hand was replaced by his arm coming to snake around me as if he was afraid that I'd fall over.

"You'll be able to turn it down, soon." He reassured me, adding, "I'm right here," as if he could sense that I was having trouble believing him.

The interior embraced the warehouse church theme from The Pulpit featuring red glowing signs like "Sell your soul", and "We are all sinners." Faux confessionals, once phone enclaves, now housed drinkers. A hipster with a PBR chatted with a pastel goth, while a beautiful elder goth in an eighties style sat alone, sipping a dark drink and observing the crowd. A quick scan revealed a few colored clouds or shimmers, possibly hidden by flashing lights. Ahead was a spiral staircase to the second floor.

A second bouncer stood by a small black velvet rope, blocking access. A velvet rope can't deter a vampire or a human. I wanted to roll my eyes but focused on maintaining my senses.

"Rhys." The next bouncer nodded, his figure lacking any color, smoke, or glitter that might have signaled he was one of us. Still, he was able to identify Rhys in the shadows.

"Armes." Rhys responded. "Us two, please. Call the wine list up, would you?"

"Of course," Armes responded, opening the velvet rope to allow us entrance. "I'll be on it next week."

"Ah," Rhys said as we ascended the stairs. "I'll see you then."

"Wine list?" I mouthed, grimacing at my naivety for not figuring it out. Bleeders, wine list...they meant blood.

The higher we climbed, the more I concentrated on the odd vampire episode of Cheers I had been thrown into. I could have sat imagining what visiting The Pulpit would be like for hours upon hours, but I never would have guessed vampires greeted each other with the campy flare of a sitcom. On the thin spiral walkway, I looked as far down at the first floor as my eyes could see without damn near falling over the railing. The decor featured numerous religious elements. The main room held a full island bar and seating, with a massive DJ booth disguised as an ornate pulpit, resembling something from Notre Dame or The Vatican. Neon colors danced across the polished surface in vibrant shades. Beams of light pierced the darkness, illuminating faces in various stages of enjoyment. Some danced vigorously, sweat beading on their foreheads, while others swayed with drinks clutched tightly. Groups circled tables featuring Catholic motifs in the centerpieces. As we neared the end of our climb, I looked around, eager to discover more.

My eyes widened as I nearly stumbled from the metal staircase onto an unusual fabric that definitely wasn't carpet. As my left foot slipped, I let out a squeal resembling a distressed seal, causing an unintentional split.

Before things got embarrassing, Rhys grabbed my arm. I clung to him like a drowned cat until I steadied, then he let go. "The floor is a velvet carpet."

"What the fu—"

"If you can't walk on it, you shouldn't be on the first level."

"Second level?"

"First level," he continued to insist. He held his hand flat in the air as if mimicking a floor. "Ground level." Then he raised it. "First level."

I opened and closed my mouth three times, trying to find the words to express how it all rubbed me the wrong way.

"That's dumb." I lifted my gaze from the deep purple velvet beneath my feet to see Rhys's lips twitching as he struggled not to laugh. "Don't you dare. No one has velvet carpet."

"Velvet carpeting is very luxurious," he shrugged, and I huffed. "What?"

"That's some rich people shit."

"Come," He offered with a smile, hand extended out to me. As I gazed at it, I was tempted to reach out and take it, but something warned me against it; it was the strange pull from his body that drew me in, not my own desire.

"I'm fine."

Rhys's hand returned to his side, and the smile faded.

"I gotta pass the test." I joked, sliding on my heels slightly as if I was about to dance from side to side. The playful display lasted just a few more seconds before a scent overwhelmed me.

Blood and honey.

No, not honey. *Honeysuckles.* The kind that I had licked in my aunt's yard out in Georgia that one summer my parents let me stay there.

"Is that?"

Rhys and I both turned at the same time, catching a better whiff of it.

"Blood, yes," Rhys answered.

"It smells like honeysuckles."

Rhys had a coy grin on his face, as if he found humor in what I said, but not in a mocking way. "I can smell it, too."

"Will it taste like that?" The question came off juvenile when I first said it, true, but I found it difficult to anticipate the taste. What I had taken the night before was delicious and invigorating. And as much as I hated to admit it, I wanted more.

"Will it taste like it?" Rhys repeated, relaxing his shoulders. "It could, but it might just be the fragrance."

"That they're wearing?"

"Of the blood itself," he corrected.

My chest rose and fell deeply as my mind clouded, like fog thickening over London. The ache of shifting fangs turned into a weight pressing down. I guessed it'd take little time for the fangs to lose feeling, subconsciously like salivating.

Unable to stop searching for the scent, I moved to my left and crossed over to the other side of the building. The walkway between the other landing and where I stood was twenty feet, and maybe eight feet wide. Normally, that'd make me nervous, but I didn't care.

I had to find the scent.

That was until I almost bumped into one of the most beautiful women I'd ever seen. The whole of her body I was surrounded by yellows and golds. Unlike Rhys, whose colors didn't shimmer quite as much, she twinkled like the night sky when you got far enough outside of the city lights. I gasped and stopped dead in my tracks, eyes wide. She didn't see me in her fluid gothic dance, but I grew rigid watching her move and how her colors reacted to it.

We were inside a building, yet her hair whipped and floated as if she were outside in a field. I tried to make sense of feeling the air moving around me, but there was no reason for it. Air conditioning aside, I didn't see any active industrial fans running, and the central air would have to be whirling so hard that everyone else's hair would move, too. The most surprising part about it, however, was that the air wasn't moving randomly. It followed the rhythm and movements of her arms, as if they were guiding it... as if she were the one in control of it.

She wasn't controlling it, was she?

My hand reached out to get her attention, but Rhys intercepted me before I could touch her, and his hand enveloped mine. He leaned into me until his lips barely touched my ear. "She's a Mystic," he whispered. "You see the gold? Those colors tell you exactly what we are, aside from just vampires. The gold, the blues and reds, and the green you saw surrounding Slevin, they work as identifiers."

"Identifiers?"

"We call them auras."

I was mesmerized by how the woman's clouds and sparkles danced on a level that everyone else's I'd seen seemed to only show. "Auras," I repeated, to get the word comfortable rolling off the tongue. He had used it before. Of course, I was used to the human meaning of the word, which had a similar definition to vampires, but ours was tangible.

It was in the air in front of me, around me, surrounding me. It existed in the physical world with us, and while I didn't know what caused it to move or intensify yet, I could witness it happen with my own eyes. My brow furrowed. Did humans not experience this? Were there some who saw auras but mistook them for something else when really they were seeing vampires?

"What is a Mystic?" I asked but when the words left my lips, the woman stopped dancing and looked at me.

She gave me a mischievous and flirtatious grin. I couldn't stop myself from smiling. It wasn't until I blinked a few times and separated myself from what I was looking at that I realized my fangs were fully drawn. My cheeks tingled and heated. I didn't want anyone to see them so easily. She kept my gaze for a few seconds as if inviting me closer before closing her eyes again and returning to dance when her invitation went unanswered.

Rhys coaxed me forward and I complied. I wanted, no, I needed to know more about her and what being a Mystic entailed. The surrounding air literally reacted to her presence. I'd never seen anything like that before. I even smelled her blood in the air that moved around her. Not much, but enough to catch on instinct it was vampiric.

As we passed, I noticed pointed rings on her fingers as they moved through the air, the fingertips wet with blood although I didn't see any cuts or pricks. I had to crane my neck to keep my eyes on her as we got further away, but in doing so, I caught her snap her ringed finger, and the ring sliced her finger bed. Unphased, the woman turned so that I could see her more clearly and mimicked the motion of fluid water in front of her chest, the gold glittering brighter around her as she did.

In the air, her aura clouds followed the motions, and as she lifted her hands higher while still moving them, her hair reacted. Her blood was the catalyst that controlled the air around her. My eyes bugged wider, and I stared at her until she was behind me to the point I couldn't see her and walk at the same time.

"Come, let's get a seat." Rhys instructed softly as we crossed the last of the walkway and the ground grew more stable beneath me.

I stole one final look at the woman, her hair floating high around her head as if she had blowers underneath her. Envy knotted in my stomach. How did I learn to do that? Could I even learn? I wanted to be able to do that more than anything else in the world.

"Here."

I turned my head back to Rhys and watched him approach a black leather couch against the wall. A few other people were on the landing, with half of them being vampires. Before I moved to the couch, I took one last look down at the dance floor, hoping to count more auras, but was disappointed to see just two.

Frustrated and hungry, I found my seat and as soon as I plopped down, I huffed. I was going to need my supposed Lord to start answering some questions, and fast. "Tell me everything. Now. You promised."

Rhys sighed, adjusting his comfortable position so that one of his ankles rested on his knee. "Let's start slow. Right now, in this moment, you're brimming with energy because you're both close to me and you're close to others. Others of our kind and the lesser kin."

"Lesser kin?"

"Humans."

"Then call them humans," I corrected. "Or did you forget that I was one of that lesser kin you spoke of only a few days ago?"

"Humans, my apologies."

I still huffed and pursed my lips. "Why would I be energetic around you?"

"Well, because I made you." He answered. "But, I'll give you time to settle as we discuss some broader subjects." Rhys diverted before I could even ask for more clarity.

"Let's return to auras. These colors help us identify each other's classes," he said. "There are six distinct classes, determined by your individual traits. Mystics, like the one we saw dancing, are golds and yellows. The color indicates the class, while intensity shows power." I recalled Slevin's lighter green aura compared to Rhys and the Mystic. "Though we don't fully understand our origins, we have learned about how we function." He continued, prompting me to lean in closer to hear better.

"The colors grow brighter and denser with active ability use, especially class-specific ones." *The Mystic.* My brows lifted as I began connecting the dots. "Clouds and smoke reflect our age and power. Apprentices under a year old have a translucent haze. Ancients, those over a thousand years old, possess darker, more opaque auras. Our power and abilities wane with time without feeding, impacting aura opaqueness as well."

I nodded the entire time he spoke, my eyes focused on his but it wasn't that I was really looking at him. My mind was working too hard to process all of the information he threw at me. His face, albeit handsome, was not a priority at the moment. "But what are Mystics, specifically?"

"They're elementals. Using their blood, they can manipulate the elements. When they were human, they had a deep connection to nature. When they become a vampire, this connection only amplifies." Rhys held up his hand closer to my face and mimicked snapping, except he went at half speed, and the top of his thumb's nail slid across his middle finger's tip instead of the finger pad. He repeated the action on loop as he continued explaining the ability. "Usually they use blood from their finger to power this ability. You'll see a lot of Mystics with either long nails or with rings and other accessories that allow them to draw blood quickly and efficiently. The blood mingles with the element they want to manipulate, and they use the said element to stretch the blood out, so to speak. The more of the element the blood touches, the more they have to work with."

I thought of the rings the dancer wore and how I saw her draw blood from her own fingers using them. She used her ability to dance with the air around her. That's why I could even smell her blood in the air because it *literally* was in the air.

"And you," I paused. "You've got two colors in your aura. You're two classes then?"

"Exactly." He waved his hand around. "This," he said dramatically before letting it fall to his side, "is due to my two mutation classes. It's not extremely rare, but it's also not common. I possess two, yet I'm primarily dominant in one. While I embody the traits of a Casanova, I also have some Muse abilities. The Casanova red is more pronounced than the Muse blue."

"Casanova," I started to say something smart but stopped myself.

Vampires were real, that dancing lady had some kind of control over elements, and I had drank a stranger's blood the day before and liked it. Fighting him on the name of a class was fighting air at that point. "Fine, okay, Casanova, dumb name, and Muse. So, you've said Mystic, Muse, and Casanova. But Slevin's green; what is he?"

"Slevin is a Brute."

"Brute," I repeated under my breath, drawing the word out. I had no clue what each class entailed, but some ideas started to form from just the titles.

"But you...you are a Prole."

"Prole?" I grimaced at the word. I remembered where I had heard it much quicker than I expected. It had been used frequently in some required reading from high school. It was short for Proletariat and it was as good as an insult.

"I'm a member of the Proletariat, Rhys?" I raised an eyebrow.

"Yes," he confirmed. "Collectively, officially, the Populi."

"You're fucking kidding me." I scoffed. Not only had my fiancé left me for not being up to his standards, but I had been transformed into a supernatural creature, and all I had become was a goddamn Prole.

"There's nothing wrong with being a Prole." He tried to reassure me but I didn't need his pity.

"Can it, Oxford, save your sympathies. Tell me about the cool shit we can do" I said, trying to push myself further into the couch. My skin was bristling with whatever the hell connection we had and the rhythm of the music, strangely enough, made me want to dance. I was growing restless.

"I attract humans due to a pheromone my body produces. It's a passive ability; when humans are near, they become more docile and agreeable, especially if attracted to my gender. This effect intensifies when I tell stories, a skill we call enamoring. Every Casanova has a unique talent for enamoring, whether through storytelling, dancing, singing, or performing. When we engage, humans become like putty in our hands."

"Are all Casanova's the same?" I asked and Rhys nodded.

"Center of attention. Highly sociable. We're all the same," he chuckled. "But our official class name is Paramour."

"I think I like that more."

Rhys smiled as he continued. Then there are the Muses. They were the smartest as humans, especially those with multiple talents. As vampires, they can communicate telepathically with humans, starting one-on-one but expanding to groups through practice. Initially, they hear thoughts, then experience memories, and finally speak directly into their minds. I received a different ability—implanting. I directly influence human thoughts and actions. While I can't hear thoughts, I can alter short-term memories, convince people of lies, change their dreams, and shape their aspirations by placing my intentions into their minds. It's what allows me to drink blood from people and not get caught."

"That..." I motioned toward him, "is a dangerous gift."

"Dangerous for them. Invaluable to us."

"To you," I corrected. "I'm not a Muse, Paramour, or a Mystic."

"To us," he insisted, uncrossing his ankle to lean forward. "You're a Prole, so you have the basics like us. As long as you drink blood, you don't age. You have improved strength, reflexes, and senses, and your mind is sharper. But you lack other abilities." He paused, creating an awkward silence. The correction was too late; I knew what he meant. There was nothing special about me to mutate into other classes. "Because of that, you'll struggle post-feeding. I'll help you for the first year," he said.

I put up a hand to stop him there. "What good is helping me the first year if I'll never have the stuff you do? Shouldn't I learn how to handle myself?"

"You need to learn how to handle your hunger first," he said, and the words brought back my behavior from the night before. Operating a motor vehicle as you disassociated into your body's muscle memory was one thing, but when your new reflexes had made you turn a man into a milkshake, some self-control was a necessary lesson.

"Discipline; yes, necessary." I took a deep breath in to use the air for a defeated huff, but when I did, the smell of blood returned. Yet, it wasn't honeysuckle that paired with it. It was floral but in a different vein.

Roses.

The visual of blood sprayed over rose petals flashed like the scene from an action moving. I sat up, the line of my spine straightening.

I had to find it.

Before I could stand, Rhys's arm came to stop me from moving forward and I looked down at it with indignation. Why did he bother taking me to a place like this if every corner was going to be a test that I didn't have a shot at passing?

"Wha...just...come on..." I droned out, continuing to push against him, but I wouldn't be able to move him without exerting more strength and effort than I wanted to give.

However, that quickly changed the longer the scent of blood lingered in the air. "You can't turn into a bloodhound every time blood is spilled around you."

"I'm not, I'm just..."

"Just what? Curious?"

"Yes," I answered too quickly for it to be taken seriously. "I just want to know why it smells like roses," I answered under my breath. "Does it taste like roses?" The words slipped out, and I drew back when I heard them. The absentminded addition only further proved his point.

"Sometimes it tastes like it smells, but you've drank before. You know it isn't always a taste that blood provides but a feeling. An emotion. A memory."

Oh, I remembered. Quite vividly, I could recall how I fell into a memory and the warmth it provided as if it were a scene on a movie screen.

My mind raced. What would blood taste like if it smelled like roses? Or honeysuckles? Did I want it to taste like it smelled more than I wanted

131

to experience it? I only realized I'd begun to press harder against Rhys when he started having to exert force to keep me down. I turned to look at him, stopping my advance.

"I'm not curious; I'm craving it, aren't I?" I pulled a hand up and opened my mouth, aware of my fangs. I knew they had receded into my gums while Rhys was talking, but after blood was mentioned so explicitly, they had slid right back out.

What if I'd been talking to a human? Human.

Humans were filled with blood.

And the blood was so delicious.

Humans...lesser kin?

Kin.

The vision of me sitting on my parents' couch stole my attention, the brown sofa oddly vintage and reminiscent of the 80s despite it being the 2000s at that time. Only in the last five years had my mom replaced that worn-down thing. The memory was from 2006, back in high school when the kids played with toys on the rug while my father and I watched The Love Boat.

I blinked, hoping to improve my vision of the memory. I felt like I was currently there, even smelling my mother making pot roast in the other room. It had been cooking all day, ready when I returned from my first job at The Shoe Palace, still in my uniform. The vision faded, and I gasped upon returning to the present. My back dug deeper into the couch until Rhys withdrew his arm.

"Dove?"

Lower. Kin. Humans. My family.

They were vulnerable to this world like I was, a victim to be reaped at any moment. Maybe even by some untrained baby vampire like me, maybe by someone worse.

Fuil.

My eyes clamped shut so hard I started to see colored static behind my eyelids. My hands came up to cup my face. Air skipped into my lungs, and I wondered if I'd forgotten how to breathe as soon as Dom's voice came to haunt me.

"Are you—"

"What?"

I had heard him perfectly and knew he was checking on me and my sudden change, but I was having difficulty processing any of my thoughts or emotions. It all mingled together into a boiling and bubbling mess of volatility. Seconds passed in silence before I finally pulled my hands down.

"I'm sorry."

"You need blood." Rhys said curtly.

There was a part of me that knew it. My past, present, and future raged inside of me, fighting with my anger, sadness, and lust. A nuclear concoction on a supernatural scale simmered inside me. That made me dangerous.

"Yeah, I think I do," I muttered the words and gave him a sad excuse for a smile, one that would elicit pity.

Though, all of them were laced with an undercurrent of need. A hunger.

Rhys's eyes left me to catch someone across the landing, and I followed to find him lift his arm and signal for someone who looked like a server to come forward. I squinted, struggling to see the colorless glitter of their aura that signaled to me that they were like the desk clerk, like me, a Prole. It didn't take long before they stopped in front of us, holding a menu printed on ivory card stock, the weight of the paper visible in the lowlight thanks to its lack of a bend.

"Thank you," he said, taking it and giving it a glance before handing it back. "We'll share the Merlot, please. Send it right up."

"Of course, anything for Sovereign blood."

I made a face at the reference, having heard it twice in such a small time frame. What the fuck did it mean? Rhys offered the server a gracious smile as they turned and walked off before turning to face me and noticing the expression. "Sovereign blood?"

"Figured you'd have called out the merlot bit, but yes. Sovereign blood," he said.

"I can gather what merlot means. I may be a Prole, but I'm pretty smart. But, two people have said you've got Sovereign blood. You explained the Sovereignty a little so I can gather that it's got to be related to that, but what does that have to do with your blood. Are all vampires sovereign? The way they say it doesn't sound like it. They say it like it's a privilege, even for our kind. And if you have some kind of special blood, then you had it when you made me; so I have it too?" I started off with a more confident one that wavered dramatically at the end. I knew he still had two other mutation classes to explain to me, but I was throwing the questions at him in the order they were coming in. The other classes could wait. If people were going to be using titles and stuff around me, I needed to get a better handle on what they meant.

"The man who mutated me is a member of the Sovereignty, and not just anyone in the Sovereignty, a Sovereign Leader," he started.

"A vampire king made you?"

"God no, not a king. Though he might disagree with my contesting that," he said with a huff of laughter, the joke going over my head. "While the Sovereignty are our version of a government, it's not a monarchy. Within the organization is three branches. The Legion, the Institute and the Order. Each has a purpose. Each is crucial to keeping our existence intact and safe." He readjusted in his seat, trying to get more comfortable, and I mirrored the action. "At the top of the Sovereign Order are leaders. Each leader has their right-hand man, which is their emissary. What I used to be. I was my Lord's first protégé; we were close. He trusted me. So he made me his emissary. This isn't why people say I'm of sovereign blood. It's my Lord being the leader that does. All leaders are addressed as My Sovereign. I have his blood, and so it is Sovereign blood."

"And I have yours, so mine is too." Again, with the growing hesitance. He nodded, and I started to consider the implication that if people found out Rhys made me, they might start saying something about it. It was an odd thought. Did it come with privilege? I, myself, had never been one to have any inherent privilege before being a vampire, I hadn't expected there to be any I would gain afterward. Most people don't get more of something after they die.

"Who is he?"

"He?"

"Your..." I was about to say maker, but the term from before sprang up. "Lord."

I couldn't pinpoint a single muscle that moved or twitched on his face, but his expression changed. His eyes darkened, which I would have thought impossible considering they were endless in their blackness. But, it was unmistakable.

"He isn't important. Not to me and not to you."

"He's important to the people bringing up his blood," I pointed out.

"As much as anyone given a silly title and doesn't deserve it," he countered.

My brows rose at his reply, and I made a mental note that his maker...Lord...was a sore subject. "Okay then." I drew the first word out and while I pulled at something to say. "Tell me about the other two classes then."

"I'll be brief, it won't be much longer."

I nodded in approval. It didn't matter how long it took, as long as I got to learn more about the real world out there. "Brutes. Their auras are green, which is what you saw with the bouncer at the door and with Slevin." He started. I rubbed my hands together in my lap, eager to hear more. Slevin had quickly become an ally and maybe a friend, and I wanted to learn more about him.

"Brutes are the strongest of our kind. They are also the ones among us that can change their form. You don't see it as much in modern westernized tales of vampires, but a lot of the older stories from around the world have vampires who can change the form into animals. We call it shifting."

My mouth stayed open, but if I wasn't trying to hold it all together, it'd have been on the floor. "Shifters?"

Rhys nodded this time. "Yes, but not all animals. They can only shift into mammals, and it has to be mammals whose blood they've tasted. It's not human-esque versions of the mammals, either. A human would never be able to tell the difference between the vampire and the actual animal. We, however, would still see their aura."

A million different things ran through my mind with the newfound information about Brutes. For one, I considered how incredible their ability was. Not only would being able to turn into another mammal have some amazing applications, but also, it would be so fun. I could lounge around as a cat sunbathing or romp around with foxes in the forest. Were there vampire zoologists out there in the world, studying animals in the most intimate ways by shifting into them and living amongst them? Please, someone tell me there was.

"Those with a natural magnetism to animals, both wild and domestic, tend to mutate into Brutes. But they also have their Brute strength. Bodybuilders, dancers, those with immense power...they can become Brutes too."

Strength and shape-shifting.

Was Slevin a Brute because of his strength or because of the animal magnetism? I hadn't known him long enough to assume either one on appearances. Plus, his jacket obscured the muscles I assumed were underneath, going off the vague build of him that I could see. I knew he was broad enough to fill the jacket out, but I wondered if it was more than that. If he had muscled arms and more beneath it. If he had the strength to lift a car or maybe something bigger. I whistled.

"What else could there possibly be after all the others? Mystics had the elements, Muses had their literal telepathic powers, Paramours made humans putty in their hands, and Brutes were so cool they had the strength to turn into lions, tigers, and bears. Did that leave anything else?

"Creepers." Rhys said, a defeated tone to the word. When I heard it, I remembered how he'd said it to me at my town home and how he was happy I wasn't one. My stomach dropped at the negative context. "Also called Cadavers."

Cadavers, as in dead bodies.

I was starting to get ideas and none of them were good.

"Creepers are a newer nickname for them, but officially, and more respectfully, call them Cadavers."

"Both sound awful."

"Yes," Rhys agreed. "Cadavers are those that mutate too late. Whether it is due to timing or the state of their body when they become vampires, it's not quite done right. The vampire blood isn't what kills them when it should be, as it needs to be the catalyst to start the mutation. It doesn't happen every time but there's always the possibility that those who are too close to death when the blood is exchanged will become one. You, very well, could have become one. I took a huge risk with you, I admit."

My heart sped up. I didn't know what they were, but I had been minutes, maybe seconds, away from being one.

"What are they?"

"They are the dangerous ones," he started. "The mutation takes in its own way, but they lose a lot of themselves in the process." I gulped as he explained. "They're mute. Old tales say that their voice is the price they pay to the ferryman of the dead to bring them back."

My hand came up to touch my throat.

"They're also feral. The closer to death they were, the more feral their behavior is. It's impossible for them to go back to life as it was before their mutation because of it. Human social behaviors start to fade away because they live on the outskirts of society. They'd never be able to live within it. Their skin looks waxen, and they can't retract their fangs. They also smell like fresh corpses. There's a blanket of death to their musk. It puts off both humans and animals...even us."

I didn't know why, but the more he told me the more uncomfortable it made me. I had been so close to become something like this. What would have happened if I had turned into a Cadaver?

"How close was I to being one?" I asked.

"I don't know, dove," he said, voice low. "We'll never know. All we know is that you aren't one. Prole, yes. But never a Cadaver. You don't become one after the fact. You'll never be one." My heart slowed a little. The prospect of being one scared me, but his words sent a reassuring warmth into me.

"They are also the quickest of our kind. Some move so quick you can't see them...so quick you'd swear they were flying. They can't fly, but you'd almost bet they could." My brows rose at the additional information. So, even Cadavers got an extra ability. Yet, here I was as a Prole, with the basics.

"That's six."

"That's six, yes." He leaned back into the couch as if he needed to rest following all the information. "Delayed mutations do happen. Aside from Cadavers of course. You either have that class at your initial mutation or not at all."

"Oh, okay."

137

"So, technically you could become something else later. Not that there is anything wrong with being a Prole."

"Yeah, yeah, yeah, I get it." I blew a raspberry at him. "There's nothing wrong with me, right? I'm perfect just the way I am."

"Precisely."

I rolled my eyes. My envy was overflowing. All of the other mutation classes had amazing abilities, but I was stuck with the bottom of the barrel. Even the Creepers were fast. Although, I didn't think I'd appreciate that kind of existence. How tragic, to try and save someone so close to death only for them to come back as a feral living corpse.

Just then, the server returned with someone else in tow. A human.

CHAPTER FOURTEEN

I BLINKED AND WIDENED my eyes far too much when I opened them again. I expected a donor bag or perhaps a beverage glass filled with blood, not a whole ass human person, just living and breathing, to be delivered to us. While people were dancing downstairs, they delivered some of them to vampires upstairs, out in the open. The landing didn't even have walls. The *audacity*. Supernatural creatures were out there all through history doing shit like that, and we never noticed. I never noticed as a human?

I didn't notice Dom.

I shook my head to return to reality. I didn't need to think about Dom when I was about to drink blood. My guilt swelled in me without needing any assistance, especially not from the asshole who caused me to become a vampire in the first place.

"Your merlot, Emissary."

My mouth opened, but nothing came out, although I continued to give exaggerated blinks where I switched between looking at Rhys, the server, and the human.

"Uh—"

"Thank you, darling. I appreciate it," Rhys said. "And you don't have to call me Emissary. It's been decades. I don't take offense, I promise."

"My apologies, sir."

"Please, none are needed."

While I heard the exchange, my eyes stayed caged on the human. They stood silent, hands to their sides, not acknowledging the three of us with even a glance. "Are they hypnotized?"

Rhys turned and looked at me, perplexed. "Hypnotized?"

The human then turned to me, expression stumped. "I'm right here. You could ask me."

When they spoke, I gasped, and my shoulders jumped up, which caused them to do the same. At the sudden movement, I flinched. "Jesus Christ!"

"Joceline, are you okay?" Rhys asked, but before I could answer, he turned to the server and thanked her again, insisting he could take it from there.

"No, I am not. Because what the fuck is this?" I gestured to the human flamboyantly.

"My name's Korbin."

"Oh, of course it is."

"What is that supposed to mean?" Korbin asked, insulted.

"I don't know." I threw my hands up, defeated. "It just fits for a place like this."

"I'm not even goth. And my parents named me." Korbin explained, gesturing at his modest attire of black slacks and a white golf shirt. I studied his face and the suburban banality of it. He wasn't goth. Not even a little bit. I looked down, embarrassed.

"I'm so sorry, Korbin. It's her first time with a Bleeder."

I snapped my head up to Rhys. Did they call them that to their faces? My brain spiraled. Bleeder wasn't exactly complimentary rolling off the tongue.

"That makes a lot of sense. She's new-new?"

"Glaringly obvious, isn't she?" Rhys joked. I watched them interact as if they were old friends at a barbecue in stunned silence. Korbin gave him a look that answered the questions and I frowned.

Korbin sat between us on the couch, and I fought the impulse to scoot away to the edge. "Do you have a preference?" He asked, facing Rhys.

"Let's go traditional, for Joceline. Nothing fancy."

"Shirt?" Korbin pinched the fabric between two fingers.

"If you wouldn't mind, let's take it off. Just in case. I wouldn't want you to have to take it to the cleaners," Rhys insisted.

"It's machine washable."

"Lovely," Rhys started, "Still, blood can be temperamental. No need to risk a stain. She's still learning."

"Be careful, now." Korbin turned to me when he gave the joke warning, a mild Texas accent coming forward the more comfortable he got with small talk.

Without another word, Korbin took off his shirt to reveal a white sleeveless undershirt. He gestured to it, but Rhys waved it off as if to say that he could keep it on. Suburban banality aside, Korbin hid a lean, cut figure, shoulders solid and rounded like a casual sportsman.

"You gonna let her..."

"If you're alright with it, and she's alright with it." Rhys answered, then looked at me. "Dove, are you comfortable with—"

"With any of this?" I interjected, flustered but not only from Korbin's unexpected muscles, and not in a hot and bothered way. My cheeks were warm and tingly, and my heart hammered away much faster than it had been when with the shirt on.

"I'll pour."

Without any pomp or fuss, Rhys looked away from me, then wrapped his hand around Korbin's neck and pulled him closer, lips descending. Though I couldn't see it, I knew the exact moment he bit him. Korbin's blood smelled like liquid smoke. Dusky and flavorful in a savory way, not like the floral scents I had gotten from the other blood I smelled. It was heavy, something to keep you satisfied for longer with a fuller belly.

I got all of that from a single second, one solitary moment, of bloodshed.

I took a deep breath, allowing the scent to seep into my chest and fill my lungs with its complex notes. Warm and full-bodied, his heart resonated with a melody that was unfamiliar to me. It escalated with the first bite, likely fueled by pain, yet never exceeded what I imagined to be a steady hundred beats per minute. He remained calm. Despite my discomfort and awkwardness, nothing about this frightened him; he felt no threat.

My stomach dropped.

Korbin knew what was happening. He was willing. He wasn't being attacked. Rhys wasn't going to hurt or kill him.

The realization hit me like a brick to the face, and fifty pounds of metaphorical weight lifted off my shoulders.

We weren't hurting him.

Korbin moaned in what sounded like pleasure as Rhys's hand held firmly to his thigh. My cheeks grew hotter, but not as hot as my bloodlust, which I had been using so much effort to repress because of my unease.

I leaned toward the two, processing my trauma and situation in tiny bits as best I could. When Rhys pulled away from Korbin's neck, the space allowed blood to spill into the crook of his neck. It made it more fragrant, but in an effort to not waste or ruin any undershirts, Rhys's hand went to the wound and applied pressure.

"We don't have much time, please." The encouragement came gently, and without condescension. "Drink."

I hesitated, but Korbin's hand came and coaxed me forward to taste him. Though wordless, his consent and eagerness meant so much. My fangs lowered to their peak, a dull ache present because they couldn't go any further. I allowed myself to relax into my new instincts, and Rhys backed away, noticing my muscles soften and my body move closer.

"The bite is enough; you don't need to open it any more than that. Simply put your mouth to it and let it flow. A clean bite will bleed enough to satiate. If you feel you need to bite down, then you are being overindulgent. Or you need to tighten up your bitework."

I heard the words, every one of them, but I couldn't make myself acknowledge them with a physical action. Everything was laser-focused on what was now budding into a small red streak. I loosened my jaw and let it slacken open as I got closer, then my tongue came and traced the blood that spilled before my lips surrounded where Rhys had bitten to accept the crimson.

As soon as I tasted it, I moaned. My body awkwardly posed so it was not quite on top of him, just a little to the side. I tried not to put all my weight onto him as I drank, but reality melted into a strange corner of itself.

Rhys's words echoed in my mind, but I knew I didn't want to be aggressive. Though not exactly run of the mill, the entire situation wouldn't be traumatic to any of us. I was conscious enough to be sure of it.

I pulled on the wound, and more blood lazily flowed along my tongue until I had enough in my mouth to swallow. The volume of it wasn't the only thing filling me up. There was something there, something I could only describe as magical, that charged. It energized me down to the cells and atoms of my existence. Peace came over me, and the expression on my face relaxed until it was neutral. Korbin, beneath me, was also calm, which I guessed fed into how comfortable I was. His emotions influenced my own; it was surprising that he had that much of an impact on me as the human in the exchange. I could feel him weakening. Startled by the sensation of it, I drew back.

"Perfect." Rhys's voice interrupted my haze, and I reacted by quickly pulling myself further back as if breaching water. Before I could say anything, my hand came up to cover my mouth, wondering if I had spilled any but my hand came in contact with only skin. Nothing was wasted.

Rhys put his bleeding open palm to Korbin's mouth for a second, then pulled away. He only offered the bare minimum of his own blood for whatever that was. Healing him?

Korbin took Rhys's blood and shivered, licking his lips. I tried to pay as much attention to what was happening as I could, but I felt high, drunk, and loose all at the same time. It was so perfect. My belly wasn't full; no, my soul was. Some invisible tank became full, and I reveled in the pleasure of that sensation, like eating a cake and savoring it before the sugar rush kicked in.

"Thank you, Korbin," Rhys said softly.

He slipped Korbin a bill of some kind, but I couldn't tell what it was. "I'd say compliments to the chef, but you're right here." He added, and Korbin smiled as he put his shirt back on, his heartbeat popping up a little from moving so much after losing blood.

Even as I watched and listened to them interacting, I rode the euphoria. It ebbed and flowed within every inch of my body, energizing the very fiber of my being until I had to bite my lip. With the strength of the stimulation, my mind tried to convince me it was sexual, but it wasn't.

I knew it wasn't. It was intimate, but it didn't pass the threshold into sexual or romantic territory.

"Joceline?" Rhys's voice shook me free of the trap Korbin's blood had dropped me into. I took a sharp inhale and centered my attention on him, eyes wide like a drunk trying not to spiral inward into themself.

"Hm...yes?"

He smiled and huffed a laugh out under his breath, entertained by the lazy amusement of my expression. I wanted to give him a retort back, but I couldn't conjure up the effort. My whole body took the bounty it had been given and turned it into whatever it was that made us work. But why did it have to feel so good?

His smile brightened as Korbin walked away, ending the exchange with a nonchalance that showed how experienced he was as a bleeder, whatever the scope of that was. "Good, isn't it?"

"That's one way to describe it."

CHAPTER FIFTEEN

IT TOOK TWENTY MINUTES before I had the mental clarity to get up off the couch at The Pulpit. For another forty-five minutes after that, I stood leaning against the railing and watched clubgoers dance, unable to stop myself from swaying to the darkwave music. Then, Rhys spent another five minutes convincing me that I didn't need to join any of the dancers below and that we should leave. I agreed, but not happily.

The rest of the night blurred into obscurity, but I knew Rhys had dropped me off at my apartment. And, reluctantly so. The entire car ride, he rattled off reasons why he wanted me to stay with him at his loft, and I refused every single one of them, citing that I was an independent adult when I met him and that I'd remain one. I wouldn't let him win the debate, even though he had saved my life two nights prior. Saved and ended it.

Respectively.

On the nightstand, my digital alarm clock blared its robotic tune at me, and I swatted at it. Unlike the previous evening, I'd been sure to set it for what my weather app had told me was sunset, that way I could get a full day of sleep.

"Don't forget, we don't die because of sunlight, but we are weaker, practically human, in it. Not only are we allergic, our abilities wane the longer we're directly in it."

Rhys's reminder on the way home came to mind as I peeled open my eyes to stare at the time. 5:42 PM. From there, I glanced over at the three large windows on the other side of my bedroom.

While riding the high of my recent meal, I jumped from the top of my bedroom's half-wall to the window ledge. On the second attempt, I did a much more effective job of covering them up. From what I could see, and the fact that I hadn't woken up to my arm burning, it was a success. Rhys didn't need to buy those black-out curtains as he insisted. The old blankets I'd been hoarding for the last fifteen years from the flea market were all a Texan vampire needed. So much for my mom telling me to get rid of them.

I stretched and sat up in bed, holding back a yawn with the back of one of my hands. Thanks to some foresight, I had emailed my supervisor before sunrise to let him know I'd contracted a nasty case of the flu while taking my long weekend off and would be out for the week. Thankfully my paid time off had reset at the beginning of the month, but I had a sneaking suspicion I wouldn't be peddling specialty art supplies much longer.

Feeling the opposite of urgency, I dropped back onto the bed and stared up at the ceiling, trying to muster up motivation. Following my breakup, work was the main thing that kept me on a stable schedule. Remove that from the equation and I became one of those big cats released into the wild after a life in a cage, looking in all directions and not moving in any of them.

I puffed my cheeks out with air and held it for several minutes in silence, wondering how long I could hold it in. My eyes stared bored at the alarm clock, watching each minute pass, and after ten minutes, I released. I didn't need oxygen anymore, that was certain, but it took a conscious effort not to breathe. It seemed easier to keep doing it.

Going through the motions, I pulled myself out of bed and took a shower, dressing for the night although I had no plans. All I knew was that I had to keep doing something, or I ran the risk of looking inward, and I wasn't ready to do that yet. Everything was still too fresh. Dom's voice still mocked me every chance it got.

Hair washed and conditioned, I looked at myself in my vanity mirror as I swirled strands around my fingers with hair product. Each time I released a new curl, it bounced up and settled, looking too perfect. I'd always wanted to get rid of my frizz, but never would've imagined mutating into a supernatural creature was the cure for my hair blues.

Finishing up, I shook my head and let the pampered coils settle naturally around my head right as my phone buzzed on the countertop.

Without looking at the screen, I already knew who it was. When we were still together, I had changed the rhythm of the vibrations for his texts and calls to mimic the theme song of a popular post-apocalyptic time travel movie we watched and poked fun at. After he left, I forgot to change it back to the regular vibration.

Matt.

My stomach sank until it reached the cushion of my small vanity chair. The groan I gave forth was deep enough my windpipe hummed.

I didn't have to answer, right? He had no place in my life after he took off that engagement ring, and he certainly had no place in my vampire existence past that. He could, non-respectfully, go fuck himself for all I cared.

The vibrations cut off and I sighed, eyes caged on the screen after it went black. The silence only lasted a few seconds before it started back up again, in the same rhythm. A hand balled into a fist with enough force my forearm shook.

How dare he call me back to back, as if he had any agency in my life. He wasn't important to me, nor I him. Did he really think I'd answer? I took a few deep breaths and released my fist.

I'd sooner see hell freeze over than answer that motherfucker's call.

A text lit the screen up and I snatched the phone up to see what he thought was so important. Facial recognition unlocked the phone as soon as it lit up, bringing me into a brand new text conversation window with "Don't answer, fuck him." I was adamant that I didn't want to keep a running text conversation with him because we had nothing to discuss. I didn't need to see reminders of him whenever I opened up my messages.

"I left something at the apartment?" I read the text out loud, under my breath. What did he think he left at the apartment? Left some stuff, my ass.

I typed out a reply that harbored far too much hostility, then back-spaced the entire thing, before staring dumbfounded at the tiny key-board on my screen. There was no way I could say what I wanted to, but the blood singing in my veins made it hard to resist the temptation.

"What do you think you left here?" I spoke out loud as I typed, stressing the word think. I sucked my canine after typing, as three dots appeared, letting me know he was about to respond quickly.

"Social security card." I read, brows lowering. "Are you fucking kidding me right now? Oh my god."

I breathed, putting the phone down before typing anything out. I didn't recall having seen any of his important paperwork anywhere when I'd cleaned, but then again, I didn't specifically remember throwing it out or packing it up for him. He very well could've left it.

No.

Even if he did, he couldn't come to the apartment. Not with me in it. He surrendered his keys to the leasing office, so he didn't have a way to get in, otherwise. Shit. I'd have to find it and leave it out for him. However, the thought of him suffering in the Dallas Social Security office tempted me. He deserved it.

I picked up the phone and opened the text conversation again, just as he started typing more.

> Where'd you leave it?

> I think I remember. I'm at the door.

"At the do—"

A knock came from downstairs, matching the vibration of my cell phone. I didn't know how long this would last, but I needed to stay away from that man until I gained control over my emotions and impulses.

I grimaced and pushed my head down toward my shoulders. Not that the action would make me invisible or matter as I was on the second floor, but I sure hoped it would. Anything to make him go away.

The knocks came again, but in no specific rhythm. My eyes moved from side to side while I tried to think of some way to get out of the situation, then I gasped at my idea. Slevin.

> I need a huge favor. Can you call me in like three minutes and say that you need me to meet you somewhere for something important. Just make it up. Need to get out of something.

I would've asked my brother or sister to do it, maybe my mom, but I didn't think I could start talking to them now and cut it off. They'd have a million questions and would want to know why I'd been avoiding them like the plague. No, it had to be someone else.

I turned the phone off silent and slipped it into my pocket just as I finished sending the text. It was a Hail Mary if he got it fast enough to be helpful. Was there a vampire god or goddess I could pray to?

I heard him breathing on the other side of the door before I opened it, positioning my arm to act as a bar through the middle of the doorway. "Tell me where it is, Matt. I'll bring it to you." I greeted with no warmth in my voice as I opened the door. My gaze landed on him for a millisecond before I diverted downward to the metal kick plate of the door. My jaw jutted side to side. I hated everything about that moment, and that anger bubbled to the surface.

The emotional devastation he caused didn't only extend to a breakup. He abandoned me at the lowest point of my life, apart from my father's death. He even started talking to other women before he left, because, God forbid, he had to wait.

My gums ached, and I set my jaw back into place and hissed as it tightened up. I had to get control, or my fangs would shift out. He'd notice immediately.

"Just let me in, Joce. It'll take three seconds."

"It'll take three seconds for me to grab it. And don't call me Joce." I spit out through teeth pressed hard against each other.

In my pocket, my phone dinged, but I didn't pull it out. I needed to stay focused on ignoring the heat in my core. Anger. Disappointment. A lust for nonsexual things. Was it violence, or retribution?

"Look Joce—line." He barely managed to correct himself but tried to push his way in against my arm. He expected me to be the woman he knew before. A passive Joceline. A weak Joceline.

Able to easily keep myself in place, my head raised up to stare defiantly at him. He wasn't getting inside. "What the fuck do you think you're doing, Matt? This isn't your apartment anymore. You don't get to just walk in."

"Yeah, well I need my stuff..." he trailed off the sentence as his eyes focused on my face as we were close. "You're—"

"No. Nope. No fucking way." I used the arm pressed to his chest to push him back, trying to restrain myself but still moving him back a few steps.

"Joce, come on. Let's just talk."

"Talk? You're kidding right? You've gotta be kidding or maybe you've got amnesia because there's no talking with us anymore." All the background noise of electronics and cars, the neighbors in my complex, all of it quieted. My heartbeat began throbbing in my ears as my temper flared.

"Don't be like this."

"Be like what, exactly?" The inside of my chest vibrated as I fought to keep my fangs from coming out. My arm returned to the middle of the doorway, fingers gripped tight enough to the wood frame it indented.

"It wasn't easy for me to leave. I know you think it was, but I was hurting, too." Matt's voice was even, calm. It didn't hold the supposed hurt he claimed. And even if it did, he could drown in his pain. He deserved it.

"Don't you dare," I threatened. "Don't you fucking start that shit with me. You lost the privilege to attempt to lie to me." I released the wood and placed my body in the open space of the doorway, not just my arm.

"I'm not lying." Matt's pulse quickened, his carotid artery bouncing within the side of his neck. The thump of each beat played in my head as I stared. "I still loved you at the end."

"You did, did you?" The temperature of my whole body rose, even in my eyes. If things didn't dissipate soon, I'd start shaking. "Could have fooled me. Or do you show love by DM'ing women while I'm out of town?"

"You ain't gotta bring that up," he said, dismissing his infidelity with the ease of self-delusion. My brows rose as high as they would go, eyes bugged out.

Kill him.

When the idea hit me, I blinked. Not once, but a few dozen times. That wasn't me. I didn't wish death on my exes, just because they broke my heart.

"We can be amicable, Joce."

"Don't call me that!"

I hadn't yelled it, but it was damn close to it. The huff of my breathing had gotten deeper. Not only did my chest move up and down, so did my shoulders.

"Damn, sorry. Joceline. Come one, let's just go inside and talk."

"We don't have anything to talk about. You abandoned me."

Hurt him like he hurt you.

No. That wasn't me. That wasn't who I was.

Is he not owed pain?

He was an asshole, not a war criminal. He didn't deserve the wrath of a supernatural creature.

"I'm sorry," he said. He reached out to me and I slapped his hand away, backing up a step. My gums ached. I didn't think I had the strength to keep my fangs from dropping much longer. Did Slevin get my message? I needed help. "I'll just grab my stuff, then."

He moved a step forward, but with visible weariness in my new-found strength, he'd never seen in me. Before he left, I was a mess. I was emotionally and physically weak after my diagnosis. The fertility drugs left me fatigued at times and in pain the others. All so that I could get pregnant with an egotistical prick's baby while still working full time at a job that required constant travel. But, what he was looking at was not that woman.

My mouth opened, but before words followed, my cell phone started to ring at full volume. Both of our eyes went to my pocket, and I pulled it out and swiped to answer, without bothering to look at the screen and check who it was. My Hail Mary was in play. I lifted the phone up and used muscle memory to turn the speaker on.

"Yeah?"

"Joce!" Slevin's energetic voice greeted.

"Hey, Slevin. What's up?" I stared down Matt as I talked, daring him to try anything.

"You rushed out of here this morning and forgot your debit card. I know you were a little distracted. That's my bad. As much as I'd like to think we'll see each other soon, you better come get this. I'm going to be busy for the next few days. Although, I'd much rather be busy with you."

Although my stare didn't waver, my cheeks flushed. Of course, Slevin would use the opportunity to do something embarrassing. But at least he called when I needed him to. "Ye—yeah. Of course, I'll leave right now. See you soon."

"Can't wait." Slevin's voice softened when he said the last bit and I hung up the phone before he had a chance to say anything else that might make me blush hard enough that my complexion couldn't hide it any longer. Matt's expression changed, gaining an edge of what I guessed was jealousy. How ironic.

"Bye, Matt." I said, "Be sure to go fuck yourself next time you think about showing up unannounced at *my* apartment."

"But my—"

I backed up and slammed the door in his face.

Chapter Sixteen

I MAINTAINED MY TOUGH demeanor until the knob clicked securely, and I engaged both locks. A long sigh escaped my mouth, my fangs sliding out as I let my emotions free. He shouldn't have come. I had no idea what possessed him to think showing up without an invitation was a good idea. He'd never done that before. Perhaps it was the passage of time. A few months must have seemed adequate time to get over wasting six years of someone's life. He was, terribly, mistaken.

I pressed my eyelids together, trying to avoid collapsing to the floor, but I only succeeded in leaning against the door. I heard Matt's car reverse and drive away. He wasn't going to hang around for me, which was for the best since I had nowhere to go.

What I needed to determine was what to do next. I had to get accustomed to my new existence and species. I needed to discover ways to feel at ease in my new skin. Yet, what I truly wanted was to run to my mother and weep in her embrace.

I longed to settle into the living room, on the cozy couch that felt both familiar and unfamiliar, surrounded by siblings who would appreciate my presence but not enough to put down their phones. Just being close by would suffice. That connection would nourish my spirit. Then I could caution them, warn them, that the world was a treacherous place steeped in blood and magic, and a supernatural threat hovered over them like clouds on an April afternoon. Ever present, yet not always unleashing its storm upon them. They needed to understand the importance of remaining vigilant.

"Joceline Fuentes is dead. You're no longer your mother's daughter or your siblings' sister. You need to pull away from them. They won't understand, and you can't force them to try. They can't be a part of your new life.

If you try to hide it from them but keep going around them, they'll figure you out faster than you'd think. You can fool the world, but you can't fool the ones who love you. At times, they see you more clearly than you see yourself."

Rhys's advice from last night flooded my mind as I tried my hardest to gain control over my feelings. The old me was dead; he was right about that but it didn't mean I could turn my back on my family when they were the one constant in my life that gave me peace. If I saw them for a few minutes, what trouble could it cause? A family of three in the lower middle-class suburbs of North Texas wasn't a threat to the vampire community at large. Were they?

In a moment of desperation, I pulled out my phone, unable to contain myself. My fingers raced as I struggled to find my mother's name in my contacts. As I sank to my knees, the call connected.

The second trill made my breath quicken, and I pulled my head down and let my body down on its side, so I was in the fetal position, phone to my chest. I didn't need it to my ears to hear it.

Maybe Rhys was right, maybe it was a terrible idea.

The third trill made my hands clench around the phone until the glass and metal of it started to resist, as if it would give way under my strength. Strength that had multiplied substantially from what I was used to. If only I'd lighten my grip.

"Hey, baby girl."

My mama's soft voice reached my ears, bringing tears to my eyes. Finally, my fingers relaxed.

Air filled my lungs, audible proof that I was crying. She'd know I wasn't okay immediately.

"Baby?"

"Yeah…" I lifted my head from my chest but remained on my side. I lost all the words, unable to conjure a single one to say the million things I needed to. "Mama…" I had to say something…I had to. But, how? I started to sit up in time for the screen to catch a tear of the water from my cheek. The screen illuminated from the movement. The red tint of the water pushed me further into my sadness. I was so alien. "Are you...are you home?"

"Yeah, baby. I'm home. You know that. It's a school night; I got work in the morning." Her voice grew concerned. "Did something happen? What's wrong? Is it Matt again? Oh, that boy. I'll sick your uncle on him if he doesn't stop breaking your heart. We can throw him in the Trinity. No one will know."

"No, it's not Matt." Not entirely. "I just..." I sniffled. "I'mma come over, okay?"

"Of course."

"Okay, just...I'll be there soon." The house was a forty-minute drive away and I wasn't wasting any time. Blinking past tears, I grabbed a jacket, slid on my flats, and ran out the door.

The drive was silent; only my breathing and heartbeat breaking the silence. I was just a daughter needing her parents. I wished more than anything for my father, who stayed strong and was my best friend, knowing me better than anyone.

He would've known what to do.

But, he didn't have the luxury of being saved from death. Slowly, painfully it consumed him until the very end. If I had been then what I was, a vampire, could I have rescued him the way Rhys rescued me?

I could almost hear his voice in my head say, "No one should live forever, baby girl." He would have let his time end when his God intended it to.

He wouldn't want me to cry either, but I sobbed as I drove. Growing up, I tried so hard to be like my father, holding back tears when I could, as if I needed to show some semblance of strength close to what he did. I saw him cry twice in my entire life, and here I was, having cried a handful of times in just two days.

Seeing mama would help. I didn't have to tell her everything; I didn't have to spill the secrets of the world or try to get her to understand. I just needed to see her. The rest would figure itself out later.

The modest home I pulled up to looked exactly like it always had. Built a half-century before, it was kept well with pride. Pride that it wasn't much, but it was what we had. We kept clean inside and out. Even the paint on the sidings got refreshed every seven years or so. When someone looked at it, nestled into its forgettable little neighborhood, they knew the family inside appreciated what they had.

I parked behind my mom's weathered sedan and exited the car after checking my reflection in my rearview mirror. Wiping away trails of bloodied tears, I expected to look worse for wear, but my eyes were clear and bright. How disappointing. I wanted to look like I felt.

A myriad of details stuck out as I walked up to the front door. Aside from the smell of the lawn and grass, I could smell dinner, or at least the remnants of it. It was too late now for them to still be eating. I put my house key in the lock and took a deep breath when I unlocked it. I turned the knob, walking in despite the desire to run in the opposite direction. Inside, the smell of food intensified. Opinions and garlic, some beef. Maybe a roast. It should've smelled good, as it always had, but it didn't. It wasn't foul like the expired food in my kitchen and pantry had been, but it didn't bring me happiness, either.

Neither did the familiar scents of home. Every home, every family living under a single roof, they had a familial scent like a fingerprint. I lost it over time when I moved out on my own. I could tell because every visit home I started to notice more and more, which meant I wasn't smelling it anywhere else. By my mid-twenties, I loved coming home to be greeted with it when I walked in the door. Now, I took a deep breath of it and my stomach flipped.

"JoJo?" My mom's voice called from the kitchen, dishes clattering as she washed them.

"One second." I called back. Yearbook pictures and family portraits lined the tan walls of the hallway. The yellow bulbs of the lights casting a warm glow and giving off a comfortable atmosphere. Until mom updated the house, it would always stay stuck a couple decades in the past. I stopped in front of framed collage of my senior photoshoot. The Joceline in those pictures had energy and dreams. She had gotten accepted into an art program at the University of North Dallas, where she hoped to master drawing and animation. Maybe she'd work for Disney or Cartoon Network in a decade. She definitely wasn't the Joceline who dropped out after a year due to tuition and rent issues, plus car payments, without crying about it because art lost its fun when it became a necessity.

I couldn't remember the last time I opened a sketchbook without intending to discard old ones. Now, I only draw enough to test my company's markers at art stores in my area—just quick line art of a face and a stylized cat sketch here and there.

I touched the cheek of my senior photo. My skin looked just as it did back then, but the spark behind my eyes had faded after the events three days earlier.

My choppy haircut took me back to the late 2000s. I aimed for a balance between the popular emo style and the flashy scene kids while trying to model the outfits I saw in mall windows, with clashing patterns and layers. I squinted at my over-plucked eyebrows and shook my head. The amount of heat damage I inflicted was criminal.

"You'd never imagined you'd be here, did you?" I asked myself.

The song changed in Marley's room, pulling my attention away. The door to her room had been left cracked offering me the perfect peak inside without bothering her. All I saw was the back of her braided pony while she worked on some homework on the floor. She always defaulted to the hairstyle, but she'd have her braider put a new color in each time, just to keep people guessing. This month it was a deep green. It looked pretty against her warm honey complexion. My mouth opened to greet her, but I stopped myself. Nerves knotted in my stomach at the thought of talking to her face-to-face.

Maybe after I talked to mom I'd be more comfortable with interacting with my siblings. I could go check on Byron, then I'd go to Mama and get some hugs, have a heartfelt conversation, and maybe a few happy tears. Later I'd be right as rain.

I turned away from the door and walked the few steps to Byron's room. His door was wide open, but his TV had been mounted on the opposite wall, so he faced away from me. With his headset on, he'd never notice me standing there behind him, even if I stayed there an hour. Not unless he went to grab a Dr. Pepper or a snack from the kitchen.

"Bruh, what the fuck!" he yelled into the mic, and I rolled my eyes.

I never understood what was so fun about playing shooter games and screaming at your friends for hours on end, but then again, I never had a gaming console before Byron. I only ever played stuff at the arcade.

I wanted to hug him.

To walk up behind him and wrap my arms around him, which was starting to become harder and harder because he wouldn't stop growing up. I sniffled and wiggled my nose to settle the sudden sadness at the thought.

This wouldn't be my last visit.

Even if I didn't tell them about all of the supernatural stuff, I didn't have to vanish that quickly. I could be a part of their lives a little bit longer. I wanted to watch them walk across the stage while making a fool of myself in the crowd. It didn't have to be time to let go yet. I squandered months of my free time because of my ill-fated doctor visits. If I had known that they would all be in vain, that Matt would leave me before giving the medication time to work, that I'd become something out of bedtime stories. I'd have spent all my time here.

I reached forward and grabbed the doorknob, then closed his door all the way so that his cussing wouldn't upset Mom if she heard it. After we became teenagers, she stopped acting like cussing was some sacred social sin we wouldn't do. Everyone around us cussed, and naturally, we did too. Hell, she cussed from time to time, though not like a sailor. Still, this look would cross her face when she heard the kiddos do it. Maybe it meant they were growing up too fast for her liking. Or she wondered how people would perceive them with all those words coming out of their mouth. Either way, I'd do everyone a favor, while I could.

I found myself returning to the kitchen, eyes taking in all the details of the knick-knacks. Everything was in place, familiar yet vibrant with new colors through my eyes. "Mama."

I stopped short when I saw her through the doorway. The middle-aged woman before me resembled her home – both were fixtures. Her strong, soft body reflected years of hard work and parenting. Greys heavily marked her black hair, which she never dyed, usually tying it in a ponytail so tight I joked it spared her from needing a facelift.

The same woman. The same house. The same existence.

I had been the one to change.

The water cut off and I gulped. I didn't want her to turn around and face me. When she turned around, everything would be different, and I knew it.

She turned and I took in the weathered face in front of me. Despite having dark skin not without wrinkles and smile lines, time hadn't been cruel to her. Her body took the brunt of her age, but she always told me that love kept her beautiful. She looked beautiful to me at that moment. It was a beauty that brought me a wave of sadness.

When her eyes reached me, she smiled. "Well, now, you sounded like a mess on the phone, but you look good."

I moved forward, taking in every detail of her face. "Hi, Mama. I'm just going through a lot, and I missed y'all." "Well, c'mere. It's okay."

She reached out to embrace me but I didn't move forward. Just like I'd been nervous to call out to Marley and too nervous to embrace Byron, I was second-guessing if I could do the same with Mom. Her arms stayed lifted, and I struggled to get my feet to close the distance.

Did I tell them?

I could tell them, but they wouldn't even believe me if I did. I knew they wouldn't. They'd say I was drunk or high and tell me to go get some sleep. My mom would blame the medication, even though she knew I stopped using them after the breakup. The kiddos would probably text their friends about how their older sister went crazy after her ex left her.

I swallowed the hesitation that rose in my throat. I wanted that embrace just there in front of me. I wanted...no I needed my mom. My mama. My family. Pushing through the reluctance, I moved forward and accepted her, letting those familiar arms get closer until she pulled me into her for warmth and comfort.

When she wrapped her arms around me, I wanted to feel relief. I wanted it more than anything, more than life itself, but it never came. There was a sense of comfort there, but it was a wave that crashed against me, not able to penetrate my exterior. The tension in my body never released. I pulled away from my mother to look her in the eyes, her doing the same.

"Baby girl?"

There was a flash of confusion on her face as if she didn't know who I was anymore. My heart raced, and my eyes filled with tears. My mutation made me different; I felt different, I experienced the world around me differently, and I looked a little bit different, yes. But this...this stuck like a knife in my gut.

"Mama, I..." I took a step backward, mouth hung open. A million things to say and no words to say them. "I..." I took a second step, hands rising to cover my mouth as my gums ached.

"What happened to you?"

My chin quivered. "I don't know. I just, I have to go. I'm so sorry Mama, I gotta—"

I needed to turn and leave, to run out of that house, but we both looked at each other for a moment, frozen in a purgatory we didn't understand. My mother's hand came up to cover her own mouth and the expression of fear and confusion on her face broke me.

I ran.

I got in my car and got the hell out of there as fast as inhumanely possible. Seeing her should have calmed me, it should have given me a connection to who I was and grounded me. My mother should have looked at me and known who was standing there, who she was holding tight. Neither of us knew the other in that embrace. Not in the way we were supposed to.

I wasn't my mother's daughter. My father's daughter. I wasn't the big sister who helped raise my siblings. The blood inside me wasn't the same blood that shaped me in my mother's womb.

Joceline Fuentes died at the Avery Hotel.

I had become something else.

Someone else.

The exit for my apartment came and went, but I continued south on the tollway toward Uptown. The further I drove from my mom's house, the further I felt from them emotionally but the heartbreak at the fact kept the tears coming. I plugged in the address I'd seen on the card Rhys had left me.

When I turned into the parking lot of the luxury mid-rise building, I shook my head. Of course, he lived in some swanky place that cost more than my rent and my mom's mortgage combined. "Right..." I sniffled, navigating the visitors' parking lot.

One deep breath turned into two, which sped up into sobs. With my head low, everything came out in a flurry of cries that rocked the whole of me. The warm fuzzy feeling I should have gotten at my family home finally came. There I was, sitting at a loft I'd never been to where a stranger lived, and I felt like I was supposed to be there. Like, I arrived home. Not the location, but to him. To Rhys.

Was he my home now?

He said he took what I had left to save me...had he taken that, too?

The intoxicating feeling of Rhys's presence grew stronger, but I didn't turn to see if he approached. I didn't have to. As it built up and sent warmth into me so intense I felt flush, I heard feet on the pavement running toward the car. The car door flew open.

"Joceline?"

His voice showered down on me and I choked out more cries. He didn't say anything else or ask any questions when he found me weeping. He stood and let me cry for as long as it took, guarding the outside world from getting any closer.

Eventually, I stopped. I had no idea how long it took—forever in a moment. When I did, he helped me out of the car and grabbed my things with an arm around my shoulder. But still, he said no words.

I didn't recoil from his touch. I didn't think I'd ever recoil from it again.

"Sometimes you have to find out for yourself, I suppose," he whispered as we entered the garage elevator, his arm still around me.

"Did you?"

"Yes."

On the short ride up to his floor, I left my head resting against him, emotionally exhausted. If I was no longer human...if my body had turned into something else...if I was forced into a new existence with no turning back, then my mind was made. I lifted my head and looked up at Rhys, who returned my gaze.

"I'm going to kill Dom."

CHAPTER SEVENTEEN

"You sure about this?" I asked.

"No," Slevin answered.

He bounced on his feet the way a fighter warms up before a fight. He took jabs at the air in front of him, switching left to right, left to right, and then giving an impressive left hook. Whether it was magic, power, or straight-up energy that shimmered like stars in his aura, I didn't know. All I knew was the more he moved around, the brighter it became.

After we stopped in front of a dingy metal door, I reached out and tried to touch the green particles, but my fingers moved right through them. The air that they occupied was charged with energy, but not tangible. I waved my whole hand through the aura, but the feel of actual electricity never came how I wanted it to. My countless other attempts to experience a tactile reaction with either the shimmer or the smoke had been fruitless, too.

"So, what is this place again?" I asked, huffing.

He turned to me, both feet on the ground and shook out what he had told me was his battle jacket. That's what they called them. The jackets, either leather or denim, were decorated by punks with lots of metal and sentiments on their personality. Bands. Political statements. Crude humor. All of it was on there. All of it worn with pride by those in the community.

"If you're serious about what you're going to do when you find Dom, this is the place to help you with that."

He knocked twenty times on the metal, creating a rhythm that would be random if we weren't two vampires outside a seedy building off Division Street in Arlington, far enough from Six Flags and the Cowboys stadium to avoid affecting the mid-city's appeal, yet close enough to spot a motel every minute or two. It was a code.

I looked back and forth between him and the door, the door and him. My lips pursed out as we waited for the next thing to happen, whatever the hell that was. Details were purposely omitted from when Slevin invited me on our little adventure to us standing in the modest cold of mid-January. All he said was to dress comfortably and wear sneakers.

A series of knocks answered after almost a minute in a similar fashion as Slevin's. He answered with twelve spaced-out knocks, then seven quick ones. After the secret exchange was completed, the door groaned as it was opened from the inside.

"Slevin, how are ya?" A Mystic greeted.

The density and brightness of his aura was a middle ground between Slevin's and Rhys's, but he was shimmering with the most activity I'd seen. Not that I had been around many of our kind at nearly a week post mutation.

"Good, good. Got a new one here with me."

Their eyes met mine, and I waved, smiling broadly. The Mystic nodded and gestured for us to enter. Inside, the building resembled a warehouse, with concrete floors stained by decades of labor and bare metal walls. All prior equipment had been cleared, leaving open space. My brows lifted to improve my view as we proceeded further.

Blood, smoke, and earth fragranced the air, and toward the back I could see flashes of light like flames appear and disappear. At first, I assumed it was someone playing with fire pois but upon further investigation I realized the Mystics in that area of the warehouse weren't holding equipment.

A Brute and Mystic stood about twenty feet away from each other, two men, and they were panting. We stopped walking about ten feet away from the middle of their space, and each of them turned to look at us, then nodded up at us to give acknowledgment but quickly returned their attention back to each other. Drops of blood surrounded their circle, especially near the Mystic, whose blood-covered hands contributed to the heightened energy of their auras, which bristled and swirled more than the Mystic who let us in.

I opened my mouth to say something, maybe a hello, anything to kill the silence but before a sound escaped, both men exploded into movement. The Brute had his shirt off and was healing a burn, which finished just as he lunged toward the other man, hands posed like claws. He swiped at the Mystic, but his opponent jumped back using a pointed ring on his thumb to slice open his other palm in a movement that looked as simple as swiping one hand over the other.

As soon as the blood started to drip from his hand, it stopped, suspended halfway to the ground and then dissipated, as if the very atoms of it had dispersed smaller and smaller into the air. Then, he punched toward the Brute, and despite not making physical contact with their chest, the Brute flew backward.

The air.

The Mystic was using it to fight like an extension of his arm.

"Whoa," I whispered under my breath.

The Brute recovered almost immediately and lunged a second time. The two of them went down and in a flurry of blood, red sweat, and groans. I grimaced at the violence of it but couldn't hide how interesting the display was. "So, they're just fighting each other?"

"Yeah, they're practicing. There aren't many places you can loosen up and go at each other. This is one of them."

"Nice."

"We're up next," Slevin said.

I shook my head, brows lowered, nose wrinkled. "The fuck?" I argued back. "I can't fight them."

"Ya not fightin' them. Ya fighting me."

"Pssh," I crossed my hands over my chest. "Yeah right. I can't fight you either." He'd tear me apart.

"C'mon," he coaxed, a smile beaming on his face as he gave me a side glance and a wink. He shrugged off his leather jacket, revealing his muscled arms, shoulders, and chest and a worn-out, bloodied, sleeveless undershirt. I gulped at the sight of it for two *very* different reasons. "I'll be gentle."

I rose a brow at him.

"Gentle enough." He smirked down at me, the look dragging all the air out of my lungs. "I'm going to teach you how to take down a vampire."

My nerves were on edge, but I realized I needed to improve my fighting skills. Not just improve- I needed to actually learn how to fight. I had no experience, especially when it came to battling supernatural beings. I nodded, then redirected my focus to the sparring vampires in front of us. They grappled on the floor, with the Brute pinning the Mystic down and hitting him. I clenched my teeth, picturing myself in that position, receiving those blows. I knew Slevin wouldn't really hurt me, but that didn't mean I was eager to even take a light punch to the face. A controlled punch still counts as a punch.

"Okay then."

The Mystic, who I assumed would lose the fight, let go of the Brute's arm to fall to his side, where a metallic container no bigger than a flask was fashioned to his belt. He flipped open the lid while his other hand shielded his face, and water spilled onto the floor. As soon as it did, he used his pointed thumb ring to slice the fingertips on the same hand, and blood splashed onto the ground, mingling with the water.

Snarling against the pain of the Brute's assault, his hand slammed down on the red water. As it rose, the water lifted from the ground, formed into a ball, and cooled enough to freeze. My jaw dropped. The Mystic then grabbed the new ball of pink ice he had created and slammed it into the side of the Brute's head with enough force that he tumbled to the side. Having stolen the advantage with the hit, he scrambled to his feet, opened a second canister on the opposite side of his hip, and snapped with the ring on the same side, drawing blood again and dripping it into the opening. After two seconds, while the Brute tried to recover his senses, the water rose out of the metal and formed into an icicle.

As the Brute rose and prepared to assault once more, the Mystic pressed the cold weapon against his throat, causing the Brute to halt abruptly, his shoes sliding on the filthy ground.

"Yield?" the Mystic asked.

"Yield," the Brute conceded, raising his hands in the air, chest heaving deeply, mouth open as he panted. The Mystic dropped the icicle, and it shattered into a dozen pink pieces. Both vampires then slammed their hands into each other's for a handshake.

"Good fight?" the Mystic started.

"Good fight," the Brute agreed.

They stood there, looking at each other, breathing hard for a few minutes as they recovered their senses before each walked to opposite sides of the warehouse. I saw the shattered, bloodied ice that the Mystic created from water, trying to understand scientifically how it worked. But could this paranormal stuff make sense technically?

"Ready?"

Slevin's voice forced my eyes back up, and I blinked. "No."

"Great." He gave me a little pat on the back. "Real fights never start when you're ready."

He started bouncing on the balls of his feet again as we moved forward. I walked normal, my gait much slower and less energetic than his.

"What are we even supposed to—" Before after I answered the question, Slevin swung his fist at my face. I flinched but reacted quickly enough to avoid the blow, so if he intended to hit me, he would have missed. Nevertheless, his fist halted just before making contact.

"How about you attack, I'll block." His Boston accent was getting thicker, but I had started to enjoy it, if only for the fact that it was something new beside the native accent around town, but more fun than how fancy Rhys sounded.

My balled-up fists came up to block my face, knuckles as high as my eyebrows. Slevin laughed at my form, reaching over to lower my hands a little before drawing back a few feet. He motioned for me to continue.

"Alright." I drew the word out, unsure of what to do.

"Just go at it. I can handle it." My eyes rolled, and I took a swing at him without putting much weight behind it.

He sidestepped the attempt, looking a little disappointed in the effort. Another swing at the face followed, but it carried a bit more strength this time. He moved out of the way, bouncing side to side.

"Think about why you're here, Joce." I lowered my hands and considered what he said.

I was there to learn how to fight a vampire so I could kill Dom.

I lifted my hands back up and jabbed at Slevin's face, my mind pulling up the memory of Dom sitting next to me at the bar of Amaranthine. Heat rose in my chest. I swung at him from the side, and he lifted a bent arm to block.

As he noticed my effort escalating, he nodded. "Let it out. I got you."

The words. The memories of Dom. The idea of killing him. All of those sparked the fire in me that sharpened my vision of Slevin and ignited a wave of energy. Swaying side to side, the next punches came at him no bar held. When he blocked them, I could feel the resistance of his own strength and weight creating a wall of muscle to accept the assault. As I went to hit him again, his fist came around to get me, making contact with my side but stopping before it caused any actual pain.

"Two people can punch at the same time. Protect your body while you attack," he instructed.

I nodded behind my fists before attempting a cross-punch to his left side. I could see his iris flick to the side and catch the movement, but he didn't move out of the way or block it. My knuckles made contact with his jaw, and I winced at the sound.

He shook it off and smiled. "There you go."

We circled each other, each trying to advance on the other and watching as we reacted. I tried punking him a few times before swinging, but no matter whether the movement was a threat or not, he reacted accordingly, able to decipher the empty threats versus the real ones.

"Watch the arms," he advised. "Any of the limbs. They'll help you anticipate an attack versus a movement."

I nodded and switched from the offense to defending myself. He noticed the change and took a few steps toward me. I backpedaled to keep at least five feet between us, but he lunged forward so quick I couldn't avoid him. His fist came straight at me, and I closed my eyes, flinching. After a second, I looked and saw his knuckles maybe an inch from my nose. His face came around the side of it, brow raised. "You've never been in a fight before have you?"

"No, not a real fight."

"I can tell."

For hours, we spared. After a few rounds, I started sweating blood. The hoodie I'd worn had been discarded on the ground, and wet curls stuck to my face and neck. We practiced for ten minutes each and then the others would also take their turns while we watched. The warehouse was large enough that we could all easily pick a partner and fight in different areas, but we weren't trying to have a tournament. While two fought, the others studied. Sometimes, the fights would be against two vampires of the same class, and then the next time, it would be different classes. But seeing as there were only Mystics and Brutes present, it didn't allow for much diversity. The Brutes also weren't allowed to shift, to make the fight fair. Mystics had the elements, but that didn't mean that it created a level playing ground if they were fighting something huge like a polar bear or an elephant.

"We save that kind of fights for class-specific nights."

"How many of y'all are a part of this?"

Slevin made a face. "I think there's about a dozen of us on a full night."

"And y'all just come here and fight each other for fun."

"Not just for fun. We're learning, we're training. This is how we work out. Going to a regular gym is out of the question. They're not made for us."

"I guess that makes sense."

"And it's where you're going to work out, too."

I pointed at my own chest, and he nodded. "Like going forward, or..."

"Do you have a full dance card?" he asked, and I shook my head.

My dance card would be emptying real quick. There was no way I could keep up with the charade of human life. Earlier that same day I had called my area supervisor and quit my job. She'd been sad to see me go and even more sad that I didn't give two weeks' notice, but I cited medical as the reason, and she let it die pretty quickly. Sudden onset solar urticaria. Rhys had fed me the disorder as he stood by me. Sun allergy. After the countless doctor's appointments from the year before, her questions were sparse anyway.

"Dance card is clear." I wrung my hands together, and Slevin nudged my side.

"Fill in a slot. Every other night."

"That often?"

"Until you can get the hang of it, yeah."

I huffed and crossed my arms, side-eyeing Slevin for a second. A moment later, a gust of wind pushed against me from the Mystic's fighting, and I craned my head to the side and blinked away the dust in the air as it hit my face. I swatted it away and coughed. "Fair enough."

CHAPTER EIGHTEEN

I'D BEEN STARING DOWN Rhys's pet serval cat for thirty minutes. Despite insisting she was well trained and "harmless," I maintained my skepticism. Cats were fine. Dogs were fine. African wild cats that were the size of dogs bordered my comfort zone. Sitting in the spacious living room, lounging on Rhys's dark leather couch, I watched the serval, named Ubaste, meander into the room from where she usually stayed upstairs in Rhys's bedroom.

Catching the sound of my breath and the little bit of movement I made readjusting, she twitched in surprise. She was still getting used to me, too.

"Uby..." I greeted, voice light and pleasant. "How was your nap? You know, if you didn't scare the shit out of me, I'd take you out for a walk or something." I added, looking at her over the edge of my phone.

She acknowledged my words with a series of hisses and chirps I'd been taught were just her way of communicating. If her ears were faced forward with a relaxed posture, she was friendly. I'd hate to know what her hissing sounded like when she was pissed off.

Hoping to warm her up to me, I read out loud the wall of text that Rhys had sent me with important information about my new world.

"The Sovereignty is made up of three branches. The Legion, the Institute and the Order." I bit my lip before continuing. "Blah, blah, blah, the Legion are the soldiers and punitive branch. The Institute are the ones who preserve and seek out history. The Order are a mixture of judicial and executive." I sighed, defeated. "This is a lot more human than I expected from vampire society."

I lay down, my phone held above my face, ready to fall on me at a moment's notice. "Scholars are the ones in the Sovereign Institute that study the histories; they preserve artifacts and interpret it all. Scribes are the ones that go out and find the stuff to bring back to the Scholars." I nodded; lips drawn down in an impressed expression. "That's pretty awesome actually." I stole a glance at Ubaste.

"They have vampire anthropologists and archaeologists." I rose a brow. "There's a blood-sucking Indiana Jones out there." I erupted into laughter, which scared the serval whose ears went straight back. "Sorry, Uby. But, I'm asking Rhys about that later. One hundred percent."

"Vivariums are Sovereignty-funded research facilities used to house viable blood samples for animals. Although Brutes can only shift into mammals, samples of all kinds of animals are kept for conservation efforts and research purposes." I matched eyes with the cat after reading the last part out loud, and she responded by taking a couple turns in place and laying down to listen.

"You're a bit secretly a Brute, are you?" I asked, thinning my eyes as if a hint of green aura would show itself.

"You're not Slevin, are you?" I squinted more, but nothing showed. She chirped at me. "Right?" I added, craning my head back. No, she couldn't be. I would have seen an aura. Plus, Slevin played too much, but he wouldn't spy on me like that. He didn't even come into my apartment when I had invited him in. *Not that I would have minded him there.*

No. I wasn't thinking about that.

I groaned and threw the phone down. I didn't want to sit in the loft studying the crazy world around me like I was one of the Institute's scholars; I wanted to be out in it. I wanted to explore the pockets of society where we flourished and did our spooky shit, like what Slevin had shown me. I also wanted to find Dom.

The serval didn't bother getting up when I got up from the couch. I then stretched my arms over my head with a moan and walked toward my new makeshift bedroom on the lower level. After the scene at my apartment, I finally agreed to stay with Rhys for a little while. Just while I got on my feet in my new lifestyle. I was out as soon as I found an overnight job and a new place and got a handle on my abilities and emotions. Rhys maintained a human job, a very successful job at that, doing PR for some public-facing figures in the Lone Star State at a firm called the Collective Group downtown. Steady, lucrative pay and flexibility with hours afforded him whatever he needed, although I had been assured that he had money from decades of medium-to-high-risk investing. I could find something that suited my strengths as much as his jobs did him.

I huffed thinking about Rhys as I cleared my door frame. I appreciated him...I did. He was thoughtful in a general sense, yes. He helped me whenever he could, but it was on his terms. Still, every time I brought up Dom, he shut it down. According to him, I wasn't ready.

The only thing he shut down faster than Dom was his Lord, who sired him. Sorry...mutated him. It had become customary to use less whimsical language, as science generally won out how people spoke daily. Humans didn't talk about blessings and miracles like they used to. I'd been told the Sovereignty adapted the term in the last twenty years. On the receiving end of a recent "mutation", the transition didn't feel scientific or medical. Either way, mutated or sired, changed or evolved, damned or blessed, the person who turned Rhys into a vampire was the closest thing he had to an enemy. It must have been quite the messy breakup. He'd have to tell me about it eventually, considering the vampire resided somewhere in the metroplex.

I groaned for several seconds then sat on the edge of the bed. My new room, my only sanctuary in my new existence, was decorated like any boring guest room. It made me miss my apartment where at least I had some decorations left that Matt didn't take. Now, all I had were hotel quality prints of famous artwork and gray walls.

Rhys had an engagement after his regular work hours, and I was stuck. Well, I wasn't actually stuck. I had a car, I had a key, and I had free will. With him being otherwise spoken for, I had an unsupervised window of opportunity, too. A smile crept onto my face, growing until my cheeks raised. Rhys could only pinpoint my location when we were physically close. If he wouldn't help me find Dom, then I'd do it myself, using the only clues I had.

The Avery Hotel.

If the search was fruitful, I'd be back in the loft before he knew I was gone. Easy-peasy. I went to the full-length mirror facing the open doorway to my left. I needed some adjustments, but I could pass for someone who was supposed to be there. I'd been there before, after all. A few minutes later, I returned in the overpriced athleisure-wear I'd been gifted from my ex. With five minutes of effort, I returned to the mirror with light makeup and a high ponytail. I smiled at my reflection. Perfect. Sheep's clothes were the most important item in the wolf's closet. A lump formed in my throat. Changing how I looked to get into places was very "vampire" of me.

No, that wasn't it. I wasn't going hunting to torture some innocent person. I was hunting the monster who did those things to me.

Ubaste chirped at me from my door frame as I gathered my things into a small purse. She needed to watch her tone. "It's just recon, okay." I started, then gave her a dramatic glance.

She hissed with her ears forward, but I understood what she was saying. She was on to me. "I'll be right back." I paused. "If I can make it in the door, anyway."

I hadn't returned to The Avery since the morning I'd woken up as a vampire. Would I have the strength to walk in? I had to. The hotel was my only lead.

Ubaste hissed again, her tail vibrating behind her as she pawed the ground. "Don't be a narc; you play nice, and I'll take you for a walk tomorrow or something." She made a noise I took as an agreement. Without another word, I left the room. Ubaste followed behind me until I got too close to the front door. She never tried to escape. Slevin had trained her well. "Stay." I teased, pulling my house key out of the bag.

Twenty minutes later, I stood at the valet stand outside the imposing structure that was the Avery Hotel. The brick building resided there for at least eighty years, one of those early downtown buildings that stood the passage of time. It's Art Deco style showed in the decorative brick frames to the windows and the geometric curves added wherever possible. The long gone design style wasn't my favorite, but it did look stunning nestled into the diverse exteriors of downtown. Under the valet cover, I stared at the sliding glass doors, blood rushing to my ears.

He wouldn't be in there.

I didn't know, but I knew.

There was no way he frequented the same bar where he nearly killed someone. In his mind, he probably thought he had killed me. I could manage. I had to manage. Where would I get the information I needed if I couldn't go in? I exhaled a deep breath with extreme control, taking ten seconds to get it all out. I wasn't Joceline Fuentes. She died. I was better, stronger, quicker.

As I entered, it wasn't just the stark contrast of the cold January air with the warmth inside that struck me, but also a feeling of dread in my stomach. Vampire or not, I hadn't fully processed what happened to me, beyond being murdered, so to speak.

My eyes landed on the door of Amaranthine and its glass wall facing the lobby. Seeing inside was virtually impossible, but I still tried. My jaw shook, but I turned my attention to the front desk.

Just breathe. You're okay. Stay focused.

The same desk clerk from the morning I checked out was working. I thinned my eyes, focusing longer on the glittering aura of the fellow Prole. As if sensing my gaze, he looked up, and we locked eyes. I followed with a nod and walked over. He nodded back.

"Miss Fuentes."

Oh, that was nice. Our mental dexterity could get sharp enough to recollect a stranger's name from days before on a dime.

"Hello, good evening. I think you remember me staying here last weekend." I explained. "Well, I need your help identifying someone like us that was here. I don't know if you worked that night, but I believe they had a room." As he listened, his expression shifted, making me feel uncertain. "They were less than friendly."

"Depends. What information do you got?"

"They were white, with light eyes, and brown hair. About six feet, maybe. Skinny, but not a stick."

"You got a name?"

I pushed my lips to the side and looked down. "It's not much of a name. Dom."

"Dom. No, I don't know anyone by that name."

"Okay, look. Maybe you saw him check in or out or something. He's a True Alpha and an Ancient. You can't miss him."

His eyes widened, and he leaned forward. "Look, I know you're an Apprentice, I can see that. And I know you've got Sovereign blood, but you don't ask questions about Ancients or Alphas. If they didn't tell you, you aren't supposed to know."

I craned back, my brows furrowed. How did he know I had Sovereign blood? Then it dawned on me.

"Lord's got it under control."

Rhys.

He had taken care of my room incidentals ahead of my check-out and told them I was his Protégé. It appeared the local vampires knew Rhys was Sovereign, so they assumed, by extension, I was, too.

"Look, that vampire attacked me. He's the reason—"

"Sh." He exclaimed, grabbing my arm to pull me down toward the counter. "Don't talk so loud. A chunk of the staff are kin, but The Avery don't employ people who talk too much about their guests. Even if I knew, I wouldn't tell you."

"Are you fucking serious?" The words were whispered, but I cut them with acid. "This is bullshit."

"I'm not putting my head on a silver platter for anyone. Not Sovereign blood, not a friend. No one."

I snatched my arm back and huffed. "Thanks." I snapped.

Time for Plan B.

I hoped I didn't have to go into the bar, but maybe the bartender from the night of my attack would be more forthcoming than this asshole.

I stepped forward, making my way to the doors. Dom's voice echoed in my mind, recounting his time in Italy. His storytelling captivated me, but it was merely honey in a trap. My intrigue was probably due to his charming abilities and magnetic presence, not any genuine attraction.

No. He had no control over me anymore. The me who walked into Amaranthine was a phoenix from the ashes of his wake. I ignored every nerve in my body trying to stop me. Cold sweat formed on the skin of my forehead and my fangs drew out, but I kept my lips closed. I just had to walk in. I'd walk in and he wouldn't be there, then I could move on with my search. How did I expect to face him when I was supposedly ready to fight if I couldn't do that? I had to face him to kill him.

I wanted to be so close to him, I'd see the light go off behind his eyes. Only then would I be satisfied.

My anger propelled me forward. Without allowing it to wane, I walked into Amaranthine. Fewer patrons populated the bar. Only a few of them looked up as I entered, and the expression was trivial when they did. I wasn't on the menu. They must have pegged me for a housewife trying to catch a cheating husband.

My eyes scanned from left to right. Dom wasn't there, and neither were any vampires. I pursed my lips, considering my options. I didn't recognize the bartender at the far end of the bar, but I could always ask after the one from that night. I walked up to the counter but gasped when my hand casually came to rest on the quartz countertop.

Aren't you delicious?

The memory of Dom's voice cooed in my ear, but it was a new memory, one I hadn't recalled before.

"I can't wait to taste every inch of you."

I clenched my fist and pushed it aside. When the bartender came over, I managed to smile, and they smiled back. "Hello! I'm looking for the bartender from last Friday night. I can't recall his name. Do you know when he'll be back?"

"Is there a problem with your check, miss?"

"No, no. Nothing like that. I need to ask them something, see if they saw someone. It's very important."

"That's Clancy. He'll be in later tonight. So, like, two hours or so."

"Oh my god." My eyes lit up. "Thank you so much. I'll just wait here for him."

"Would you like a drink while you wait?"

"Huh?" Realizing how strange it would be to sit in a bar for two hours without drinking, I flinched. "I'm sorry, yes, I'll have an IPA, in a bottle." IPAs usually came in dark bottles, just as Rhys preferred. Humans often overlooked whether they were full or not. Beer was cheaper to waste since we couldn't drink it.

I grabbed my debit card and placed it on the counter. When the card came back to me, I moved to sit as far away from my previous spot as possible. In the back, there were tables lined against the wall, which had built-in wall seating. I took the cornermost table and planted myself there. Anyone who entered would come within my field of vision, but there was enough distance to hide if someone came in who I didn't want to see me. Namely, Dom himself.

For the first thirty minutes, I watched everyone in the building. None of them were vampires or supernatural beings that I could recognize. The place crawled with businessmen who'd concluded their work but refused to retreat to their rooms for the night. Standard five-star fare. It was the kind of crowd I wished had been present the night I'd sashayed my ass inside in that cream dress. All I got were fucking vampires.

I sighed and pulled my phone out as a welcome distraction. All movement and conversation in the bar were easily tracked, so if anyone so much as mentioned Dom, vampires, or me, I'd clock them instantly. When the phone lit up, there were twenty-six message notifications, but no phone calls. No phone calls meant no real emergencies.

Opening my messages, green dots showed next to the sibling group chat named "tHe LOVE booooooaaatttt" and the rest were in a separate text conversation with my newer contact I'd affectionately titled Ole' Dirty British, for Rhys. I had a sneaking suspicion the majority of the unread texts were in my siblings. I prayed the majority of them were Marley and Bryon. I'd never tested Rhys's patience or graciousness like I had decided to. Generally, I just annoyed him because I was bored and he was there, but he took it in stride. I may have been pushing the boundaries a bit. But, even so, what was he going to do? Kill me? He just put a significant amount of effort into making sure that didn't happen a week before. There was no "I brought you into this world and I'll take you out" for us. Not yet.

I pretended I didn't see the text preview under Rhys that said,

> Where are you?

The meeting got out earlier than I expected.

I opened up the group chat, scrolled up to the beginning of the latest squabble and started reading.

> Byron: Hey, idk what happened the other night but mom was being weird when we asked u to pick us up after the game on next saturday

> Marley: Ya she said smth abt u bein weird when u were over. r u on drugs??

> Byron: she wouldn't do that wtf

> Marley: she's almost 30, i wouldn't be surprised if she tried it, idk

> Byron: omg marley, stfu

> Marley: u don't have to be a fuckin square

I rolled my eyes hard, trying to maintain the slightest interest in their back and forth. I guessed they were sitting next to each other in perfect silence as they texted the conversation to me. I'd put my money on it. I scrolled past more bickering before I got into the meat and potatoes of the conversation.

> Byron: Mom said if we could find a ride back from the game we could go, she didn't say u, which she always does. that's y i'm asking

> Marley: Ya can u come get us? games over @ 3

Marley followed the questions with a slew of emojis and my heart sunk. I'd never let them down before, and that wasn't going to change. Vampire or not, they were still my babies. My "firstborns" as I liked to joke, much to my mother's chagrin.

No. I'd never let them down.

I rubbed my forehead and typed with my free hand that I'd be happy to pick them up. Even if it was at three in the afternoon on the weekend. A groan accompanied my accepting reply.

Moments later, a chill crept down the back of my neck, lingering briefly before surging down my spine. I looked up for Rhys, but the sensation wasn't warm; it felt electric. I set my phone on the table and examined every corner of Amaranthine. No one had come or gone; the patrons continued their trivial chatter or watched a barrage of man-focused social media on their phones. Yet there was something... someone had disturbed my reality.

Was it Dom?

My heartbeat quickened, canines aching to retreat so that my fangs could come forward. I slid my phone into my lap and then pocket, ready for a swift exit if necessary.

Something was moving through the lobby at Amaranthine.

CHAPTER NINETEEN

MY BREATHS QUICKENED AS I scanned for details. Moments later, the door opened, and the breath I'd been holding fell from my lips.

In walked a larger man, aura green with traces of black swirling around. So, he was a Brute. Mostly. Brutes were green, right? But the black, that meant he was a Creeper? My mind raced to understand what I was looking at. He wasn't a Creeper, because he didn't look like a corpse. He looked very much alive. I breathed in deeply. No new scents of death. Maybe he was a Brute with a Creeper ability.

Rhys had explained how something like that could happen to me once before. A Beta, he called it. Omnipotent in that he had more than one class, but Beta because it was only a singular ability.

The man's outfit and mannerisms screamed private security as he walked in. But my analysis stopped when the next person entered. All my thoughts and assumptions faded. I struggled to breathe as if I needed to pause everything to take him in.

In walked an actual True Alpha. Red, blue, green, gold and black mingled lazily in different densities and intensities, seeming to caress the air around him in a sensual dance. The black did not sparkle but instead deepened an abundance of shimmering red and blue. Which meant he used mostly his Paramour and Muse abilities. The gold and green smoke twirled through the dominant colors, the black barely visible. He hardly used his speed. From looking at him, I knew he never had to rush a day in his life.

As the True Alpha cleared the threshold, I drank in his appearance. While the one before him had been physically imposing, he was all encompassing.

He was beautiful. Beautiful was never the word I used to describe men; I admit. But, when I looked at him, it was the first and only thing that came to mind. He looked to be in his late mid-twenties, but the darkness in his aura revealed he trumped Rhys in years, his skin untouched by the envy of age.

His blonde hair was a length that I would have called too long on anyone else. It didn't quite reach his shoulders and the light strands held a bit volume. The strands were straight until they curled and waved at the ends.

Then there was his eyes.

From fifty feet away, I caught their color. They shined vibrantly like a glass of honey being held up to the sun. I couldn't find the words to describe him if I tried – I had never seen a man like that before. The muscles in my thighs tightened as I found the urge to go up to him, to be a little closer to him, to talk to him. He wasn't my usual type – that honor belonged to the first vampire – but this one? This one had my body begging for his touch. I watched him enter and begin to canvas the place as if he were searching for someone specific. I had a sneaking suspicion it was me, being the only other vampire present, but I wasn't holding my breath. Behind the blonde, another vampire stepped in. Tall, dark, and obviously a Brute, he moved with the grace one would expect from a creature capable of shifting. He personified a panther, his skin a dark umber that was as smooth as dyed silk.

A two-person detail meant Blondie was someone not to write off. He reeked of importance. I considered what I gathered about him in that quick moment. Bring a True Alpha would put him at the top of the social totem pole. I returned my attention to the aura, admiring how it framed him, complementing his tan suit—the jacket somewhere between a suit jacket and a cape, with sleeves too long to be worn conventionally and cut to drape and billow. On anyone else it may have seemed like it was trying too hard to be fashionable, but on him, it fit.

I wonder if that's what it was like with Dom?
Is his aura just as mesmerizing?
Did he enchant and intimidate other vampires.
No...

The vampire before me was definitely not Dom but, my enchantment with him made it hard for me to decipher whether that was good or bad. As my eyes followed the True Alpha who turned and smiled at me, I raised the warm beer to my lips. My body moved on instinct, distracted by the group, accompanied by a similarly dressed human, approaching my table. I nearly took a sip, lost in thought.

"You know, our kind doesn't stomach those very well. We have a limited palate." Blondie spoke and took a seat next to me in the booth seats of the table to my right.

It felt odd how effortlessly he positioned himself next to me, despite having three men protecting him from everyone else in the bar. This confirmed what I already knew – he was there to see me. I tried to steady myself, placing the beer down while keeping my gaze straight ahead to avoid facing him.

"Good evening, fräulein."

"Hi." The greeting was simple, but it was all I could muster.

Our kind had titles and pomp, but I hadn't been exposed to it enough to know if we had specific greetings. Rhys and Slevin had taken me around our kind, yes, but it'd been casual, friendly – no need for me to learn German and Austrian or whatever the hell he was speaking to me currently.

"Pretty little thing, you are."

While his comment was technically a compliment, it felt condescending. Either way, I couldn't help but smile when I heard it. His speech had a deliberate cadence, and the accent added an enticing edge that made me eager for him to say more – nice words, harsh words, anything at all.

I cleared my throat and straightened my back, slowly losing my battle to not give him my attention. "Are you sitting next to me for a reason?" I asked.

"Precisely I am." He answered as I looked at him, my body tense with curiosity. I needed to understand why he had taken a seat. His back straightened, causing me to flinch and him to laugh softly. "Please, do not worry. I am simply an interested party." He leaned closer. "Tell me your name."

"Joceline Fuentes."

As soon as my full name came out, I cursed myself. My human name should have remained secret. I didn't have to offer it to the new world I'd been thrown into and here I was serving my old self up on a platter for a fine man in a suit.

"Ah, Ms. Fuentes. Yes. You are exactly who I need you to be." He licked his lips. "You must excuse the show." He gestured to the men around him, who didn't react. "One can never be too careful these days. Tell me, pretty little one. What brings you to Amaranthine?"

"Why? You own it?" It came out snarkier than I expected, but his laugh let me know he thought I was all bite and no bark.

"I deal in hospitality of a different nature, of our nature."

As much as I wanted to ask what he meant, I refused to show the naivety that we both know existed from someone as young in the world as I was.

"Then, why ask?" I managed. The question earned me another laugh, more of a chuckle, from the stranger. He anchored his elbow on the table to help him cup his chin with his fingers, then leaned toward me.

"Curiosity brings the cat both demise and satisfaction, doesn't it?"

"Uh..." I wanted to reply but fumbled my words as his accent filled my ears.

"Tell me, fräulein. Do you always talk to strangers in this manner or have I offended you in some way?"

My cheeks warmed. "I'm not trying to. I'm sorry."

"Please, do not apologize for your nature. It entertains, not insults," He chuckled once more. "I wouldn't be opposed to an answer as to why you are here."

"I don't see why you need to know, but if you must, I'm looking for someone."

"So the wind whispers." He replied. "What a shame it is that I am not the one you seek. Not yet, at least. But *you*, I never would have guessed that I would be looking for someone like you. Alas, here you are and here I am. Unfortunately, I cannot give you more of my time. Work calls to me. I simply couldn't resist letting my eyes fall on you, if just for a moment."

Startling me in the process, he stood from his seat and turned to face me. His open palm came up to me, in which I instinctively put my hand, much to my own surprise. The willingness to do it without a thought was scary.

"What do you mean?"

"Come to me...at the Fountain of Youth." He lifted my hand up to his lips and planted a gentle kiss. "I hope you do not waste time in doing so." I drew a breath in so quick, it startled me.

"Your blood, it sings," he whispered, releasing my hand. As soon as he cleared the table and made it into the open space, his security detail moved to surround him. The Omnipotent Brute returned to the front, while the human and Brute took the back.

I took a moment to gain my bearings. My whole body reeled from the experience, trying to conjure a reason for anything that occurred in the last five minutes. Before he reached the door, I snapped out of my haze and ran after him.

The Brute reached for his hip, where I presumed a gun holster was, but the blonde came from behind and stopped him with gentle hand on the arm.

"Wait," I started, "I wanted to ask if you knew an Ancient named Dom? Or, maybe they have a similar name? I'm not sure. He's a True Alpha, like you."

"An Ancient True Alpha named Dom." He chuckled while he considered his answer. "I can't say I have that answer right now."

My brow arched; it wasn't a straight denial. He reached out and traced his fingers down the side of my face. I should have flinched but didn't. Instead I stood my ground, hoping he would give me more. "Let's hope next time we speak, we both leave more satisfied than curious, ja?"

He turned and walked out, his lackeys in tow, while I stood there like an idiot unable to will myself to move.

When I did move, I found myself at the bar top for another ten minutes, lost in my haze, unable to even scroll through social media.

"Ma'am." The bartender called and I blinked, trying to put the experience behind me. "Clancy called in, he won't be here tonight. I'm so sorry."

My stomach turned. Of course, he wasn't; it seemed the perfect thing to happen after that weird interaction I had. I hung my head low for a moment but forced myself to look up at the bartender.

"Right. Yeah, okay. I'll just try again," I replied but my mind wasn't on Clancy anymore. It was on the man – could I even call him a man? – who had left me speechless.

Why would he need to look for someone like me?

My mind instantly drifted to Rhys. Maybe that had something to do with it. Or maybe I was the gossip, the hot tea that scolded the tongues of my new so-called kin.

Reeling, I walked out of the bar to the front valet stand in the drive-way, pulled my valet ticket out, and handed it off. "How much do I—"

"It's already paid for, ma'am."

I "Uh, thanks." I climbed into the driver's seat and buckled in, reaching for the gear shift, but before I put the car in drive, the passenger door opened.

What the –?

As Rhys got into the car, I forced a smile to hide my guilt, but his serious expression quickly erased it, leaving me frowning. It was clear to me what thoughts were swirling in his mind. He looked ready to give me a piece of his mind, but thanks to our connection, I knew underneath that anger was nothing more than frustration.

"Okay, look—"

"No, listen first." He cut me off. "I know you want to find Dom, I understand that. I promise I'll help you when you're ready, but..." He exhaled hard. "You're not even a month mutated. You have no real control of yourself or your abilities yet. You've hardly gotten any combat training. This is impulsive. Running off playing Sherlock and ignoring my calls isn't going to get you anywhere. Can't you have some patience?"

"I am not a child." I rolled my eyes as I put the car in drive.

"No, you're not a child. You're a volatile creature let loose on the world."

As I pulled out of the driveway, the downtown streets were bustling with traffic. I let a moment pass before I answered. "He tried to kill me; I'm allowed to seek my retribution. I'm owed what's mine. That's not fair."

"Life isn't about being fair," He glanced over at me. "And you know that."

"I don't need a lecture, okay? Can you just be plain?"

"Oh, I don't think plain looks good on you, dove," he quipped. "You're anything but plain or simple."

"Yeah, well you don't know what this is like. You have no idea what I'm going through and no matter what you say, you're never going to stop me. I may be your Protégé, but I'm not bound to act as you think I should."

"I can see that," He scoffed. "You have no idea how our world works, how things are handled. Do you think we can go around killing each other? That it's as easy as having a personal vendetta and using that as a license to kill?"

"Are you insinuating that he can try to kill me and that's okay but when I attempted to do the same to him, I'm in the wrong!" I yelled at him. "That's bullshit."

"It's not bullshit; it's centuries of culture."

"Centuries of culture!" I screamed. "You call victimizing innocent people culture? . Last I checked, it was unchecked entitlement and shitty learned behavior." I took a deep breath. "What he did is inexcusable. I don't give a fuck what you think about it, what he thinks about it, or what vampire fucking culture thinks about it." I gripped the steering wheel tighter as a dinging noise grew louder from the dashboard. "And put on the goddamn seat belt."

Before he could think to give me some snarky ass response, my expression made him pause. He buckled in and took a few controlled breaths. "I'm not here to argue."

"That's debatable. If you're not here to argue, I really don't know why you're here."

Rhys sighed, defeat filling his tone. "You weren't answering. I was worried."

"Worried? Aren't I a vampire? What do you have to be worried about?" I grumbled.

"One of the things I remember most about being an apprentice is the roller coaster of emotions. Elation, despair, relief, rage. A storm always brewed in my being," he hung his head as he continued to speak. "I gather you're likely experiencing the same. I don't want you to make the same mistakes I did."

"I get it, but I'm not you." My mind struggled to imagine him unstable and erratic. I turned down a street that led to the loft. A line of deep breaths pulled me out of my anger, letting it subside into a bubbling annoyance for the time being. "Can I ask you a question?"

"Yes?"

"What's the Fountain of Youth?" I looked over at him, wanting to gauge his reaction to the words.

His eyes widened. "What did you say?"

"The Fountain of Youth, what is it? I mean, I know the magic water stuff. I don't think he meant that, but—"

"Who told you that?" Anger spread through our connection and I almost winced from the intensity of it. "I need to know where you heard that, Joceline. Why would an old fable elicit that kind of response from him?

"Someone said it to me in Amaranthine," I shrugged, not knowing if it would be smart to tell him all the details. "They told me to meet them there."

"Damn it, Joceline," He ran a hand across his face. "Who?"

"He didn't give me a name. That's all he gave me, Fountain of Youth."

"What did he look like?"

I stopped short when a light turned red in front of me, causing us to jerk forward in our seats. "Blonde hair, not short, but not super long, either. Hazel eyes, or at least I think they were. I couldn't really describe them if I tried. He was older than you in vampire years but looks younger than me in human years. True Alpha. He wasn't Dom, I can tell you that much."

"Fuck."

My heart sped up as the word fell from his lips. The light turned green, but I didn't take my foot off the brake.

"Who is he, Rhys?"

He didn't answer, so I kept my foot down. Behind us, a car honked, but I wasn't going to move until he said something. More honks followed. He didn't want to respond, but we could end up in a road rage incident. The honking persisted, coming in quicker succession, highlighting everyone's annoyance with me. Even with them in a different vehicle six feet behind us, I could hear the person yelling obscenities.

"Rhys."

Nothing.

"Rhys!"

"It's Dietrich."

My eyes moved to the back of my hand where he'd placed that kiss, but I forced them back on the road as I began to move the car under the light. "My blood..."

"Felt him?" He continued my sentence. "I've never felt a second-generation blood coupling myself, but I'd imagine you must have felt him near."

"It wasn't like you." I didn't have to give him that detail but I couldn't stop myself from telling him. "It wasn't warm; it was magnetic. Like I was being called to him instinctively."

"His blood recognized itself in you. He's not your Lord but there's still a connection there."

I chewed my inner cheek and turned down another street, mind racing. "Do you feel warm when you're near him?"

"I do." He started words laced with acid at the mention of his Lord. "But it doesn't stop how much I want to rip his bloody throat out."

CHAPTER TWENTY

"WHERE'S THE FOUNTAIN OF Youth?" I asked a week after my run in at Amaranthine, my voice sing-song as I sat on one end of Rhys's couch, staring into Ubaste's unblinking eyes. The serval stared back at me with the smallest hint of understanding. I couldn't pinpoint the understanding, but it was there. I guessed she knew I wasn't human, that I was another predator like herself. She never let me walk behind her, and that's what tipped me off to her magical sixth sense. I blinked and turned away from her when I got no response, causing the cat to give a friendly chirp and walk away.

"It's in Florida, I believe," Rhys lied.

"No, it's not."

"No, it is not," he agreed, staring at some work documents on his tablet.

"This is so annoying. I'm hungry." I sunk into the couch even more. "Can we get something to drink at the Pulpit? Do we have to get a bleeder? Can I just, like, have a glass this time?"

"You just fed."

"I'm hungry though." I groaned.

My appetite was uncontrolled. My training with Slevin didn't help the ache. Every time I left the warehouse, I'd have taken any red I could find. Last night had been a grueling training session and here I was hungry... again.

"If we're going to go out, you're going to practice feeding properly from the vein."

"I haven't fucked it up."

"A few good feedings doesn't mean you're the best at it now, does it?"

"No." I grumbled. "I just...drinking is already weird enough."

"Well, we're going to do it until it's not weird."

I raised an eyebrow. "If I agree, can we go?"

Rhys glanced over at me. "We can if you stop complaining and do things my way."

"Fine." I stood up, facing my room. "Give me five minutes."

Fifty-five minutes later, we entered The Pulpit, despite it being a ten-minute drive. After two centuries, I trusted that Rhys understood what five minutes meant in terms of getting ready. He didn't complain when I spent thirty minutes in the bathroom. If my lips were going to be at someone's throat, I wanted to look less like I was going to the grocery store and more like the presentable vampire I needed to be.

Not even five minutes after walking in, we sat upstairs in our exclusively vampiric section. On one of my earlier visits, I learned that the only humans allowed up there were either bleeders who got paid to provide a service or were accompanied by a vampire. The latter was less likely, because loose lips sink ships and who was going to play around with the risk?

Lounging on a chaise couch, we waited for a Syrah to arrive. The current menu had been exhausted, and a fresh menu was arriving within the hour. The double meanings were easier than expected to keep up with thanks to the increased mental dexterities, but I still found myself annoyed at the charade. I'd rather have been upfront about it.

A light Pinot Noir, ye' were.

My relaxed posture turned rigid as I straightened my back. A shiver coursed from the base of my neck down my spine. The moment I let loose and lowered my guard, that asshole's voice slithered in like a snake in the garden. Were hallucinations common for the newly mutated? I could've asked Rhys, but he would only warn me that my obsession with Dom consumed me. I didn't want to deal with that after our last fight about it. Dietrich had been heavy on my mind, but Dom would never miss the opportunity to weasel his stupid ass into my mind. How did someone so briefly in my life take up so much real estate?

I pulled my arms in and crossed them over my chest, as if to protect myself from a phantom. But, he wasn't really there, just a figment of my imagination that I didn't have the strength to fight. I rolled my lip over my fangs, which had lowered a little in anticipation of a meal. The thoughts of him rolled smoke over my skin, the feeling trying to engulf the warmth Rhys provided.

I can still taste it on my tongue.

"Fuck." I whispered, clamping my eyes shut.

Rhys adjusted his position so that he faced me, his hand coming to rest on my shoulder, but I jerked away. I knew it was him, not Dom, but I didn't want him touching me when that asshole's voice was in my head. The two had to be separate. If they became combined, I'd hate them both, I'd hate everything about being a vampire. That was more than I could handle.

"Dove?"

"No." I spat the rejection out and jerked further from him. "I just need a second."

Behind my eyelids, a vision of crimson and violence sprang to life. White sheets and blood fresh enough to be bright red. In the memory, I tried to lift my hands to push him off me but I couldn't do it. All my limbs were useless. I couldn't do anything but cry.

My fingers fanned out and I flexed them, losing sense of my location. I fell into the sensation of that floating blood loss. As soon as tears flooded my eyes I stood up. The action brought me closer to reality, but I needed to be a hundred percent before I fed. The intrusive thought stung my mind. I'd just kill a human like Dom had tried to do to me.

No.

I wasn't Dom.

I wasn't a killer.

I was Joceline, but not Joceline Fuentes.

I remember the night of my attack and the name I had given Dom in Amaranthine, the name I had unintentionally given to the world that lived in the shadows. The world that looked down on humanity like we looked down at the clubgoers in The Pulpit.

Joceline DeLon.

"Give me a second," I explained to Rhys, who looked ready to stand up with me. When I finally opened my eyes I turned to him.

"Please." His jaw flexed, but he relaxed, and I tried a smile. "I'm going to take a lap."

I walked toward the nearest spiral staircase, which opened up to the first floor, much closer to the dance floor than the one at the entrance. A chill ran down my spine before I reached the landing and I shook my shoulders out and descended. He slithered in and out of my subconscious, leaving my body reeling as much as my mind.

Stepping onto the dance floor, a sea of faces I didn't recognize flooded around me, all dancing in a way that seemed unique to the gothic atmosphere. They were having fun. They were comfortable in their skins within these metal and concrete walls when most couldn't boast the same outside of them. Rhys felt the same and for the same reason. His ease rolled off him into me as soon as we walked in. Outside those walls, Rhys was the handsome, suave business man who ran The Collective Group. But, not the vampire. I figured that played into why he acted so buddy-buddy with the staff.

I moved into the middle of the floor. Everyone else faded into the background around me, even though my senses picked them up on scent and sound with unnecessary precision.

I wanted what both the alternative clubgoers and Rhys had: to be comfortable in my skin. I'd been a vampire, a Prole, a victim, for almost weeks. At no point in that time had my body gained harmony. Something new always reared its head and threw my new world further askew.

One moment I had some new flashback, a glimpse of that hotel room, the next I figured out that I could cut out a scar from my arm and it would heal without it being there. Or, I jumped high enough to touch the ceiling of the loft-like child's play. For no reason at all, I remembered what I ate on a random Thursday at seven years old. None of that would compare to simply being sure of who I had become.

I found myself in the midst of a dozen or so people who danced with abandon, and I joined in. I had never considered myself much of a dancer, so my moves to an industrial song lacked finesse, but the bass reverberated in my chest, allowing me to feel every rhythm. My hips and thighs lifted and dipped, my head swayed, and for a moment, I simply existed. If a moment could be measured as about a minute or two.

I didn't have to be Joceline Fuentes or Joceline DeLon. All I had to do was move. I'd never heard the music before, nor did I have to impress anyone with my simple moves. I only existed without interior or exterior presumptions.

When the song ended, I opened my eyes and stopped. I had finally experienced that calm I was searching for. There were no rules to the dancing, there were no expectations of what it had to look like, no way I had to feel about it. I was just dancing. No thinking. Just dancing.

I caught the icy stare of my personal phantom in the crowd around me, colorful shadows swirling around him. Shocked, my fangs dropped, and I covered my mouth. But as soon as he appeared, he vanished. I whipped my head from side to side, searching for him again.

Chest heaving, I started to make my way off the dance floor and toward the back hallway, which housed the restrooms and various other side doors. I had no idea where I thought I was going, or if I was trying to find or run away from Dom, but I needed to move. The song changed to something electronic with a quick, pulsing beat. My heart reacted by speeding up and I pressed my back against the side wall.

He wasn't there.

I squeezed my eyes shut and focused on breathing slower than my heart rate. In front of me, someone's hand brushed across my chest, then something struck the wall next to my head. I sucked in the air and popped my eyes open, but no one was there. The hallway was empty.

"Fuck." I spat, hands coming up to rub vigorously at my face.

I needed to get a handle on myself. And I needed to feed. If I fed, I'd be able to sharpen up my senses. I'd have the focus to differentiate reality and whatever the hell I was experiencing.

Drown in that blood. Feel the pleasure I felt when I ripped...you...apart.

The words disgusted me, my body heat rising until I swore I could see red. My fingers pushed onto my eyelids until stars burst behind them.

He wasn't there.

I was just hungry.

I was at The Pulpit to drink and I would be okay.

I wouldn't kill the Bleeder.

I was okay.

He wasn't there.

I was just hungry.

I wasn't going to kill the Bleeder.

I took a series of deep breaths with my eyes still closed, repeating the phrases over and over again in my head until my heart slowed and my skin cooled.

I was okay.

He wasn't there.

I was just hungry.

I wasn't going to kill the Bleeder.

I wasn't going to kill anyone.

No one but Dom.

A hand touched my shoulder, and I jumped, eyes wide. Rhys stood before me, concerned; he felt my panic.

"Joceline." The use of my actual name assured me of his unease. "Are you alright?"

"Yeah, yeah." I shrugged it off, despite our coupling telling him that I was far from it. "I'm fine. Let's go upstairs."

He wanted to ask more after my dismissal but kept to himself. For that, I was grateful. I needed a pint in me and some quiet. Especially because I had to pick up Marley and Byron in two days. If I couldn't get a handle on myself, I was putting them in danger, and I refused to do that.

"Alright, dove. Off we pop."

CHAPTER TWENTY-ONE

DESPITE THE COOLER TEMPERATURES of January, the sun sat high in the sky and I found myself squinting behind the darkest tint of sunglasses on the market. Most people were in attendance at the football game so the pickup line wasn't terrible. Judging from the parking lot, half the people seemed to have left halfway through the last quarter anyway. Why wait to watch defeat when you can beat traffic?

The school wasn't known for sports, which is unfortunate for a Texas high school. However, the stomp team and marching band made watching the kids get their asses handed to them by the neighboring schools worthwhile. It had been that way for over a decade, and it was the same for my siblings during their time there. At least it was a consistent thing.

Unlike the events of my life.

Parked in the middle of a line of cars, I looked around the post-game crowd for Marley and Byron, who hadn't answered the five text messages I sent them when I arrived. I didn't mind that they were having fun, but it was bright out and I needed to get out of the sun.

I blinked hard twice, fighting the desire to rub my eyes, so I could keep my hands clutched to the steering wheel. Almost every inch of my body was covered except my lower face, but I still felt a little warm, as if a hay fever was about to set in.

After a few minutes later, Marley and Byron walked out with other students and their parents. I scrunched my nose, wondering why those parents couldn't take them home, but I pushed the thought away. My chances to do this for them were limited. They were human, growing and living safe mortal lives. My time in their lives was numbered. If only that number would show itself. Single or double digits? The knowledge it wasn't triple digits weighed heavily in my gut.

Behind the small group, a figure loomed. At first, it was obscured, but the hair... I'd recognize that hair anywhere.

Dom.

My mouth opened, fangs dropping at the possibility of danger.

Not the kiddos.

Anyone but them.

I unbuckled my seat belt and rushed halfway up the sidewalk before realizing it. Luckily, the crowd hid my speed. Convincing my siblings I'd taken up cardio would've been harder than claiming to be a paranormal creature. I could no longer see Dom. When Byron and Marley paused to find my car, they turned back in surprise at how close to them I was. They separated from the group as I closed the distance and urged them forward by placing my hands on their backs.

"JoJo, why are you rushing us?" Marley tried to hold back my pace, but I pressed harder, leaving them no choice but to quicken their steps to keep up with me. "What the fuck?"

"Dude," Byron huffed, but their protests didn't mean a thing. If there was even a slight chance Dom was there, we needed to get the hell out of there.

"Sorry," I apologized, getting into the driver's side. Once inside, my fangs receded, and I took a deep breath. Both of them yelled shotgun at the same time and proceeded to run for the passenger door.

Byron was awarded the front and Marley begrudgingly entered the back on the same side. Sore from her loss, she kneed the back of Byron's seat. "Watch the leather." I grumbled, despite having cloth seats.

"Yeah, yeah." She replied, and I gave them both a moment to buckle in before leaving the parking lot.

"You okay?"

I stole a glance at Byron while he spoke, chewing the inside of my cheek as I considered my reply. I cleared my throat and gave a half-hearted fake cough, rubbing my sunburned nose. The fact that I wore long sleeves and pants wasn't the issue. It was the hoodie I had on with the strings drawn, allowing minimal exposure through the opening, along with the oversized sunglasses. The gloves also made me look like a damn fool. "Yeah, I'm just getting over a really bad cold."

"You're sick? Nah..." Marley started. "Why didn't you say that? I don't want to get sick."

"It's fine, I'm getting over it. Just still getting chills and shit. Relax."

"Tell mama that then." Marley interjected. I sighed, grip on the steering wheel tightening. I'd never be able to tell my mother, or them, anything.

A silence settled in the car as they played on their phones. Unlike my observant mother, they couldn't see my monstrous transformation. What if I found Dom? What if my retribution failed? Would he hurt them after killing me? Would my relationships with Rhys and Dietrich jeopardize my human ties?

The idea sickened me.

Choice had been taken from me too often, and I despised losing the chance to protect those I loved. Their importance meant I had no choice in safeguarding them either.

"I love you guys."

I knew I came off suspicious as soon as I said it, but I wanted them to know. How many times did I have left to tell them—a handful, a dozen, or one? Whatever way I decided to disappear, the fact that it had to happen wasn't going to change. Not if I wanted to make sure they never became a part of my world. I didn't even want to be a part of it, myself. None of it was a positive experience, to say the least.

"I wish you came to dinner more. Since that asshole left, we hardly see you." Marley's honesty was like a dagger to my heart.

"Damn Marley, tell her how you really feel."

"What?" Marley replied, not realizing how harsh that was.

"I'm sorry; I've been a shitty sister."

"Not really," Byron said. "You're an adult. You don't have to spend all your free time with us. Marley's just needy."

"No, I'm not needy. I just want to see her. Don't you want to see her?"

"Look," I interrupted. "I'm just going through a lot right now." I explained, pulling into their subdivision. Months before, I withheld my medical problems from them in favor of bringing it up when they were older, and here I was, withholding worse. "I'll be around more later. "Let me just get my shit together. I'm so all over the place, I can't even fend off a cold."

I parked the car on the curb and turned to face them. They both looked back, seemingly waiting for some valuable piece of older sister advice or insight into my life, but I had nothing to share. My jaw clenched tightly before relaxing enough for me to say, "I'm fine; mom's fine. I love you both, but I have to go. Please, take care."

"Take care where, at home?" Marley shot back.

"In life," I clarified, feeling helpless. She rolled her eyes at my response. Byron reached for the door handle but paused to meet my gaze, his expression sparking a memory I wouldn't forget, just like my mother's face from nights past.

"Let's go, Marley," Byron commanded, as if trying to reassure himself more than her.

They muttered to one another before stepping out of the car, prompting an exasperated sigh from me. I stared at their departing figures until they entered the front door. Just as I was regaining the courage to drive away, my phone buzzed with a text from Byron, separate from the group chat.

U okay?

He noticed the body snatcher parading around in his sister's body.

Yeah i'm fine. don't worry. just a cold.

Immediately after I answered, three moving dots appeared. He was really worried.

I overheard mom a few months ago say smth about doctors, are you sick sick?

When I read the message, my stomach crept up into my throat and I put the phone down and then drove off. Halfway down the block, my phone vibrated again, but I didn't check it. No matter what he said, I didn't have an answer to give him yet. But what a fitting question. I, most definitely, was sick-sick. I could name a handful of reasons in just as many seconds on the different ways. Not that Byron would hear any of them.

Hopefully, he'd never know how right he was. That would lead me to another problem.

How could I keep my new world from my old one?

Chapter Twenty-Two

IF SOMEONE SEARCHED FOR the Fountain of Youth in Dallas, they'd find a new spa or skincare regimen. Which would be helpful if I was a human needed a soak or a massage but that wasn't what I needed.

I needed an Austrian vampire.

I ground the bottom of my palms into my closed eyes and rubbed them for a while until vaguely colored darkness made patterns. If only I had an extra clue, but searching for The Sovereignty and Dietrich's name also didn't do anything for me, except maybe add me to a watch list somewhere.

My hands stopped, and I pulled away.

I pulled up a translator on my phone and found out that 'fountain of youth' in German was Jungbrunnen. Excited to continue down my rabbit hole, I searched Jungbrunnen, Dietrich and Dallas. A few forums popped up and a link appeared for a German site about halfway down the page. It was an outdated website, resembling something that had been created when the internet was still in its adolescence. However, if the internet domain was functional, it meant it was owned and kept in 2020. I scrolled down, noting little that stood out except the name Dietrich Starhemberg and some random numbers scattered throughout. At the bottom of the page was an address—an address in Dallas.

I looked from side to side as if I had to make sure no one watched me, although I knew Rhys was out on a dinner date. Dinner for him and a date for the human. Both would leave satiated in one way or the other. With a smile creeping onto my face, I typed the address into my Maps app. The area of the city it popped up in made me scoff.

Highland Park.

Old Money Dallas. The neighborhood wasn't the flashy downtown area or the swanky gentrified regions. No. It lay hidden in north Dallas. The affluent built it back when the area had potential and was considered distant enough from the city to feel separate, yet close enough that the trek into downtown for work wasn't too arduous.

Now, decades later, the outer area had become rundown. The surrounding suburb was filled with aging apartment complexes, dingy businesses, and small homes occupied by the working class. Millionaires were on one block, and not even five minutes down the road, people lived paycheck to paycheck. Even in terms of location, my new world was just on the other side of the looking glass, hidden in plain sight. I turned off my phone screen and made my way to the shower. If I was going to arrive invited but unannounced, I'd better look and smell like roses.

An hour later, I got into my car sporting light makeup and the closest thing to appropriate clothing I had at the loft. Black slacks, black silk camisole, black boots, and a black leather jacket. It all screamed vampire a little loud but at the end of the day I needed it to.

I spent the drive rehearsing hypothetical conversations with Dietrich. When I met him in Amaranthine, I forgot my words. The pomp and show of his entrance took me by surprise. I didn't have that excuse anymore. Although, judging by the aerial view of Jungbrunnen, his house might do that instead.

Gaudy estate aside, I had questions for my Lord's Lord. Most of them pertained to Dom identity, but some were personal. Rhys divulged so little but my patience was wearing thin. Plus, every time I pressed him about his past, he clammed up so tight that I thought he'd shit pearls. Did he keep it under lock and key because he feared I'd think differently of him if I knew? If humans in high government positions had much to hide, how many skeletons were stashed in the closet of a top-level official of the Sovereignty?

As I approached the subdivision, I tried not to dwell on the cultural shift from sparse foliage to an abundance of towering, aged trees. Their large canopies obscured the estates behind them. Initially, plots occupied a quarter of a block, then half, and eventually entire blocks. Thick landscaping made it hard to see where one property ended and another began, marked only by different fence styles or a guard shack.

Each glimpse of multimillion-dollar mansions hidden down winding driveways made me roll my eyes as an unimpressed sound escaped me.

The electronic voice of the navigation instructed me to turn to my destination on the left, where I noticed the fence line took up the entire oddly shaped block. A manned guard shack lit up by the glow of surveillance equipment greeted me as I turned in.

The car window slowly rolled down to reveal my unassuming smile, which was not returned by the Brute with no visible emotion on his face. I noted the way his aura held a light green tint, but not much density. Then again, he wasn't doing anything that would be causing it to brighten. Even from the sight of it, he didn't seem especially strong or old.

"Good evening," I greeted.

"Yes, Prole."

His condescending tone caused my smile to fade. "Nice to meet you as well."

"What brings you here?" As thankful as I was to hear a native accent from a Texas vampire, I didn't appreciate his attitude. The lower-class Prole shit had gotten old really fast.

"I'm here for Dietrich Starhemberg," I replied. His eyebrows raised in surprise. "I'm the blood of his blood."

The Brute picked up a landline phone, and I seized the opportunity to glance at a camera positioned at eye level next to a small, dark monitor screen aimed at me.

I caught Dietrich's voice at the end of it saying, "Ah, I hope my eyes do not deceive me; the beauty before you is a Prole, is she not?"

"Yes, Sovereign."

"Well...I do not let beautiful things waste away sitting on driveways, do I, Tommy? Let her in. You really can be quite the Brute, honestly."

Tommy scoffed into the phone before hanging it up, aware that I could hear the conversation. I offered him another broad smile and rolled up my window. He pressed a button and waved me through.

As the gears to the iron gate turned, it opened to a long driveway. I drove forward and wiggled my fingers as a gesture of facetious thanks to the ever-lovely Tommy and started down the drive.

The more I drove, the more the spectacle that was Jungbrunnen came to view. I didn't know if the place was for business or pleasure, but it was definitely big. Big and ostentatious. It honestly looked as though it belonged in the French countryside as some chateau a wealthy family spent their summers. I had to consciously keep my mouth closed.

What kind of place was this?

I parked my car in a circular drive behind the others that made my own look like a pile of, for lack of a better word, shit. I stepped out of my car and straightened my clothes, psyching myself up to approach the door. I felt out of place—not because of my skin color, tax bracket, upbringing, or my newly acquired vampire mutation class. It was the blood in my veins, however, that pulled out a small sense of belonging.

Before I made it up the stairs, the oversized front doors opened and revealed a vampire with a noticeable golden aura. A Mystic, like the woman from The Pulpit. "Please come in, Joceline."

Great, another stranger who knew my name before I'd even introduced myself. At least he wasn't another European guy, I noted as his deeply rich dark skin almost glowed in the moonlight. "Hi." I made it all the way up to the threshold but hesitated before I crossed it. As I entered the foyer, I looked up and was awed by its grandeur. Everything gleamed in white and gold, yet the colorful murals on the ceiling captivated me. At the top of the grand staircase leading to the second and third floors, I spotted familiar blond hair and a charming face.

Dietrich.

Before I knew it, I moved closer as he descended from the third floor. He smiled down at me, my eyes instantly drifting to his sensuous pink lips as I bit my own. He seemed perfectly at ease in the luxurious surroundings. Seeing him almost made me forget myself. Blinking, I forced myself to move onto a large rug, waiting for him, determined not to let my emotions control me. We both watched each other as he approached, curiosity clear in our expressions, until he finally reached the landing of the foyer.

He seemed more relaxed here than he was at Amaranthine. At the bar, he had been dressed in business clothes, but in Jungbrunnen, he wore much more casual clothes. I marveled at his royal-colored slacks and robe, both made of silk. His shirt was translucent cotton in the same shade, and he was barefoot. I had never seen someone embody the word 'soft' so completely. Even his slightly pale skin had a peach undertone that gave it a supple quality, and his face didn't show a single wrinkle. Still, even without his security team, he demanded respect in the room.

I didn't know how, but I knew I had to stop staring at him.

"Mm, our beautiful fräulein has discovered the Fountain of Youth, like the famed Ponce de Leon." His voice was light as air when he spoke. To close the distance between us, he reached out and ran the back of his hand down my cheek, his skin warm to the touch. "You are so fresh, your scent still carries some human notes. This must be why my insolent protégé refuses to bring you to me. The spiteful thing he is, keeping you all to himself."

His hand fell to his side, and the blood in my face almost vibrated when he did. Dietrich's pull was similar to what I shared with Rhys but completely different. I pulled myself away from him before I completely gave into his touch. "Why didn't you tell me who you were at Amaranthine?"

He smirked and walked around me like a cat circling its prey before it pounced. "It is not my responsibility to tell you. Rhys would do well to warn you of pertinent information about your kin, especially Sovereign matters. Even so, I must say that I enjoyed meeting you not as your Sovereign, but as a peer."

"I could tell you weren't a peer," I corrected. "But, if you're one of our leaders you can tell me about Dom, right? That's why I came."

Dietrich tisked and then stopped in front of me. "Who is this mysterious Ancient True Alpha who has your attention more than your Sovereign?"

"You see, Dom...he assaulted and murdered me." I sighed. If I was going to barge in and demand answers, I could at least give a few of my own.

"Murdered? I may be a little confused, as you are standing right here in front of me looking quite lively. You're definitely not a Cadaver. Tell me, as I assume this attack brought you into your new life, what does it matter how you received your immortality so long as you're gifted it?"

I sucked on my canine with my tongue at the ease with which he dismissed me. "It may not matter to you or anyone else, but it matters to me."

"I see." His voice perked up. "Come, let us speak on these things in a more fitting atmosphere, ja? Perhaps some quality blood will have your mood elevated and agreeable."

At first, my instinct was to refuse him, but being rude would afford me no favors, and he'd been nothing but welcoming in his own way. "Sure."

Dietrich's eyes lit up and a wide smile lifted the ends of his slightly plump lips. His hand wrapped around my waist and guided me forward up the grand staircase. He didn't say he had no information for me when I brought Dom up. He could have found out who Dom was and he'd been waiting for me to find my way to his home since I'd seen him a little over a week before.

I noticed details about the gold and marble surrounding me with each step. Antiques were displayed in cutouts in the walls, perfectly spaced every ten feet or so in any direction. Paintings, vases, and busts lined the space, serving as an obvious display to ensure that everyone who entered recognized the type of person inside.

I took a deep breath as we cleared the second-floor landing, but the sound of my action was louder than it should have been. Jung-brunnen was nearly silent. I could hear his feet against the polished floor, my inhales contrasting with Dietrich's absence of breath, and the cadence of his slow heartbeat against my more accelerated one. The silence startled me, reminding me of the night terror I had experienced after my mutation. There were no real odors, only fragrances. Even Rhys carried the normal scents of being in a building with humans in the other units. But not here. The entire place smelled exactly as he intended, from the top of the ceiling to the tightest corner of the floor.

"Why is it so quiet?"

He chuckled, his hold on my waist tightening slightly as we made it to the third floor. "Quite the apprentice, you are. There are so many sounds within these walls." He gestured around him. "I hope you get to hear them...and to make them."

I opened my mouth but couldn't manage to get out a reply. He knew what he was implying. Hell, I knew what he was implying, but I didn't know if I was ready to go down that rabbit hole with Dietrich. "Come, let me show you what Rhys lacks the courage to."

I crossed my brow. The passive-aggressive insult intrigued me, revealing Rhys wasn't the only one with animosity after their relationship. Its complexities were cloaked in offhanded comments, but I was eager to learn what happened between them. "What hasn't he shown me?"

"So many things," he answered. "I can give them to you, you know." Every word from him was laced with sensuality. I hadn't experienced much flirting in the past decade, except for the last two weeks, but I definitely knew the signs. Or was it just my vampire hormones? No, I wasn't misinterpreting; he was flirting with me.

We began down a long, wide corridor, the decor and architecture consistent with the neo-Baroque style. Faux antique lights and candle holders gave the place the desired antiquation despite the fact that it couldn't have been more than sixty or so years old, per the history of the neighborhood. No matter what the age, it screamed old and reminded me of Versailles.

Dietrich used the leverage of his arm around my waist to stop us outside a large set of doors just as an aroma knocked the sense out of me. Despite the blood I smelled, my jaw tingled as if expecting something sweet like cake or chocolate. Unable to control myself, my fangs shifted out.

"I cannot speak to the quality of the blood you have had in the past, but allow me to present to you what I have to offer." He gently took my hand to lead me forward. "You see, there is not a singular fountain that brings youth."

We closed the remaining distance and as the white-painted wood came within arm's reach, I finally heard something besides my breath and our voices. The rushed breaths, moans, and giggles in the room ahead spread heat until it reached my ears.

"Jede einzelne Ader...jeder Tropfen Blut geht in den Jungbrunnen." He smiled after he spoke, fangs peaking from his top lip. "Every vein, every drop of blood, that is Jungbrunnen. The finest Conditioning Sept in the country."

The drawing room he led us into was littered with vampires and humans alike. They were all in pairs, one vampire to one human and all in some stage of feeding and possibly other sensuous acts. If my face was a little warm before, it was on fire then.

The blood in the air mixed to create a sweet medley new to me.

Caramel.

Honey.

Almond.

All the flavors and aromatic notes that dripped thick with indulgence. My fangs lowered to their peak. A Muse, with its lips against a beautiful woman's throat, lapped lazily at a small open wound. Her fingers wove into the vampire's long blond hair, grasping it firmly, both of them half-clothed in their place on a chaise.

The next was a pair on a chaise opposite the other. The Paramour licked at a cut on a young man's unclothed thigh, who moaned in either pleasure or pain. Maybe both. I'd bet on both.

Last, an omnipotent Muse and Brute rubbed what I assumed was her own blood on the throat of a girl who couldn't have been older than twenty. The girl eyed the vampire as if she wanted to devour her in other ways.

"Oh my god," I whispered.

Dietrich chuckled, urging me further inside. "The only god here is me, Dunkle Geliebte."

We approached the middle of the large room and all six people stopped what they were doing, their gazes heavy. I kept my eyes trained on my feet. "I, um—"

"It is perfectly acceptable to be at a loss for words. I cannot fault you for that." He made a motion with his head and all six people cleared the room. No words exchanged, no protests, no time wasted.

Once the room had emptied, my attention spread back out to the room itself. In doing so, I spotted Dietrich making himself comfortable, sprawled on a chaise lounge that had recently been a dinner table. His pouty lips and devious expression perfectly complemented his pose, making him a statue in an art museum.

"Tell me, Joceline," he began as he propped himself up on his elbow, his eyes taking me in. Though I was mostly clothed, every inch of my skin bristled under that amber stare as if I were bare before him. When he looked at me like that, he assessed my value, keeping that estimation close to his chest, adjusting my worth whenever he wished. All of this from a solitary look. "Is this path of vengeance the only way you pass the time, or are there other things in this new life that bring you pleasure?"

"I don't need pleasure; I need to find Dom."

Dietrich let out a low laugh, leaning forward when he did, his charming visage lighting up with amusement. "Over three centuries I have been on this Earth, Miss Fuentes. In that time, I have found that everyone seeks pleasure." He stood up and made his way over to where I stood. "You see, the question is, what do you want to be the thing that brings you that pleasure?"

It took actual physical effort to stop myself from turning to watch as he walked by me and around the room, admiring the splendor of his own possessions. I tracked his movements by his bare feet's soft contact with the marble floors. The cords of my neck strained, so I focused on the ornate gold frame of the large baroque painting directly in front of me. The artwork, rich in color, seemed overshadowed by a dark overcast that gave it a moody feel. The blues and reds stood out against the darkness and shadows, revealing woeful expressions on meticulously painted faces. Despite my artistic background, I still surprised myself by recognizing the style. Art history bored me most days, but this piece was definitely baroque, just like the entire estate we inhabited. The parallel it had with Dietrich was a little too pointed. Was that what drew me to him—the way his appearance mirrored art?

"Pleasure, fulfillment, indulgence, gratification. These are interchangeable things. Are they not?"

I considered the words but didn't answer his rhetorical question. The idea of Dom paying for his crimes against me and anyone else he'd done it to, just the possibility of that kind of justice, brought a wave of satisfaction from my head to the anchor of my hips.

Clean skin, the faintest hint of sandalwood fragrance oil, and flavored alcohol filled the air as someone entered the room. I closed my eyes. "I am well versed in the many ways to coax that special feeling from a person. A human, a vampire...from Prole to Ancient," he said.

My breath stuttered out and I pursed my lips to exhale, fangs teasing against my lower lip. The person who entered was human, their scent masculine and humming with the energy of uninhibited metabolism. I hadn't even seen his face, but I wanted to taste him. My bloodlust, my ache, it took my insides and dragged them down. It wasn't sustenance I wanted; it was pure lust. A distinction I'd never had before but couldn't mistake. I didn't need it; I *wanted* it.

"Ah, Jansen. My Familiar, my consort, my beautiful little Dutch accompaniment." He greeted the new addition. "Come forward, and let her see you," he urged him, and the footsteps moved next to and then past me. That's when I opened my eyes again. Dietrich stood next to a man with light olive skin, his ocean blue eyes relaxed in their half-open gaze, lids heavy with dark curled lashes.

"Vegetarian. Peak physical condition. Blood as smooth as silk down the throat. He drinks two glasses of Steinhäger in the evenings. It warms the blood, gives it just enough movement," Dietrich explained as Jansen wrapped his arm around him to hold onto him like a kept pet. "He likes the buzz while we have our time together, I must say."

I wasn't sure if the smell of him was his authentic scent or if his blood had been spilled in some small way and I was associating it with other things, as I'd grown to do. But whatever it was, I couldn't stop the ache inside. I pressed my thighs tight to each other.

My thoughts were clouding. Lust hijacked my reasoning, begging me to bite him, to leap on top of him and to share the delights of the feast that he'd supply for both Dietrich and I. I craved a sort of sexual carnage I'd never taken part in but could visualize with absolute precision the way his blood would coat my chin, throat, and breasts as I took him right there on the floor. So much skin covered in red. Warm, supple skin drenched in the wine of life. The sounds of pleasure and pain. Every indulgence of the flesh and our kind's desires satiated beyond measure when that human's veins opened.

I forced myself out of the fantasy only long enough to speak. "What do you mean, conditioned?"

"I know that Rhys is guarded, but has he really not explained this to you? Especially when he profited from it for a time before running off."

I furrowed my brows. "What?"

212

"Yes. He was a highly skilled recruiter and handler, not just an emissary. I admit I struggled to find a comparable replacement until Asher came along. What a disappointment Rhys has grown to be. Centuries we had each other. Business, pleasure—it was all the same to us. And the pleasure we made...exquisite. Undeniable. Coveted. And then suddenly, one day he grows a conscious. A waste of a beautiful thing."

My brows rose.

"But about conditioning...it is our most lucrative business as vampires. We shape the lower kin to mutual standards. It truly helps both parties." He was being cryptic, but I picked up on strong undertones of mental programming and brainwashing.

I repeated my earlier, "What?"

"Everyone is motivated by something. It is our job to find that in a human and use it to make them the best versions of themselves." Dietrich explained with a chilling nonchalance. "This, of course, has its benefits to our kind. We must find a way to profit off our gifts, just as humans profit from the skills and abilities they are blessed with. Those at their healthiest are the ones whose blood is the most beautiful."

"You brainwash people into being healthy so you can feed on them?"

Dietrich made a noise of amusement, and Jansen's gaze moved from studying Dietrich with adoration and desire to look at me with much less than that.

"Brainwashing? How could you attribute what we do to something so lowly as simple brainwashing? How human." He turned to Jansen and cupped his cheek, making the man turn back to him and smile, lowering the cupped cheek so it almost touched his shoulder. In doing so he exposed his delicate throat, the skin supple and begging to be bitten. "Did I do any such thing to you, my beautiful Jansen?"

"No, my Sovereign."

"Would you educate our apprentice as to what I did for you?"

For you, instead of *to* you. He changed the wording on purpose. I wanted to fight back against the whole performance, but the ache only grew the longer I stayed in both of their intoxicating presences.

"You saved me."

213

"How is it that I came to do such a thing?" Dietrich traced Jansen's lower lip as he asked and the Familiar waited until he removed his finger before replying.

"I was nothing. I was an addict. I was hopeless. I would sooner end my life than improve it. You taught me to love myself, my body, and how to love other people's bodies. And I love you." The way he spoke put Dietrich on an impossibly high pedestal. My brows furrowed. I could hear the sincerity in his voice. I didn't need his thoughts to verify it. He believed everything he said with his whole self. Dietrich beamed at Jansen's confession, revealing an intimacy that felt almost too personal for me to observe.

Dietrich's gaze shifted briefly from Jansen to catch my attention from the corner of his eye. The playful expression on his face ignited a sense of excitement within me. Regardless of what he said or what I saw, I couldn't shake the magnetism between us and the artful beauty he possessed. Then, he inclined his head toward Jansen's throat and bit into it with the control expected of a seasoned vampire. Moments later, he withdrew and let the blood ooze from the wound, refraining from lowering his lips to drink.

I sighed.

Jesus Christ, it smelled better than anything I'd had before, blood or otherwise. A juicy steak, a perfectly baked pie, the lips of someone I loved—nothing compared to what my mind imagined Jansen tasted like. I stepped forward toward the pair, fangs and gums aching in their need.

"Oh God," I whined, breathless.

"Denk dran, meine kleine, I am the only God here." He dragged his finger through the trail of crimson and extended it, dripping, out to me. "Come take the sacrament, my child. Our altar is the body, and we worship at it."

I reached my hand out to him, and he took it, wrapping his fingers around mine, smearing the blood on his skin onto mine. He urged me forward until we were pressed together, our breaths warm on each other's cheeks. Those breaths came jagged, doing little to mask our pure desire for one another. Dietrich's touch against me begged me to come closer so he could explore me...to worship every inch of me with his lips...to tease every crease with his fangs until I squealed and begged for air.

The world around me blurred, darkened and faded. Dietrich's lips whispered in my ear, "The price for what you desire is pleasure. Show me what you will do to find your elusive ancient. Give tribute to your Sovereign, and I will serve you." His hand came to collect more of the blood that trailed down the crook of Jansen's neck. I watched him do it with my heart hammering in my chest before he brought it up to my parted lips. Breathing in, I could practically taste it, but my body knew that wasn't good enough. My tongue longed to drown in it. I needed it inside me.

My mind tried to resist, asking me what would happen if I dared to open my mouth all the way. If I drank from him, with him, what else would I do? At that moment, all I wanted was to be with both of them in the twisted ways that Dietrich had earlier suggested and that Rhys would reprimand me for. My eyes closed and my head tilted back, my tongue coming through the part in my lips to taste the blood. As soon as I did, a shock went through my system. Every nerve ending fired off as I melted into how succulent it was. His finger moved into my mouth, and I wrapped my lips around it to suck away every trace of blood, falling into a state of pure euphoria. I never knew anything could taste so good. Nothing compared. Not my first drop of blood, not the bleeders from the Pulpit. Nothing.

"Taste it. Take him." His words were far away, but his other hand came to cup the side of my face, more blood cool against my skin, drowning me in the aromatic pleasure of breathing in that crimson. "Take us both."

Despite being a whisper, the urgent edge to his words gave the feeling it wasn't a request, but an order.

"I—"

"Joceline!"

CHAPTER TWENTY-THREE

THE WATERFALL OF RHYS'S voice rained down on me, extinguishing the heat the blood ignited. My eyes popped open and I snapped my head to the entrance of the drawing room. The fog cleared enough that I realized what I was about to do. "Rhys?"

His dark eyes held a heat like nothing I'd seen in him before. "How dare you corrupt my protégé with your hedonism," he said, voice acidic. Shocked and embarrassed, I stepped away from Jansen and Dietrich, but not toward Rhys.

"You speak as if my blood has not corrupted both your veins already." Dietrich amended, lifting his hand to his mouth to casually lick away some of the blood coating it. I took in a long, nervous breath and, in doing so, caught more of the scent, trying to push down my animalistic desire amidst the awkward encounter. Dietrich then gestured from Jensen to the door and the Familiar exited without a word, a hand pressed tightly to the wound in his neck. "You are both products of my Sovereign blood."

I noticed Rhys's jaw clench at the edge of my vision. He resembled a tightly wound spring, ready to unleash his fury, like a ball of rage being toyed with by a playful cat. I searched for words, but fears crept in that neither would listen, as their mutual disdain filled the air around us like a heavy fog.

"Rhys, I'm—"

"Not now." Rhys's stern voice sliced through my words, plunging me into an involuntary silence as he glared at me. Just as quickly, he turned his gaze back to his Lord, whose expression revealed his indifference.

After all, Dietrich was older and stronger; he was Sovereign. 'We are not your playthings."

"If I wish it, anything is my plaything." I noticed the slightest change in Dietrich's face, a darkening of his features before a smile took place, which he directed at Rhys. "I do not delight in the prospect of taking my blood back, but I will drain every drop of it from your ungrateful veins."

"Your egotism is breathtaking, my Sovereign. It never fails to amaze me." He used the title with the worst intentions.

"I—" I tried.

"Even a Protégé as insolent as you can understand your place."

"That's laughable."

"Guys—"

"Du unverschämtes Balg! Your quest for redemption has made you forget your very nature."

"Your nature is not my nature—"

"For fuck's sake!" I screamed the words. "Damn it, I know y'all are pretty but can y'all look away from each other for one fucking second?" I managed to get out, surprised they hadn't interrupted me again. "I came here on my own." I gestured widely at myself. "Me. Myself. On my own. He—I pointed at Dietrich. "—didn't force me here."

"Listen to your Protégé, Rhys."

I put a hand up to gesture for Dietrich to shut up. "Na-uh. That's not fucking helping."

Dietrich raised an eyebrow at my stubborn change in demeanor toward him. Judging by his expression, he seemed more amused than disrespected. He could likely kill both me and Rhys before his security arrived in the room to help.

"I'm so tired of everyone around me thinking I can't and haven't made my own decisions." I took a deep breath. "I came here to get information on Dom. Okay. And if feeling good...really good...for a few minutes is the price to pay for finding out where that piece of shit is, then I'll pay it."

I pointed at Rhys. "And you." Rhys's eyebrows shot up. "If you could just be forthcoming enough to tell me what you know, I wouldn't have to go to Dietrich in the first place. Why does being a vampire have to be so goddamn complicated for no reason?" I inhaled deeply again as I lifted my hands to my chest to emphasize my next words. "All of this could be so easy. I could move on with my new life if you all just let me kill this guy. But everything has a price or a stipulation or a rule or some other bullshit." My hands danced in front of me as I lost myself in my frustration. "He. Tried. To. Kill. Me. He ripped into me. Literally. I deserve his heart in my hands." I motioned between the two of them. "Fuck your ex-lover quarrels. Fuck your overbearing, helicopter Lord thing." I gestured at Dietrich. "And fuck your weird seduction thing. Like, why? Why?"

"So, you both can sit here and continue your stupid fucking anger circle jerk, but I'm done." The words were coming so fast, I had no time to consider them, only to feel them. "I'm over it." I ended up throwing up my hands and walking out of the room. "Don't you dare think of following me." I added, eyes on Rhys.

The car damn near flipped when I whipped open the door. Maybe not flipped, but it rocked in place, for sure. I snatched my hand back and looked at the car in front of me, then at my hand. A deep breath followed. My frustrations needed to fall below the surface, but they came off me like steam.

With the door closed, I sat inside but didn't move. I didn't know where to go from there. I wouldn't be caught dead going back to the loft. What did the line of questioning look like when Rhys made his way back there? No, not there.

But where else was there?

My hands traced over the leather circle of the steering wheel multiple times as if my car required the kinetic energy generated to start. Around and around, I kept going, the motions the only thing grounding me. I'd withdraw from reality otherwise, so I refused to stop.

For a few minutes, I synchronized my breathing with the motions, and temporary relief arrived, but it was brief, as anxiety and anger returned. As it always did. It was more of a surety than my own humanity these days. My new kind, my kin, weren't we supposed to be better than humans?

My hands locked in place at ten and two on the wheel as I pulled myself away from my introspection. Although calling it such was liberal, my mind struggled to focus on any line of cohesive thought for long. I closed my eyes, grabbed my keys, and turned the engine over.

No, I wouldn't go back to the loft.

For thirty minutes I drove. Thirty minutes of orange lights passing in a calming visual lullaby. Thirty minutes with the window down, pushing air onto my face and whipping my curls around, reminding me that despite how out of body it had felt becoming a vampire, a Prole, a so-called creature of the night, I was still connected to the same body. The body had *mutated*, yes, but it was mine.

My body.

My mind.

My life.

These things had changed in some way, but they remained mine. Right?

My family.

> I'm outside. usual spot.

That was the whole text.

Yeah, I was at my family's house. The place I swore up and down that I'd distance myself from. The place that I ran out of when my mama had been close enough to see the darkness now under the surface of my skin, but I didn't want to be anywhere else. If I hadn't gone here, I would have stayed in the car at Jungbrunnen, thinking about how much I hated my new existence. I would have punched the steering wheel until it no longer resembled a circle. I would have screamed until I pushed the boundaries of what my rapid healing could do with my vocal chords.

Not even ten minutes later, Byron and Marley both got into the back seat. I figured they were tired of my prolonged feigned illness.

"Look, if you're dying, this is a weird way of telling us," Marley said, her face illuminated by her phone. At this point, it seemed like a permanent extension of her left hand. My spine cracked about ten times as I turned in my seat to look at her, hoping she would see how unamusing her statement was.

"Do I look like I'm dying?"

Earlier they'd seen me in layers and layers of clothing. Even my face had been mostly obscured. Marley examined me for a second before sucking on her teeth. Without all that clothing, my newly improved complexion and bright eyes were on full display, my hair silken and bouncing.

"Aight." She conceded. "You don't look like it."

"Marley, why you always gotta do too much? Like...chill, bruh," Byron said.

She rolled her eyes.

"Y'all hungry?" I asked, putting the car into drive.

"You paying?" Byron asked.

"Yeah, I got it."

"Whataburger's open," he suggested.

I smiled. There was one off the highway; 183 and Valley View Lane. Just the thought of the location brought back several memories. Eight years before, after a night of heavy binge drinking at a high school friend's house, a couple of old friends and I were bumping the radio at the drive-thru. We were damn near yelling the lyrics to those songs while we waited for our milkshakes. Whataburger shakes when drunk just hit different. I blinked a couple of times to clear the nostalgia away. A month ago, I would have struggled to remember the name of the girl in the back, as I didn't know her as well, but with my newfound mental agility, I remembered her first and last name, even her birthday. She wore a birthday ribbon senior year, and by the end of the day, she'd collected about fifty bucks in one. "Whataburger it is."

As the kiddos sat in the backseat scarfing down their food, I watched them eat in the rearview mirror. My envy festered until I swore my eyes were green. I missed fast food so much already. Blood was great...in its own weird way. But ya' girl just wanted a honey BBQ chicken strip sandwich. A deep breath in brought me as close to consuming it as I would get. Their burgers smelled divine.

"Why aren't you eating? You said you felt better?" Byron asked, shoveling a palm full of fries into his mouth after smothering them in spicy ketchup. I licked my lips before lowering my gaze, not wanting to tempt myself with the sight of their bountiful feast behind me.

"You are missing out. This shit slaps. It's hitting the spot right now," Marley added before taking a large swig of her soda to wash down her bite. She shimmied her shoulders in her enjoyment of the food. "Whataburger tastes so much better when someone else is paying for it."

"I feel better, yes, but my stomach is still recovering. I can only drink right now, and only certain things."

"Why'd you come get us then?" Marley asked.

I sighed and ran my hands down my face. "I miss you guys, that's all."

"How could you not," Marley joked again.

"I know she don't miss that mouth of yours, always running," Byron teased.

"Damn y'all. Don't make me regret my words," I warned. "No. It's just that Marley, you were right; I'm not around enough. And I went home, rested, and felt a lot better, so I thought I'd hang out. My mind's a mess right now. I didn't need to stew in it, you know?"

"Yeah," Byron answered. There was understanding in his one-word reply. "I got you."

"But I don't want to talk about it," I added, clearing my throat and readjusting in my seat. "Tell me all the gossip. My socials are dry as fuck right now." I slipped right back into myself around them.

The me I was before The Avery Hotel.

Before Dom.

Before Rhys and Dietrich.

Before blood became the driving force of my waking hours.

To drink it. To spill it. To understand its new importance.

For a couple of hours, Joceline Fuentes, the real me, the me both my siblings and I missed, sat in the car with Marley and Byron, chopping it up, giving each other shit, and simply enjoying each other's company.

For a while, I forgot I was a vampire.

CHAPTER TWENTY-FOUR

THE SUNRISE WAS SET for 7:31 AM.

Suncheck, an app I downloaded that had been developed by a vampire that Rhys personally knew, made sure I knew it. It sent notifications to my phone every hour after two o'clock to make sure I didn't forget. By the time I dropped Marley and Byron off, the last hourly reminder buzzed my phone.

"Yeah, yeah," I mumbled as I approached my old apartment complex. I still wouldn't dare return to the loft. On the other hand, my apartment remained vacant. An agreement for me to stay with Rhys was that I kept the apartment, and he actually agreed with me for once.

When I walked in, the place smelled stale, even though it hadn't been sitting unattended for long. Stale was still better than what I met after my mutation. Anything was preferable to a rotten kitchen for us. Now, nothing in the house was perishable, including me. And all I needed anymore was blood. Living blood. From their veins to my dead lips. But was I really dead? In my chest, my heartbeat, which meant I was alive.

As I walked into my living room, I felt genuine and valid emotions wash over me—something the dead certainly lacked. I threw myself face-first onto my couch, the air rushing from my lungs. The inexpensive beige fabric felt cool against my skin, and to my surprise, the overwhelming mix of scents didn't bother me; rather, it offered a sense of relief. I rolled onto my back, pulled out my phone, and opened social media. Mindless scrolling would distract me from my emotions long enough to drift off to sleep.

I woke up an hour after sunset, my hands still clutching my phone, which had fallen on my chest. I may not have been able to have regular hangovers anymore, but the emotional hangover I was feeling was way worse. I didn't know what I wanted to feel. The reprieve of spending time with my siblings filled me with true happiness, but what about the lies? All night I told them to their faces I was okay. Nothing was going on, just regular adult stresses. Nowhere in there did I let out any of the frustrations and problems that plagued me. Now, I drowned in my melancholy about it.

With no urgency to rush anywhere, I resumed where I had left off, reconnecting with the lives of all the casual acquaintances and family members I had neglected. Those who were once close to me. I would have been present for some of the stories and photos I scrolled through. I could only glimpse their lives through a mobile app, double-tapping icons to show that I was still around. But eventually, even that would come to an end. I would have to fade away from everyone I knew or from me.

I groaned and closed the app. Those kinds of thoughts were taking me in the opposite direction I needed to go. I stared at my home screen and all the possible distractions before opening an app I remembered I had tucked away in a random folder. The thing was riddled with personality quizzes and pop culture, and I couldn't stop the urge to consume it.

The first quiz I took told me I was the color green, which felt far away from me. But the reasons were nice, vague enough to relate to most people, but nice. The second quiz revealed that I would be married in five years with three children and a big house. The answer prompted a fit of sarcastic laughter. Marriage and children were no longer in my cards, or anything remotely close to that. More and more, I took frivolous quizzes without breaks. What Halloween costume I should wear that year, my celebrity husband, the perfect job for my personality. Ridiculous as it was, maybe, just maybe, one of them would give me a result that I'd accept. The perfect combination of questions and answers to lead me to a result that rang true...anything I'd agree was who I'd become. Otherwise I was lost.

I almost clicked on another one that promised to tell me which superhero I was when I stopped myself. I wasn't going to find myself with this shitty method. I threw the phone at the other side of the couch and buried my head. For minutes, I lay there, chest motionless, as I let the air stall in my lungs. But, I could hear the hum of the empty refrigerator. That, and my insecurities didn't allow me any tranquility. The growl that rumbled out of my throat was animalistic, and I sat up.

No, self-pity wouldn't do.

I reached for my phone again and pulled up my texts with Slevin.

> Its joce. I'm having one of those times where I don't feel very much like joce. U said I could text you if I ever felt like that....so im texting you

My fingers moved so quickly that I didn't have the chance to second-guess myself or scrutinize the fact that I hadn't used proper grammar. Sent and delivered instantaneously. I shrieked out my frustrations and fell back. I hoped he was too busy to bother with me, but my phone vibrated in my hand after barely a minute.

> Joce! Glad to hear from you!

The enthusiasm took me back before I remembered how large his personality was.

> Have you had a drink yet?

The thought hadn't even crossed my mind after I'd gotten to the apartment; I was too busy reminiscing about how good fast food tasted.

I huffed.

> 15905 Wisteria Lane Denton TX 76201. Hurry, I'm hungry.

I sat up straight, and looked dead at the address. At most, I expected him to maybe text me for a while and lift my spirits or give me some wisdom to ease my insecurity, but hunting? How could hunting help me feel any better about the creature I'd become? It'd only make me feel worse. Three dots appeared on the screen to show me he was typing.

> C'mon little vamp, you've gotta learn more about who you really are. I think I can help you with that. ;P I haven't steered you wrong yet, have I?

A smirk curled my lips at the outdated winking emoji he typed out, and I rolled my eyes.

> Give me like 45 mins

I didn't bother checking if he replied to me and sprang up from the couch with a newly refreshed sense of purpose. Slevin was worlds apart from Rhys, Dietrich, or any other vampire I'd met. Authentic and self-assured, not arrogant. Definitely confident in who he was as a person, and who he was didn't seem to be consumed by his vampirism. I could try to resist all night, but that was exactly what I craved. I had to at least try.

Minutes later, when I had already started the drive up to Denton, I allowed my mind to wander. There was a multitude of things that rattled around up there from moment to moment, and much to both my amusement and grief, I was getting glimpses of previously lost memories. They were only a few seconds in length, but my father came to life in them. None were significant, most of them just us relaxing after dinner, fighting off sleep thanks to my mama's cooking while watching our show. I'd never been invested in it, none of us kids were, but there were so many pieces of my childhood where my father and I would lay watching, content on the couch with a blanket, when the rest of the house had

226

been resigned to their rooms. Those little pieces of my past had become invaluable, and being able to call on them after I thought I'd lost them gave me solace.

The happy reminiscence lasted only twenty minutes before flashes of less desirable thoughts began to demand my attention. Violent flashes of Dom and the things I'd also forgotten then returned. The abrupt change from happiness to terror caused physical and mental pain I wasn't sure how to fix. That face covered in blood, grinning at me. The fangs. The pure menace of him. It was a revolving door of terrifying images. My hands nearly bent my steering wheel out of shape. He laughed, smiled, and reveled in my fear, flashing his fangs to make my heart beat faster. My mind reeled as it saw a monster I'd only thought lived in stories.

My eyes blurred pink; I tried my best to keep driving. Even though I didn't have to breathe, I felt starved of oxygen, and I didn't know if I could keep going. I looked down at the open navigation app. Five minutes.

I was already off the highway, I just had to make it a little longer. I'd be okay if I could keep the dark thoughts at bay long enough to pull in and park. The phantom touch of Dom's hands on my body, wet with blood as they roughly grabbed at different parts of me, were enough to trigger my gag reflex and I shivered.

By the time I pulled into a small residential parking lot, I breathed like an overheated dog. I focused on my breath and my heart, working to bring them closer in rhythm. Slow it down. I took a few breaths in a rehearsed cadence, managing to pull away from myself. I inhaled for four seconds, held for seven, then exhaled for eight. Then again...and again. One more time.

I'd be okay, maybe.

The count continued until it regulated the rise and fall of my chest. After a couple of minutes, I returned to myself. I was surprised to see that only bloodstained tears on my cheeks showed my panic attack when I checked myself in the rearview mirror. I used the back of my hand to wipe them away, then smiled. I nodded my head. It was convincing enough.

I'd be okay.

CHAPTER TWENTY-FIVE

MY PHONE SLIPPED FROM my hands as I heard knocks on my driver-side window, my shoulders shooting up to my ears. I turned to see Slevin, as expected. Despite the chilly temperature, he wore a tattered Bad Brains t-shirt that looked like he may have even made it himself twenty years before, and from what I could see of his pants, they were patched up in the same fashion as the others I'd seen him wear. At least he was consistent.

"Joce." He greeted, waving at me in a silly, over-animated fashion to get me to smile.

I rolled my eyes and shook my head. He grinned down at me, but all I could muster was a half-hearted smile. I didn't have it in me to do much else. After exiting the car, we started toward a building that may have been a small dormitory or perhaps a form of shared living. It was too small to be an apartment complex. I tried to be objective of the fact that Denton was a college town for a lot of its population, but the dorm assumption kept returning.

"Welcome to my sept." He motioned with his hands to the building. My eyes thinned and took in more details. The aged brick facade was nothing to write home about, like many places older places in the city. The visible windows were covered in blinds, some with curtains or small objects peeking between the slates, like plants and decorations.

So very *ordinary*.

I was taking my idea of what a vampire was supposed to live in from terrible references, though. The vampires in my coupling were not a good starting point. Dietrich lived in a mansion straight out of some European historical romance, and Rhys lived in a high-rise loft downtown that people my age couldn't afford. On top of that, all the movies or stories I knew of with our kind usually had either nomadic or rich vampires. There were generally no spaces in between. Then again, I'd just been turned into a vampire and my apartment was nothing fancy. Still, the term sept went beyond vampires in a single building. Micro-septs were single-family houses with maybe two or three vampires sharing the dwelling. Dorm-septs, much like what I was looking at, were what vampires in larger numbers had. Everyone had their own private rooms but shared communal areas. Packs-septs were what Brutes had and coven-septs housed Mystics, almost exclusively. Then, of course, you had organizational-septs, which were businesses operated at a higher level by our kind. From what I understood, calling something a sept covered a lot of bases.

"It's cute, in a college sort of way." The words escaped me before I could censor them and I resisted the urge to clamp my hand over my mouth. How humble. "So, are we leaving from here to go eat?" As soon as I said it, I didn't like using "eat" in that context. Were we zombies waiting to devour the flesh of the uninfected? I grimaced, making a note to stop using the word immediately.

Slevin huffed out a laugh. "Not exactly, no."

My brows scrunched up, and my nostrils flared. Had I missed something? I opened my mouth, but closed it when I had nothing to say.

"C'mon, I'll introduce you to my roommates."

Entering the sept, the empty remnants of a reception desk and the entirety of what should have been a lobby greeted me. My instincts weren't that far off after all. Dorm-sept it was. At some point it housed students, but not in the last twenty years. I sighed. I was not prepared to meet other vampires tonight. A little warning would have been nice.

"You see, we're a...uh, breeder sept. We breed deft animals for adoption around the country." I wasn't sure if he was lying or struggling with his words, but there was a cautiousness there.

"Deft?"

"Rhys didn't tell you about deft animals?"

"I haven't been around that long, so it's not like we've covered every single slang word."

"Slang for some terms but this one's official. I got you, though." He answered. "Defts are humanely bred pets or service animals."

I took a deep inhale and picked up the hints of cleaning supplies and animals somewhere nearby. "Is that your version of humane or a general consensus?" I didn't think him the type to torture animals into performing tricks or services, but Dietrich said the same thing about his operation.

"General consensus, for sure." I caught the coy smile on his face as we continued forward. "We don't do things like subject breeders."

I was happy to hear it, but still I had my reservations. Anyone with common sense would. Jansen had looked in my eyes and said how much he wasn't being manipulated, but Dietrich was smart. That whole encounter reeked of pageantry. As a leader of The Sovereignty, he couldn't show me anything less than a positive picture. There was no way that mentally reprogramming a human's behavior could be done by benevolent means. Dietrich had a lot of work to do to convince me otherwise.

As we stopped at the entrance to a communal living room, I took in the largest congregations of our kind in a small space. There were six vampires, all occupied in leisurely activities, and most were lower-level mutation classes by the Sovereignty's standards. My eyes thinned as I used their auras to identify them. All but two were Proles, and the two who weren't were Creepers. Sorry, Cadavers. Creeper sounded rude. One was only a Creeper, and the other partly so.

Living corpses.

I studied the full Cadaver as he sat silently on the couch next to a Prole, and by close I mean that they were cuddling. I took a deliberate inhale through the nostrils and caught the whiffs of death Rhys said there would be.

"Alright, guys. This here's the one I was telling you about, Joceline. Her blood may be Sovereign, but she's still a Prole and she's good people. At least for now." He gave me a wink. "I figured I'd show her a more realistic side to all this."

"Hi." The word barely squeaked out as I lifted a hand and gave a curt wave, hardly moving my palm from side to side. I really, really wish I had been more prepared to meet people.

The first to get up and approach were the Cadaver and Prole sitting together. The Prole, a Hispanic woman in her late teens or early twenties, looked everything like the scene kids of the early two thousands, complete with lime green and black hair. The vision of her took me right back to my high school days. Beside her, the Cadaver followed, holding her hand. I tried not to make a face, but masking my puzzlement didn't come easy. Cadavers were supposed to be feral vampires. They were mute beings that couldn't control their hunger, I'd been told. But he was timid and gentle. The look in his eyes was more humane than some vampires I'd met. Definitely more human than Dom.

As the couple closed the distance, I clocked the appearance of his tan skin, which, though I could tell it was deeply tan, was so muted compared to the Prole. "I'm Dani," the girl extended her hand. "This is my husband, Daniel."

He didn't speak, of course, but his eyes focused on me, and I acknowledged it with a nod. No matter what he looked like, Daniel wasn't feral. There was nothing other than the dead-like appearance and smell that allowed me to agree with what his mutation classes had been called. Even his clothes were clean and current.

"Hi, I'm Joceline. But you can call me Joce."

"Welcome." Her warm voice made me smile. Then they both turned and returned to their seats on a worn-in leather couch with stretch marks and stains. When they did, the room took a breath.

"Around the room," Slevin started, not wasting a beat. "There's Dalton." The Cadaver-Brute Beta lifted a hand but didn't look away from the television.

"Mitch." He gestured toward a Prole wearing reading glasses, who glanced up from a book and waved back.

"Madison, we call her Wisconsin." An adorable Prole, appearing no older than seventeen, waved from a large bean bag near the big mounted television.

"Ximena." A fierce woman nodded silently while scrolling her phone, and I mimicked her action. "The rest are out. My Lady, Mary, left a few hours ago."

The room groaned when he used the formal title to address his sire and my brows furrowed. Everyone I knew had used it as if there was no alternative.

"Hey, hey now. She's been brought up traditional, okay. Remember, Sovereign blood over here." Slevin joked.

"I prefer to call them mentors." Ximena's thick Mexican accent corrected.

"Or Sire." Dalton chimed in as well.

"Their name's good enough, but to each their own," Mitch added. Still, Mitch gave me a wink, then went back to the words on the page below him.

"Nice to meet y'all."

"Anyway." Slevin started back up again when his eyes caught me, crossing my arms over my chest, and rubbing them. As nervous as it made me look, I couldn't shake nerves that fired off at how much Dietrich's bloodline and status drove an immediate wedge between the group and me. "I just want you to see what us normal people are like." Madison and Dani both snorted a laugh out at being called normal. My eyes landed on Dani and Daniel without trying, my interest stolen by their dynamic.

Rhys said Cadavers were still themselves in a way, but not much. Dangerous, he said. And here one was, watching a sitcom about a dysfunctional law firm while his wife laughed and swatted at his arm. He wasn't dangerous. I didn't feel repulsed. Despite its oddness, I found it comforting.

"First Creeper?"

Slevin whispered, catching on to what stole my attention. I blinked and turned back to him. "Yeah."

"Daniel's not as affected as others out there. He wasn't abandoned by his mentor." I caught him shift into the more casual term. . "Dani's never left his side, not a single night. You don't see that with Creepers. When the mentors find out they've turned into them, they leave them. Some kill them to save them from that miserable existence. But, not Dani." I glanced over at Dani who continued to enjoy her show, cackling away like it was the funniest thing she'd ever seen. Every time she'd laugh, Daniel would smile as if the sound was music to his ears.

233

"Let's grab a drink." He escorted me into the kitchen. "I'm sure you drink flesh, but not all of us have the money, time, or the privilege." We walked to a small refrigerator next to a much larger one, and when he opened the door to an array of blood bags. They were like the ones I saw in hospitals, or more accurately on show and movies of hospitals. I doubted I'd seen an actual blood bag in person. I noted the crude labels slapped on the front of them all.

Apparently, I'd been living in a whole different world from these vampires.

Slevin grabbed one with his name and showed it to me, mimicking an auctioneer. I laughed. "We have a plug. It's twenty a bag."

I nodded, keeping in the fact that I didn't know if twenty dollars was a good deal or not. . A bag lasting three or four days was a bargain, but one a day was too much.

Being a human was pricey, but, so was being a vampire.

He grabbed a small saucepan from a drying rack beside a double basin metal sink and placed it on a stove burner, which he turned on medium heat. My eyes searched out and found a microwave built under a cabinet not far from him.

"Microwaves ruin the blood."

I watched as he ripped open the bag and poured its contents into the pan, the slightest hiss of protest coming from the stainless steel. With the blood's colder temperature, it didn't have a strong odor at first, but the slight hints I got weren't nearly as appetizing as what I'd sampled from Jansen at Jungbrunnen. Then again, the whole reason I didn't walk right back out of the building when I'd been faced with a room full of vampires I didn't know was because I needed perspective. As it warmed, the aroma heightened, forcing my fangs to shift.

My hand flew to cover my mouth. "Sorry."

"For what? It's a natural reaction. We can't stop it." He gave me a toothy grin to show that his own fangs were out. The length of his lateral incisors were a little shorter than my own, but they were sharper, and he had a lower set of fangs. Neither Rhys or I had lower fangs. *Interesting.* Slevin started to move around through cabinets and pulled two coffee mugs out of the third one. Returning to the stove, he stirred the blood one last time, before taking it and evenly distributing it into the mugs. One mug was decorated with a local law office's information, the words The Texas Sledgehammer in bold, the other wished an unknown parent a Happy Father's Day back in 2011. He handed me the Texas Sledgehammer and my eyes dropped to the cup.

"The trick's to get the temperature just right. Go ahead and try it," He urged as he placed the pan in the sink, then returned to grab his own cup. "Sometimes, if you overheat it a little, it gives you time to sip it, but other than that, get it down the hatch. Also, don't burn it, it smells fuckin' awful," he advised.

I gulped down my saliva unsure if I wanted to taste it. Something about drinking it out of a mug pushed me into a supernatural Twilight Zone. I'd only drank from the vein so far, as Rhys insisted. Taking it in its freshest form, pumping into my mouth by the beating of a heart felt natural. Drinking it like a warm cup of my morning coffee humanized it, but not in the way that made it more comfortable. Drinking blood couldn't be humanized, could it? I pushed the discomfort down.

Afraid of losing heat, I opened my mouth and took a large sip. At first I coughed a little as it made its way down my throat. The taste wasn't amazing, but it wasn't terrible, either...a reheated entree from a beloved restaurant. As it settled, the supernatural energy in my veins hummed with power. My eyes stayed caged to Slevin as he took three large drinks and finished his off. I followed suit and downed mine as quickly as I could.

"Thanks."

I offered the cup back and he took his and mine to the sink and washed them out along with the pan. The three items made their way onto a drying rack as he walked back toward me, the chore domestic in a way that gave my world grounding.

"C'mon." His favorite word. "I'll show you around more. Show you what you're usually going to see with us. Well, with Brutes and breeders anyway."

"Why don't you just say vampire?"

"Why don't humans say human?"

"Well, it's assumed. They don't know there's anything else."

"And we can see each other's aura, so we know the difference between a vampire and a human. It's assumed. Just like humans, or culture changes over time, it evolves. It wasn't always mutations and classes. Mine were Bestia before we were Brutes, there were the Populi before Proles. We change and grow, just like they do."

"The lower kin?" I tried to use the formal phrase, despite how it rubbed me the wrong way, to see how he'd react.

"Lower," he paused, "maybe?" Then he shrugged. "But, we don't exist without humanity. We have to be human before we can be what we are now. It's backhanded to think of them as so much lower than us when they are the basis of our whole existence, right?"

"But we're supposed to call them that, aren't we?" I asked.

"Call them whatever you like, Joce. I don't care about that," he answered softly and I smiled.

He walked me through the building until we passed the living room again and into a wide hallway, to the front of elevator doors. My body tensed up when he clicked the button to hail the car down. My throat squeezed and energy raced into my chest.

"Do you have stairs?" I barely managed to get the words out, my voice higher as my body tried to seize in on itself.

There was no way I could get into an elevator, even if Slevin had been a friend. His hand swept to the side toward a door with a placard for stairs in both an icon, text, and braille. He remained quiet, and I relaxed. If he had questions, he chose to keep them in and I appreciated him so much more for it.

We continued up the stairs, and I tried my hardest to assume the silence was because there wasn't anything he felt he needed to tell me. Stairwells were stairwells no matter your species. The air bristled with a noticeable weight, though. He must have seen my panic, and he was trying to give me space. If only that made me feel better.

Halfway to the next floor, I paused against the railing. Clearing my throat echoed upward, prompting Slevin to climb two more steps before halting. He glanced back, silent. I lingered, hoping to understand my pause, searching his eyes for a clue. He looked indifferent—neither annoyed nor amused, just present. This compelled me to open up; if there was someone I would tell it would be Slevin. Rhys reacted strangely when I mentioned it. Other than those two, there wasn't anyone else I'd tell. I hadn't focused on it, trying to suppress the memories, yet they stirred.

were surfacing increasingly, whether I wanted them to or not. There was no escaping it. Maybe talking about it would help me start the journey through those feelings.

"He toyed with me in an elevator." I started, voice weak. "I was barely able to keep my head up after the roofies and he danced me around that fucking elevator car like a doll." I averted my gaze to the concrete below my feet, unable to look at him. In the recesses of my mind, soft light bounced off bright gold, the colors falling through the air and landing on the figure of Dom, his smile radiating with wild abandon. Those clear blue eyes watched me struggle to stay off the floor as he twirled me around. It was a troubling memory, but I couldn't shake it. My vision seemed to blur and drift away, but I forced myself to focus and saw Slevin descending until he stood on the stair just above mine.

"My dad went to Vietnam when I was young." He leaned against the wall, standing with me in solidarity. "I don't know what happened over there. He didn't tell Ma either, but he acted differently when he returned." He sighed. "I didn't notice while it was happening, but when I mutated, I could remember things I thought I lost. I thought about it more, too." He crossed his arms. "Sometimes things happen *to* you. No one can blame you or expect you not to change as a result of it." His head rested back. "I'm not owed an explanation, nor is anyone else. We can take the stairs for a century if that's what you need." He pushed off the wall and started up the stairs. Tears trailed down my cheeks as I followed him. I wanted to thank him, but he already knew. My sniffling gave me away. Like me, he didn't say anything more. He said all he needed to say.

We entered a hallway with six doors, three on each side, after exiting the stairwell. I suspected they were private living spaces. Approaching the second door on the left, he used a key to unlock it. Did a key seem necessary for vampires? Couldn't we just kick it in? I guess a deterrent is based on convenience, not impossibility.

I hesitated before entering but went inside. I never had a dorm room at college since my parents couldn't afford it, so I lived at home. However, I knew from movies what dorms looked like. Upon entering, I saw the rooms had previously been small dorms but were now modified for more space. "Don't worry, I'm just grabbing my jacket. And I figured I'd show you a sept room while I'm here." As he retrieved his heavy jacket from a corner chair, I took in the room. He clearly made this space his own.

The middle of the room held a rough-textured rug resembling a commercial doormat, with black fabric marked by various band logos. Between two windows, I found spray paint and stencils in milk crates. The walls were lined with old band posters dating back decades. Though logic suggested they were reproductions, I doubted it since he was a vampire. "It's really like a dorm here, isn't it? No bathroom or anything."

"Hey, Don't knock it 'til you've tried it. Free rent helps." He threw on his jacket and left, while I absorbed his anti-capitalist sentiments from the wall statements. I read them, along with names of punk and grunge bands. "We can stay here if you like. I can show you plenty about our kind," he teased. I snapped to the door and jogged out, my cheeks burning, wondering if the blush was from excitement or embarrassment—maybe a mix? At the bottom of the stairwell, my temperature lowered again as he led me into a new part of the building. The scent of animals grew stronger; I didn't dislike it, but it overwhelmed me. I hadn't had a pet since I was seven, so I struggled to adjust to having a cat, especially one as big as a dog. House cats aren't meant to weigh over forty pounds of muscle.

The scent wasn't excrement but fur and a unique animal odor I couldn't name. As a vampire, my sensitivity to it was heightened.

Slevin remarked, "You get used to it...Brutes are never bothered, but you're young, so it can be strong, even if you live with Ubaste."

Was this his usual disclaimer for guests?

"Try breathing through your nose if it gets too much."

His Boston accent grew more apparent as he spoke. I found it oddly attractive, perhaps because it suited him. I felt my face warm again but pushed the thought aside; my emotions had been on high alert lately.

He glanced back, and I smiled at him, receiving a smirk in return. He stopped at a glass door, saying, "This is the feline room."

I imagined a large animal shelter but was surprised to find exotic cats. "We usually have Bengals and servals; Ubaste was bred here. Larger cats need special housing." As expected, several servals lounged in the common area, but the cat trees were much larger. Some savannahs played in the back while two Bengals watched. Floor-to-ceiling glass cubbies lined the walls, allowing the cats to access their litter boxes and water bowls. I only focused again when I caught his mention of the larger ones.

"Bigger?" I repeated, head inclined back. "How much bigger?"

"Big enough to stay segregated." Was all he offered back and my eyes bugged out. Servals were the largest cats I'd considered cozying up to, what else were vampires in need of?

"Are you serious?"

"Let's see the dogs."

My body relaxed under the quick diversion, showing he liked to push my buttons at every opportunity. He escorted me to the other side, away from the cat area. We passed through another glass door into kennels that were nicer than any shelter I'd seen before. These kennels had glass doors and housed sleeping canines. Of the eight kennels, half contained German Shepherds and the rest were Dobermans, which felt accurate for vampire guard dogs. Up close, the dogs had a stronger odor, but I wasn't deterred; I noticed it without being repelled. The dogs appeared well cared for, possibly spoiled, with toys and clean areas. Each dog was comfortable enough to merely open their eyes and sniff at our intrusion. Slevin extended his hand. "C'mon, let me show you something." I hesitated before placing my hand in his.

Even with its natural and otherworldly creatures, his sept was happy. I knew nothing of their past hardships, but they lived in a peculiar domestic bliss in a small Denton, Texas building. If Slevin was part of it, I trusted it. Aside from some light teasing, he remained the only vampire who didn't irritate me, a feat some humans couldn't manage. I couldn't imagine a better friend after my mutation.

He gripped my hand and led me through the back door to a half-indoor, half-outdoor enclosure, releasing me as we entered. I couldn't help but smile, expecting large birds or exotic creatures to amaze me. Once inside the building he unlocked, I regretted the ease with which I followed him.

The door swung shut, and I gasped at the wide-open interior designed for much larger animals. Two fully grown mountain lions lazily looked up, their sleep interrupted. I froze, my body tense.

Locked in place, my left eye twitched, and my jaw quivered. Vampires could endure a lot of damage, a fact Rhys drilled into me, but I'd never experienced it. I didn't want this to be how I discovered my limits. Recovery from a mauling was one thing, but we still felt pain. My eyes darted to Slevin, unfazed and relaxed as he approached the wild cats, who regarded him with casual indifference, eyes half open.

"What in the actual fuck?" I whispered.

"I warned you," he said, approaching the closer of the two, who didn't even bother getting up from their place despite him being within arm's reach. When he leaned down to pet them, they made a noise I assumed was contentment, but I wasn't sure I knew what sound they were supposed to make, no matter the emotion. "Come closer. Don't worry, they're fully bred. They only attack on command or self-defense," he said.

That didn't make me feel any better. All that I registered was that they were trained to kill at some point.

He waved me over, his exaggerated gestures startling only me. I relaxed and approached slowly, eventually reaching Slevin and his cougar. The animal sniffed the air, seeming to sense our disconnect from nature, like Ubaste. But would that calm them?

"Slevin, you son of a bitch," I whispered, close enough that volume didn't matter. He affectionately rubbed the animal's belly as it rolled over.

"Carol McFadden is a saint," he joked. "No, I get it. It's unnerving at first, but smaller ones are easier." My face contorted at his term for mountain lions as the "smaller" ones.

"Is there a fucking tiger in here Slevin, I swear to God."

"No, no, no. We don't have a tiger right now. It's just these two. They're going to a friend in New Mexico."

"Friend?" I didn't believe that title at all.

"Client?" he tried.

"Client," I accepted.

I focused on my breathing, unsure what to do in the presence of such a beast. I looked down and watched him pet the animal from their head to the base of their tail. After a moment, he motioned for me to pet them, but my head immediately began to shake.

He replied with an exaggerated expression, telling me he wouldn't let it die until I touched the cat. I warred with two instincts. One told me that it was a wild animal below me and I needed to back out of the enclosure while also making sure the other one, wherever it was, didn't attack me. The other told me I could still trust Slevin and that he didn't bring me in there to hurt me, nor would he let it happen.

I sighed.

If the night would end with me being mauled, at least I had a meal in the recent past, so healing wouldn't take too long, depending on the damage. Hell, if the damned thing attacked, I had enough strength. Maybe I could fight it off.

Breathing slowly, I kneeled down and extended my hand out. The animal first looked to Slevin, then to me, and back to Slevin. Slevin, in turn, gave a curt nod to the cougar, and when they saw the command, they relaxed their head back down and rested.

As soon as my skin contacted fur, my heart rate doubled. I ran my hand down the length of its side, and it huffed but calmly, its body and muscles shimmying so that it could roll over further and expose even more of its underside for affection.

"I..." My voice trailed as I marveled at the experience. "I can't believe..." I had been turned into a vampire not even a month before, which had spiraled me into a million experiences I never would have guessed I'd have. Still, petting a mountain lion in a training habitat with a punk, now that was not on my bingo card for twenty-twenty.

For a few minutes, we stayed there on the ground. I continued running my hands down the animal's fur as they fell back into a sleep-like state. By their ears and heartbeat, I knew they weren't unconscious, but their guard was down in the presence of who I assumed had trained them.

From beside and behind me, I turned to see Slevin. He had planned to take me in here the whole time, judging by the shit-eating grin on his face and the twinkle of success in his eyes. No matter the planning, I was grateful. I smiled at him and relaxed even further. Despite being sandwiched between a two-hundred-pound wildcat and a shape-shifting vampire likely of the same size, I didn't want to leave.

"Thank you, Slevin."

The fear melted away, leaving me in awe. For once, I had found a moment that lived completely in positivity. No catch, no manipulation, just the knowledge that there was beauty in the gifts of the supposed immortality I'd been given.

"This is Leon." He introduced, and the cougar huffed and shook its head upon hearing their name. "Introduce yourself, don't be rude." He nudged me with his shoulder, and I laughed.

"Uh...hi Leon." I started, focused on the way my hand rose and fell with the breaths they were taking. "I'm Joce."

"Joce who?"

"Joceline Fuentes," I stated without hesitation. The moment I spoke, I felt a pull back. I thought I would shed that name, distancing myself because I wasn't her anymore, yet here I was using it again after days of trying to discard it. "Nice to meet you."

My smile spread, thinning my eyes and scrunching my nose. Even with my eyes closed, I sensed Slevin's gaze on me. When I opened them, his smug expression sent butterflies throughout my being. How could he make me feel like my old self when I didn't realize she was still there, that anyone but my siblings could coax her out?

As my awareness spread, I realized that Slevin's body radiated warmth, much like Leon's. A similar but separate warmth than Rhys. The feeling was so comforting that I found myself leaning back against him, my back nestled against the solid wall of his chest. His breathing was calm and steady beside me, and I happily fell into a rhythm, letting my body rise and fall in sync with his. I lost track of time in those moments, completely absorbed but feeling a gentle urge to explore the softness beneath my hand. With a flutter of anticipation, I lifted my hand from the wildcat's fur. I knew exactly what I wanted to do, but I wondered if I had the courage to take that step.

"I knew Joceline was still in there." He said the words at a low volume, almost a whisper, but the sound caressed my ear and silenced everything else in the enclosure. He could've been right about it, but how did he know who I really was? Did he see me, who I really was, on the surface like the clothes on my back? Even when I doubted anyone else did? When I doubted I did?

With his breath warm on my neck, he moved closer so that he was flush against me, the points of metal spikes teasing along my spine and shoulders. The sensation was gentle enough to only tickle my skin, but tickle seemed too innocent a word for what stirred within me.

His hand came to snake up from behind my right shoulder, and his fingers lightly traced my jawline. My jaw slacked at the delicate touch, and my fangs drew themselves out to their peaks without my being able to stop them. My breath slipped out slowly, timed with the feeling of his chest heaving upward. My left hand moved to ground me against the concrete slab of the floor, and my fingers flexed, aching to grab something. They couldn't grip concrete like they wanted to grip skin and muscle.

He was so warm. From the grin plastered on his face whenever he looked at me, or the blush he spread on my cheeks, the words that he said at just the right time, all of it radiated heat.

I moved my left arm to my right side, so that I could turn further into him. Despite my earlier fear and fully aware wild animals were present, his body invited me closer.

Against the better judgment of every wildlife documentary I'd ever seen which told me to never expose my back to a wild animal, I did exactly that. I turned myself completely so that I faced Slevin, the action forcing him to lower himself to the ground so we were sprawled on the concrete. Slevin was the biggest predator in that enclosure, and I knew it. No matter Leon, the other mountain lion, or anything else that might have been there, I needed to see him before me, below me.

His steely blue eyes fixed on mine as his grin spread into a mischievous smile.

We stayed there for an unclear time, locked in apprehension. Neither knew if we should act first or if we hoped the other would. Our eyes couldn't leave each other, sealing the moment.

"You see me?"

His eyebrow rose at the question.

"Joce..." His voice trailed, making me lower my face closer to his. "Joce." He repeated, slower, his thumb resting against my bottom lip.

"Don't stop saying it."

His hand moved so that he grabbed my chin between his thumb and pointer fingers and urged me lower until the skin of our lips grazed each other's but didn't go further. The longer we held out, the sweeter it would taste.

"Who am I?"

He rolled us, his hand bracing my lower back so that he was on top of me, his other hand anchored to the ground.

"Joce." He teased out before he came down and pressed his lips to mine with a restraint I didn't expect. His arm pulled me up so that my hips were against his. Eventually we pulled away not to breathe, but to look at each other.

"Slevin." I finally said his name back to him, and hearing it, he kissed me again and again. His lips moved against mine with a hectic rhythm. My head swam when he did, unable to concentrate on a single thing. I wanted to keep going forever, to live my new eternity with him in that enclosure. Or pause it all. Turn off the world so we could hide away in a pile on the floor, our names the only things we dared to say. Any other words would ruin it. But, neither of those things happened because instead someone else's voice filled the air.

"Well, I must say it is quite a surprise to meet the newest of Dietrich's sovereign blood tangled up on the floor of my habitat. With my protégé, no less."

CHAPTER TWENTY-SIX

"HELLO." THE SOFT, HISPANIC accent floated in the air as my fangs receded back into my gums. Scurrying, I flipped myself so that I was on all fours, Slevin doing the opposite and rolling himself onto his back and elbows.

"Mary." He greeted with energy in his voice, energy he undoubtedly got from the events so close to transpiring. "Good to see you." He added as I scrambled up to my feet, hands frantically dusting off the knees of my jeans.

In that moment I wanted to rescind into myself and out of existence. "Uh...hello." The greeting couldn't have been more pitiful if I tried.

"Mary - Joceline. Joce - Mary." Slevin gave the not-so-formal introduction right as I extended my hand for her to shake. That was, of course, before I remembered that some vampires weren't keen on the idea of physical touch with strangers, especially handshakes. At least not the ones I'd been in contact with. When she looked down at my hand and smiled but didn't offer her own, I withdrew and stuffed it in my pocket. She did, however, offer me a wide, inviting smile.

"Welcome to my sept, Joceline. I'm Mary Cortes."

Mary stood a few inches shorter than me, but in front of her, I was small. Like myself, she was a Prole, but the title seemed meager in the presence of her aura. It mesmerized me the longer I looked at it. If the heavens pulled the stars down so that they were shown on Earth, they radiated around the beautiful woman standing in front of me. Her olive skin glowed and her dark brown eyes were sharp. Her smile beamed at me from sensuous, plump lips. Absolutely stunning.

She was Slevin's Lady?

"Thank you." I bowed my head, unsure of what else to do. Slevin smugly looked between us, clearly aware she was approaching. That or he hid his surprise well. Regardless, we were both distracted.

"Please excuse my rude protégé. He is not one for formalities." Her accent was smooth, and I struggled to place it as it wasn't one I commonly heard despite being Hispanic.

Slevin slowly got to his feet as Mary urged me forward. "Come, let's find more comfortable accommodations," she said, exiting the habitat. I sighed, feeling embarrassed. Looking back, I saw Leon yawn and head deeper into the enclosure for some sleep. Slevin approached the door, and not wanting to be last, I jogged ahead.

While not his goal, Slevin was impressively skilled at keeping me humble. Was it a game to haze newly mutated vampires to prevent inflated egos? The sept clearly had feelings about my bloodline: was this the result? Entering the building, I tried to dismiss these thoughts. Despite my insecurities, Slevin had been remarkably helpful, even if his methods were unconventional. As long as it worked, right? He also trained with me in Arlington every other night to prepare me against Dom, if I ever found him.

Back in the communal living room, the group had thinned out so that only Mitch remained. Mary sat in the beaten-up recliner that had certainly seen better days, weeks, and years. The material groaned beneath the weight of her, despite it barely being any weight at all. Following suit, Slevin and I found a seat on the once full couch.

"Tell me, Joceline, how long have you been on this side of the veil?" Mary asked.

"Two or three weeks, something like that." I answered, eyes moving to the floor.

"Not even a month." She nodded. "This new life, is it something you chose?"

"I don't know. Kind of, I think. I don't really remember much of it, but I think I did." My shoulders shot up. "I was roofied. Most of it's still gone up there." I gestured to my head. "Some of it's coming back in pieces, but yeah..." I trailed off, trying not to think too hard about those terrible, nightmarish pieces.

"Rhys Llewelyn would do such a thing?"

246

My eyes popped open. "No, no, no." I corrected her assumption, throwing my head from side to side. Mary sighed. "No, not Rhys. Someone else did it. Someone called Dom." I explained. "Rhys is the one who saved me. But Dom, he's one of us, but an ancient." I looked at Mary's aura and the sheer depth and power to it, considering if she was one herself. "He's a True Alpha, too. He brutally attacked me and left me to die."

"I am sorry, but you say a True Alpha? Ancient no less. He drugged you?" Mary hesitated there. "He could have easily implanted your docility in the blink of an eye. It is so odd for him to do otherwise."

My brows furrowed at her words. The events of that night were indisputable. The lethargy, the confusion, brain fog, how little control I had over my body, it was all textbook symptoms of Rohypnol. "No, there's..." I started, but my voice died as I shifted in my seat. At the same time, the speed of my breath jumped up and I clenched and unclenched my fists. "He..." I was trying to affirm my certainty of the memory. An awkward laugh skittered out of my mouth. "I know he did, he said he did." I gnawed at my bottom lip.

"Drugged, not drugged, whatever. Who cares, right? The asshole attacked her. That's the important part." Slevin must have noticed my change in demeanor because his swoop-in was immediate. Gratitude washed over me, and I let in a deep breath.

Mary waved her hand in the air. "Apologies, I can be abrasive at times. You see, I am, too, an Ancient. I am sometimes, how you say, out of touch?" Clearly she struggled with it, but at a thousand years old, I also knew she'd learned hundreds of things that no one would ever repeat in many different languages. "As soon as I learn a turn of phrase, then poof..." She gestured again and chuckled. "Then we can not say these things anymore. Conversation is not my strong suit." She gave me a sultry smile, her dark eyes and full lips confusing my desire to be her or be with her. I didn't know which, and I'd hardly ever felt that way about another woman. I blinked and forced my gaze off somewhere else.

"It's fine." I tried to play it off as easily as she had, but I doubted it reached the mark.

"So, Joce," Slevin started, "you said the guy was an ancient True Alpha. That's not something you see often, even in Dallas. He's not affiliated with the Sovereignty? Do you know?"

"Rhys and Dietrich said they didn't recognize him or his nick-name."

"I can't say that I know of a Dom either, I'm afraid." Mary added, tone softened, eyes thinned.

"I'm starting to think Dietrich may know more than he's telling me, but he wants something from me for information." I gave an exasperated breath, remembering how easily swayed I'd been by his presence and charisma. "I'd probably get myself killed anyway, if I found him." I dismissed.

"And why is that?" Mary asked.

I chewed the inside of my cheek as I considered my reply. "He's got to die, and I want to be the one to kill him." I chose to be plain. "He can't get away with what he did to me, what he's probably done to thousands more. He's still so much more powerful than me. I don't know if I'd be able to walk away from that fight." The answer was direct, but I knew I had every intention of taking Dom out, and anyone could see the same on my face when he was brought up.

"Do you truly think you are capable?" Mary leaned forward in her seat, causing me to lean back in mine, as if the ancient's aura would smother me. Even as a Prole, she intimidated the shit out of me. "Have you taken a life before?"

My mind flashed to the stranger outside Lenny's Spot and I gulped, eyes averting down to my hands as they made their way into my lap. "No, but if doing it puts a mark on my soul, I'd say it's worth it."

"That I can not argue." Mary smirked as if she remembered a life worth the red on her own ledger. "However, I don't question that. It is capability."

My head leaned ever so slightly to the side, trying my best not to be insulted. If she was insinuating that I didn't have the fortitude to see my proclamation through, she was sadly mistaken. "Like I said, I'll die doing it, but I'm taking him with me."

"I hope for your sake you are successful. His life is yours to take." She leaned back again, the chair groaning when she did. "I may not be able to help more directly, however I know someone you may have better luck with."

"Yes?" My eyes lit up and I leaned forward.

"There's a Casanova that owns a boutique bar near downtown Dallas. It is in Oak Lawn?"

"Yeah." Slevin chimed in. "Oak Lawn."

"His name is Charmed Thibodeaux. You would do well to see him. Charmed knows all the gossip of the city. Anything worth knowing will reach his ears. Let him know that I sent you."

My posture straightened, an excitement buzzing through me at the information. Finally, someone was upfront with me, not trying to keep it from me or manipulate me for the information. "Thank you." I almost shrieked. "I'll be sure to do that as soon as possible." My phone buzzed in my pocket for a phone call as I gave Mary a nod to show my gratitude. I ignored it and asked, "what's the place called?"

"Le Jardin." Slevin answered for his Lady and I turned and nodded to him. The area they were talking about wasn't far from Rhys's loft, so I could sneak out and find Charmed without being gone long. If I had to keep my visit from Rhys, I would. It wasn't Dietrich, so what did he care? I finally had a lead. My phone buzzed again, but I ignored it.

"Tell me, Joceline, what do you think of the world as it really is? Everything is so new to you, have you had enough time to have formed an opinion of it? I am so old, I love to talk with the young ones." Mary's brow lifted to emphasize the question and I cleared my throat.

"It's, uh, confusing." I said it, but realized I needed to be more specific. Where did the confusion really lie? Was it with what everything else was around me or my inability to find my place in it. Why else had I run to Slevin when he invited me there? Not that they needed to know all of that. "I mean, it's just a lot. Everything is so connected but separate."

"You mean prejudiced?" Slevin asked, a tone to his voice I could almost put my finger on. Contempt, maybe?

"Yeah, kind of." I'd only seen bits and pieces, but they definitely treated certain classes and ages with more respect.

"It is human nature to divide itself and fear those that are different. And we were all humans, once." Mary mused out loud. Her sentiment matched Slevin's in the necessary connection to humanity.

"Well, yes. I get that. I'm just trying to figure out where I fit in all of it."

"Do you believe you must pick and choose where you belong, Joceline?" Mary's question caused Mitch to stop reading and look up from his fine print. I tried not to let my noticing it affect what I thought, but I faltered on my reply. The spectacled vampire turned his face between the familiar faces of the room, before settling on me and waiting for what I said.

I swallowed and looked at the most familiar face. Slevin looked to me with nonchalance in every muscle of his being. "Everyone wants to belong somewhere. It's human nature." I faltered noticing the mistake. "I mean, it's not...I guess...not just human. It's people-nature. Social instinct? Is it not vampire nature? Y'all have septs so—"

"Please, child." Mitch finally entered the conversation, his deep English voice a contrast to Mary's Hispanic one, and my own. "Don't let them scare you into blubbering on," Mitch said. He gave me a sincere smile and softly placed his book down on the weathered table by his side. "They are not trying to test you, or best you. There are no wrong answers." He pulled the glasses off the bridge of his thin nose, and watching him do so, their being there finally struck me as odd.

"There is nothing wrong with wanting to connect," he said. He gave me a closed smile which thinned his eyes and extended his prominent crow's feet, aging his face for a moment. "All creatures crave it; when we lose it, we mourn it." His eyes lost focus momentarily, as if recalling a memory. "If you are newly sired, you will mourn it, too, when the time comes to." I was fixed on Mitch, but I didn't see him. Not really. My mind turned down my senses to process his words.

He was right.

I mourned my human self and the connections I was losing. Each attempt to connect pushed me further away. My absence affected both my family and me. Stolen moments with my siblings didn't compensate for all family dinners I missed.

Mary's voice interrupted my thoughts. "Give yourself time. There's no rush to find your place when you don't know where you want to be." She gestured to me. "Discover how you want to spend eternity before seeking those who will join you."

I nodded, not ready to speak. Though, I didn't think they really expected me to. A fact I was grateful for. Being there in the presence of other mere Proles and other kin, even Cadavers, it forced perspective on me. Slevin was right.

"It was a pleasure to meet you, Joceline. But, you must excuse me, Antonia must be taken for a run before the sun comes up." Mary got up from her seat, and I promptly followed suit, while everyone else stayed seated. This left me second-guessing my decision, yet she was an elder. Despite our norms, I felt compelled to show her respect. Maybe it was ingrained in me from my upbringing.

"Have a good night, and thank you so much. Your sept is beautiful."

"Thank you, Joceline." She turned and smiled at me, just as a Xoloiyzcuintli dog came to stand beside her. That wasn't a breed you saw often. The Mexican hairless dog looked up at its owner, tail wagging in excitement after it had heard the word run earlier. "May fortune and I meet you again." Then, they were gone out the door.

"I think I'm going to go, too." I decided walking toward the front. Slevin stood up, and his arm reached out toward me.

"Joce, wait." He jogged up to me just as I reached the door, but I didn't turn to look at him.. "Joce." When he repeated my name, it made me weak in the knees, and I finally pivoted to look at him. "You don't have to go."

"I know, I just..." The words surprised me as they flowed from my lips. I needed time to process what nearly happened. I didn't think I could process anything with Slevin, no matter how much I wanted to. I yearned to embrace him, but that wasn't an option- not yet. Between Rhys and Dietrich, I had enough complicated relationships with men. I lacked the bandwidth to figure out how Slevin fit into the mix. They were right; finding companions came second to finding myself. I wouldn't discover myself in his arms. There were other things I'd find, but those would complicate our friendship. "What happened out there, I mean—" Slevin began.

"No, it's fine." I struggled with my confidence in refusing him. "We were both caught in the moment."

"I wasn't." His voice held steady, not surprising me. He was unapologetic, the way he said my name, how his eyes drank me in, the feel of his lips on mine- those were not things to apologize for.

"Maybe I was."

"Joce." It was the softest time he'd said it.

"Slevin."

He moved forward and grabbed me by the waist so he could pull me into him. Our bodies melted against each other, and I sighed, looking up into his eyes. "Tell me when the next moment rolls around then, so I can make sure to make the most of it."

I almost leaned up to kiss him but barely managed to control myself. "I will."

CHAPTER TWENTY-SEVEN

THE CRISP AIR CHILLED my cheeks, the wind whipping my hair into my face as if to punish me for my embarrassing exit. I pushed my curls behind my ears and unlocked my car. A month ago, I would have given anything for a handsome man like Slevin, imagining him beneath me, eager to devour me. But there I was, walking to my car in the cold.

How stupid. Frustration pulsed within me, amplifying until I bristled. "Fucking shit," I spat into the night. I entered the car and pulled my phone from my pocket. There were text messages from Rhys, but I didn't feel like reading them yet. I'd head to his loft anyway; I needed to ground myself. Just being in the same room as him leveled me out. I could weather the rest.

I needed to understand Dietrich, too. Apprenticeship aside, the vampire intrigued me. When I saw him, my mind waved a red warning flag, but my feelings made me question if I was colorblind. His seduction went unchallenged by me, which was unsettling. Was that similar to what I experienced with Rhys? How much warmth did they share back then? Based on what I'd seen, there was no spark now, despite their past. Did my feelings for Rhys differ because I didn't hate him? Or was it simply mutual respect? Frustrated, I hit the steering wheel.

I had just made out with Slevin and almost had a blood-soaked threesome at Jungbrunnen the night before, yet I still questioned my connection with Rhys. What was wrong with me? After a few more hits to the wheel, I started the engine. Clearly, I was on overdrive. Sleep and reflection on the past twenty-four hours were next. I hadn't allowed myself a break yet; everything was chaotic. I'd burn out soon, if that was even possible. Who knew baby vampires needed so much rest?

I took a few deep breaths before starting my drive home. At that moment, I wrestled with feelings of lust and desire. The emotions I experienced for those I craved might have been genuine or not, yet they were still rooted in lust all the same.

The vision of Slevin splayed out on the concrete appeared in my mind, replaced by Rhys, comfortable and smiling on the couch in the living room with papers in his hand, but his attention was on me. I breathed in long through my nose and even longer out through my parted lips.

"The price for what you desire is pleasure. Show me what you will do to find your mysterious Ancient. Give tribute to your Sovereign and I will serve you…"

Dietrich's words resurfaced as I drove south on I-35. He was a leader; I was just a baby prole, an insignificant apprentice. They called us apprentices, novices, and babies to highlight our unimportance. Did my simplicity amuse him? He was dangerous, and it puzzled me why someone so powerful cared about my pleasure. Our bond could only mean physical intimacy, but why would that matter so much to a member of The Sovereignty? I snapped out of my thoughts; I needed to let my recent events simmer on the back burner before I dissected them. The hour drive to the loft was silent, both in the car and in my mind.

Before I even made it to our parking spaces, I knew Rhys was home. At that distance, it was faint, but my body recognized him. I cut the engine and hung my head low. I didn't know what Rhys would say, or if he would try to say anything at all, but I didn't want to deal with it. When I pushed open the door to the loft, most of the lights were off and Ubaste was nowhere to be seen, which meant she was with him in his room. As I stood in the foyer, I listened.

The quiet allowed the appliances' electric hum to fill the silence. I cursed myself for not checking my messages before entering. Tiptoeing to my room on the first floor, I still tried to avoid noise, despite him knowing I was there. I closed my door slowly, twisting the lock carefully. If he heard me, he respected my space.

For hours, I played on my laptop. Rhys had given me step-by-step instructions for accessing what he called the vampire internet. I figured it was time to try it. Still, I was scared to access a dark web-like browser.

Would the U.S. government put me on a watch list? Rhys had assured me that The Cave browser differed from the traditional dark web. Though vampires might use the regular dark web, they had to avoid spreading sensitive information about our kind, so an alternative was born. It used onion routing, yes, but was solely maintained by the Sovereignty. Rhys joked about the fate of vampires who discussed our kind not in the proper online channels. The Sovereign Legion had a reputation.

I wasn't using the vampire web for nefarious purposes. I only wanted to find Dom and maybe look up Dietrich. First, I needed to get it working on my laptop. There were a few websites accessible only through the Cave browser, which had its own ".cav" domain, and the list was next to me while I sat crossed legged on my comforter.

I searched the public Sovereign records, a Wikipedia-like database, for three hours without finding Dom. This suggested either Dom wasn't in the records or they were locked. Part of me wanted to ask Rhys about his emissary clearance, as he mentioned having almost complete access. No, I didn't want to talk to him yet. I needed time and could ask later. For now, I'd see what I could find alone. Another ten minutes, and I had given up. I glanced at the list and saw BatBook at the bottom. Not long after the emergence of social media in the human realm, vampires had developed their own. My brow lifted as I typed it into the address bar: Batbook.cav. My fingers drummed the keyboard as I waited for it to load, which took longer due to the many pictures. Which was already pretty bad. Rhys had warned me about it, saying that the way onion routing worked meant that everything was being bounced off multiple locations so everything was moving around the world before or after making it to me. If I wanted to browse safely from the eyes of humans, I had to have patience.

It's not like I didn't have forever.

By the time the home page loaded, my laptop screen flashed, and the low battery icon showed up in the middle of my screen. Frantic, I popped up to look for my charging cable. In less than a minute, I had my room turned inside out but no charger. Shit. It was at my apartment. I wasn't on my laptop much, so I bet it was still plugged into the surge protector on my bedside. I grimaced when I checked the time in the corner of the screen. It was getting late and by late I meant early. In the morning. I'd have to get it after a good day's rest when I woke up.

I'd barely hit my bedsheets after changing out of my clothes when my phone buzzed on its own charging stand. My gut told me it was Rhys.

> I'm sorry, dove.

> I had no right to treat you like a child and I recognize that. Please, accept my apology.

The texts from earlier in the night earned a smirk. I hadn't expected an apology so quickly from him after the way he acted, considering how much he assumed he was right.

> Goodnight, Joceline.

The new text made the smile fade. Did I say anything back? I wanted to, but a part of me retained annoyance at the entire situation as it went down. I stared down at the pixels of my phone, unblinking. A minute later, my fingers replied and sent it, before I placed the phone back on the charger and turned around.

> Goodnight Rhys.

"Can you feel me, Fuil?" Dom's voice echoed in pure darkness. "I can feel *you*." He continued, and my eyes popped open, only to reveal that the world around me stayed shrouded in blackness. I tried to get up from where I lay, to move a muscle, but my body ignored my commands. My mouth wouldn't even open to speak. 'You haunt me. Just as I haunt you."

I used all my energy trying to open my mouth to scream, but nothing came of it. My shoulders and arms randomly twitched and my neck tensed.

"You're mine." He whispered, his voice by my ear but I couldn't see him. Everything remained black.

I struggled, refusing to give up my fight to move and scream. Inside my chest, my heart hammered, but I didn't breathe. My chest remained still. Despite being able to function without oxygen, I craved air. I needed it in my lungs, and the fact that I couldn't breathe only heightened my panic. I attempted to scream, repeatedly. I failed to scream no, to cry for him to stop.

"Mine. Mine. Mine. Mine."

These visions, these hallucinations, they were killing me. I hated them. His phantom presence tortured me as much in his wake as it did when he hurt me. Was I doomed to suffer for an immortal eternity because of him? If I could shake my head enough or move my arms, maybe it'd trigger me to wake up from this day terror.

"You will always be mine, now. Mine to haunt." He continued, volume rising. My panic increased. "Mine to haunt." He repeated, his voice so loud my skull would split. "Mine!" He screamed. "Mine!" I needed to scream, as much as my heart needed to beat, I needed to scream. "Mine!" He assaulted my senses.

The memory of his touch groped at my arms, chest and legs as if he had a dozen hands. The scent I'd noticed when I met him, the one that I had been so drawn to invaded my nostrils.

"Mine, Fuil."

Desperate, I tried to scream to Rhys. He could save me from Dom. He saved me before, he could save me again, right? Even if it was all a dream. I repeated his name in my head over and over again repeatedly, my heart beating so quickly it caused physical pain.

"Dove!"

"Rhys!"

I started punching and swinging as my eyes opened. I snapped my head side to side, taking in everything, searching for Dom. He was there. Was he there? Fuck, was he there? My room was uninterrupted. My chest heaved, and I realized I had woken up saying Rhys's name. My skin was drenched in pink sweat.

"Rhys?"

His hands were on my shoulders, having shaken me awake. "Joceline, dove. Are you alright?"

"What?" I looked from side to side, expecting to see Dom lurking in every shadow the curtained room provided, but there was nothing. "I...Dom was touching me, and he..." I squeezed my eyes shut and leaned forward to embrace Rhys in a hug. "I can't do this," I whined out, nuzzling my face into the curve of his shoulder. "Please help me."

"It's okay. I'm here."

His hand rubbed up and down on my back, and I leaned into the embrace. I didn't want to, but tears started streaming down my face, quick in their descent so that they slid down onto his bare chest.

The warmth of his torso, the skin-to-skin contact, and the proximity of him eventually calmed me down enough as the tears ceased and my breathing leveled. When I had the strength to move away from him, I pushed myself off, and his arms dropped, letting me put a small amount of distance between us.

"I'm so sorry."

"You don't need to apologize to me," he insisted.

"No, I..." I rubbed my face with the palms of my hands. "I don't know why this is happening to me." My tone faltered. "This is why. This is why he needs to die. I'll never stop having these visions until he's gone."

Rhys cupped the side of my face with his open palm, and I stopped my eyes from shifting long enough to set my gaze on his. "I should be apologizing to you. If I'd have stopped him from ever talking to you, if I had gone up to you first, I could have saved you from this pain." My brows crossed, the film of tears returning to my eyes. "Please, forgive me."

"You don't need to be forgiven. It wasn't your responsibility." I don't know why I said it, mainly because I didn't know if I believed my own words.

His hand dropped, and I looked down at it, unable to hold his stare any longer. Did I blame him for letting it happen? I wanted to say I didn't. Of course he wasn't to blame for my attack and subsequent mutation, and it was unrealistic to put that on him. However, when he warned me in that back hallway, could he not have ended it all? He knew something was wrong when I stumbled. Everyone there knew, but they let it happen. For weeks I went back and forth in my mind between the two.

"It's fine, really." I continued, feeling myself withdraw. I was grateful for him waking me up from the day-terror, but I still needed time. His barging in on me at Jungbrunnen and the subsequent dick-measuring contest with Dietrich only happened because he refused to help me find Dom.

I may not have blamed him for everything, and his little save was nice, but it didn't magically fix everything. I wanted time from him, at least a full day's rest. Maybe even into the evening when I woke up, some time to think things through.

"I'll be fine, Rhys. Thank you. Goodnight."

Sensing my withdrawal, he cupped my cheek one last time, stood up, and started for my door. In the doorframe, he stopped and turned to look at me. "Goodnight, Joceline." Then he walked away, leaving me sitting up on the bed, my sweat cold as the fan blew air down on me. I groaned and rubbed my temples, then shimmied back down so I was lying flat under the covers. I'd face the world tonight, whenever that was. For the time being, I slept.

Chapter Twenty-Eight

I woke not long after the sun had set. My body sensed the change in daylight after about a week, and it seemed to get more and more accurate each day. With my recent drama, half of me wanted to roll over and sleep for longer. The other half knew I had too many things going on to push any time aside. My phone greeted me with a few new text messages from my family. I wasn't about to add their stuff on top of the mix. I had to table that and read them later. Next, a new text message from Slevin grabbed my attention, and heat went straight into my cheeks as I opened it.

> I meant what I said. u let me know, Joce. I'm always here for u no matter what you need. ;)

I rolled my eyes and clicked out of the conversation and messaging app.. Slevin was a lot of things, good-looking, and sweet, but he was also a distraction. A distraction that I didn't need to have.

I huffed and wiggled in my bedsheets. I may have been conscious, but I could give myself a few minutes to exist but not have to do anything about it. It was the least I could afford myself after the shit show that was my last two nights. I don't know what I was thinking going from Dietrich one night to Slevin the next. To be fair, my evening with Slevin turned out different than expected. And how the hell did I end up getting more information from my time with Slevin than I did with Dietrich? Something was up with that blonde, and I'd find it out eventually. If he wasn't helpful, he wasn't worth my attention. If Charmed Thibodeaux proved unhelpful, a return to Jungbrunnen might be necessary. Though the price for his favor was enticing, would it bind me to him? What fear did my Lord have of this Austrian that turned him monstrous? Rhys was always controlled, except with Dietrich.

I groaned and pulled myself up into a sitting position. All these subjects were well and good to look into later, but not yet. Not when I had a lead. I'd go and see Charmed first, then figure my other shit out after. It was a logical sequence of events. First, shower, then clothes.

An hour later, I stepped out into the living room, knowing full well that Rhys had left the loft at some point while I'd been getting ready. Good. He couldn't ask me any questions. Not to my face, anyway. Try as Hollywood might to convince the world otherwise, vampires were very comfortable with technology. Hell, they had their version of the dark web. Rhys assured me he'd witnessed firsthand how it advanced over the decades with accelerating speed. How could someone hoping to survive the changing of time not adapt?

I bid Ubaste adieu and headed to the car, already having pulled up the address for Le Jardin in my navigation app. With the light congestion of downtown streets after the workday, it took me roughly twenty minutes to get there. Not bad at all. Having found a spot half a mile away in a pay lot, I walked toward the gastropub feeling productive.

Oak Lawn had always impressed me before, and as I navigated it, the opinion remained unchanged. Dallas made strides in separating itself from the stereotypical western image of a Texas city, unlike Fort Worth to the west, and Oak Lawn, being the LGBTQIA+ hub of the DFW metroplex, aided it. The neighborhood stood clean and maintained with great nightlife and restaurants even those not within the queer community enjoyed. If I hadn't been so nervous, I would've taken time to walk around and enjoy it.

As I walked, however, I googled Charmed and found that not only did the vampire own the bar and restaurant, but he ran a clothing boutique out of the second floor of the building. My brow shot up as I looked further into it. Charmed Apparel was no small shop, celebrities from Milan to New York City flew in to visit and purchase from the vampire designer. Photos from fashion weeks in Paris, Italy, New York and London littered the image results under his name, but finding a picture of him didn't prove easy. Articles described him as a visionary. Inspiring. The perfect blend of couture and nostalgia. He channeled the androgyny of the 80s and early 90s into pieces which fetched prices starting in the thousands.

I whistled and killed my phone screen as I approached the entrance. An expectedly fashionable Mystic sat on a stool by the door, checking IDs. Not only did the golden hue of his aura seem to liven his complexion, but his skin was so smooth and dewy, it glowed with its own youthful vibrancy. As they saw me coming up, our eyes locked and they gave me a curt nod. Finally, a vampire in a higher class who didn't greet me with contempt at seeing my Prole aura. Oak Lawn was even welcoming on the vampire side of things.

I entered and noticed that the place looked more like a cafe than anything else. The beams and paneling were all white wood with forest-green walls. It gave off a fresh, lively vibe that made it inviting, even to someone not the normal clientele. A dozen or so couples sat at small, circular tables littered around the place, enjoying polite conversation. A small, full-service bar was off to the side, full of men conversing with mixed drinks in hand.

I had no idea where I needed to go, until I spotted a Paramour sitting at a high-top table toward the back, next to a set of stairs leading to the second-floor which had been roped off.

There it was.

Closing the distance, I smiled, trying to be as inviting as the place was, but the Paramour looked at me as if I was of no consequence. With how dark and powerful his aura was, I could likely agree. He had to have been over a hundred years old. Still, he didn't have to be snooty.

"Good evening," I tried not to let the smile waver too much. "I'm looking for Charmed."

"And who are you?" The pretentious tone made my nose itch.

"My name's Joceline. Joceline...DeLon." Perfect, I remembered not to give my last name out. "I'm of Sovereign blood." I hated the title drop, it was such a shitty thing to do especially considering the relationship Rhys had with Dietrich, but if it got me in, I'd do what I had to.

"I'm sorry, name doesn't ring a bell, hun."

"I didn't think it would, to be honest." As I spoke, I caught the echo of footsteps from above us over the background ambiance. Was that Charmed up there?

"Then state your intent." His attitude was palpable and I wasn't a fan.

"Mary Cortes advised I come speak with Charmed. The matter is quite personal. If you just let me talk to him, she insisted her name would get me an audience with him." I turned on my confidence and heightened my voice so Charmed may have heard it from where he was. The footsteps stopped in the descent away from the stairs when I said Mary's name. That interested him. The Paramour's and my eyes moved upward, and we waited.

Approaching the stairs and descending them, I spotted the shadow of a figure about to round the corner. As they came into view, the first thing I saw was an immaculate white fur coat that stretched from shoulder to floor as it peaked into view. Then, the thin, androgynous vampire dressed in a black eighties-styled suit followed.

He was good looking, clean shaven, and radiated confidence. And not unearned confidence, either. He was a head turner, and not because of those good looks. He walked into a room and people stopped to admire the *whole* look of him. His light bronze skin tone and facial features screamed mixed, too. Full lips and an upturned nose accented high cheekbones and thick but shaped brows. His Paramour aura was lighter than his guard, but I doubted that mattered. The lines of his suit, although the fur coat obstructed some from view, cut angles on his tall frame. I guessed six and half feet, and the leather, pointed boots he wore added another inch or so. I watched him with a mute sense of awe. He gestured a manicured hand dismissively toward his guard, who moved the blockage out of his way.

"Well, that's a name I haven't heard in quite some time. Tell me, who are you again, baby?" He reached the last stair and stopped, looking down along his nose at me from a foot up.

"I'm Joceline DeLon."

He extended his hand out, palm down, to me and introduced himself much like a southern belle might. "Charmed, really."

Taken back by the unorthodox introduction, I awkwardly placed a kiss on the back of his hand, his nails reflecting the little light around them. Was that what he was hoping I'd do? I hoped so.

He accepted the greeting with a wide, but closed smile. "Please, miss Joceline. Follow me." He added a level of pomp to my name that I wasn't accustomed to hearing. There was an accent there, but I struggled to place where in the south it was from. Not Texas for sure, but maybe Louisiana.

Charmed didn't speak as we made our way up to the second floor, so I didn't either. I was too busy taking in everything around me, while also trying to think of what to say.

Reaching the landing, though, he got the first words in. "Joceline DeLon, of Sovereign blood, has come to my establishment at the behest of Mary Cortes. Now I assume you must have a reason, but I am at my wit's end on what it is. All I know is that it must be deliciously intriguing." He said and I placed him, he was Creole. That explained the surname. If it wasn't real, it was at least regionally accurate. "And tell me, is it DeLon? Really? I heard something different."

I stammered, wondering why on Earth he'd heard anything at all about me. "You've heard of me?"

"It's my specialty." He looked at me. "Information." He raised a brow. "Sorry, I assumed you were here for the talk of the town. You mentioned Mary Cortes. I love her to death, but she doesn't recommend me for...this." He gestured at the mannequins adorned with his creations. "You're the blood of Dietrich's estranged protégé." He pointed at me. "I will say, we were all surprised to hear that Rhys had made a coupling of his own. At least the Rhys we have now. Emissary Levett has matured quite a bit since leaving the Sovereignty. Before his estrangement he had become the perfect copy of Dietrich." He turned back and we walked deeper into his fashion studio, filled with large cutting tables and spools of fabric for unfinished looks. "Ironic, isn't it? He left the Sovereignty, only for it to take up residence in his backyard."

"What do you mean?"

"The North American Sovereign Campus?" He rolled his eyes when I didn't immediately respond with a show of understanding. "Oh honey, how old are you?"

"I would've turned thirty this year," I answered.

"Mutated."

I blushed at my mistake. "About three weeks."

"Fresh blood." He smiled. "The North American Sovereign Campus is the brainchild of one of their top scholars and several millions of dollars and years in the making. It will be the largest campus for Sovereign use in the world and it's opening in Fort Worth. They've been buzzing about it for months."

My eyes bugged and I dropped my jaw to say something. Nothing came out.

He raised his brows at me and clapped, bringing the hands close to his chest in a show of exasperation at my ignorance on Sovereign matters. "You have got to get more informed. I take it the reason you're here is the reason all of this information evades you."

"Yes."

"And that reason is?" He made small circles with one of his hands, urging me to divulge. "I simply must know why you're standing in my studio right now. I'm well and truly intrigued."

"I don't think it's as intriguing as you're imagining. I don't think anyone but me finds it important, honestly."

"A self-fulfilling personal crusade by a baby Prole, who can't get help from her vampy grand-pappy?"

"Where'd you get self-fulfilling crusade?"

"You came here to gather tea from me. That's what everyone does. But I ain't mad, baby. It keeps me relevant." We took back up walking, and despite my eyes wanting to wander, I kept them trained to Charmed's back.

"I'm looking for an ancient, but not just any ancient. A True Alpha ancient."

Charmed stopped walking and turned to face me. "Now, I could've sworn you said it wasn't interesting to anyone but yourself. What business do you have with an Ancient Alpha that Dietrich nor Mary can help you with?"

My natural desire to withdraw came, but I pushed it down. "It's important and personal." I said, then added, "deeply personal."

"Well now, I don't doubt that." He continued walking and I followed in tow. If it was rude, I couldn't take it back, but I deserved some privacy. We stopped at a desk with fashion designs and sketches scattered over the top of it. Charmed moved so that he could sit behind it in a large, ornate wooden chair.

"If you're going to keep the fun stuff secret, the least you can give me is enough details to be useful. I need more information than that to be sure."

"To be sure?" I gulped, my body bristling at the tease. He may have known Dom.

"Well, he's white. Not pale as a sheet, but not tan either. Blue eyes, light brown hair, or maybe dirty blond. I can never tell the difference between the two and styled short. Probably around six feet. Thin."

"How very specific." He wanted more.

"He's..." I struggled, the vision of that monster coming to mind. "He's between handsome and average. Just barely good-looking, but he's got memorable features." I concentrated on the memory of him when I first entered Amaranthine. "His eyes are so clear and light blue that they trick you into thinking you can see through them into the soul of him, see his intentions and motivations. But, you can't."

They were walls of ice, those eyes, obscuring the real soul- or lack thereof- from anyone naïve enough to get caught in his stare, warping the image of the hideous thing behind them. "He's chaos, switching between charming and evil. Dancing that line, dancing and dancing." My voice began to trail off until it was as light as air. "He dances with you closer and closer to death. To pain. Until you can't go back." I had been gazing off to the side of Charmed, toward the window, but turned my gaze back to him when I finished talking.

"It doesn't take a genius to see he's done a number on you." He offered me a sympathetic expression. "Do you have a name?"

"Dom."

He cocked a brow at me. "My suspicions are right." The words gave me a shock to the system that reverberated throughout my entire body.

"You know who he is?"

"I don't think anyone really knows who that man is, but I know of him." He said it with such nonchalance. "I have met him." My hands began to tremble, body moving closer to him without even realizing it.

"Please, tell me. You have to tell me." Tears were on the verge of falling from my eyes at the emotions that swelled up in me.

"Ah ah ah, now. Let's keep cool heads." I took a step back. I couldn't control myself. Any inch that I found would become a mile. But I needed the inch first. "This is what I can tell you, Joceline DeLon, of Sovereign Blood, who fraternizes with Mary and the little operation she's got going up there." The last bit caught me off guard. I boxed it up to think on later. There were bigger first to dry then cryptic statements about Mary. "And you didn't get this from me."

I nodded, mouthwatering as if a glass of fresh blood had been offered to me.

He visited my place weeks ago to buy some pieces. There was something dangerous behind those pretty eyes." He suddenly straightened his shoulders. "But I don't choose sides," he warned. "He left with some boys from downstairs. We don't allow feeding at Le Jardin; take that elsewhere." He gave an unnecessarily cautious glance around the room, for theatrics. "He said he'll be around for a while; something caught his interest. He wants to see it through. Said he enjoys Texas more than expected, thanks to a new friend." My eyes widened.

He meant me.

I wasn't his friend, but I knew he was referring to me.

"I will say this, ma cherie." The casual pet name felt warm, despite the implied warning to come. "If you are that someone and I'm not the first person you've been asking about him, I don't think you'll have to look very far. Truth be told, you've been on his radar for as long as he's been here."

It was only when I opened my mouth to reply that I noticed my jaw quivering. "He's here, he's still here." I stepped toward him again, anxious, but immediately withdrew. A million thoughts swirled around my head; if my exterior looked like my interior, I'd be jumping around.

He raised a manicured finger at me in response. "Dallas is very large. I am not the only place he can find a drink in Oak Lawn, either. He may not be close." He huffed out a casual laugh. "As I said, I don't pick sides. I will also say though, that you need to be careful. You may have powerful names behind you, but they won't always be there at your back to hold you up. The only thing that can hold you up when you finally find him is your own spine."

I blinked, taking another step back as I processed his words. I hadn't expected anything so poetic from him. "Th—thanks." I should've said more, but I couldn't muster a response. His expression told me I didn't need to. The corner of his lip lifted in a smirk.

"I'll be watching from the middle ground. I hope you're victorious in your crusade. We all love an underdog." The smirk spread. "Darken my doorway again any time you need to, Joceline Fuentes." He dropped my real name, as a show of credibility. Then he motioned to the stairs for my exit. Despite the abrupt end to the conversation, I abided. He had nothing else to offer and had already given me a wealth of information. My head swam with what he said. Dom was still around, watching me. I didn't need to look for clues; I needed to let him show himself. I bowed my head and walked out of the room, down the stairs, and out of Le Jardin, trapped in the cloud of my discovery, ready for what would come next but not sure what to do.

CHAPTER TWENTY-NINE

WALKING OUT OF LE Jardin, an emotional haze hung over me so heavy, I swore it was visible. I didn't even acknowledge the Paramour at the base of the stairs or the other two vampires that had entered. None of them mattered. A couple sidestepped me with a grimace as I walked down the sidewalk, but I ignored them. Everything was so trivial.

Dom was watching me. All those times I had seen him, what was real and what was a product of my trauma? All the day terrors and nightmares, the visions of his face amongst a crowd—could they really have been him?

How close was he?

When I reached the parking lot, I continued walking. I didn't have it in me to end the night there—not with my mind swirling with possibilities. Because it was a weekday, not many people were on the streets, but Oak Lawn always had a bit of life to it, no matter the day. A stranger would pass by with a dog on a leash, and I'd look at them and offer a courteous smile, but I was miles away. If the face looking back at me wasn't Dom, I didn't care. And it didn't matter if the face was across the street, jogging by, or hidden under a hood; I'd spot him. His image had been burned into my mind, like a brand on my subconscious not yet healed, and every time I touched it, it stung. If only I could stop touching it.

My skin prickled up with gooseflesh as I passed a mid-rise apartment building, every instinct on high alert. My eyes shifted as I expected to see either Rhys or Dietrich. "Centuries it's been since I've felt something beneath the surface that didn't have to split my skin first."

The words fell on my ears like weights, and I whipped my head around and stopped dead in my tracks. People moved around me, but I stayed planted. Where was he? That voice was Dom's. Nothing sounded like him. I wouldn't even be confused by another Scotsman. That voice that was once so interesting and charming made my skin crawl.

I turned toward the alleyway between the apartment building and a retail shop, walking halfway into it. My gut urged me further in, and I closed my eyes to understand the feeling. Was it my coupling? Had Rhys come to warn me about Dom? Were they both close at the same time? "Rhys?" I stopped, but the proximity of the coupling diminished, as if the vampire had moved closer behind me. "Rhys?" I repeated, though the silence told me how mistaken I was, along with the lack of warmth.

There was a huff of laughter. "I'm sorry to disappoint you, but your Lord is 'na here."

"No," the first word fell slowly from my lips, but the others didn't. "No, no, no."

I had been searching for him, following every lead I could find, and all the while my blood reacted to him. The fact that neither Rhys nor Dietrich was there meant that I could sense him nearby. I couldn't mistake it.

It was light over the skin, making my hairs stand on end but it was there. Which meant that my blood was tainted with that of the monster I hunted. Those times I had felt that smoke roll over my skin, it wasn't anxiety...it wasn't my imagination torturing me. It was him.

"You uttered those words at me, like a song, our first night together," he teased. His calm voice echoed off the concrete walls around us. My heart pulsed in my ears, blood begging to come to a boil. Had he been waiting until I got close enough to reveal himself? "I'd much rather hear something sweeter fall from those lips."

Outside of Lenny's Spot? At The Pulpit?

My stomach dropped, nausea hitting me like a slap in the face.

He had been standing behind my sibling when I went to pick them up? I wanted to fall to my knees, but I refused to bend. Not to him. Even with my revelations. "I'm going to fucking kill you."

"A little dramatic, Miss DeLon. Or is it Fuentes?"

The more he spoke, the more I panicked. He had been there outside the football game, hadn't he? How did he know to be there?

"How can I feel you?"

The shuffle of clothing came, but half a second later, he was already in front of me a few feet in the darkness. He wasn't too close, but with my vision, I could make him out clearly. His aura glittered in the darkness, all the colors present in equal measure. The dark cloud of his cadaver black was so thick and dark. Yet, every color's depth was unlike anything I'd seen on a vampire before. Dark indigo, the deepest pine green, the gold so dark it appeared almost orange, and the red deeper than dried blood. And blackness. So much blackness. An aura had never struck fear in me until then.

"Now, I know that's a question you can answer," he mocked me. Of course, there was a logical reason, but there was no way it could be true. The only valid reason couldn't be true.

Sire coupling.

"No, it's...you're not my Lord. You're not of Rhys's blood."

"Oh no, I'm not his blood, nor the blood of his predecessors."

I swallowed, eye twitching at my inability to accept the logical answer. Dom smiled a smile with no visible teeth but an overwhelming amount of malice. Seeing his face so close again, it brought back so much dread my temples pounded.

"Do you still not remember?"

"How could I remember after what you did to me?"

He shook his head and tisked, taking a step toward me. I took two steps back toward the mouth of the alley. His smile twitched upward when he watched me do it. He enjoyed my fear, just like he had the night of the attack.

"Come now, Joceline." His voice hushed to a whisper. "Do I need to jog that memory of yours?" He reached out toward me. "Coax it out of you." His hand retracted. "I'd have thought your vampire nature would have revealed that for you by now."

My head inclined to the side. What memory would explain a coupling between us? He drugged me, attacked me, and left me for dead. It was pretty cut and dry.

He rolled his bottom lip between his teeth, stopping the corner of his bottom lip on his unsheathed fang, puncturing the skin so that blood beaded the small wound. When he finished rolling his lip out, he used his thumb to smear the spilled blood along his lower face. Still smiling, the change darkened his expression.

The sight of crimson on his face, smeared and messy, jolted me. It sent cold lightning through my mind that tensed every muscle in my body. His bloody face. The jovial expression smothered in gore that came into focus as seconds passed. The horror. The memories that teased at me, milliseconds of tied-up moments coming undone, were hiding some detail, but what?

His blood in the air begged me to remember. With each hurried breath of panic I took, I smelled it and wanted to have it closer. Inside of me. That blood bristled and stirred beneath my surface, a whirlpool in the oceans of my veins. "You didn't give me your blood. You didn't give—" I screamed.

He moved a step closer to me. "No, that I dinnae do," he said. His clear eyes fixed themselves on me, giving gravity to everything about him. "You *took* it." Pink blurred my vision as I did everything in my power not to buckle. I'd had his blood in my system when I mutated. Not much, but enough, and it connected me to him forever.

He moved forward again, but I didn't withdraw. My breath trembled out, and I clenched my hands to fists at my sides until my arms shook and my eyes closed. He moved even closer, his shoes barely making noise on the pavement. The sounds didn't matter, and neither did I need to see his figure grow larger with each step. Not at this proximity.

I felt him.

He stopped when he was close enough to reach out and touch me. One of my hands relaxed, its fingers stretching. All I could think about was wrapping those fingers around his neck. He could easily overpower me if I did, sure, but I had to try. Maybe, I could snap his neck to immobilize him and tear the head from the body. That was my only shot at killing him.

Before I could act on the impulse, my eyes snapped open from the shock of my body being slammed by the throat into the wall beside me.

The concrete bit into my shoulder blades through my clothes, and I let out an anguished cry, fangs bared at the danger.

"Over a millennium and a half, I've kept this blood sacred." He inched his face closer, nostrils flaring as he took in the scent of me. He spoke of his essence as if he was the only one with a right to it. As if he was its keeper. "I should take every drop of it back from your unworthy veins." He raked his hand from my neck up to my cheeks to grab them, which caused my lips to purse open. "Take it back," he said forcefully, "but the way your blood sings to me..." He inched even closer, lips almost touching mine when he spoke. I remained frozen, feeling too much like the scared human I'd been when he came into my life and changed it forever.

With his proximity, when he licked his lips, it moistened the already congealed blood, and I smelled it. It smelled good. I hated that it smelled good. His hand returned to my neck and tightened, cutting off my air supply. Unable to draw a breath, however unnecessary, caused me to choke up and my tongue to push out of my mouth as I started to struggle against him. He continued to squeeze harder, my windpipe straining, pain creeping in fast.

Powerless to resist or fight, his lips crashed against mine, his blood mingling with my taste buds. In the midst of the violent kiss, he bit my lip to draw blood before deepening the one-sided kiss and reopening his own wound. The action forced our blood to merge. As soon as it did, fire coursed through me. Every part of me was alight.

So much anger, the fire of it burned like the pits of hell. But there was something else there. Forcing itself on me. Was it pleasure? Not my own. His emotions, his arousal, violated the fibers of my being, making me sick, violating me through the coupling.

When he pulled away and sighed through his open mouth, the smell hit me again, the age and strength of his blood unmistakable. "Very interesting." His tongue dragged lazily over the smeared blood on his lips, eyes rolling into the back of his head as he lifted his face up to the night sky.

Trying to push past the shock of what was happening and the pain in my throat, I knew I had to escape while he was distracted by the pull of our coupling and empathetic connection. I couldn't allow myself to get lost in it with him. His blood was strong like moonshine, and it wanted to keep me close. The amalgamation livening the bond. I had to resist it. I couldn't fall into the feeling. The anger and pleasure were so different, but the passion of them both became a sea that drowned me. My head swam.

"So fascinating." His head hadn't moved, still faced upward. He breathed in deeply, taking in more of the scent. His rapture only grew, flooding that sea of emotions. I couldn't fight it off much longer. I started to buzz, unable to decipher the difference between my own panic and the visceral excitement forced on me. I slowed my breathing down as much as I could with his hand on my neck. My heart bounced in my chest and my fingers twitched. I didn't know if he wanted to fuck, fight, or free me after the violation of my lips, but I wasn't going to give him the luxury of time to find out.

I huffed as much of my breath out as I could muster and readied myself. The hum of anticipation grew louder and louder in my ears. My stomach tensed. My mind sharpened. My weight shifted into my feet to anchor me.

I couldn't beat him. I was unprepared and caught off guard by our bond. I had to run. But, despite the fact that he had centuries on me as far as strength, I had the volatility of my apprenticeship. That was my one saving grace.

As I pushed off my heels and rocketed into him, I barely caught his eyes when his chin fell. Pure, unadulterated power and undisciplined rage collided with his body, breaking his hold of my neck enough I could get away. I used the split second and pushed him forward, running toward the street in the time he staggered.

I watched him gain his bearings as I escaped. That face and the amusement that washed over it when I got away from him sent ice into my veins. I snapped my eyes forward as I emerged onto the sidewalk, dodging two men holding hands on a romantic walk down the street.

I spun and stopped myself when I faced the direction of my car, acutely aware of where I'd parked it even in my predicament. From behind me, booming in volume, so much louder than I'd ever heard it before I heard his guttural, feral scream.

That was all I needed to hear.

I sprang into motion like a bullet. Anything to get distance between us. I didn't care if I startled the humans around me. If I didn't get space between us, it might end up being my last night alive. The further I got, the more my mind clouded with my weakness.

Charmed was right.

When I was faced with Dom, being alone with my bogeyman in the shadows, I couldn't do it. I screamed from the mountaintops that I'd kill him, but there I was, running for my life. I'd been as easily bested as I had as a simple human. All my training, what good was it if I panicked at the moment of opportunity?

I panted, hoping the breaths would cure the cowardice that consumed me. Something to help me fight off the over-one-thousand-year-old psycho chasing me down. He had screamed, but I didn't know if he was pursuing me. Not until a moment later, when every nerve in my body bristled with electricity. He was near. I couldn't tell what direction, but he was getting close. I continued running, either way. I didn't care where the asshole was as long as I got away.

Without warning, a hand grabbed me as I passed the opening between two buildings only fifty feet from the lot where I had parked. He pulled me into the darkness of the alley. His nails dug into my skin in a grasp that would hurt like hell to break, ensuring I wouldn't easily snatch it out. Not with his strength.

Tears welled in my eyes at the pain of then being swung into the wall, my arm forced outstretched beside me, his chest almost touching mine in the small space. "And where do you think you're going? I've not decided what I want to do with you yet, blood of my blood."

Those words, that connection being used by him...it sent shivers down my spine. I gritted my teeth. "You're not my Lord."

"Lord?" He smiled. "No, that I'm not. But my essence flows through you and I dinnae ken what to do about it." He forced his fingertips harder into the meat of my forearms, the blood it spilled pooling onto his skin, giving fragrance to the air between us. He slacked his jaw so I could see his fangs slide back out at the smell of it.

The presentation of his fangs aside, I knew how he felt. I knew that smelling my blood, spilling it, and making it race within me brought him more pleasure than he'd had in hundreds of years. More than it had when he tortured me. Because he could experience my terror and pain, not just witness it. The empathetic connection went both ways. I knew it because I fucking felt it too. That perverted ecstasy. Despite how little of his blood might have been in my veins, an emotion that intense seeped into me. He was ancient. It could've been a single drop, the smallest trace, but I'd always feel him. As long as he was still alive, he affected me. His tainted, powerful blood poisoned me.

He took from me, I took from him. It didn't mutate me, but kept me alive long enough to be turned by Rhys. If I took it all back? If I stole every drop of blood from him, would that sever the bond? Would that leave me only with a coupling to Rhys?

My fangs unsheathed at the thought. The image of his pale, lifeless body beneath me, blood everywhere but inside him. His eyes no longer a chaotic galaxy of ice, but vacant.

Our eyes met. In the near silence of my breaths and his composure, we stood there deciding the other's fate. The gravity of our sentences weighed heavy in the air, so palpable I could taste it.

It was bitter.

It meant death.

He smiled at me before dragging his tongue over his elongated canines. "Don't you make it easy, Fuil." I repeated the Gaelic word, under my breath. "Blood..." He finally translated it back at me. Finally, knowing what it meant, knowing that from the moment he met me he referred to me as less than a person, I ignited. He dared to call it to me as a joke before he slaughtered me and then, having destroyed my life forever he used the fucking word and had the audacity to keep it as a pet name.

No.

My upper lip curled into a snarl, teeth gritted tight, eyes narrowed. From my core, a pressure began to build, an energy that intensified until it spread through my core and limbs. It continued until it reached my extremities, and I thought I would burst. As I bubbled over, he held my gaze with a glint in those clear eyes. "I'mma make it fuckin' impossible." I spat back at him. "The closest thing I'll ever feel to death again is when yours releases me."

"Don't make promises you cannae keep."

Unable to contain myself any longer, I opened my mouth and let out a brutal cry. With the sheer volume of it, Dom recoiled, lightening his grip. I took advantage, and pushed forward into him so hard we hit the opposite wall, the small distance not giving me clearance to use much strength.

A low, amused laugh echoed out as I held him to the wall, unaware of the trails of red dripping from deep scratches on my arm where his nails were no longer embedded in me.

I bared my teeth at him as he continued his condescending chuckles until my hands wrapped around his throat to quiet him. Even as I crushed his neck, he remained unphased. I growled and then screamed through my teeth at it. He could have fought back, but he allowed me to punch him. Over and over again my knuckles came down on his face, the impact of them against his cheekbones driving me further and further into my assault. There was no stopping. The skin below his eye split, spilling more of his blood then I broke his nose and red gushed out from his nostrils. I wanted him to hurt, to experience all the pain he inflicted on me. He licked the blood from his upper lip, his eyes staring me down.

"My turn."

Before I could try and get distance between us and counter his retaliation, he reached up and grabbed a fistful of my hair. I yelped at the sudden pain of having him yank it, my scalp protesting how much strength he used in his grip. I wanted to scream, but I didn't want to give him more satisfaction that what our coupling provided.

"Scream for me."

"Fuck you."

His fingers, braced like claws, went to my stomach, and I lurched down, hands coming down to try and keep them from breaking skin. "I said scream for me." God damn it, the pain of him trying to grab my insides seared through me. It blinded me. I bared my teeth and clenched my jaw, but I still didn't do as he commanded.

When I didn't think the skin at my gut could resist much longer, I dropped my left hand so that I could get leverage then brought it around with all the strength I could muster to the side of his head, connected my wrist to his temple. His hand dropped from my stomach. My hands went straight for his throat, but he grabbed my own before I got to him, and I tried clawed at his hold. Without much effort, he pushed me back until concrete fought against my shoulder blades. Harder he pushed, my spine protesting the pressure of the building on my back. I gritted, still refusing to scream out. He could kill me before I willing screamed for his sadistic ass again.

"So much blood to play with." His free hand came up to wipe his face, the blood from his healed nose and cheek coating his palm. "Do you want to see what I can do with it?"

He used his hold on me to throw me to the side, down into the alley, until I hit the ground, awkwardly wedged into the small space he had dragged us into. My eyes found him as I tried to get to my feet. He placed his bloodied hand into a puddle that had formed in a small pothole.

The water.

My eyes widened, anxious about his next move after witnessing numerous sparring matches at the old warehouse. I scanned the surroundings, comparing the distance to the opening on the other side with the side we had entered through in the alley. I didn't want to put my back to him, but I needed to get distance before he used his Mystic abilities to attack. But he wasn't only a Mystic, he was an Alpha. He had speed and strength on me, too.

I started to back up, one hand behind me making sure my path was clear while the other was extended in front. I hadn't realized it earlier, but I was panting. His hand lifted from the puddle, gripping an icicle shaped like a blade.

Fuck.

He smiled at me. I could feel the excitement from him. He wanted to use it on me. He wanted to use it to flay the skin from my body. I needed a fucking weapon, but I didn't have anything. I looked around me, desperate but there was nothing within reach. A 2x4 wooden plank leaned against the building about ten feet away. I looked between him and the plank. It was worth a try.

I sprang in its direction, and he did the same towards me. When the impact of his body sent me to the ground; the plank was inches away from my head. The blade of ice came down into the meat of my forearm that he held down. I gasped, still trying not to scream. I wanted to scream. It hurt so much: electric pain from the wound sent stars flashing in my vision. My hearing faded for a moment. The world blurred into the background. Then he stabbed me again in the same spot. The pain knocked the wind out of me, and I struggled against his body, which straddled me. Now that his blade, spreading cold where it had been embedded in me, held one arm down, his other hand held my other arm out.

"If you could see how beautiful you look," he said as he slid the knife out of my arm, I opened my mouth in a silent scream but made no noise. My chest bounced as I panted, my heart hammering away. "So pathetic beneath me." He brought the cold blade up to my face, pointing the tip into my cheek. It didn't take much pressure for it to break skin, but he didn't push hard. "I'm going to rip the skin off of every inch of your body and lick it clean." Then he pushed harder, the tip going through my cheek, nausea dropping bricks in my stomach, tears welling in my eyes.

I started to thrash against him, while my free arm reached for the plank. I could almost reach it, it was so close. His warm tongue licked the blood that he spilled on my cheeks, and I tried to turn away from him. If I could just reach the plank...

The hurried voice of a stranger from the alley opening caught me off guard. "Are you okay, what's going on—" I snapped my head toward the closest alley opening to see what was going on and Dom retracted the blade from my face.

"Run!" I screamed.

But Dom was so fast, he had the man by the throat before I even got off the ground. The man's feet dangled a foot in the air as he struggled to breathe, Dom walking him into the darkness where I was. The man struggled to call for help, unable to even pull air in with how hard Dom held him. Dom's buzz of excitement invaded me.

"Tell me, Fuil, do you think you're fast enough to kill me?" My body tensed. "You'd better be," he continued with a smug tone, "because you're going to have to kill me before I kill him."

My heart dropped. I didn't waste a second before springing into motion. It may have taken the length of a single heartbeat, an intake of a breath, but no longer. I grabbed the wooden plank, and my body turned to run at them.

He pulled the man down and ripped into his neck with the ferocity of a rabid animal. The man tried to scream, but the sound was unable to fully form as it gurgled in his throat, drowned in his own blood. The way he coughed through the violence was both deafening and quiet. Even with how short it was, it nauseated me. I swung the wood into Dom's back, but he didn't even flinch. His mouth was still at his throat as he greedily took every drop he could. The spice of the crimson was thick in the air as it spilled and spurted everywhere. I shoved and pushed at him, but Dom didn't move. He was planted there.

"No, please no." I repeated, pink sweat dripping down the sides of my face. I swung again, but it was as if he had tensed his body into a statue.

The scene was savage and violent. The most violent thing I'd ever seen followed only by my own attack, by the same monster. Then Dom dropped him; the man's body crumbled to the ground, blood spurting rhythmically from the gore in his neck as he twitched. I fell to my knees, eyes barely able to rip away from the sight long enough to catch the gleam of satisfaction in Dom's eyes. It drove me mad.

Dom took off running, but I took off after him, dropping the plank. Seconds felt like hours, everything around us blurring into nothingness, but I hadn't even gotten that far. Dom disappeared, and I stopped running when I heard the screams of a woman from where we had been. The breath caught in my lungs.

Without hesitation I left that man on the ground to die alone just to chase him. He died confused in pain, just like I should have. The pavement ground into my knees as they hit it, eyes filled with tears at the realization of what I'd done.

The stranger only wanted to help, but I'd sealed a fate for him worse than my own. If I'd have stayed, applied pressure to the wound, maybe I could have given him enough blood to survive.

My head clouded with pressure, and I swayed. I stayed frozen there on the sidewalk, looking forward, blood cooling on my body. I couldn't get myself to move, not an inch. A minute before I had so much anger in my heart, rage and feral energy rampant within me, but it all rushed out in a flurry of grief, sadness and guilt.

I'd never seen violence like that before; I'd never witnessed a murder. My eyes fluttered as I tried, to no avail, to push the thoughts out.

I had a murderer's blood in my veins, and because of him, an innocent man died.

The feel of someone's hand on my shoulder made me jerk away and twitch. No one could touch me, I was dirty. Everything in me was dirty. My whole body dripping with the filth of consequences and things I'd never be able to change. I started to cry.

"Ma'am?"

My shaking breath was audible.

"Ma'am, are you—"They grew quiet as they noticed the blood all over my arms. Up the street, another scream rang out. The person released my shoulder, their heartbeat doubling.

"Go." I roared, pointing behind us. "Go, help them." I didn't deserve their assistance. My reasoning returned to me and panic crept in. I had to get away from the scene. "Go now." I pushed the stranger away from me as I got to my feet. "I'm fine, just go." I wiped the tears from my face. I gave them another push, so hard they nearly fell over. Scared, they backed away from me.

Then I ran.

CHAPTER THIRTY

I RAN AWAY FROM it all.

Miles and miles I ran with the heat of emotions in my chest and head that couldn't form themselves into cohesive thoughts. By the time I stopped, I stood outside Rhys's building, huffing.

What had I become?

Or was it what I had always been since my mutation? In saving me, had I only become another hidden, monstrous thing tainting this city?

Chest heaving, I fixed my gaze on the windows and balconies carved from the red brick of the sixth floor. Rhys was home. His presence spread over my skin as soon as my feet stopped pounding on the sidewalk. My eyes shifted back to the grimy concrete. The connection I felt with him wasn't pure. Dom had diluted it. Maybe that was why I couldn't bond with him as intimately as I should have. Still, through our coupling, Rhys shared in my shame and guilt. I didn't know how to stop the empathetic transfer, nor if stopping it was possible, which I despised. I didn't want to share it; I wanted to take it all into myself and let it fester until it consumed me. He didn't deserve my punishment.

Only I did.

My hands patted my bloodied jeans as I walked up floor after floor of the parking garage, searching for my keys. Of course they were nowhere to be found, and my spare was upstairs. They probably fell out in the commotion of my fight with Dom. What a horror I must have looked. Good thing no one was there to witness it. By the time I made it up, leg raised to kick in the door to the interior of the building, it swung open.

"Rhys."

His eyes widened at the sight of me, which made tears start back up in my twitching eyes. "I'm so sorry." I whispered, lifting my hands up to show him the drying blood. "I didn't listen." I sniffled.

"Joceline." He called my name, then froze. After a moment, he blinked and pulled me into the hallway. "Dove..." he started, leading me to the loft like a scared child. "Are you okay?"

"I didn't—I didn't listen."

"What happened?"

I collapsed onto the floor as soon as the door closed behind me and we were safe in the privacy of his foyer. "I took his blood Rhys," I blubbered out, face pointed down, tears splashing the hardwood.

"Took whose blood? Is this from feeding?" His confusion seeped into me, edging me into a breakdown when it mingled with what was already there.

"No," I ground out, baring my teeth. "It was Dom." I slammed my fist down. "I took Dom's blood that night." I pushed away his arms as he attempted to wrap them around me, trying to offer comfort. Comfort would serve no purpose. I needed rage and fire; I needed to expel it all from me because I couldn't expel Dom's blood.

"What are you talking about?"

"Goddamn it! Don't you get it? I had his blood in my system when I mutated," I screamed, bringing my head further down, forehead close to the floor, chin to my knees. "The only reason I didn't die before you got to me was because his fucking blood was in my system. It kept me alive until you got there."

It all came back to me. The pain, the fear, and the fleeting nature of my mortal life as I ventured further toward an inevitable demise. A red hell resided in the memory, one that made the violence of the stranger's end in the alley seem like a courtesy. Dom was capable of far worse things, and he did them to me. Every detail flooded my senses. Every second that evaded me before returned.

"You can't be—"

"Serious?" I interrupted. "How could I have stayed alive? How? He butchered me. You saw. I remember now...the look on your face when you made it through the door." I was speaking as fast as I remembered when Rhys arrived in my hotel room. Chunks of his time in there were still missing, like the act of exchanging blood to become a vampire, but I was getting it back.

I remembered my head had been turned toward the door, and as I faded in and out of my last moments of consciousness, Dom's blood in my system was attempting to heal me, though it'd never have been enough to save me on its own. It did keep me coherent enough to see the look of horror on Rhys's face as he burst into the room. "I saw you."

I tried to speak but struggled as I processed the memories. Rhys's hand came to gently grab my chin and lift my head to him. I took him in as my eyes moved up. His face expressed so much in the small details. He didn't have to exaggerate anything. I read the emotions as easily as our bond broadcasted them. Even then, his trepidation glared at me with his mouth hung open just a little bit and the smallest degree of wider eyes, as if it hid the fact that his breath sped up.

"Why didn't you just save me at the back of the bar?"

He had explained it before, but I needed to hear it again. I needed to grasp why I had to be a part of that man.

"He'd have killed us both, you know that."

"But now...now I'm his. He's in my blood and I'm in his and I hate it. I can't."

He cupped my cheek. "What happened tonight?" he asked.

"I was at Le Jardin; I met Charmed Thibodeaux."

"What were you doing with Charmed?"

I flinched, battling the urge to pull away from his chiding tone. "I was looking for Dom. No one would help me, but Mary said Charmed could. And he did. But then Dom showed up when I left, and we fought. I tried hard, but I was losing." The image of a dirty ice blade flashed in my mind. "Then, someone got caught in the middle." Silence hung as he seemed to want to speak, but nothing came out. "He killed someone in front of me, daring me to stop him. I wasn't fast enough. I don't regret going to Charmed's, but he didn't have to kill them. That innocent person didn't have to die," I added, almost pulling back.

"I know."

"I just—" I tried to finish the sentence but instead the air rushed out with an exasperated sigh. "Do you have any idea how much I need this, to see him dead? To be the reason he's dead. I can't move on without this. I can't have my life back."

"You'll never have your life back, Joceline," he replied, tone firm. I pulled away that time. "And it wasn't only him who made sure of it." My brows lowered. "I made sure of that as much as he did."

"It's not the same."

"It is. I changed your life irreversibly. You'll never be the same Joceline that checked into The Avery Hotel. You'll never be the same Joceline I met that first night. Or the Joceline that walked into Amaranthine."

His words stung, and I hated that he felt the need to say them. "Stop."

"You can't go back to being the person you were before your mutation. None of us can."

My jaw clinched but I released to spit out my reply. "I said stop it. I don't want to be his."

"You're not his."

"I am, okay." My stomach turned at saying it. "A few drops of his blood—."

He backed up from me to exclaim, "Fuck his blood. Fuck his blood and fuck him. His selfish actions don't mean he's entitled to you."

Thrown off by his sudden movement, I lifted myself up from my crouch but remained on my knees. "He was right there, and I couldn't even do it. I couldn't kill him tonight."

"He's a True Alpha, dove. Of course you couldn't. That's why I didn't want you running around like this."

The desire to shrink inward grew, but I wouldn't make myself smaller for him, no matter what weird connection we had or the truth in his words. Every time I tried to let my hurt go, it came back with more passion. It thrived inside me like a hydra. "I'm never going to stop looking for him. You can't expect me to. He's in my blood."

"*I'm* in your blood." He didn't yell it, but he said it with an urgency in his voice that vibrated through me.

"I know, it's just—"

He was suddenly down on his knees in front of me, one of my hands in his, clutched to his chest. "It's not *just* anything. It's everything. Our coupling is everything."

I looked down at my hand in his. Was I that important to him? All that happened, all of the pain, confusion, and horror...it tainted my relationship to him from the moment he showed up at my door. But that was one-sided, wasn't it? My body grew heavy. "I..." If only I could articulate the weight that came when I finally took the time to see Rhys. To really see him in front of me, desperate to ease me. "You..."

"Tell me what I can do. Can I make you remember the night we met?"

When he said it, I went back to the corridor in Amaranthine, to the way he called me dove and the bells ringing in my mind at the sound of it. But I didn't remember meeting him the night before in my drunken stupor. There was so much wine. Wine and self-pity. "I can't."

"I shouldn't have asked you to save me a drink. I should have saved you one, right when you walked in. I should have had it waiting for you. I'm sorry."

Save me a drink...

My eyes closed and I grimaced at the sudden intrusion of images in my head.

"Save me a drink, Joceline Fuentes."

The night before Amaranthine, the hallway outside my room swam and swayed, bathed in yellowed tined lights. And I wasn't alone.

"You..."

"I had left a room not five doors down from yours. Some nights when I miss the hunt I go to the Avery. And there you were."

I centered my focus on his hands, but I wasn't looking at them. Lost in resurfacing memories, I saw the hallway that had been ahead of me as I walked, my body wrapped in the comforter from the hotel bed, an ice bucket tucked in my arm. I was singing and dancing along to a song stuck in my head. At one point, drunk as I was, I think I stopped and threw it back to what I thought was empty air, proudly exclaiming raunchy lyrics.

"You were behind me in the hallway?"

"Yes."

My vision blurred as the memory materialized.

I had run out of ice to cool my white wine and was on a poorly-decided trek to get more at the machine. I didn't really need more ice or, for that matter, wine, but I had passed the point of reason. When I got to the machine, it dawned on me that I had forgotten to take my hotel key card with me, and that's when every negative emotion I'd suppressed gained the upper hand. I started bawling, standing there, wrapped up like a blanket burrito.

"Are you alright, love?"

He had startled me. But in my state at the time, anything would have done the same. The shock of someone witnessing my very public, very drunken breakdown forced a noise out of me. A squeal. For a moment I thought he had been a figment of my imagination with his sudden appearance, but no. He was real. His hand placed gently on my back, in an unsuccessful attempt to keep from scaring me, solidified his existence. I spun around to look at him. "Did you just call me a dove?" I asked while trying to suppress my sobs, because what could be worse than having a meltdown in a hotel hallway with a stranger, a very good-looking one, calling me a fancy pigeon?

In that moment, it wasn't the hushed volume of his voice or the disarming English accent that calmed me, but the smell of him. It smelled nothing like lavender, but it pacified me as if it had. The hurried breath I took in during my interrupted crying deepened that pacification and made me trust him. If only I'd known it was his Paramour pheromones at work, much like how Dom ensnared me when normally someone like him would have thrown up a red flag the size of Texas outside a car dealership.

But Rhys...he stayed with me in that hallway as I unloaded all my woes. I went from my piece of shit ex leaving me using the excuse of not being able to have kids of his own blood to the death of my father long before that. All of it tumbled out of me in a metaphorical rockslide of traumas. He became the unfortunate and unsuspecting stranger who runs into the wrong woman in the ladies room at a busy bar.

But he never appeared burdened by me. He even made me laugh a few times. On top of that, he not only called the front desk to have someone let me in, but he also stayed until he was sure I got back inside my room. Before I closed the door on him, after confessing my terrible plan to go down to the hotel bar the next night to regain the confidence, he asked me to save him a drink.

"Save me a drink, Joceline Fuentes."

He smiled at me, a smile as wide as the one I saw disappear behind the door that night. "I always wondered why you saved me."

"Because I met a woman in a hallway, wrapped in a blanket, who thought I called her a bird," he answered. My nose tingled and the sensation traveled up to my eyes. "And my life's never been the same since."

I wanted to cry again, but I wasn't sure if it was an accurate expression for what I felt. I didn't know if there was a way to convey it. There was relief in finally understanding, but also sadness in having lost the memory for the time I had. Maybe if I remembered it, I wouldn't have given him as much grief when he came to me. Or, if I remembered it, I'd understand what we were to each other. But, then again, the "why" still lingered. "Why did you save me though? I was just a dumb drunk girl who talked your ear off. You still didn't have to."

"I don't know." He shrugged, releasing my hand. "From the moment I saw you, I felt something there. You were unapologetic, and a bit silly. But all that I was after that... was yours."

My breath stuttered. Warmth spread within me; I was unsure if it came from Rhys or myself. Happiness, gratitude, and maybe pride?

Pride in myself... no, his pride in me. He was proud of me? For what? I shared the emotion, though its source was locked in his thoughts.

My brows scrunched up as we looked silently at each other, permeating in our shared empathy. "I still don't remember our coupling; things are coming back, but not all of it. I wish I did, but I don't—"

"Then we can rewrite it. One day it may come back, or perhaps you never have to open that door again. Either way, our coupling remains intact. You are not Dom's. You belong to no one. But I am yours."

"Blood of *my* blood?" I hadn't intended for it to come out as a question, but I couldn't help the inflection in my voice. Was it just a title, a privilege, or a leash? What did it mean for us in our relationship that I struggled to define? Despite our deep connection, I couldn't label us like I wanted; all I saw were shades of gray between us.

Strictly platonic? No? I was attracted to him, as many people were just by looking at him. He was clearly attracted to me too; he said as much. However, having been robbed of the memories that formed our first interactions, I didn't feel close to him. The intimacy wasn't there. The instincts I had to trust him after I mutated—were they just a coupling, or did a part of me, somewhere inaccessible, remember that time in the hallway or him saving me before I succumbed to my injuries?

"*Your* blood." He said it with a distinguishable firmness that resonated in the depth of his voice. "I wanted to be yours. But it wasn't my place to take your night away, even when you looked a vision. I saw you walk in... just the sight of you, no one in that bar could look away...that cream dress, your hair like a halo around your head, your skin glowing. You deserved to have your own night, not hijacked by my desires. No matter how stunning I thought you looked. I'd always have the time from the hallway."

"So, I resigned to allow what happened happen. If no one bought you a drink, I'd spend the evening with you, but I wouldn't be selfish. I've spent so much of my life being selfish. Then Dom approached you. He was an Ancient. He was a True Alpha. I let him have you when I shouldn't have given him the chance. I should have been selfish."

My head swam with heat at his admission.

"Can I be selfish, Joceline?" He leaned forward and took my cheeks in his hands, not squeezing, but holding me still. Not that I would have moved. "As much as I should have been that night enough to ask you to rewrite the blank page."

"Rhys," I whispered, unable to reply. My volatility pulled me in different directions; focusing enough to reply felt impossible. "Is that—"

"You're sacred to me. I never wanted to be a Lord, never, but you...I am only Lord to you, for you, because of you. It doesn't have to be anything other than me being your Lord if you'll have me."

"My Lord?"

"Do you want me to be?" With his eager eyes fixed on me, he laid his sire title down and gave me the power to sanctify it. My breath shook, and a nervous smile emerged. His head tilted slightly to the side, a brow raised as he awaited my response. "Am I your Lord?"

My fangs unsheathing caused my jaw to slacken before I replied, "Yes." I surprised myself with how easily I answered. For years, I wanted to be someone else's, for them to want me, to claim me. But, Rhys...he sought my claim.

He was *my* Lord.

"We were robbed of the proper consummation of our blood. We can change that," he offered. I nodded. He came forward, one hand snaking around my midsection and the other around the back of my neck to pull me closer to him. Our bodies were almost flush against each other, and when his head nuzzled into the crook of my neck, I closed my eyes. "Do you trust me?"

"Yes."

"Will you rewrite that page with me?"

"Yes."

"Lean into it."

The sting of his fangs puncturing my skin forced an exclamation out of me. Before long, the pain it caused faded into something straddling the line between throbbing heat and pleasure. Using the little time he could before the punctures healed, he pulled back and drew at the wound to take my essence into his mouth. When my blood left my body and entered his, I felt it as if it was connected to me like nerves. I could feel my magic fracture- if " fracture " was the right word- and fade into him, but it was happy to do so. It widened the cord of empathy that tethered us to each other. The satisfaction of not only feeding on blood but of taking it from me specifically caused the cord to vibrate.

Lost in the feeling, I barely noticed the electric pulse of my skin and artery healing. It didn't last long; within a minute, it was completely closed. He pulled away and I took in the sight of him, his aura brighter around him, his cheeks reddened slightly. Not a drop had been wasted, safe for a wet sheen on his bottom lip that tinted it darker.

"Take me."

Was it an order? Or request? A plead?

I lifted myself up, and then moved so I straddled his hips, neither of us caring that we were hardly a few feet from the front door. The horror show of my dirtied clothes, the punctures through the fabric from my fight, he acknowledged none of it. None of that mattered. Looking down at him, fangs drawn, my body hummed with anticipation. The attraction I naturally had for him that I tried to fight through, the one that I chalked up to our coupling, but I accepted now as authentic, ached.

"My Lord." And he was. When I said it, eyes locked with him, his fangs lowered to their peak. They weren't long, but I could see them as his mouth hung open, much like mine.

Dom would never have that title. But Rhys, he earned it. For all his overbearing protectiveness, his know-it-all attitude that drove me crazy at times, and the worlds apart we were in more than just personality type, he never hurt me.

He exposed his neck to me, a mutual consent from him to be taken and for me to choose to take him. I lowered myself and bit into his carotid artery, not as I would if he were my prey, but with a gentle grace. My fangs didn't tear at the artery, only puncturing it enough for a drink. His arms enveloped me and drew me as close to him as he could manage. As soon as the blood spilled past my lips and onto my tongue, my restless soul found peace. The guilt, the shame, the rage quieted. The world quieted.

He was my Lord, now.

I didn't want it to end. The blood, the bond, the pleasure of that moment. I coveted every second of it. Sacrilegious as it was, we exchanged the sacrament of our bodies on a level I'd never experienced before. Not with anyone or any imagined entities. He may have been my Lord, my

Sire, but from just one taste of his blood, I knew I had become the whole of his creation. He would scorch the Earth for that silly girl he saw in the hallway of the Avery. The drunk girl who was twerking one minute and bawling her eyes out the next. For *me*.

My breath shook when I finally pulled away from the bite, surprised that it wasn't fully healed. Before I could react, he used his hold on me to roll us so that he hovered over me, the movement causing blood to splash onto the hardwood. The aroma of it intoxicated me as it played off the euphoria of the exchange.

He lifted himself up as he unbuttoned his shirt, and I brought my palm to my face, biting hard into the space between my thumb and pointer finger, tugging the wound open before I released it so that the blood flowed. Shirt falling off his frame, he reached out and grabbed my hand, lifting it to his lips so that he could take it in. All of it didn't make it into his mouth, and it dripped down his chest, exciting my view of his sculpted chest with the stark contrast of porcelain and crimson. Our blood stained the floor, our clothes, our skin. But it was ours and no one could take that from us.

"May I?" He gestured to my ruined outfit.

Heat flared my cheeks again as my eyebrows shot up and I nodded with unneeded enthusiasm. Even at a moment like that, I could manage to be just a little unserious. But that was the me he saw in that hallway, the me I wanted to get back.

He nodded, mimicking me, making me bite my lip and giggle.

"Yes," I whispered.

His hands came down and relieved me of every article of clothing I had on, one by one. He took his time, barely grazing my skin if he made contact at all. The small traces of touch from him were tantalizing after he had pulled himself away from holding me moments before. Every time his fingertip touched me, an electric sensation surged to the anchor of my hips, intensifying our shared desire. His aura had not only strengthened, but so had mine. The vibrant shimmer of them became more intense.

Completely bare before him for the first time, I was surprised to find myself comfortable. Free, even. All of my exposed flesh laid out meant that I'd experience his voltaic touch on every inch of my body he explored. At first, he ran his fingers along my sides, and I moaned and giggled at the stimulation the actions caused through our coupling, my eyes closing so that it enhanced my sensitivity.

Ever since I'd been turned into a vampire, I wondered what sex and carnal pleasure was anymore, if they were anything compared to drinking blood. As his fingers traced my breasts and down my navel, I knew it was just as good.

I couldn't remember the last time I'd experienced as much exhilaration without even getting to the actual sex. Would I be able to handle it? When his lips took the place of his hands, I was on the verge of the purest form of ecstasy. Then, drops of blood came down onto my hips and my eyes opened at the sensation.

Looking down, I watched it drip from his mouth. Our coupling amplified the feeling of the liquid hitting my skin, morphing every physical sensation into bliss. My mind clouded, so close to losing myself in him. The fog within it was thick and hazy, so heavy I couldn't concentrate on anything but our two bodies.

"Rhys."

My voice was different things at once. It was a whine. A call. A beg. An order.

"Yes?"

"Yes."

Absolution was in my voice. He heeded it.

Making quick work of his slacks, my mouth gaped open when he entered me. The satisfaction of penetration was mutual; the ability to feel it from both sides forced me to whimper, my brows furrowed as I struggled to stay afloat in the pleasure of it. The feeling of him rocking into me, inside of me, connected to me, consumed every piece of me. The world only existed within that feeling.

"My—" He wavered when he was buried deep inside of me. "Blood." Then his thrusts picked up with urgency, working to satiate that hunger in both of us. Our breaths grew faster and faster, until I was left panting, skin covered in bloody sweat mixed with the pure red coating us.

As he took me, I tried to keep my eyes open, watching him as he did the same, his eyes venturing to adore the movement of my breasts and hips, his hands holding me by the thighs. But my eyes kept closing as my head fell back until he slowed again, as if he knew exactly what I needed without me having to say it. Speaking would have proven too difficult. I was too busy letting myself expel every other noise his body coaxed out of me with each thrust.

I gasped as he slowly, deeply pushed himself all the way inside me. His body lowered so that he could hold me to him and feel the shock of the contact as we were entwined.

"Rhys, it's—"

"Close..." he panted, but there was a questioning inflection there despite my certainty we shared the same build up. I bit my lip, and he strengthened his strokes, his breaths getting faster while his rhythm quickened. I bit down even harder, fangs breaking skin with no resistance, and I cried out as I let myself lean into the pain it caused.

Before a drop could be wasted, his lips crashed into mine, the collision of our kiss the most forceful act he'd committed the entire time. I tried to gasp into his open mouth, but my instincts instead forced me to bite his lip instead, desperate to have our blood become one again as our lips danced against each other.

As soon as that crimson hit my tongue and polluted my own, it was too much. I yelled out, eyes clamped shut, body rigid. My entire being lit on fire as I surrendered. Rhys groaned as his own orgasm approached, but it wasn't until I had recovered my own senses and opened my eyes that I caught the moment of sheer pleasure on his face barely a second later.

As he collapsed beside me, breathing hard, I lifted myself onto my elbows, looking down at our bloodied bodies and the mess on the floor. Unable to stop myself, I erupted into laughter, which caused him to roll so he faced me. Looking at his face only caused the laughter to grow, shaking my hair and shoulders.

"Dom and I just swore we'd kill one another, a human died in the crosshairs, and this is the way I ended my night."

"What?"

An exasperated breath escaped my lips as I began to gather my clothes. I knew he wouldn't be pleased to have learned the information, but I also wasn't sure if I was ready to unpack it fully either. I likely said it so flippantly because I knew I'd psych myself out if I had time to think it through.

"Very soon either he's going to kill me or I'm gonna kill him."

I stood up, clothes bundled against my chest and walked to my room. A heat started reaching me from Rhys, but he didn't say anything. I was grateful. I needed a shower, and showers weren't usually accompanied by lectures from someone you just had bloodied sex with on the foyer floor.

As I stood in the bathroom, eyes watching water pour from an over-sized rainfall shower head, the emotional high from our shared sexual experience started to wane. The vulnerability of my nudity sent the available heat to my cheeks and stomach. The longer it stayed there, the more my recent actions made my stomach knot up. As steam began to fog the mirrors, I stepped into the water, relaxing clenched muscles.

I didn't regret sleeping with Rhys.

Neither did I regret the events that had transpired the night before at Slevin's sept.

That didn't mean they didn't muddy the waters. I'd been so lonely; suddenly, it was as if I needed fewer men. Even the supposedly elusive Dom wasn't as far away as I thought he had been. I stood motionless under the water, eyes trained on the floor and mulled it over, circling back again as soon as I thought I was done.

My gratitude and trust for Rhys had been solidified, yet it didn't change the small part of me holding onto angst at his letting my attack happen in the first place. That piece of me took hold and pushed against his decisions. Inaction allowed my attack. Inaction allowed so many attacks. Inaction would let Dom get away.

If our blood was consummated, he understood why I made my choices. My apprenticeship may have amplified my emotions, but one year, five, ten, one hundred years couldn't dull my rage.

He'd have to trust me.

An hour passed until I forced myself to escape my steaming oasis. As relaxing as it was, I had to get some rest. Tomorrow was the beginning of Dom's end.

CHAPTER THIRTY-ONE

THE NEXT EVENING, I woke to an empty loft.

While I did appreciate the space, I also expected the complete opposite from Rhys, but that likely came from my very human past experiences. Either way, when my eyes opened, I had a tighter grip on who I was and what I wanted.

Unlocking my phone, I went into my texts with Rhys to see new notifications.

> I have a work thing but will return right after. I'd say to wait for me if it'd do any good. At least tell me if you do anything ill-advised, please, dove. XX

I gnawed my bottom lip and exited the conversation. What I was about to do was incredibly ill-advised by his standards, but I had to do it nonetheless. I didn't have the luxury of taking my time. Dom knew my real name, likely since the moment we met. He'd been following me the whole time. I didn't need to give him any more advantages. Not when I planned to be his reaper. I dressed in an outfit that both accentuated my curves and also didn't make it seem as though I was trying to draw attention to my body.

I had a particularly licentious Austrian to visit.

Dietrich insinuated that he had information for me because he told me the price. While my visit with Charmed technically brought me closer to Dom, it didn't give me the details I needed, like locations. Dietrich had leads to the locations I was after, I knew he did. I wasn't leaving until

SONIA BLADE

I got what he knew. No one else would die because I was unprepared. What happened last night in Oak Lawn would never happen again.

When I pulled up to the guard shack of Jungbrunnen, the same Brute sat behind the glass and when I rolled my window down, he gave me an unenthusiastic raised eyebrow.

"Tommy." I greeted, smiling ear to ear. He didn't give me the courtesy of a response but pressed a button and opened the wrought iron vehicle gate. I winked and closed my window, prompting him to roll his eyes. As a Brute, he only had me beat by one rung on the totem pole, which should have humbled him. Perhaps that single gap was wider than I imagined.

I parked in the circular drive by the entrance, where Dietrich stood at the open doorway to welcome me. Despite his smaller stature next to the fifteen-foot doors, he radiated presence. His aura shimmered in shades of mostly deep indigo and burgundy, bits of magic sparkling in the early dusk.

When I exited my car, his pouty lips turned upward into a smile, our coupling spreading his satisfaction for my return into my chest as a latent sense of victory.

I sighed and smiled back.

I needed to form my own opinions about the Sovereign Leader whose blood ran through my veins. Rhys had to trust me as I did him. Dietrich was a means to an end. I wouldn't be distracted by his estate or its riches, whether objects or people.

"Hello, Dietrich." My voice heightened enough to convey a false sense of elation. Of course, my body hummed at our proximity, but I needed to make it seem like I leaned harder into it, that being near him had me giddy. Approaching the open doorway, he received me with out-stretched arms, and embraced me as he kissed my cheeks.

"My evening started quite hum-drum, but seeing you approach has revitalized my old soul. And what I see..." He motioned to the outfit, made up of black flare jeans and a black corset style vest over an opened white button up. "Beautiful, my blood. You are a vision."

I did appreciate the careful way he spoke, making every person think they were the center of his attention. And maybe we were for a single moment in time. I had an inkling he could make a moment feel like a lifetime. "Pleasure seeing you again, too." His smile spread. He ushered me inside, closing the heavy doors as if they were feathers, though they groaned at the movement of their immense weight.

"Tell me, what brings you to me?" He stole my gaze and held it as he asked, stopping so we remained in the cavernous grand entryway. "What pleasures do you seek?"

"Yours." I answered, with all the confidence of an actor on a stage. "The price for your service was my tribute."

His eyes lit up and he took a step toward me. "Yes," he whispered.

"Dom is still in Dallas and he's watching me. If you're Sovereign, you know where he's at. I know you do. So, I'll pay your price." An unspoken excitement charged the air between our bodies.

"Don't you care to know how expensive the price is first?"

"I don't have time for bartering and playing coy. Name it."

He closed the space between us, his arm holding me to him by the small of my back. The scent of frankincense enveloped me while maintaining a subtlety in its strength, the fragrance on the crook of his neck and his wrists. "The promise of a taste."

"A taste?"

"Exactly as much," he verified. His other hand joined the first at my back, locking me to him.

The embrace itself didn't bother me, I knew my part to play. Carnal pleasures and touch were not only the means he used to seduce others; they were the means I could use to do the same to him. I could easily play his target, the newcomer ready to be corrupted. The public exposure of the entryway heated my face in earnest, though. "Of what?"

"Each other," he answered. My head craned back and he laughed at the reaction. "Fret not, kleiner liebhaber." His voice lowered, playing on the intimacy of our position. He walked us backward a few paces until we were against the front door. "We need no privacy in this exchange."

"Are you—" I cut myself off, trying to collect myself. "Are you sure about that?" I fought the urge to fall into his snare. The intensity of his honey eyes tied knots in my core I wanted him to unravel like a cherry stem in his mouth. My fangs lowered. No. I had control. There wouldn't be a repeat of my last time at Jungbrunnen. I hadn't lost sight of my goal.

He huffed, then slacked his jaw so I could see his own fangs were lowered. "I know where your mind resides. You are Dom's tonight. When a door closes behind us, and it will, your undivided attention will belong to me, Meine Liebe." My mind swam and I tensed my legs. My core temperature rose ten degrees. I nodded. "Tonight, give me your bloodied lips in a kiss as a promise that I will see you again."

It just had to be a damn kiss. It had to be intimate. Fuck.

"Yes, my Sovereign."

The acceptance stung, and I pushed aside my guilt. If he was a Sovereign Leader, I could not deny him the title. Rhys understood that. Hell, he had come to terms with the culture of titles to the point that he accepted them being used toward him in public. And no matter what, Rhys remained my only Lord. These were just words.

"How sweet it is to hear those words from your lips," he said. "Those beautiful lips." He grabbed my chin with two fingers. "Since he took his leave from my sept and from the Sovereignty, I have found little reason to be proud of my protégé, but you..."

I bit my lip first, to show my eagerness to cement our transaction. His eyes dropped to watch the beads of blood form on my bottom lip, the corners of his lips curling up. He wasted no time in doing the same, puncturing both sides of his bottom lip with his fangs. As the blood from my lip began to slide down my chin, he kissed me. Our blood mingled together, and I moaned not only at the taste of it. His pleasure invaded me, and the strength of his age and power reverberated through me. A firecracker lit in my chest. He deepened the kiss, a hand trailing down until it made its way to the back of my thigh, which he used to hoist my leg up while pushing me harder against the door. I yipped in surprise at how smoothly he managed the action, and hearing that he forced a noise out of me only excited him further. God damn it. He was skilled with his lips. His hands gripped me harder as he kissed me, never imposing his tongue. The interplay of our lips felt desired, not forced.

When he pulled away, I furrowed my brow and exhaled, barely abstaining from leaning forward into him. I hated to admit it, but I didn't want it to end. He sighed, the breath slow as it escaped his reddened lips. I swallowed and straightened up as he released me.

"Where is Dom?"

He laughed, looking down at me with something different behind his eyes that hadn't been there a minute before.

"Five years ago we bared hunting exercises. Controlled hunting they called it." He started, his hand still holding my leg up in place. "As if the name made it sound any less barbaric. And barbaric it was," he continued. "The locations, however, are still property of The Sovereignty. Three of those locations are in north Texas." My breathing stalled. "If I were looking for an Ancient True Alpha with a penchant for hunting things, those three locations would be the first on my list. I'll send them to you." He released my leg to use the hand to wipe away the trail of my blood from my chin, which he then brought to his lips. "Save my number, won't you. You'll need it."

"Do you—"

He rattled off my phone number with ease, the display a show of political reach and leverage. "Please, do try to not get yourself killed. Saying it'd be a waste is an understatement. Rhys's eye for beauty has not dimmed. Ich liebe schöne sachen. Du bist eine echt schöne. But I can not deploy my resources for a vendetta. You two are on your own. Contrary to what humans think of us, we have checks and balances in places. There is order." He took a step back. "Keep your schedule free in April." He didn't ask if I could free the time up, he instructed it. Then he turned and walked away, with effortless swagger in every step. I blinked and rubbed my mouth clean on the back of my hand.

Chapter Thirty-Two

As I DROVE AWAY from Jungbrunnen, my lips buzzed where they'd been in contact with Dietrich's, the aftertaste of his blood on my tongue. My phone vibrated on the seat beside me three times in quick succession. I didn't need to look at it to tell who was texting me. Dietrich had already sent over the addresses, as promised. Not that I expected him to lie, as it wouldn't benefit him, but he'd skirted the truth about knowing Dom when I first met him in order to hold his cards close to his chest. It wasn't beyond him to manipulate. And now I owed him.

On the list of those I owed, another person sat at the top. My mama.

The world didn't end when I spent time with the kiddos, and I owed her a visit. An explanation. A chance to see her daughter before I may or may not get myself killed. After what Dom had done to me, I had no assurance that I'd walk out of there. I wanted to see her one last time before I attempted the impossible.

When I pulled up to the house, my stomach had somehow made its way into my throat. I shook my hands out, knees bouncing. "It's fine, you're fine, it's fine." Despite the reassurances, I couldn't shake the nerves. She knew something was different with me. What if she rejected me? It'd break me. I loved her so much. She and Dad meant the world to me. And that meant it didn't matter what the outcome was.

I took a deep breath.

After my mutation, I didn't stop loving her. She wouldn't stop loving me. I was different, yes. But, as Slevin had said at his sept, things happen to us, and we can't be expected not to change as a result of it. My mutation was a result of my attack. But I was still Joceline Fuentes. Rhys

305

saved *me*. He didn't kill me. And the me he saved wanted to be with her mom.

I swallowed my fear of rejection and walked into the house. I held my breath as I waited to pinpoint where everyone was. TVs buzzed in bedrooms, but the main one in the living room played something that sounded an awful lot like my comfort show. The lump returned to my throat but for a completely different reason. There wasn't a thing on the planet that sounded better at that moment than what I was about to do.

My shoes were off and scooted into the corner of the foyer before I tiptoed into the living room. On my way, I caught the lingering scent of meatloaf and mashed potatoes. Everyone was watching tv as they let their dinners settle. My lip trembled as I approached the open doorway. Mom sat snuggled up on the corner of the L-shaped couch in the same spot she always was. The spot that had been hers since they'd gotten the things years before. The closet spot to the TV had a recliner built into it. There was no way anyone but her was going to get that prime real estate. She had her hair wrapped and her pajama dress was covered by a large quilted blanket. Grandma Loritta's quilt. Seeing such a familiar vision finally brought me the warmth of happiness I craved from my human side.

She caught me as soon as I passed the threshold of the room. At first, she sat up, mouth opening to say something, but after looking at my face, her mouth closed. A mama saw one of her babies that needed her. She lifted her arm up and I took no time in crawling under it.

For an hour, we watched The Love Boat without saying a word, laughing at the camp of it all like we always did. I remembered each episode word-for-word, thanks to my mutation, but as much as I wanted to say the lines out loud, I couldn't do anything to distract away from hearing her voice. I wanted to pay attention to everything about that time with her. The smell of her fading perfume barely lingered on her skin after a long day. The feeling of her stomach as she breathed, because I had moved and laid my head in her lap. Her rubbing my upper arm mindlessly. The way her laugh was a lot higher than her speaking voice but still sounded like it fit the way she looked. All of it.

As an episode ended, the need to talk to her bubbled up in me until I couldn't ignore it any longer. "I'm sorry." Was all that managed to get out. It wasn't enough. She deserved an explanation, and she deserved the truth. But that didn't mean she deserved to have everything she knew snatched from her, including her peace of mind. The real world didn't have to steal my family into its darkness. I would remain its only casualty.

"You don't have to apologize to me. What you've been through, what's happened, it's a lot."

I pursed my lips as if it would keep my eyes from watering. Then I sniffled. I couldn't cry in from of her, she'd see the pink tears. She only knew half of it, the tip of the iceberg, but she still gave me so much grace. "I know, but I panicked. I ran."

"It was a little weird, the running."

I laughed and she chuckled.

"I know," I said. "I wish I could tell you how crazy everything's been."

"I'm here when you want to, if you want to." She rubbed my arm. "Or we can just watch TV. We can do whatever helps you through it. I'm here for you, baby girl. Always will be. No matter what happens." She squeezed my upper arm. "I know you miss your father, I know you and him were close. You're such a daddy's girl. I was a little jealous when you were young." I laughed again to keep from crying. "I know you miss him."

"I miss him so much."

"Me too," She added. Her eyes glazed over with tears that never fell.

"I miss you, too," I said back. "So much. I just...I can't come over as much, right now. Things are changing. I'm getting back on my feet. It's complicated. I can't really explain more than that, but I'm not avoiding you because you're not dad. I promise. I'm still your baby girl. It's not because I don't want to tell you, it's because I can't yet." Or ever. "I'll get better. I'm healing. I'm sorry."

"I love you." She patted my cheek, and I put my palm over her hand. "You ain't got to say a damn thing else. That's all that matters. I'm here for you. Okay?"

I nodded, sniffling again.

"I love you, too."

I leaned my head back and watched TV with her until she dozed off. Even without looking at her, I could hear her heartbeat and breathing become slower. I glanced at her serene face and smiled before returning my focus to the TV. I didn't feel the urge to leave—not just yet. Although my body didn't biologically recognize her as it once did, my heart still did. That connection was what I needed to hold on to.

At nearly three in the morning, long after the noise from Marley and Byron's rooms had died off and the season of the show ended, I got up from the couch with enough grace to keep my mom from waking. Not that a light touch was needed. She slept heavy as all get out. It's what allowed the kiddos to sneak out with ease when they ventured to.

I snuck over to their rooms, opening their doors just enough to peak inside but not enough to wake them. They were both passed out. Their rooms were messes. Even Byron, who thought he was pretty organized for a teenager, had stuff strewn around and half the contents of his backpack on the floor. I rolled my eyes and smiled. Teenagers.

I locked the front door behind me and took a deep breath. The neighborhood was dead quiet. When I inhaled, the cold had a distinct smell. One I couldn't describe but also couldn't ignore. The lights of the streetlamps were a light orange, casting a warm glow despite the chilly air. Far off, a car drove by. I didn't have many nights like this left. Quiet, peaceful nights with human family. But, while I could, I would have as many as possible.

CHAPTER THIRTY-THREE

> You busy?

Define busy...

> I could use another pair of nostrils. Can you meet me at an address?

Nostrils? You trying to sniff something out?

> Kinda.

Send the address, depending on the distance, give me an hour. Is there imminent danger?

> Idk yet.

Got it. Wait for me. See you soon.

AFTER THE QUALITY TIME with my mom, the next night I was refreshed and ready to tackle the addresses that Dietrich had sent me. Rhys insisted that he'd be back in a few hours following a meeting with a client, something his assistant Gabriella had scheduled months ago that couldn't be pushed back. That was fine. A Brute may have been better suited for what I was doing, anyway.

I plugged the address into the navigation after passing it off to Slevin. It calculated an easy forty-five-minute drive north, almost to the end of the expressway, past McKinney. Judging by its relative location north of the metroplex, Slevin might beat me there if he wasn't wrapped up too long in finishing his prior engagements. Either way, an ominous weight sank into the pit of my stomach.

Having pushed ten over the speed limit the majority of the drive up, I arrived at the location a few minutes early. The vast, flat parking lot sat empty, occupied only by light poles with yellowed plastic covers. I surveyed the lot from my car. At some point, it must have been an industrial building. It had two stories but was massive. The only thing that trumped its size was how decrepit it was. The once white or grey of the exterior was now a creamy color, and mustard stains dried in their path of dripping down the sides. None of the exterior or interior lights were on, and where once had been some business logo, the gray outline of the sign long removed remained.

As I focused on the details of the doors and windows, boarded up, Slevin's muscle car roared up the access road behind me. He parked next to me, a couple of rows from the front. Having him there dissolved the bile in my throat. I exited my car at the same time as him.

"Joce." My name fell from his lips with a partial tone I tried not to read into. Too many men, too much other shit to do.

"Slevin." My attempt to sound casual hardly worked. "Thank you."

He gave me a single nod, his lips drawn into a hard line as he assessed where we were. "You smell it?" He asked.

I turned back to the building, which was a good fifteen yards ahead of us. I took a deep breath in and released it out of my now parted lips. It was difficult to place, but something smelled bad in there. A memory came to mind, something forgotten, or more accurately, pushed away. It was a summer weekend from years ago when we had some steaks left out in the backyard, uncooked, because my father experienced an emergency cardiac episode that took us all to the hospital- one of his first heart attacks. We turned off the propane grill but forgot about the meat as we packed into the car to follow the ambulance. The steaks remained there for a couple of days while we worried about more pressing matters, but we quickly noticed them when they turned.

Things inside that building were rotting.

"Is that..."

"Dead bodies." He answered, rolling his shoulders. I sucked my bottom lip in. Stones dropped in my stomach. "Is he in there?"

"Dom? I don't think so. I don't feel anything." I regretted the admittance until I remembered it was Slevin to hear it.

"Joce, are you?"

"Yeah," I answered. "Apparently I had a few drops of his blood in my system when I mutated."

His expression faltered. "I'm sorry."

"Thanks." I wanted to tell him not to worry about it, that it wasn't a big deal. But that was a lie. Instead, I diverted. "Dietrich gave me three addresses, this is the closest one." I chose to let the words lie, without explanation.

"What are the other addresses?"

"Why?"

"Because I'm familiar with places that smell like this," Slevin answered, his eyes as serious as I'd ever seen them, his trademark goofiness nowhere to be seen.

I pulled my phone out and read the other two addresses out loud. One was a farm-to-market road off a small highway I'd never heard of before which was not uncommon in a state as big as Texas, and the other was an address in Well Springs, which was west of the far side of the metroplex.

"That's what I thought." he grimaced. "It's controlled hunting."

"That's what Dietrich said." I started. "Is that what I think it is?"

"Where they round up humans, sometimes Creepers, Proles, and Brutes, and hunt them for sport? Yes, it is."

The stones in my stomach doubled in weight. I couldn't imagine hunting people as if they were animals. I didn't even like the idea of hunting them for their blood with the intent to keep them alive. Since my first night at Lenny's, I hadn't gotten my blood from anything other than a willing donor or a bag. Hunting animals wasn't even a pastime I explored in my human years.

"Why do you know that?"

"I barely made it out of one alive, myself."

"Here?"

"No, up in New England," he corrected, and my brow furrowed. "Then why do those addresses mean anything to you?"

He ran his tongue over his teeth in contemplation, which worried me. "My sept isn't only a breeder sept. We used to crash hunts before Dietrich prohibited them." With his answer, my brows shot straight up. Is that what Charmed meant when he commented about Mary and her little operation? "But that's beside the point. Hunts haven't been organized in Dallas in any official capacity for years."

I stuffed my hands hard into my pocket and gestured with my head to the building. We both began walking toward it. The heavy stones of disgust and anxiety shifted and moved about my insides, making me nauseous. Though, that could've been attributed to the growing stench of death. I spotted an industrial-sized lock as we closed the distance to the front entrance. Before I could even attempt to kick it in, Slevin moved ahead of me and did the honors, breaking the lock and the door on the first try. The debris went flying inside from the force. Dust and even more odor than I expected rushed toward us. I gagged, my mouth salivating as a warning. I pulled an arm up and covered my lower face with it. My eyes tried to take in what I could outside the doors.

As I lifted a leg to walk forward. Slevin, who was a few feet inside, held up his hand to stop me from entering. "What?" I mouthed the word. He took a handful of exaggerated deep breaths that brought his chest up inches. As I tried to replicate his breaths, I could only smell old gore, the flurry of it all too much to gather information for the obvious death that had once taken place here.

"The blood is not entirely fresh, but it's not very old either."

"What does that even mean?"

"It's days and weeks, not months or years. And there's also..." He trailed and took a few more deep breaths. "Cleaning supplies." He shook his shoulders out. "I need to shift."

My eyes widened and I hitched my breath for a moment before releasing it. While the idea of him shifting briefly came to mind, I hadn't thought he'd do it. "What? Right now?"

"Yeah. So, I need some space. Take my clothes and put them together by the door." He shrugged off his jacket as he gave me the instructions. My cheeks tingled.

"Uh, yeah, sure," I stuttered out. "I can do that." My heart rate spiked a little as he handed me the jacket and the t-shirt he then removed. I folded the items against my chest, failing to stop staring at him. "What are you going to turn into?"

"You'll see," he answered, leaning down to untie his boots and then kick them off. All the modesty in me screamed to look away as he then removed his belt and started undoing his jeans. If I looked away, I wouldn't see him shift, and I desperately wanted to see how it happened.

"Do you need me too—"

"Turn away?"

I nodded. He chuckled, leaving a lingering smirk on his lips afterward. "Do you want to see?"

I nodded again with unnecessary enthusiasm, and then my eyes bulged for a moment, brows shooting up. "Shift," I specified. "I want to see you shift, not your..."

"I know." He laughed again, and I had to focus on the dark space behind his head to thwart my embarrassment. "Just focus on my face for the first part."

My head bobbed up and down, and I did exactly as I was told, except for the moments he leaned down to lower and then kicked off his pants and underwear. I couldn't look that low, no matter the curiosity. As his head came back up, he caught my eyes, and we stayed there for a moment before I mouthed the words, "Thank you."

It was his turn to nod, then he backed up a few steps and rolled his head first, then his shoulders got a few turns before he shook out his arms. The green aura that floated around him, with its calm lime color, became more vibrant. The density of it grew thicker until it nearly swirled with clouds like Rhys's. My mouth slacked open, words lost to me, as the air bristled with electricity.

His skin darkened as he kept rolling his shoulders, spreading over his back and onto his chest, moving downward. But, as my eyes adjusted, trying to focus on his face, it dawned on me that it wasn't darkening, but sprouting hair. His muscles bulged and contorted to create a new shape.

313

Hand of my mouth, my eyes widened as he grew in size, hunching down until he was on his knees. The longer he shifted, the more I recognized that it wasn't a dog or a cat that he resembled but something larger with a lot more bulk to it. So much more bulk.

"Oh my god."

He snarled his lips back but didn't appear to be in pain, maybe in mild discomfort or something like a deep stretch. But there wasn't pain in his dark blue eyes, which remained the same color even as they changed shape to fit in their new skull.

The skull of an American black bear.

Slevin finished his shift, and I tried to relax my eyes, but they remained wide. He shook out his head and made a noise that was not human, but I could tell he was saying some variation of a greeting, to be silly. I inhaled deeply, the scent still reminiscent of Slevin, with the slightest wild edge. As if an animal had been bathed in the soaps and colognes Slevin used.

His large head came down and nudged the remainder of his clothing toward me, and I returned to reality. "Shit, sorry." I got down on my knees and scrambled to sweep the rest of the items into my arms. In my lowered position, Slevin's head craned forward and nuzzled into the valley of my shoulder, and he grunted. The noise wasn't like the human grunt I'd grown accustomed to, which showed impatience, but a noise of familiarity or contentment. He shook his head and bumped me again until his meaning dawned on me.

My arms relaxed before I brought my hand up, and I rubbed the soft fur at the top of his head, leading him to exhale a huff of air before pushing his head into my hand. I lowered my head to nestle against his cheek and he pushed back lightly to show approval.

"Thanks."

Satisfied with my gratitude, he then took a few steps back. I gathered the clothes again and placed them neatly in a pile by the doors, then turned the flashlight on my phone to full power. I may have had exceptional sight, but it couldn't hurt to catch the details.

We ventured further in, but despite getting closer to the death and decay, I struggled to place its location relative to ours. In the silence around us, I followed the sound of Slevin's heavy paw pads as they scraped the ground, which was dusty, but surprisingly free of the amount of clutter and debris I expected. The place was abandoned but not junky. I couldn't even place how long ago it had been since business had been conducted there. If it had been used for hunting people before it was well and truly abandoned, it would be decades ago.

Past the lobby were a couple hallways, stairs, and an elevator leading to the second floor. We started on the bottom floor and the opening closest to us. Although I didn't particularly smell blood on our path, we still walked the hallway before entering into a large suite that must have had dozens of cubicles at one time. Now, only a few were left over along with some empty offices around the perimeter of the space.

The next suite was about half the size of the last, but the same. Empty space, offices, but the faintest scent of old blood. Slevin grunted and led me to one of the further offices, almost to the back wall of the suite and the building. He grunted outside the door, and my stomach knotted as I slowly opened it.

On the ground was a bloodstain so old it had turned a dark shade of brown, damn near black. Slevin walked forward and gave the stain a sniff but shook his head in a very animated way. It left no room for me to misinterpret that he cleared it.

By the time we made it through upstairs, I was beginning to lose patience. A call from Rhys activated my phone screen, drowning my face in light. I stopped moving, but Slevin continued forward up the stairs to the second-floor landing. His large body surprised me with how well it navigated the small steps. Did bears have a pretty flexible range of motion or was that all Slevin?

"Hello?"

"Where are you?"

"I'm checking out a possible lead of 75."

In the silence after my answer, I started walking forward with the phone to my ear, confident in my vision that I would catch anything important.

"North Central Expressway? How far north?"

"Pretty far. Used to be a hunting ground."

"I know the address."

315

I doubted it until I remembered that he had been an Emissary in the Sovereignty for some time. Controlled hunting hadn't been outlawed all that long. It would have been legal during his tenure.

"Of course you do." As soon as I said it, the stench of rot got stronger and Slevin roared, nothing boisterous but enough to get my attention. "I think we found something."

"What? Joceline, don't try anything. I'm on my way." I clicked off the phone, catching up with Slevin with a hand over my nose and mouth. He braced up and bared down on a door, breaking it open. As soon as the wood splintered inward, noxious smells rushed out at us. I wretched. My hand pushed harder against my mouth, the pads of my fingers making my gums ache with their force.

The bodies of about a handful of victims were inside, bloated and discolored, liquids and foam seeping from all orifices. I gagged again and turned away, forcing my eyes shut as I leaned against the outside wall by the doorframe. I'd never seen or smelled anything like it. What in the fuck was wrong with Dom? How could he just use and dispose of these people as if they were like fast food wrappers?

Anger spread until it pulsed in my temples.

"I can't..." I started to say but was overtaken with the need to dry heave. I wretched for a few seconds, but nothing came up. Recovering, I continued. "I can't go in there."

Slevin gave a low growl, motioning with his head to the area behind me. He chuffed and gave a series of noises, but I got the gist of it. He wanted me to take some space. He'd look inside. Even though he had shifted into a bear, I didn't struggle to understand him as much as I thought I would. The sounds he made, paired with his movements, communicated effectively. No matter the physical changes his brain made to fit into the skull it now inhabited, it still functioned to allow him to "talk" to me. I appreciated it more than he knew. I couldn't go any closer.

He disappeared inside for a period of time I couldn't pinpoint. After a few minutes, I wiped the spit from my mouth and chin. No bloody vomit came out but I damn sure tried. Every time I thought the worst of it had past, I catch a glimpse of the bodies through the doorway and the world would wag and wiggle until my stomach spasmed.

Inherent evil as a concept had been something I had discussed at points in my life. Hypothetical conversations my ex or my siblings and I brushed on when late nights couldn't lull us to sleep. Was anyone truly evil? Did evil, in the form from story books and folklore truly exist? I thought I knew the answer before. I thought it was learned. People couldn't just be evil in the very soul of them. But what I saw in front of me...what Dom was capable of. I knew no way to describe his malice but pure, unadulterated evil.

I rested my back against the far wall of the hallway, panting to keep the need to wretch some more at bay when Slevin reemerged. He gestured back to the front with his head and made a few grunting noises.

"Back to the front?"

He nodded his large head.

I didn't have to be told twice. We headed straight back to the entrance and as he situated himself by the clothes that were inside the door, I turned my attention to some point off in the distance with my back to him.

Moments later, Slevin's hand rested on my shoulder, his touch especially warm. I turned to see him already clothed, minus the jacket, which was thrown over one shoulder. His aura danced around him, as if excited by the two shifts it had done in a short period of time. The sparks of magic in the area glittered and shined, the smoke of it a little more opaque than normal.

"Did you get anything useful? Do you think Dom killed those people?"

He offered me a smirk, but it lacked optimism. It was almost sympathetic. "There's no way for me to know that without having smelled him first, but I can say that it wasn't a regular hunt. So, it's probable. I could smell someone else there, on all of them. Likely the killer, and judging by their wounds, or at least what I could still see of the wounds, it was a vampire." I perked up. "But," he added, "the scent is fading and judging by those bodies, he hasn't been here in days."

"Fuck," I groan out. We'd have to check the other addresses. How could Dietrich let him come into the city and toss bodies around, leaving them to rot? Was that how our kind acted? If this was a representation of what the Sovereignty considered tolerable, then I had a long list of grievances to air. Humans didn't deserve to be treated like expendable targets. They weren't deer in a forest. They weren't playthings. Lower kin my ass. I'd never treat humans with such disregard. Dietrich's honeyed words weren't going to sweet talk his way out of this. I couldn't wait to see his ass again so I could read him the riot act.

"It's okay. We'll figure this out," Slevin said.

"Your sept stopped these?"

"This isn't controlled hunting. Controlled hunts were orchestrated on the highest levels with deep pockets. Bodies weren't left behind. The Legion cleaned everything up when the last target was killed. You could walk into an arena the next day and never suspect a thing."

"Jesus...you survived that?"

"Barely. I took a couple years to myself after I mutated. I wanted to find my own way. That way led me to the Boston faction." The world faction set off a million warning bells in my head. Factions objected to the Sovereignty. I had read as much in all of the articles in the public records available in the Cave browser. Factions were violent groups that attacked the Sovereignty for existing, despite their efforts to only help our kind and provide resources. It read like propaganda. I take everything the Sovereign posted publicly as true, especially if someone like Slevin worked against them. Slevin was the kindest vampire I had met aside Rhys, and his sept mates had been nothing but welcoming. "Just my luck on the timing. They were raided and the members became targets for a hunt. A neighboring faction crashed it. Only three of us got away, me included. Everyone else was killed."

"I'm sorry."

He huffed a laugh, but not of happiness. "Yeah, I know." He put a hand on my back. "I know." Was all he offered. I couldn't press him on it anymore. I wanted to. There were so many sides to this world, so many things to understand. But...later.

"Thanks for—"

Before I finished speaking, my phone buzzed in my pocket to a very specific rhythm, my family's vibration pattern. I forwarded the call without looking, not ready to talk to them after facing such a grisly scene. The trivial teenage escapades of my siblings could wait until I didn't see dead bodies behind my eyelids.

Seconds later, the phone buzzed again; I forwarded it. Marley always called twice. The baby of the family thought everyone waited at her beck and call. She'd have to be patient.

It was when the phone buzzed a third time that a lump formed in my throat and traveled through the rest of me. Three meant an emergency. Marley's name illuminated the screen, and I answered it on speaker phone. Noticing, Slevin came to stand next to me, concern overtaking his features.

"Marley?"

"Hello, Fuil."

The heat drained from my head, sending a shiver right through me. "Dom. Goddamn it, is she alive?" My eyes stayed trained on the phone screen, but my vision blurred pink. "Did you hurt her, you sick fuck?"

Dom laughed. "Sing little bird," he ordered before the shrill sound of screaming erupted from the speakers. My grip tightened on the phone until it started to give resistance, as it threatened to lose shape. "Such a beautiful brown bird, shall I make her fly," he teased, a sadistic edge to the words.

"Don't you hurt her."

"Her? Do you mean *them*?"

Then multiple screams rang out before the call went dead. I called the number back, over and over again, but he forwarded them. "Fuck." The word barked out of me, and Slevin put a hand on my shoulder, prompting me to match his gaze.

"We'll find them."

"We don't have time to check both locations if we pick the wrong one first."

"Is there any way to track her?"

I opened up my family tracker app, which showed the last update was days before at the house. That damn thing wasn't updating live. "Damn it," I hissed. Then, my eyes went wide. "Wait, there's that one app she's always on. Snaps. If she's got it turned on, it'll show the location, too."

I opened up the Snaps app, which I only had because of my siblings. They always sent me weird video clips on it that they thought were funny, but I didn't really understand the humor. I opened up the map of my mutual friends, which were only two users. Marley and Byron.

Both of their profile picture avatars stood almost overlapping each other a ways west of the metroplex. I zoomed in and read the town name in gray writing, Well Springs.

Slevin looked down at the screen then back up at me, "The Brayer Hotel."

My brows furrowed. "That haunted abandoned hotel?"

"Not haunted. It's a hunt location. Not so much anymore, but I crashed a few hunts there in the late nineties. The town went through a rough patch in the eighties. The town square was abandoned, and the old hotel became a hunting ground until Dietrich and the rest of those assholes decided they didn't like hunts anymore. Officially."

As he finished, a car pulled up to the curb. I turned to catch Rhys jump out of the idling car and run up to us. His quick approach and urgency set me on edge more than I already was following Dom's phone call. I gasped. It wasn't until I caught the look of horror on his face, I realized I was crying.

"What happened, are you hurt? What's wrong?"

"Dom has my family."

"Your family? Inside?"

"No, in Well Springs. We only found a pile of bodies here. Old. Then he called from my sister's phone, and we tracked it. It said they're in Well Springs."

His pupils darted side to side for a few seconds before he spoke again. "I'll drive."

"Thank you for all your help," I said, turning to look at Slevin. "I owe you."

His reaction caught me off guard as he stepped forward and pulled me into his chest. Some of the residual heat from his shift remained, making it easy to melt into him as I fought back tears. We had ground to cover, there was no time for crying. "I'll see you there," Slevin said, the depth of his voice rumbling his chest against my face.

I pulled back to look at him. Did he think I expected him to come with us? I couldn't begin to expect or ask him to risk his life. Not for me, someone he hardly knew.

"No, Slevin, you—" I started, but he grabbed both of my arms at the elbows to stop me talking.

"Joce..." His signature confidence shined from behind his eyes. "You're not going in that place without me."

"No, absolutely not. You could be killed. It was risky asking you to even come here."

His responding expression was incredulous. "I've crashed hunts at that location before. I'm coming."

I swallowed my frustration. He wasn't taking no for an answer. He'd been the one to also take me to Arlington for training. He spared with me and taught me how to fight. Having him there would give me an upper hand, even if it put him at risk. I sighed, brows knit. But, I couldn't risk him. "Slevin, I can't."

"You're not stopping me."

I whined. "Don't."

"I'll see you there. I know the address."

"Fuck," I conceded. As soon as I got in the car with Rhys, he'd be following behind us and there was nothing I could do. "Fine." He nodded.

"We need blood." Rhys said as we started toward the cars.

"Is there anything on the way?" Slevin asked.

"We don't have time to hunt," I interjected.

"Ft. Worth Presby?" Slevin offered, and I frowned at the thought. Did he expect us to go rob a hospital on the way out of the metroplex? "We need guaranteed blood and a lot of it. Three pints a piece."

"Heaven help me. I'm going to regret this," Rhys said with a sigh. "Meet us at the old T&P Warehouse off 30."

"T&P Warehouse? That huge ass building outside downtown Fort Worth?" I thought aloud, and Rhys nodded. "What's at that place? Hasn't it been sitting empty for like fifty years?"

Slevin gave a laugh. "When was the last time you went that way?"

"I don't know. Maybe like eight years. Fort Worth isn't really my vibe. I barely go that way."

"Rhys already had his phone out of his pocket. "The Sovereignty paid a pretty penny to get that old train depot and they've been converting it into the largest Sovereign campus in the world. It's almost fully operational. The grand opening is in April," Rhys explained. Charmed was right.

"Please tell me we're not calling that favor into Starhemberg?" Slevin raised a brow with his question.

"Absolutely not. I've still got a few connections. The last thing we need right now is to be in Dietrich's pocket with the Sovereignty coming to Dallas."

I bit my lip. Rhys's hatred for Dietrich was one thing, but the way he said that about being in his debt...well, that had me worried. I sealed a deal in blood to get those addresses. How deep in his pocket did I just fall?

CHAPTER THIRTY-FOUR

RHYS DROVE OUT OF the lot as soon as I buckled in, and as we put distance between us and that industrial complex, gravity weighed heavier and heavier on my lungs. It pinned me to my leather seat, and I slumped down and tried not to let my imagination wander. Dom didn't see people as individuals. They weren't even food. Thinking about it, I struggled to place how he treated me now that I remembered the feral carnage he delighted in while he had me alone behind closed doors. If he did that to me, what could he do to my family?

My eyes stayed fixed on the same point on my passenger window as I attempted to distract myself from the terrible possibilities with other memories. I tried not to think about it more, but that night at the Avery Hotel wormed its way right into my headspace. I considered where I was then and where I'd been in my life the night my fate was sealed. A woman on her way to a hotel to take back her identity on a night that would change her life forever. The expectation that this would have turned out any different was laughable.

"Dove?" Rhys's voice floated into my mind, but it was so faint I assumed it was an echo of my subconscious. "Joceline?" When he spoke again. I tried to get out of my head, but I couldn't. "Joceline." He raised his voice.

My eyelids fluttered when I finally broke free of my haze. In the time I'd been lost in thought, Rhys had made a phone call, but the details of who he'd spoken to and what was said completely evaded me. I focused on Rhys, who moved his head back to the road as we approached the once-abandoned depot warehouse. My jaw lowered and my brows shot up. I sat up straighter in my seat. This was not the vacant derelict building I remembered. Not by a long shot.

We pulled up around the back of the warehouse to a newly paved parking lot lined with a tall wire fence topped with barbed wire. I had never paid much attention to the lot behind it before, but I knew this was all new. The gray concrete was without blemish, the spaces and the directional lanes were bright white. We pulled up to a small guard shack where two Brutes were lounging comfortably, but one stood as we pulled up.

"How can we help you?"

"Yes, Rhys Llewelyn for Director Nayeon."

The guard turned and clicked a few times on a laptop whose screen was obstructed from our view. "Identification, please," she asked, her eyes looking between the screen and Rhys back and forth a couple of times. Rhys pulled his driver's license from his wallet, and I craned my head to look harder at it before he handed it over. I'd never seen his ID before, and curiosity got the better of me. She studied the picture for barely a second before handing it back. "Thank you. I'll let Director Nayeon know you've arrived."

The red and white barrier lifted and before driving off, Rhys handed me the ID, having caught my attempt to see it. "Never seen a vampire's driver's license?"

"I have not."

I had assumed that they all had fake names or some bastardized version of the human names of their past, but seeing his face on a real Texas license threw me for a loop. The name was there. His smirking picture stared at me, and the address on there was correct. I reached down and put it back in the wallet. What was a trip to the DMV like for vampires?

Slevin pulled up behind us as we approached the building, the shadow of the huge thing towering over us. The yellow brick was clean, and all the windows were new and reflecting back all the nights of the surrounding area, especially the lights of the highway parallel to the south side. I marveled at the sheer size of the art deco designed historical landmark. How did the Sovereignty swing purchasing something so big and front and center to not only Dallas history, but the public in general.

Was the integration of vampires into society really so advanced? From the exterior, it didn't look nefarious or spooky. If I had driven by it with no knowledge of the paranormal, I'd have assumed the landmark had been converted into an office building. A six hundred-foot-long office building, which took the prize as the largest one I'd put eyes on, but one, nonetheless. I whistled, twisting in my seat to look all the way up the face to the eighth floor at the top, ornate tall windows decorating the corner offices. So, this was the campus opening up in April? Was that what Dietrich wanted me to keep my schedule clear for?

Rhys parked the car in the closest row to what I assumed was the back entranceway. There was a brand-new awning that ran about a hundred feet long in the middle of the building, and extended out to a valet strip of a lane where people could drive up in case they weren't going to park. As we exited the car, Slevin parked and jogged up to us. "How much do you think they sunk into this campus?" Slevin asked, jokingly. Millions. Millions upon millions.

As we approached the sliding glass doors, they automatically opened and warm air rushed us, in contrast with the winter chill we had been in. Not that it was especially cold, but the contrast was obvious, no matter how mild Texas winters were. "Behave, Slevin," Rhys ordered. Slevin put his hands up in a mock gesture of concession. We got about ten feet in and were greeted with the monotone interior, sharp angles cut into every surface available, all except a semi-circle desk with two Proles working security.

"Emissary Llewelyn?" A woman's voice broke the sterile silence that drowned us. I spotted a Korean vampire, visibly no older than twenty-one with straight dark brown hair that went down to her middle back, her skin without a single wrinkle, her dark eyes brightly reflecting the white interior around her. Her aura told a completely different story. She had to have been hundreds of years old and the shades of blue around her were deep sapphire.

"Director Nayeon, how are you?"

The two embraced in a hug, which made my brows decide to nearly hug my hairline. Older vampires didn't like physical greetings, right? The embrace was short-lived, and they pulled away from each other with wide smiles.

"I am well. And busy." She shook her head, and the smile spread. "The consolidation of forces into this campus has been quite the undertaking."

"Nothing your team can't handle. The Sovereignty is lucky to have you as their director of personnel resources."

Personnel resources?

"Such flattery, Llewelyn." She batted at his arm, loving the attention he gave. "You're the only Paramour I let try it."

Watching the way they interacted brought me back to The Pulpit and the way vampires and humans alike reacted to Rhys. Paramour wasn't just a mutation class, it was a way of life. It was a personality. I'd never seen someone so at home with talking to other people. He didn't even have to say much, but Rhys lit a fire behind their eyes.

"I'd like to introduce you to my Protégé, Joceline," Rhys pivoted and gestured to me. My cheeks flushed, and I tried not to appear meek, despite feeling about as small as an ant next to a Muse hundreds of years my senior. If she was capable of helping to run this operation, she was impressive.

"Pleased to meet you, Director."

I didn't extend my hand to her, as I had no idea if she was only touchy-feely with Rhys due to a history unknown to me. However, when she offered her own, I took it and gave it a firm shake. "The pleasure is all mine. It's such a pleasure to meet you, Joceline. Truly, a pleasure."

A Hispanic Muse with a much lighter aura that shimmered with recent activity emerged from an elevator, three bags in hand. He wore a white lab coat and had a name badge clipped to the lapel, featuring his picture and the words Sovereign Institute in bold letters at the top, a barcode below his name, Javier Torres, along with the job title hematology. Blood research.

"Nine pints of human blood. Healthy and fresh," Director Nayeon said, making a sweeping gesture between Javier and the three of us.

"You have no idea how much I appreciate this," Rhys said as Javier handed the bags over. The blood in the bags sloshed around and my fangs threatened to drop at the promise of satiation. "I'll come see you soon."

"For the summit, I hope. Or at least the gala." She responded. Rhys bowed his head. "Now, if you'll excuse me, I have a meeting with the

Sovereign Credit Union in ten minutes." She bowed her head slightly and backed away before both she and Javier hailed an elevator. The same one that Javier had come out of opened its doors, and they disappeared inside, the beginnings of small talk heard as the metal closed behind them.

"Wow," was all I could muster.

"They've really gotten good at making this seem benign," Slevin commented. I stole a glance at him and saw something darker than I usual in his eyes. Then I remembered his affiliation with factions. He would sooner see this place burn than anything else. Him being inside the newest campus, the biggest one they had...that must have set him on edge.

"Have you considered that perhaps The Sovereignty isn't the monster you think they are?" Rhys said, handing me my two bags and giving Slevin the last one. Slevin looked closely inside the bag before relaxing his arm so it lowered to his side.

"Not by a long shot."

Rhys rolled his eyes. "Come on, we've got ground to cover."

As we returned to the car, I eyed the contents of our bags, unsure about the amount I had to drink in such a short period. "Three pints?" I asked, falling into my seat and shutting the door next to me with a little too much gusto.

"We have to be strong and attentive."

"I get that, but isn't it gorging?"

"On three pints?" He chuckled, while throwing the car into drive and taking off back toward the highway. "Not quite, especially if you're going to be using a lot of your talents."

I looked down into the bags again, watching the crimson as it swayed in its packaging thanks to the movement. I didn't know if I could drink all three pints at once. Even as a human, I couldn't sit down and eat breakfast, lunch, and dinner without stopping. Looking at three of the medical bags, which I realized were warm in my lap, I imagined myself as a participant at a county fair pie-eating competition who had entered but found they lacked the appetite.

"If it's any consolation," Rhys added, "it's far more difficult to fall into a frenzy from the bag than from the vein. Something about the beating of the heart. It's different."

My lips scrunched to the side. "I guess it wouldn't be a bad thing to go absolutely feral on Dom."

"Precisely."

"But, I won't attack my family, will I?"

"I wouldn't let you." That wasn't the answer I wanted. I sighed. "I don't think you will after only three pints. It takes far more than that to attack those you love, even in that state," he explained.

He extended his open palm to me, and I grabbed a bag and slapped it into his hand, before grabbing one for myself. Blood cooled too quickly for me to take my time. "Bottoms up," I whispered.

We both used our elongated canines to rip the bag open at the hose piece. A minute later, we finished and he handed me his empty. I replaced it with a second. He waited for me to grab my second, which I did with some reluctance and pursed my lips out to show him my apprehension. He tipped up his chin as if to say, "Drink." I sucked my bottom lip in, unsure. Two weeks before, I'd drained an unsuspecting man enough to render him unconscious and the euphoria it caused terrified me and seduced me in equal measure.

I gave a loud breath and we both sucked down the second bag in record time. After thirty seconds, I pulled it from my lips panting. The heft in my gut spread warmth and otherworldly electricity throughout my body, which brought a tingle up from my chest to my jaw. The feeling spread like butter melting, gliding from my throat to the tip of my tongue behind my front teeth. For a brief moment, everything faded away. Sound, sight, taste, the surface of my skin, everything vibrated but only by the slightest margins, like the molecules of food in a microwave. Even the shimmer of my aura grew dense. I swayed forward in my seat, dropping the bag into my lap.

"You okay?" Rhys's voice changed from far away to clear as a bell in only two words. I whipped my head to face him, embarrassed at how visceral I reacted to only a second pint.

"I'm fine."

His eyebrow rose at the answer, and he handed me his spent bag. I gave him a lopsided smile and handed him his last one. All my concentration centered on controlling whatever it was that was happening in my body due to the indulgence.

I needed to drink all three bags, I couldn't afford anything less than my body and mind at top performance if I expected to throw hands with someone at least fifteen hundred years old. I had to get through the last one.

My eyes found the road as I grabbed it. Even though my concentration stayed on the way the streetlights of the highway passed in quick succession, I soon receded into my head. The sound of my family's screams through the phone made my eyes twitch and water. Every time it repeated, my body grew hotter, the high from the blood only increasing the temperature.

It wasn't until we were off I-20, on US-180, that I pulled myself away from the horrors of Dom's imagined tortures of my family. I blinked and wiped my eyes, hand still on the cold bag in my lap. I ripped it open and drank it with less vigor than the second, but still fast enough it didn't turn my stomach.

I gathered the bags, including the one Rhys had placed in my lap while I was miles away, and put them in the back seat as I fought the tingle in my jaw and cheeks. My breathing and heart rate had increased, despite my being at rest in my seat. My pupils darted around to catch glimpses of random buildings or lights that I noticed as we drove down a smaller highway. Everything was so dark this far out of the city. In the night sky, hundreds and thousands of stars shone down on us. I wanted to admire it, but I couldn't.

"Don't get yourself killed for me. If it gets bad, you and Slevin need to run," I broke the silence. We weren't far for now—maybe another twenty minutes according to the navigation app on Rhys's phone.

"While I appreciate the instruction, you know neither Slevin nor I are going to let you die in there."

"This isn't your battle."

"It is my battle. It became my battle as soon as I saw him walk you out of Amaranthine's doors. I fucked up, I know that. But, I'm not afraid to die for you. I never should have been before. I can't speak for Slevin, but

I know he cares for you. Not only that, he's never been one to abandon someone in need. I may not agree with his stance on the Sovereignty as a whole, but I do know that he will do anything to help those who need it."

I huffed.

"Both of you have done enough. You've known me for what, a month, not even? I can't expect more than what you've already done."

"For someone who doesn't want decisions made for her, you're eager to make them for others."

"That's not it," I corrected and huffed again. "This is my mess. My suicide mission. Dom's a True Alpha. He's ancient. Going to that hotel is basically a death sentence. So, I'm not expecting or asking you to do it. If anything, just get my family out of there. That's all that matters."

"We'll find your family, we'll get them out. But I need you to remember, keeping you safe is what I want more than anything in the world."

"Get them out, first. Okay? You have to. That's the most important part. I've been training with Slevin, so maybe that'll give me the edge I need. But, I have to do this. I don't leave until he's dead. No matter what, he dies."

His pupils darted back and forth from the road to me until I made my plea. He didn't reply, only nodded and redirected his attention back to the road. We remained silent all the way into Well Springs, and even in the darkness of night, the imposing height of The Brayer Hotel loomed over the town. Nothing nearby compared to it. It cut an ominous yet impressive silhouette in the nearly black sky. I had pulled up the town on my phone during the last fifteen minutes of the drive, and it was the only structure that rose above four stories in the entire area, standing tall at eleven stories. Well Springs was so small that I wouldn't even consider it a city. It was merely a town, one of countless others scattered across Texas, almost dead but somehow still inhabited, even if it was by dozens rather than thousands.

The closer we got, the tighter my throat felt until my fangs shifted out. My temples pounded by the time we reached the barbed wire fence surrounding the block where the hotel stood. Most of the lot was occupied by the building and the rest by a derelict Olympic-sized swimming pool that had been collecting rainwater for decades, along with a pathway covered in overgrowth and dirt.

There was no turning back now. It ended tonight.

CHAPTER THIRTY-FIVE

MY PHONE VIBRATED AS soon as we exited the car. I knew that rhythm. I answered the call on speaker, pulling the screen up to my chin. As I answered the call, Slevin parked and joined us.

"I must say, I'm thrilled you picked the right location. How disappointing it would have been to kill your family before you could get here."

"They're alive?"

"For now, as alive as any human could be. Is anyone truly alive if they don't have the blood of gods in their veins?"

"You're no god."

"Am I not? Are we all not the gods of death? Do you not agree that it follows us, that it's ours to command?"

The call went dead in my hand. I surveyed the face of the building all the way up, looking for light or any indication of where he was hiding, but found nothing. There were dozens and dozens of broken glass windows, boarded up rectangles where windows should have been and none of them were illuminated.

A swift kick to the lock on the fence from Slevin sent it and the opening flying inward. "Get them out safe. No matter what. They don't deserve to be a part of this."

"Of course," Slevin said.

"Yes," Rhys added.

The closer we walked, the more the facade changed from an almost cartoonish illustration to just a building. A building made of bricks, doors, and windows. A building that could crumble. The weathered brick may have been a more vibrant color in its youth, but it had become the dusty color of sand. I was more terrifying than any imagined specter that walked those halls.

Rhys moved ahead of us to push open one of the boarded up front doors and the satisfying splinter of wood echoed into the gutted lobby. As we entered, my lungs filled with dust, mold, and a multitude of toxic remnants from lead-based paint and construction supplies outlawed before I was born. I stopped to let the dust settle. I needed a clearer canvas of my senses.

Despite its decay, the interior remained a testament to its era. Remnants of chandeliers and extravagant light fixtures loomed overhead. Even the walls, defaced with spray paint, were lined with molding and accents and still bore the ghosts of their past splendor.

I closed my eyes and lowered my chin to my chest. My next inhale gave me hints of blood from different directions and sources, but it was fresh. Fresh enough to know it'd been spilled the same night.

Rhys's proximity warmed me, but beneath that warmth, Dom's blood pulled at me. It was far enough away I couldn't use it to grab a direction, but I recognized his presence.

I clocked three distinct directions that we could take when we crossed the lobby. If the layout from the outside was any indication, and going off what I'd found on the online, we needed to head straight back then find stairs.

If only I felt my family on my skin, like I did Rhys. I could even feel that monster there. When it came to them, all I had to go off were my regular senses. If the damn building wasn't as derelict as it was, those senses might have been useful. Frustrating as it was, I wouldn't have been able to find them fast if I was still human. I wanted to believe that I could tell they were near if I was one, but I knew better. They wouldn't have been in danger in the first place if I wasn't a vampire. My life had been saved, but the cost was piling higher than I had thought I could pay.

"How do you want to do this," Rhys asked.

"We need to split up," I answered. With the amount of ground we had to cover we couldn't afford to take a slower route. Splitting up allowed us to take on multiple floors at a time.

"You're an Apprentice. There's no way," Slevin protested.

I sighed. "Fine. Rhys, you're older so you go one way, and Slevin and I will go the other."

"What?"

Rhys didn't like that at all.

"You're over two hundred and fifty years old. Even if you're not a Brute, you still have the strength and reflexes that come with that age. Slevin has his muscle and a background with the building. It makes sense."

"It makes sense to you," he cautioned. "It's too risky."

"If something happens to them because we couldn't cover as much ground, I'd never forgive myself. Please, Rhys. For me," I said. A tense moment of silence passed before he nodded, despite an unspoken trepidation. "Their safety is priority over mine," I added, and again he nodded, but I felt his hesitance.

"Dove, be careful."

"I'm fine." I didn't know if I was fine or anywhere close to fine, but if willpower and conviction alone could endure what I was about to do, then I would succeed on that alone.

"I'll call you if I find anything, or find you," Rhys added.

I nodded and Rhys started away from us, his agile footsteps echoing off the tall ceilings.

"Slevin."

"Joce." He had an electric tone, an eagerness for action.

"Where should we start?" I asked.

"The place is a free for all. There's no specific place here that is favored more than another for hunts, but this is different. If I had to guess, we need to make our way to the top, not that it'll be easy to get up there."

I agreed. Dom had mentioned making them fly like birdies, which hinted at the dramatics of the top floor. "The top," I repeated, and Slevin nodded. We started walking off in the opposite direction Rhys had gone, with Slevin giving me the lowdown on the building based on his knowledge from past raids. That being said, I also knew that Dom would try to mess with me at every opportunity he got.

We approached a staircase that led from the first floor to the mezzanine, as Slevin had called it, although I didn't really know what a mezzanine was. Apparently, it was a floor between the lobby and the beginning of the hotel suites themselves. My fingers twitched with anticipation at my sides as he spoke. When we made it up there, my head whipped from side to side, and Slevin followed suit. I knew he caught more details than I did, judging by the way his eyes thinned. In the dirt and darkness of The Brayer, there were more people than we expected. I couldn't explain how I knew, but it was as if their silent presence made noise, but not breathing. Even with my hearing as sharp as three pints could provide, I couldn't catch any breathing from whatever distance I was from the strangers. Vampire, human, familiar- who knew?

Slevin turned his whole body in one direction and closed his eyes while taking deep breaths through his nose. He tilted his chin up, like an animal might when it needed to track a scent. I squinted and watched, taking my own deliberate breaths. Then, in unison, we both shot our heads in one direction, his eyes popping open.

It was blood, and it was fresh.

We took off to our right, through a small hallway toward the far right of the building. As we approached, I got a clearer profile of the blood enough to know, before we reached them, that it belonged to a human. But the unique fragrance I detected on their body and clothes was unfamiliar to me. It wasn't my family.

We rounded a corner to find the huddled mass of a woman against the far wall. Her hands were clawing at her own forearms, and blood flowed lazily from scratches that had broken the skin. Beneath her fingernails, bits of her own skin were stuck.

"Ma'am," I called, but when I tried to rush forward, Slevin put his hand up to stop me.

"He's setting distractions. He's implanted on her."

"Look at her. She's trying to open her arms up. We can't just leave her."

"Yeah," he agreed. "But, if she's still conscious, she's going to keep trying. She won't be able to stop."

I rubbed my face, trying to come up with something that we could do to stop her without losing too much time. If this was just the mezzanine, that meant Dom had more in store for us the higher we climbed.

We both looked down at the woman, my lips drawing back into a grimace at the way she went at herself like a child trying to attack a present on Christmas morning, switching sides every couple of seconds. "Ma'am," I tried to get her attention again, leaning down to get to her eye level.

"Don't, she's not going to…"

"Ma'am," I repeated, reaching out to grab her hand. When I touched her, she began to scream. Both of us recoiled, and when she looked up at my face, her mouth open in wailing, I saw nothing behind her eyes. Her bright blue eyes were as dead as a shark's. Before I fully recovered from the shock, she jumped at me, curled fingers assaulting my face and neck.

"Shit, Joce, hold on." Slevin yelled as he lunged forward. My cheeks burned with fresh cuts, but the pain lasted only as long as the lacerations took to heal. Even with his strength, he struggled to restrain her. I put my arms up in front of my face, but she continued her attack. Finally, he wrestled her onto the floor at my side. I barely caught Slevin's arm as it reared back to deliver a punch to the woman's face.

"Slevin, no. She doesn't know what she's doing."

"I know," he said, looking at me from above her. "But she can't hurt us or herself if she's unconscious."

My eyes closed tight to shield me from having to see Slevin hit the woman, but the sound of it reached my ears and I winced. It may have been a mercy, but it was still violent. I wiped my hands down my cheeks to clean any traces of blood from cuts, my chest rising and falling as if I was out of breath, but it was only adrenaline. He got to his feet and then held up his hand to help me up, I accepted it, groaning my way up.

I didn't release his hand when I got to my feet, but he also didn't try to pull it away. My blood sung through my veins, tingling the skin of my cheeks, shoulders, and upper arms. "Thanks," I said. He gripped my hand tighter and used the leverage to pull me into him. "Don't look at me like that." I said, noticing something behind his dark blue eyes.

"I know you don't care if you get out of this alive."

My first instinct was to fight him on the claim, but he was right. I bit my lip to stop myself from lying to him to ease his mind. He didn't deserve the false hope. My brows knit. "I don't want to die here, Slevin."

"Then don't."

I huffed out a breath.

"I'll try."

He leaned down and kissed me. I responded in kind, but it didn't last long before he pulled away. "C'mon, let's go," he said. The nod I gave in return was hesitant. Did he feel like he needed to kiss me because he'd never have the opportunity again? Did I reciprocate because I agreed?

"Yeah," I whispered, taking up the nodding again. We separated, turning to walk in the direction we'd come from, out of whatever back room the woman had been planted in. Because the hotel had been abandoned so long, there weren't any markers for what rooms had once been; even room numbers were missing. Despite what remained of the lobby, the more interior places were barren. "Let's head up. I don't hear anything else on this floor."

We found stairs not far into the main bulk of the mezzanine, but it wasn't the closed staircase that would take us into the rest of the hotel. It only took us up one level up. "This way," he instructed, knowing I was looking for a safe way higher.

When we entered the second floor, I coughed from the increasing amount of dust and who knew what else in the air. "You know," I started, "if I wasn't a vampire, I'd be terrified right now," I said, looking around at the ruin that was once one of the finest hotels in the country.

"You're not terrified?" Slevin joked. Dom frightened me, but it was far from the fear I used to have about darkness or ghosts. Compared to Dom, those monsters seemed trivial. If I'd known the truth about vampires, would bedtime stories be different? Or were they already distorted versions of our kind? Lost in thought, my foot slipped through a weak spot in the floor, and I yelped in surprise, nearly falling to the mezzanine below. Slevin grabbed my arm and yanked me up so fast I almost lost my footing. Eyes wide, I scanned the room.

"Good?" he asked.

"Good."

I brushed the dust off my pants and continued forward, more mindful of how much weight I put into each step. After a dozen paces, we both stopped and looked up. It was the scent of blood again, and it definitely came from above us.

Slevin pointed in front of us and to the right, leading us to the kind of stairwell I had anticipated, one that extended all the way up the building. My eyes adjusted enough in the darkness to navigate it with relative ease, but not even a stray sliver of moonlight could help me discern finer details. I pulled my cell phone out and used the flashlight to make sure that the stairs we ascended were complete enough that we wouldn't have any close calls.

Stepping out onto the next floor, we barely passed through the empty doorway when we heard the hurried breath of someone approaching at top speed. By the time we turned in the direction it came from, we were both knocked to the ground. With the force of their momentum, the pile of us skidded several feet across debris and concrete. Broken wood and glass cut through my leather jacket, embedding itself into my skin.

"Fuck." I shouted, trying to get to my feet. When I tore myself away from Slevin and our attacker, I realized that it was another vampire, their aura deep green like seaweed. "Slevin," I called, but the two of them wrestled on the ground, one getting a punch in before the other did the same.

Once I got to my feet, the sounds of the two vampires fighting took all of my attention. I tried to figure out how to help Slevin in a way that wouldn't be me getting in the way and causing him to lose the upper hand. They rolled until the vampire had Slevin pinned to the ground and as I was about to lunge at them to get him off, I was hit in the back of the head by something, and the shock and pain took me down to my knees.

I spun around and blindly grabbed at whoever was behind me, expecting to see another vampire, but the bulking figure behind me had no aura. However, they did have over fifty pounds of pure muscle and several inches on me, and their eyes were clouded with implanted rage.

I repeated expletives in my head, hoping those three pints could give me the upper hand. I may have had some strength on the human simply because of what I was, but they were huge. I prayed Slevin's sparring paid off.

My first punch got him in his gut and he doubled over. The side of my lips curled into a smirk. I didn't pull the punch. Not like I did when I trained. For the first time in my life, I could put all my strength into it. I reached forward to grab him and hopefully throw him to the ground, but he snatched my arm and delivered a punishing hit to my head before he slung me to the side. I fell to the ground but rolled so that I could get distance between us. My vision blurred at the impact of his fist and the floor.

He gave a frustrated roar.

It took me barely a second to get to my feet, but he kicked me before I fully straightened, which hit me right in the side. I cried out.

Fuck, that hurt.

Before he could land another blow, I reared back and got another punch in, sending him back several feet then to his knees. It gave me the chance to look around me for something to hit him with. I didn't want to kill him; I just needed to knock him out, but how did I know how hard to hit him that it wouldn't send him to the ICU or worse? My head rang as whatever concussion his first punch gave me healed, and I shook off the weird feeling of my brain buzzing while I located a rod that may have been used in a closet. I gripped it like a baseball bat.

"I'm so sorry," I said, grimacing as I readied myself to attack. The words didn't even faze him as he lifted himself and stood up to his full stature, at least a head taller than me. I blew all the air out of my lungs, puffing out my cheeks as I loosened up my wrists with the rod in my hands. Then he screamed and charged me, the volume of it grating on my ears. I braced, pushing my weight down into my feet, and waited to swing until he got closer. I miscalculated and swung when he was too close, unable to stop him from making hard contact with the trunk of my body.

The collision of my back to the concrete forced a cry out of me, the rod still in my left hand. I snaked it in between us and grabbed it with my right hand, using it as a barrier to give me more space. He tried to push down on it, but I had the strength to get more inches between us. My teeth gritted and groaned with the effort; my arms were shaking against him. Dom would never have given him his blood, but he could have made another vampire give it to him because there was no way he could struggle this hard against me, even at his size. I kept straining and pushing, the shaking of my muscles traveling up into my shoulders.

Frustration bubbling, I decided to change it up. I brought the rod closer to my chest, catching him off guard before then giving the rod a hard shove back and the man flew off me. Instantly, I was up above him as he struggled to get up from a pile of discarded items. In my head, I asked forgiveness of a god I was sure didn't exist and took a swing at the man's head. The rod connected and he went limp. My eyes widened at the sound of metal and flesh meeting. "Fuck, I'm sorry." I squeaked, able to hear a heartbeat. At least he was alive.

Rod in hand, I turned to find out where Slevin and the vampire were. About twenty-five feet away, the two scuffled and I approached them. Slevin had blood trailing from his temple, but even in the dim light I could see that whatever wound had been there was healed.

I didn't even bother waiting. I ran forward, tracking their movements despite their speed. I swung at the attacking vampire, hitting him across the back and pushing him down toward Slevin, who grabbed him and swung him back toward me, allowing me to deliver another hit to the back of his head. I screamed as the rod made contact, a sickening crunch echoing as his skull cracked. I didn't have to hold back my strength. If they were vampires, it meant they were helping Dom by choice. Anyone who voluntarily sided with him was fair game.

The vampire crumpled to the ground like a rag doll. The way it happened was less theatrical than the stuff I'd seen in movies, which made it more unsettling. If he'd have been human, he'd have been dead right there. But his heart still beat and he breathed.

"Give me the pipe," Slevin offered.

Instead of handing it over to him, I brought it down on the vampire's head again, another crunch sounding and blood spurting. My breath sped up and I brought it down another time, the head becoming mis-shapen. I kept going over and over again, with all my strength. I couldn't hear anything. My eyes were fixed on the body beneath me; I didn't see anything else, either. I just kept hitting and hitting until Slevin rushed forward, his hand enveloping mine where I held the rod, finally stopping my assault. Coming to, I saw blood sprayed around the corpse in all directions from the impacts. I watched as the green aura slowly faded until it completely disappeared.

I'd never seen a vampire die before.

Slevin grabbed the rod from me and threw it to the ground. Panting, I stared down at the husk of a body, mortified that I took something that was once alive and turned it into the grotesque shape beneath me I couldn't look away from.

"Joce."

I heard him, I know I did, but I didn't respond. I didn't want to and even if I did, I didn't think I could find the words. I'd never been responsible for such violence before. I'd never killed before.

"Joce."

I had become a killer.

It wasn't as dramatic as I expected.

My mind didn't relish it; it didn't realize what it was doing.

All I could do was keep hitting their head, over and over again, unable to break away. My anger and frustration took hold, and then suddenly, the vampire was dead. My jaw loosened until it hung slightly open, but I still refused to look away.

From the other side of the long hallway, clear across the building, the sound of clapping finally forced me to look away, turning to face in its direction. My body tingled and my blood buzzed with the proximity of him.

Dom.

"How proud I am to see your first kill. If only it was enough to not kill you," he yelled.

I didn't bother with a rebuttal; both Slevin and I took off toward him. We were both halfway down the hallway when we lost sight of him, his movements so fast I didn't know how he got away. We had passed the other staircase. He had to have jumped either up or down to another floor in a room. "Fuck." I exclaimed. I doubled over and put my hands on my knees to catch my breath or, moreover, my resolve. My adrenaline was rushing through me so fast my skin vibrated.

When I straightened myself back up again, I punched through the crumbling wall beside me, my fist going through the rotted drywall without resistance. "We've got to keep moving," Slevin said, but I didn't respond right away. A hand came up so that my thumb could rest against a temple and squeeze, shielding my eyes and applying pressure to my head.

"Joce..."

"Yeah, let's go," I replied, letting out a deep breath.

The vampire tried to kill me. They were in league with Dom. I was only defending myself. I wasn't a killer. It wasn't for fun.

I wasn't Dom.

I cleared my throat and lowered my hand from my face. "I'm good, I'm good." When I said it and looked at Slevin, he greeted me with skepticism, but of course, he didn't push it further. "Come on."

We jogged to the set of stairs closest to us, and when we approached the opening for it, we heard hurried footsteps headed down. I looked around on the ground for something to use as a weapon, landing on the broken leg of a wooden chair. Slevin stood beside me in a boxing stance, ready for anything. By the time I had it in my hands and braced to swing, my body grew warmer and Rhys emerged from the darkness.

"Are you okay?"

Seeing him, I lowered my head and let out an audible breath. "Rhys." I held onto the chair leg but let it drop to my side. "I'm fine. We ran into a Brute and two humans. Both humans are alive but unconscious."

"The vampire?" he asked.

"Dead," I answered. In the darkness, his expression was a little hard to make out, but I saw something pass over his features. I answered, which meant I killed him. Rhys knew I'd never killed before, because he'd have been the first person I told. "I'm okay," I added. There was no point in giving him time to ask and fawn over me about it. "You?"

"Mystic on the fifth floor," he said, but faltered. "Maybe the fourth," he added. I nodded. If he was standing here, that meant the Mystic was dead. My eyes moved from his head to his feet to see if he was hurt. The Mystic may not have killed him, but I'd feel awful if he had to heal from something bad. There were lines of congealed blood on the sides of his face, and his button-up shirt had rips on the torso and sleeves. But, luckily, none of them were large, but still they were lined with drying blood. "I came down here when I heard the commotion."

"We saw Dom, but only for a second. Lost him as soon as we took off after him. He's fast as shit," I explained. Rhys nodded. We all started up the stairwell. Rhys led the way, because he'd already canvassed the next two or three floors, but on floor six we exited into the hallway. Once we got ten feet in, my senses caught something. A smell. Blood.

I grew rigid. It was the first time I identified who a human was from their blood alone. Their musk mingled with the blood, or it dripped from their clothes. Something to give it their smell.

Their.

There was more than one person bleeding. Two people. And, going off sensory memories, I knew them both. My mom and Byron. It wasn't much blood, enough to waft down, maybe through holes in drywall and eroded flooring. They weren't on the same floor, that much I knew.

"Do you want me to—"

"No."

I cut Slevin off, aware of his implications. A bear's weight far exceeded that of his human body; if he put too much pressure in one area, he risked falling through. While he could transform into other animals, if my family spotted a wolf approaching and reacted abruptly, it could lead to a fatal mistake in a place like The Brayer.

"No, human." I repeated, but softer. Slevin nodded. We moved toward the smell until a scream rang out in the silence of the building that was positively deafening. I knew that voice, despite never having heard it let out a blood-curdling scream like that before. It was mom.

She screamed with such violence my blood ran cold.

"Mama," I bellowed out, stopping so I could wait for a reply to get a clearer idea of where she was.

"JoJo!" Byron's voice roared in panic.

Every sense, human and supernatural, suddenly hummed as a grew hectic. I raced toward his cry, nearly stumbling over rubble. They were still my family, and they shouldn't suffer because of me.

I tripped over a gap, but Rhys caught my arm, lifting me up. The three of us moved on until we stopped before a bank of heavy, faded gold elevator doors. Their sight made me wince, a wave of nausea hitting my gut.

Why did it have to be golden elevator doors?

"Mama, Byron," I yelled.

Almost in unison, the two yelled back, Byron yelling "JoJo," and my mother yelling, "Baby."

We each pried a door open. Bracing my hands on either side of the bay door of the middle car, I looked up the shaft until I spotted Byron's figure bound with his hands behind his back, suspended in the shaft. He had to have been hanging from a rope tied at the top floor and then lowered until he reached the floor he was at.

"Byron," I called out, leaning into the open doors.

"JoJo," he cried.

To my right, I heard Rhys call out, "Your mother's here." My breathing sped up, fangs lowering. I pulled my head back and looked to Slevin on my left. Just as I did, he reared back and looked my way, shaking his head. Marley wasn't there. He had her in another part of the hotel.

"Save the babies; don't worry about me." My mom called down, her voice shaking as it bounced off the tight walls around her.

"No, we'll get you both," I roared back, tears stinging.

"Rhys, Slevin. Go, please. There's no way to jump up." I looked back into the shaft, trying to gauge how many levels up it would be to open the door and grab them without having to make it to the top. "Three floors, I think. You have to go up there. I'll be here, just in case." I instructed, sticking my head back into the shaft. "Byron, Mama, we're coming." I didn't even move my head to see the two leave but heard their feet against the floor.

"Well, well, well." Dom's voice boomed down the middle shaft as he peered down to see me from a couple of floors above where Byron's eye level.

"You fucking coward."

"Hardly. I have seen more than millennia of this life, and you but a few weeks," he said. My upper lip twitched at his arrogance. "Let's save the pleasantries, shall we? We both know why we're here."

"Fuck you," I screamed.

He laughed at my rage before saying, "Make your choice."

As the words hit my ears, a myriad of emotions struck at once. Dread, fear, rage, *desperation*. He was going to cut the restraints of both my mother and brother. I had to choose who I would catch; Rhys and Slevin wouldn't be able to reach them in time.

"No," I roared, as he leaned forward and cut the rope.

"Save By—" My mother's voice started to scream but was cut off as she started to fall only a moment later.

Both of them screamed at the top of their lungs.

It all happened so fast, yet time also seemed to slow to a crawl as I sprang into action, my heart pounding like a war drum in my ears. Even the screams faded as my heart hammered. I planted my feet firmly on the

345

ground as fast as I could and leaned into the shaft, arms wide open, at just the right moment to catch the falling Byron. The two of us went flying backward as soon as I had him in my arms. Pain shot through me, but I released Byron and ran to the elevator doors to my right, and threw myself into it without a thought. I reached for her but she was too far ahead. It was only a few seconds, but the delay was too long.

She reached for me and I strained to stretch my hand out further. Time started to slow around us. Everything dimmed. Below me, my mother's face, consumed in fear stared at me. And the ground only got closer.

"Mama!" I cried as her body hit the bottom of the shaft. I barely managed to control my fall, pain shooting up from the knees I had landed on to my head. The shock of it blurred my vision as I tried to look around for my mom.

"No no no no no..."

Tears obscured my vision further as my hands reached over to my mom. I turned as much as I could. So much electric pain seared through me. I collapsed on top of her, barely able to see the bloodied face of the woman who birthed me, raised me, loved me. In the silence of that horrific scene, I couldn't hear a heartbeat.

"Mama, no. Please, Mama."

My stomach turned over, and my lips quivered.

"Mama."

Her blood was thick in the air and warm on my skin but cooling fast. So fast. Too fast. "Mama," I wept, gathering her into my arms and lifting her into me. Her pulse couldn't be gone. She couldn't be gone. Not after she recognized me again. Not after I was able to be her daughter again. "I...I can..." I whispered the words, but I didn't believe them. I couldn't save her. The heart had already stopped, and the fall was too much. The mutation wouldn't take, or worse...it'd make her into a Cadaver. "I..."

I inhaled sharply and drew my mother closer, staining myself in her crimson. "I'm... I'm still your baby girl, Mama. I promise, I'm still your baby." I pressed my face against her cheek, sobbing as my body trembled. "No, please, no. Please, Mama, no."

If anyone had been present, they wouldn't have understood my words. My wails were loud yet incoherent, echoing upward through the elevator shaft. Just when I thought I couldn't cry any harder, I began to scream. Each time, I gave it all the strength I had in my body, and when I didn't think I could do that anymore...I still did. Nothing could hold them back.

Finally, my lungs refused. "I'm so sorry, Mama," I whispered, rocking. "I'm still your baby, please. I'm your baby girl. Don't go...please don't." I begged, receiving nothing but silence in return. "Please..." I breathed.

In my hands, her body grew colder, her blood settling. I pulled her face away from mine and studied it, as if I could still see a spark of life there. But her eyes, wide with horror, were dead.

"Mama."

I leaned my forehead against hers, unable to pull myself away no matter how much I knew I needed to. It was the last time I'd ever feel my mother's embrace, even if it was a cold one.

CHAPTER THIRTY-SIX

FROM ABOVE AND BEHIND me, hurried footsteps approached. I didn't turn to look. It was Rhys and Slevin. Their scents, mixed with that of my brother, reached me through the overwhelming smell of my mother's blood. It choked the air, my lungs, and my mind.

I wanted to save her. I wished I could have saved her, but I couldn't let Byron die. She would have never forgiven me if I did. No mother would. I never would. Her final words were a plea to save him that had never finished. Still, my heart in my chest ached and burned. It lamented the only way it knew how. Physical pain. All that I could do was experience it in the midst of all that raged inside me.

I pulled away from her, slowly laying her body down. "I love you," I whispered. My fingertips pressed to her eyelids and lowered them, allowing her to take her final rest. And I stayed staring at her face for a moment longer, trying to commit it to memory. Allowing its image to sear itself into a mind that would never age enough to forget it.

My teeth bared against the pain that ebbed and flowed throughout my body. Fractures and lacerations attempted to heal, and my legs shook when I applied pressure on them to stand. It hurt. My god, it hurt to move. All of it together, every ounce of pain and anguish piled onto me, trying to weigh me back down. Trying to nail me to the floor with my mother. I looked up into the opening of the shaft to a floor about five feet over my head. I'd have to jump up, but I needed them to open the doors and grab my hand. Could I even try to jump? I didn't know. I had to try.

Marley was still up there.

"Rhys, Slevin, I'm here."

My voice was meager as I called to them. Moments later, the doors groaned open, and their heads appeared.

"Is he—"

"He's alive," Rhys answered prematurely. "I have him. Out cold, probably a concussion, but I've given him some blood. Not a lot, just enough."

My eyes watered, gratitude washing over me. As long as Byron was okay, that's what mattered. That's what made the sacrifice worth it. I acted so quickly, grabbing and pulling us back, I didn't even stop to check before I jumped down.

"Thank you." I blinked hard, tears falling down my cheeks.

"Here," Slevin offered, his arm appearing. "Can you jump up and grab me?"

I blew out a long breath. Whether or not I could jump didn't matter. I had to. And it wouldn't be pleasant. "I can try."

He leaned further in before my attempt, and I jumped with a scream, barely able to reach him. He grabbed my forearm and pulled me up, and I took one last glance at my mother before looking up again. If I escaped, if any of us made it, we would get her out of this place. She didn't deserve to be at the bottom of that elevator shaft, buried under the discarded debris that littered this place. He dragged me onto the ground floor, a bottom level below where we had entered the lobby until I lay on my stomach. Through my agony, my broken legs kept trying to heal, but they weren't set in the right way. It was fruitless. I needed to get the bones in a position to mend properly, or I wouldn't be able to get upstairs.

I looked around and saw Byron unconscious. There was a moment of panic, even though Rhys had told me his condition, but after a few tense seconds, his heartbeat reached me and I closed my eyes. I just needed to hear it for myself.

I rested my head back on the ground, eyes closed, then rolled onto my back. I growled at the movement. Slevin had let me go and moved so that he was above me, looking down at my legs and assessing the damage. I hadn't even bothered to look at them myself. No need to see. It would have made me sick to my stomach if I did.

"Here," Slevin offered, and I opened my eyes to see what he could have to give me at a time like this. To my surprise, he held out a blood bag. I furrowed my brow. "I saved it in case of emergency. You drink it. I'm going to try to set your legs."

He threw the bag and it landed on my torso, which I snatched up without another word. When he touched my left leg, I tried my best not to scream, but a pathetic noise came out of me from deep in my chest.

I ripped the bag open with my teeth and started drinking. Part of my brain registered that the blood wasn't appetizing because it wasn't fresh, having become room temperature, but it was enough. Vampire nature be damned for even thinking about the taste. All that mattered was being strong enough to end this. With each small gulp, electricity buzzed through me.

"Ready?"

I looked down at him and shook my head, then threw my head back onto the ground and braced. With all the concentration I conjured, I focused on drinking as quickly as possible. My eyes closed so hard I saw pixels of colors flash.

I didn't know what he did or how bad they were, but when he set my left leg I violently coughed, blood spurting out of my mouth. Choking a little, I kept coughing until I cleared my throat. I took a few breaths through my nose, my jaw wired shut as I experienced both anguish at my leg's position being corrected and the heat of my blood working to heal the leg right.

Seconds later, I put the bag back up to my mouth and drank the rest of it as fast as I could. Slevin's hands softly felt on my right leg trying to figure out what he was going to do. I ripped the bag away from my mouth, my arm hitting the ground with a soft thud, dust shooting into the air. "Just do it," I shouted.

Before I could change my mind, he set my right leg with two adjustments, and I howled and rolled over onto my stomach, so engulfed in what he did that my own action didn't make a difference on the pain scale. My back arched upward and I started to curl up, weight on my forearms and knees. I pounded my fist on the ground repeatedly, snarling as my blood did its work. Different parts of my body warm and humming, I healed. My thoughts raced to the fact that I couldn't have done this for my mother, but I pushed them away as best I could.

351

After a minute, the agony of the process waned. I flipped onto my stomach, face turned toward Byron, eyes taking in the way his chest rose and fell when he breathed.

He was alive. He was saved. He would be okay. My panting kicked dust up, but I saw him through it, his head facing up toward the ceiling. It was a terrifying and beautiful sight.

After another minute, the hum faded entirely. I stood up, my legs shaking slightly, not from injury, but from the rapid cycle of breaking and healing. Rhys hurried over to steady me. I waited, ensuring the tremors had subsided, but before I let go of him, I glanced up at his face.

"I just..." The words trailed off, and I sucked my bottom lip into my mouth and left it there for a second while I collected my thoughts. "Thank you...for everything. I'm lucky to have you as my Lord."

"Dove, it's me who's lucky. I didn't deserve a Protégé like you. You're perfect for all your fight, passion, and stubbornness." Turning, he picked Byron up in his arms, "Now, go. I'll take Byron out to my car, just in case there's anyone else in here. I'll find you."

I nodded and looked to Slevin, who nodded in turn. As we started to walk away, I listened to the steady sound of Byron's breaths and heartbeat against the cadence of Rhys's steps as he headed for the exit behind us, and we headed for the stairs to take us back to the first floor.

The image of Dom came to mind, malice in a wide smile. It was the smile on his face as I faded in and out of consciousness on the hotel bed at The Avery. "Let's kill this motherfucker." I mouthed the words with all the contempt in me as we made our way up the stairs.

Once we reached the first floor, now that I knew where the stairs were, we were off. Neither of us spoke. There was no holding back. At first, I jogged through the lobby and up the curved staircase to the mezzanine, but as we reached the stairwell on the second floor, I hit a run.

I bounded up the stairs, taking them two at a time with long strides. I was moving so quickly that I finally reached my limits. Dust swirled up around us as I coughed through it, but nothing would deter me from getting to that son of a bitch. By the time we reached the sixth floor, I started sweating, and as we ascended to the eighth floor, the sweat soaked my shirt. We climbed even higher to the tenth floor, only to find the stairs blocked. We pulled apart old furniture and plywood stacked in our way. "Almost there," Slevin said, as we cleared just enough space to squeeze through.

Dom's voice reached me as we neared the top floor, though I couldn't catch the words, just the tone of his conversation. He was talking to Marley. The thought of him saying anything to my little sister, who was barely sixteen, filled me with nausea and rage. Was he trying to manipulate her, scare her? She was just a child. Keeping my eyes focused ahead, we reached the top of the stairwell. I came to a halt, feeling Slevin's chest hit my back. I raised my hand to signal for him to stay still and quiet, wanting to hear what was being said.

"Young one..." Dom was ahead of us, but the layout obscured them from my view. There was a room between where they were and where we entered. Still, his proximity set off our coupling so that I pinpointed him at the middle of the building. "Has your body even known pleasure yet? Will you die before you savor that feeling? Your blood is so sweet, your body so pure. Not tasting it in both fear and pleasure would be a shame, but the blood I've tasted so far is exquisite."

Hearing the questions and comments made my heart beat in my temples and my canines dropped to their lowest peak. That motherfucker tasted my little sister. My vision reddened.

"I can't wait to gorge myself on you and your sister," he added. I walked forward, through an empty doorway. We couldn't sneak up on each other. It was impossible. "Maybe, I'll drain that brother of yours as well, Fuil, for good measure."

I knew the statement was directed at me, even though I hadn't entirely made it into his direct line of sight. He aimed to taunt me, poking and prodding at my resolve to get a reaction. I was versed well enough on his methods of playing with his food.

But he was the weak one. He let his guard down enough that I bit him during his attack. He didn't make sure I was dead before he left the room. It wasn't that he needed the blood back that I stole from him. No, that wasn't all of it. He needed to best me because, technically, I bested *him*. I survived him. I survived and stole his essence. I did the one thing he claimed no one had been able to do in over a millennium and a half.

"Don't you fuckin' talk to her."

My voice raised so that it bounced off the walls up to the ceiling of the rooftop venue. The January winds whipped through the openness of the space from windows that had long since been broken out. It howled past me and wafted scents around that I couldn't ignore. The strongest of those scents was blood.

"Is that service animal with you?" He sneered. "How fun."

We moved close enough for him to see, and I made out Marley's figure held against Dom's chest by his arm around her throat.

"Don't worry about him; your ass is mine."

"Possessive of me? How quaint."

"Fuck you."

I continued further, but when I did he drew Marley closer, causing her to gasp. The sound of it twisted knots in my stomach. My jaw clenched, lips pulling back into a snarl. It only made Dom smile into the crook of Marley's neck. "Do you think you're strong enough now? Fast enough? Do you not recall how I proved you wrong already?"

"Try me."

"I have." He raised the back of his hand and used it to move Marley's cheek to the side until the action gave him clearance to her throat. "And I've tried her. She tastes better than her sister," he said, voice low.

The walls of my chest filled with the boiling lava of my rage.

My weight shifted so that it pushed down into my feet and I anchored myself. "Joce—" Slevin's voice sounded miles away. My heart pounded in my ears and my temples.

"Get her out of here, no matter what. You grab her and run," I ordered Slevin. Even if I didn't make it off that rooftop, if I finally met the end I narrowly escaped weeks before, I needed to make sure the ones I loved would be okay.

"Joce," he repeated.

I refused to turn and look at Slevin. I couldn't take my eyes off Dom. I couldn't give him a single second of an upper hand. My left foot pressed as hard as possible into the ground and I tightened my fists with enough strength that my fingernails broke skin.

From fifty feet ahead of me, I caught him lower his head to bite Marley and launched myself forward with every ounce of effort left in my body. As I was about to collide with their bodies with his lips at her skin, my shoulder lowered. Then I panicked. The impact had the potential to break my sister's ribs or worse, kill her.

It was too late to correct my posture, but I raised my shoulder as much as I could in that last moment, and the three of us fell to the ground in a mess of bodies. Marley cried out in pain, having tried to catch herself with her hands behind her, causing one or both of her arms to break due to the speed and force.

Huffing out breaths, I lifted myself. Dom's laughter cut through the sounds of Marley and I panting. "Aren't you spry," he quipped. I gritted my teeth and rolled with the two of them.

"Run, Marley," I roared, pulling myself off Dom so Slevin could grab her. If he gave her a drop or two of blood, it might help dull the pain until we could get her to a hospital. "I love you Marley," I added, as she struggled to her feet without using her hands. I stole a glance back at her, and she looked at me terrified, blood stained on her neck and tears trailing down her face. My beautiful sister. She'd be okay. Byron would be okay. As long as Dom didn't make it out of here alive.

Turning back, I scrambled so that I straddled Dom's body on the ground before he got up, hoping to buy some time for them to get to the stairs. I looked down at him, drawing my lips back in a snarl as he beamed a smile at me, his teeth bloody.

Why wasn't he fighting back?

Panic rose in my chest until it suffocated me, and I moved to cup my hand around his throat. The sensation of choking him excited me enough my fangs ached, and I brought a fist down on his face, busting his lip open and breaking his nose. The smile never left his face as I rained my anger down on him, his neck muscles tightened to resist me. He was going to fight back. His fist made contact with my side, rolling us and earning a grunt out of me. He tossed me off of him, but I sprang up and ran at him, tackling him.

Grabbing my hair, he pulled a chunk of it from the root, and I screamed out before he tossed me again. I tumbled to the other side of the room clearing. At my back, the echo of his dress shoes on the ground came closer until he grabbed me by the arm and lifted me with one hand. With the other, he wiped his face, collecting the blood off it in his palm. As he did, I clawed at his arm and tried to pull out of his grip. Too quick for me to take advantage of the change, he moved his grip from my arm to my neck, holding me to ensure I looked straight at him.

"Let me show you..."

He snapped the fingers of his blood-stained hand, and when he did, it erupted into flames where the blood touched. As he lifted the fire toward my face, I winced, heat scorching my cheeks. The temperature was unbearable. I winced, trying and failing to turn away from it. I couldn't see his face through the fire...but his laughter. It suffocated me more than the heat. I gritted my barred teeth as he pressed the hand against the side of my face, some of it burning my hair and scalp at the hairline. Despite the indescribable pain, I refused to scream.

"Sing for me," he ordered, pushing harder against my face.

My skin scorched and audibly sizzled, but I didn't scream. I put all my strength and concentration into my arms and pushed him back with enough force to break his hold. We fell to the floor, but at least the flames no longer burned me, though the pain persisted. When we hit the ground, he got on top of me before my eyes opened after the impact.

He reached up and grabbed my wrists. I sucked air through my gritted teeth, my advantage gone in an instant. He forced my hand above my head. The sight of him on top of me, blood in the air, brought me back to the night he had taken my mortal innocence. My body froze as if I wasn't the stronger Prole, but that scared, drugged human.

No.

Not drugged.

He didn't drug me, he implanted that.

Looking up at him, the last remaining pieces fell back into place. I remembered every word he said to me at the bar before dragging me to my room and every single way he violated my body when he got me there. I remembered the methodical way he repeated words as we sat at the bar top of Amaranthine. The obvious way he used his abilities to gaslight me into thinking I was drunk before forgetting we had even spoken on it. I remembered how he spoke from both his lips and his mind to manipulate me into feeling the effects of a drug I didn't take, because he wanted to play with me like a toy and not have me fight back. Mary had called it.

"You..."

My eyes welled up with tears. I could've gotten away; I could've fought him more if he hadn't brainwashed me simply because he wanted an easy meal.

No. Not just an easy meal. The blood. He didn't want anything to hinder the taste of my blood. A horrible detail he explained to me as I bled to death. He sat on the bed once he'd had his fill and talked to me. The conversation played back.

"I had a human wife once. Pointless thing. She couldn't mother children, either. I offered her to my Goddess, and we both punished her for it on the first night of my transition. So long ago, it was. All the names I've had since those nights...but you, Fuil, you can call me..." He made me say his name, choked through blood, with my last human breaths. *"Domhnall."*

"Domhnall."

The name slid past my lips at barely an audible level, but I knew he heard it as the glint in his eyes grew brighter.

"So nice to hear it again," he said as he lowered his head, so his face was inches from mine. "But I only tell it to the dead." His free hand came up to wrap around my throat, and I started jerking my body as I came out of my memories.

The pressure he applied on my windpipe was so controlled, the way he applied it added just a bit more pressure each passing second while keeping complete stillness as my hips and legs writhed beneath him. No matter how much I thrashed, he didn't lose grip, and the hand squeezed tighter. I need him to let me go.

"How does it feel, Domhnall," I struggled with the words. "To know...that even if you... get your blood back..." I tried to adjust my head so that I could get more space between my neck and his fingers to finish what I was saying. "...I've already tainted it with my inadequate blood. My human blood ruined you the moment you tried to take my life. You didn't make sure I died and now you'll never be pure again. You can kill me, but it won't change the fact that I've diluted you. The one you thought was so weak, so inconsequential...I bested you."

As soon as the insult left my lips, his grip tightened faster to the point that speech wasn't possible. But, I said what I needed to say. His response revealed everything. Silently pleased, a grin spread across my face.

He could drain every last drop of my blood from my body, he could take the brain from my skull and smash it to a pulp, but all that didn't matter because I mutated before I died. His blood changed as soon as I did. It wasn't pure anymore, and he could do nothing to change that.

I closed my eyes as I came to terms with the fact that I never had a real chance against him in a one-on-one fight. His grip tightened even more, causing pain to sear my throat. I was a baby Prole with a vendetta, and he was over a thousand years old, gifted with every ability our kind possessed. I never stood a chance.

The smile spread on my face, and I relaxed, even lifting my chin so he had better access to my throat. Isn't that what he wanted from me? Prey that couldn't fight back. He was strong, but he'd never be strong enough see me for the ruin I would bring. My gut twitched as I suppressed laughter that begged to come out, my body shaking.

His grip loosened until I was able to get air again, coughing and laughing at the same time, making my skin jerk up against his hand. I stared up into his clear blue eyes, finally noticing something behind them. Anger. An anger that almost darkened their icy color. The coughing stopped and I brought my chin down so that he could see my expression of sheer triumph, grinning. I didn't have to say anything. I made my peace.

I may not have had the physical strength to beat him, but I won again. Taking the blood from his veins was what I thought I needed all this time. I thought I needed to inflict pain onto him so that I'd have my retribution, but my revenge had been exacted from day one. He'd never be the same after that, and that was the worst thing I could have done to him.

The simple fact that I'd been a survivor, that I'd made it through my mutation after he left me to die, meant that before the battle even started, I was the victor.

He didn't taint me.

I tainted him.

He could take every last drop of blood from my body, but I'd be with him forever. In less than a month, I had uprooted his life to the point he planned his time around *me* because my existence pissed him off enough to harass me. All that talk about my simple ass self, my unworthy self, my weak self...how great he was in towering his shadow over me. It was a lie. The shadow of my perseverance engulfed him, and he was too arrogant to see it. *Until now.*

"You want it...take it." he squeezed my neck harder for a moment after I said it. "I'll be in your blood forever...Fuil," I choked out. He stood up and lifted me with him, my feet inches off the ground. In his eyes, all I could see was death, and it made me want to laugh again. "I hope you choke on it."

As soon as I finished the words, he let out a yell that rang in my ears with the loss of centuries worth of arrogance. The sound was sweet. I'd be proud to call it my death rattle. He walked us to the edge of the room, through an empty doorway onto a balcony. The wind whipped my back. I was pulled forward and he ripped into the side of my throat like a wild animal. The violence of the bite sent pain through me but the high of my victory remained intact.

He was so insignificant.

Nothing but arrogance and greed.

He thought he could take what he wanted, that it was his to have without contest or consent. My mortality, my humanity, pieces of my soul that I thought I'd never get back. I thought he took all these things from me, but he didn't. I never gave them to him. He couldn't have Joceline Fuentes, because I never lost her. Vampire or human. Victim? **Survivor**. I was all of them: a lover, a fighter, a Prole, a daughter, a sister. I was everything.

He couldn't take it no matter what he did.

As he greedily drank, my eyes closed. I wouldn't beg or weep; I wouldn't scream. He'd never get the satisfaction. My arms lifted, skin wet as streams of my essence ran to my fingertips and dripped onto the dirty concrete. I pulled myself into him as hard as I could with my failing strength, and he took the purchase to grow more ravenous in his meal of me. I coughed and red spurted from my mouth. "Blood of my blood," I whispered, wrapping my arms around him.

There was only one thing left to do.

With everything I had left, everything that I was, I held tighter to him and pulled us backward over the balcony railing. He tried to tear away and control the fall, but I held onto him. I leaned us back into a nosedive to make sure we'd hit the ground as close to headfirst as I could manage. The brain had to be destroyed; it was the only way to kill us. The air whipping past me, loud as it roared in my ears, was beautiful. It was all beautiful.

I took a final, deep breath.

My siblings would be safe. Rhys would be safe. Slevin would be safe. They'd never have to fear Dom's retribution after I was gone. No one would ever suffer at his hands again. It was the only way to end it.

No more me.

No more him.

His blood died with us.

But mine...mine would live on through Rhys and my human family. The things Domhnall never had and couldn't take from me.

Joceline Fuentes would live on through the blood of *my* blood.

Epilogue

My hearing was the first thing to return.

I didn't know how long I'd been alive without the ability to process the most basic of things, but it made sense that sound would be the first thing to return.

Then, I could feel. A strange thing to regain, as it was jarring to realize that for a time I existed without being able to do it.

For nights, those were the only two things I could do, and on some of those nights, doing so was fuzzy. If fuzzy was the right word. I couldn't find a better word; my brain barely functioned enough to think of the first one.

Then, after being conscious for a while, one night when I assumed I was being administered blood, the memory of taste returned. Or was it actually taste? Both? I tasted blood, and my brain linked it to the memory of a taste from my past—a burger from Lenny's Spot, juicy and dripping with grease. The smell was divine, unlike the room I was in, which smelled floral but also clean.

Wait, I could smell.

My lungs filled with oxygen as I forced myself to take a deep inhale so I could smell again. Familiar scents commingled with ones I didn't recognize, creating an aromatic bouquet of being alive. My eyes popped open, and I tried to lean forward. Even in the dim room, everything was bright. So bright. But I welcomed the sting in my eyes because of what it meant.

I had survived...